TWO'S COMPANY,
THREE IS PERFECT...

Dua thinned. She thinned more than Tritt had ever seen a person thin. She thinned more than Tritt would ever have thought possible. She became a kind of colored smoke that filled the room and dazzled him. He moved without knowing he was moving. He immersed himself in the air that was Dua.

Tritt felt no resistance, no friction. There was just a floating inward and a rapid palpitation. He felt himself beginning to thin in sympathy.

Dimly, he could see Odeen approaching from the other side, from Dua's left. And he, too, was thinning.

Then, like all the shocks of contact in all the world, he reached Odeen. But it wasn't a shock at all. Tritt felt without feeling, knew without knowing. He couldn't tell whether he was surrounding Odeen or being surrounded by him or both or neither.

It was only—pleasure.

By Isaac Asimov
Published by Ballantine Books:

THE CLASSIC FOUNDATION SERIES
   Foundation
   Foundation and Empire
   Second Foundation
   Foundation's Edge

THE GALACTIC EMPIRE NOVELS:
   The Stars, Like Dust
   The Currents of Space
   Pebble in the Sky

THE ROBOT NOVELS:
   The Caves of Steel
   The Naked Sun
   The Robots of Dawn

I, ROBOT
THE GODS THEMSELVES
THE END OF ETERNITY
THE BICENTENNIAL MAN and Other Stories
NIGHTFALL and Other Stories
NINE TOMORROWS
THE MARTIAN WAY and Other Stories
THE WINDS OF CHANGE and Other Stories
THE EARLY ASIMOV—Book One
THE EARLY ASIMOV—Book Two

THE LUCKY STARR ADVENTURES
Writing as Paul French:
   David Starr—Space Ranger
   Lucky Starr and the Pirates of the Asteroids
   Lucky Starr and the Oceans of Venus
   Lucky Starr and the Big Sun of Mercury
   Lucky Starr and the Moons of Jupiter
   Lucky Starr and the Rings of Saturn

ISAAC ASIMOV

THE GODS THEMSELVES

A DEL REY BOOK

BALLANTINE BOOKS • NEW YORK

ISBN 0-345-33778-6

This edition published by arrangement with Doubleday & Co.

Selection of the Science Fiction Book Club, June 1972

Portions of this novel have been previously published in
Galaxy magazine (March 1972 and May 1972) and *If* magazine (April 1972)

Manufactured in the United States of America

First Ballantine Books Edition: November 1984
Third Printing: February 1986

Cover art by Barclay Shaw

DEDICATION

To Mankind

And the hope that the war against folly
may someday be won, after all

PART ONE

against stupidity . . .

page 9

PART TWO

. . . the gods themselves . . .

page 71

PART THREE

. . . contend in vain?

page 169

NOTE

The story starts with section 6. This is not a mistake. I have my own subtle reasoning. So just read and, I hope, enjoy.

1

Against stupidity . . .

6

"No good!" said Lamont, sharply. "I didn't get anywhere." He had a brooding look about him that went with his deep-set eyes and the slight asymmetry of his long chin. There was a brooding look about him at the best of times, and this was not the best of times. His second formal interview with Hallam had been a greater fiasco than the first.

"Don't be dramatic," said Myron Bronowski, placidly. "You didn't expect to. You told me that." He was tossing peanuts into the air and catching them in his plump-lipped mouth as they came down. He never missed. He was not very tall, not very thin.

"That doesn't make it pleasant. But you're right, it doesn't matter. There are other things I can do and intend to do and, besides that, I depend on you. If you could only find out—"

"Don't finish, Pete. I've heard it all before. All I have to do is decipher the thinking of a non-human intelligence."

"A *better*-than-human intelligence. Those creatures from the para-Universe are *trying* to make themselves understood."

"That may be," sighed Bronowski, "but they're trying to do it through *my* intelligence, which is better than human I sometimes think, but not much. Sometimes, in the dark of the night, I lie awake and wonder if different intelligences can communicate at all; or, if I've had a particularly bad day, whether the phrase 'different intelligences' has meaning at all."

"It does," said Lamont savagely, his hands clearly balling into fists within his lab coat pockets. "It means Hallam and me. It means that fool-hero, Dr. Frederick Hallam

11

and me. We're different intelligences because when I talk to him he doesn't understand. His idiot face gets redder and his eyes bulge and his ears block. I'd say his mind stops functioning, but I lack the proof of any other state from which it might stop."

Bronowski murmured, "What a way to speak of the Father of the Electron Pump."

"That's it. Reputed Father of the Electron Pump. A bastard birth, if ever there was one. His contribution was least in substance. I *know*."

"I know, too. You've told me often," and Bronowski tossed another peanut into the air. He didn't miss.

1

It had happened thirty years before. Frederick Hallam was a radiochemist, with the print on his doctoral dissertation still wet and with no sign whatever of being a world-shaker.

What began the shaking of the world was the fact that a dusty reagent bottle marked "Tungsten Metal" stood on his desk. It wasn't his; he had never used it. It was a legacy from some dim day when some past inhabitant of the office had wanted tungsten for some long-forgotten reason. It wasn't even really tungsten any more. It consisted of small pellets of what was now heavily layered with oxide —gray and dusty. No use to anyone.

And one day Hallam entered the laboratory (well, it was October 3, 2070, to be exact), got to work, stopped shortly before 10 A.M., stared transfixed at the bottle, and lifted it. It was as dusty as ever, the label as faded, but he called out, "God damn it; who the *hell* has been tampering with this?"

That, at least, was the account of Denison, who overheard the remark and who told it to Lamont a generation later. The official tale of the discovery, as reported in the books, leaves out the phraseology. One gets the impression of a keen-eyed chemist, aware of change and instantly drawing deep-seated deductions.

Not so. Hallam had no use for the tungsten; it was of no earthly value to him and any tampering with it could be of no possible importance to him. However, he hated any interference with his desk (as so many do) and he suspected others of possessing keen desires to engage in such interference out of sheer malice.

No one at the time admitted to knowing anything about the matter. Benjamin Allan Denison, who overheard the initial remark, had an office immediately across the corridor and both doors were open. He looked up and met Hallam's accusatory eye.

He didn't particularly like Hallam (no one particularly did) and he had slept badly the night before. He was, as it happened and as he later recalled, rather pleased to have someone on whom to vent his spleen, and Hallam made the perfect candidate.

When Hallam held the bottle up to his face, Denison pulled back with clear distaste. "Why the devil should I be interested in your tungsten?" he demanded. "Why should anyone? If you'll look at the bottle, you'll see that the thing hasn't been opened for twenty years; and if you hadn't put your own grubby paws on it, you would have seen no one had touched it."

Hallam flushed a slow, angry red. He said, tightly, "Listen, Denison, someone has changed the contents. That's not the tungsten."

Denison allowed himself a small, but distinct sniff. "How would *you* know?"

Of such things, petty annoyance and aimless thrusts, is history made.

It would have been an unfortunate remark in any case. Denison's scholastic record, as fresh as Hallam's, was far more impressive and he was the bright-young-man of the department. Hallam knew this and, what was worse, Denison knew it too, and made no secret of it. Denison's "How would *you* know?" with the clear and unmistakable emphasis on the "you," was ample motivation for all that followed. Without it, Hallam would never have become the greatest and most revered scientist in history, to use the exact phrase Denison later used in his interview with Lamont.

Officially, Hallam had come in on that fateful morning, noticed the dusty gray pellets gone—not even the dust on the inside surface remaining—and clear iron-gray metal in their place. Naturally, he investigated—

But place the official version to one side. It was Denison. Had he confined himself to a simple negative, or a shrug, the chances are that Hallam would have asked others, then eventually wearied of the unexplained event, put the bottle to one side, and let subsequent tragedy, whether subtle or drastic (depending on how long the ultimate discovery was delayed), guide the future. In any event, it would not have been Hallam who rode the whirlwind to the heights.

With the "How would *you* know?" cutting him down, however, Hallam could only retort wildly, "I'll *show* you that I know."

And after that, nothing could prevent him from going to extremes. The analysis of the metal in the old container became his number-one priority, and his prime goal was to wipe the haughtiness from Denison's thin-nosed face and the perpetual trace of a sneer from his pale lips.

Denison never forgot that moment for it was his own remark that drove Hallam to the Nobel Price and himself to oblivion.

He had no way of knowing (or if he knew he would not then have cared) that there was an overwhelming stubbornness in Hallam, the mediocrity's frightened need to safeguard his pride, that would carry the day at that time more than all Denison's native brilliance would have.

Hallam moved at once and directly. He carried his metal to the mass spectrography department. As a radiation chemist it was a natural move. He knew the technicians there, he had worked with them, and he was force-ful. He was forceful to such an effect, indeed, that the job was placed ahead of projects of much greater pith and mo-ment.

The mass spectrographer said eventually, "Well, it isn't tungsten."

Hallam's broad and humorless face wrinkled into a harsh smile. "All right. We'll tell that to Bright-boy Deni-son. I want a report and—"

"But wait awhile, Dr. Hallam. I'm telling you it's not tungsten, but that doesn't mean I know what it is."

"What do you mean you don't know what it is."

"I mean the results are ridiculous." The technician thought a while. "Impossible, actually. The charge-mass ratio is all wrong."

"All wrong in what way?"

"Too high. It just can't be."

"Well, then," said Hallam and, regardless of the motive that was driving him, his next remark set him on the road to the Nobel Prize and, it might even be argued, a de-served one, "get the frequency of its characteristic x-radia-tion and figure out the charge. Don't just sit around and talk about something being impossible."

It was a troubled technician who came into Hallam's of-fice a few days later.

Hallam ignored the trouble on the other's face—he was never sensitive—and said, "Did you find—" He then cast a troubled look of his own at Denison, sitting at the desk in his own lab and shut the door. "Did you find the nuclear charge?"

"Yes, but it's wrong."

"All right, Tracy. Do it over."

"I did it over a dozen times. It's wrong."

"If you made the measurement, that's it. Don't argue with the facts."

Tracy rubbed his ear and said, "I've got to, Doc. If I take the measurements seriously, then what you've given me is plutonium-186."

"Plutonium-186? *Plutonium*-186?"

"The charge is +94. The mass is 186."

"But that's impossible. There's no such isotope. There can't be."

"That's what I'm saying to you. But those are the measurements."

"But a situation like that leaves the nucleus over fifty neutrons short. You can't have plutonium-186. You couldn't squeeze ninety-four protons into one nucleus with only ninety-two neutrons and expect it to hang together for even a trillion-trillionth of a second."

"That's what I'm telling you, Doc," said Tracy, patiently.

And then Hallam stopped to think. It was tungsten he was missing and one of its isotopes, tungsten-186, was stable. Tungsten-186 had 74 protons and 112 neutrons in its nucleus. Could something have turned twenty neutrons into twenty protons? Surely that was impossible.

"Are there any signs of radioactivity?" asked Hallam, groping somehow for a road out of the maze.

"I thought of that," said the technician. "It's stable. Absolutely stable."

"Then it can't be plutonium-186."

"I keep telling you, Doc."

Hallam said, hopelessly, "Well, give me the stuff."

Alone once more, he sat and looked at the bottle in stupefaction. The most nearly stable isotope of plutonium was plutonium-240, where 146 neutrons were needed to make the 94 protons stick together with some semblance of partial stability.

What could he do now? It was beyond him and he was sorry he had started. After all, he had real work begging to be done, and this thing—this mystery—had nothing to do with him. Tracy had made some stupid mistake or the mass spectrometer was out of whack, or—

Well, what of it? Forget the whole thing!

Except that Hallam couldn't do that. Sooner or later, Denison would be bound to stop by and, with that irritating half-smile of his, ask after the tungsten. Then what could Hallam say? Could he say, "It isn't tungsten, just as I told you."

Surely Denison would ask, "Oh, and what is it, then?" and nothing imaginable could have made Hallam expose himself to the kind of derision that would follow any claim that it was plutonium-186. He had to find out what it was, and he had to do it himself. Clearly, he couldn't trust anyone.

So about two weeks later he entered Tracy's laboratory in what can fairly be described as a first-class fury.

"Hey, didn't you tell me that stuff was non-radioactive?"

"What stuff?" said Tracy automatically, before he remembered.

"That stuff you called plutonium-186," said Hallam.

"Oh. Well it *was* stable."

"About as stable as your mental state. If you call this non-radioactive, you belong in a plumber's shop."

Tracy frowned. "Okay, Doc. Pass it over and let's try." And then he said, "Beats me! It *is* radioactive. Not much, but it is. I don't see how I could have missed that."

"And how far can I trust your crap about plutonium-186?"

The matter had Hallam by the throat now. The mystery had become so exasperating as to be a personal affront. Whoever had switched bottles, or switched contents, must either have switched again or have devised a metal for the specific purpose of making a fool of him. In either case, he was ready to pull the world apart to solve the matter if he had to—and if he could.

He had his stubbornness, and an intensity that could not easily be brushed aside, and he went straight to G. C. Kantrowitsch, who was then in the final year of his own rather remarkable career. Kantrowitsch's aid was difficult to enlist but, once enlisted, it quickly caught fire.

Two days later, in fact, he was storming into Hallam's office in a blaze of excitement. "Have you been handling this thing with your hands?"

"Not much," said Hallam.

"Well, don't. If you've got any more, don't. It's emitting positrons."

"Oh?"

"The most energetic positrons I've ever seen. . . . And your figures on its radioactivity are too low."

"Too low?"

"Distinctly. And what bothers me is that every measurement I take is just a trifle higher than the one before."

6 (continued)

Bronowski came across an apple in the capacious pocket of his jacket and bit into it. "Okay, you've seen Hallam and been kicked out as expected. What next?"

"I haven't quite decided. But whatever it is, it's going to dump him on his fat behind. I saw him once before, you know; years ago, when I first came here; when I thought he was a great man. A great man— He's the greatest villain in the history of science. He's rewritten the history of the Pump, you know, rewritten it here—" Lamont tapped his temple. "He believes his own fantasy and fights for it with a diseased fury. He's a pygmy with only one talent, the ability to convince others he's a giant."

Lamont looked up at Bronowski's wide and placid face, wreathed now in amusement, and forced a laugh. "Oh, well, *that* doesn't do any good, and I've told it all to you before anyway."

"Many times," agreed Bronowski.

"But it just gravels me to have the whole world—"

2

Peter Lamont had been two years old when Hallam had picked up his altered tungsten for the first time. When he was twenty-five, he joined Pump Station One with the print on his own doctoral dissertation still fresh and accepted a simultaneous appointment on the Physics faculty of the university.

It was a remarkably satisfactory achievement for the young man. Pump Station One was lacking in the glisten of the later stations but it was the granddaddy of them all, of the entire chain that girdled the planet now even though the entire technology was only a couple of decades old. No major technological advance had ever caught hold so rapidly and so entirely and why not? It meant free energy without limit and without problems. It was the Santa Claus and the Aladdin's lamp of the whole world.

Lamont had taken the job in order to deal with problems of the highest theoretical abstraction and yet he found himself interested in the amazing story of the development of the Electron Pump. It had never been written up in its entirety by someone who truly understood the theoretical principles (in so far as they could be understood) and who had some ability in translating the complexities for the general public. To be sure, Hallam himself had written a number of articles for the popular media, but these did not represent a connected, reasoned history —something Lamont yearned to supply.

He used Hallam's articles to begin with, other reminiscences in published form—the official documents so to speak—carrying them through to Hallam's world-shaking remark, the Great Insight, as it was often called (invariably with capital letters).

Afterward, of course, when Lamont had experienced

his disillusionment, he began digging deeper, and the question arose in his mind as to whether Hallam's great remark had really been Hallam's. It had been advanced at the seminar which marked the true beginning of the Electron Pump and yet, as it turned out, it was extraordinarily difficult to get the details of that seminar and quite impossible to get the voice recordings.

Eventually, Lamont began to suspect that the dimness of the footprints left on the sands of time by that seminar was not entirely accidental. Putting several items ingeniously together, it began to seem that there was a reasonable chance that John F. X. McFarland had said something very nearly like the crucial statement Hallam had made—and had done so before Hallam.

He went to see McFarland, who was featured not at all in the official accounts, and who was now doing upper-atmosphere research, with particular reference to the Solar wind. It was not a top-echelon job, but it had its perquisites, and it had more than a little to do with Pump effects. McFarland had clearly avoided suffering the fate of oblivion that had overtaken Denison.

He was polite enough to Lamont and willing to talk on any subject except the events of that seminar. That he simply didn't remember.

Lamont insisted, quoted the evidence he had gathered.

McFarland took out a pipe, filled it, inspected its contents thoroughly, and said, with a queer intentness. "I don't choose to remember, because it doesn't matter; it really doesn't. Suppose I laid claim to having said something. No one would believe it. I would look like an idiot and a megalomaniac one."

"And Hallam would see to it that you were retired?"

"I'm not saying that, but I don't see that it would do me any good. What's the difference, anyway?"

"A matter of historical truth!" said Lamont.

"Oh, bull. The historical truth is that Hallam never let go. He drove everyone into investigating, whether they wanted to or not. Without him, that tungsten would eventually have exploded with I don't know how many casualties. There might never have been another sample, and we might never have had the Pump. Hallam deserves the credit for it, even if he doesn't deserve the credit, and if that doesn't make sense, I can't help it, because history doesn't make sense."

Lamont wasn't satisfied with that, but he had to make it do, for McFarland would simply say no more.

Historical truth!

One piece of historical truth that seemed beyond question was that it was the radioactivity that pulled "Hallam's tungsten" (this is what it was called as a matter of historical custom) into the big time. It didn't matter whether it was or was not tungsten; whether it had or had not been tampered with; even whether it was or was not an impossible isotope. Everything was swallowed up in the amazement of something, anything, which showed a constantly increasing intensity of radioactivity under circumstances that ruled out the existence of any type of radioactive breakdown, in any number of steps, then known.

After a while, Kantrowitsch muttered, "We'd better spread it out. If we keep it in sizable lumps it will vaporize or explode or both and contaminate half the city."

So it was powdered and scattered, and mixed with ordinary tungsten at first and then, when the tungsten grew radioactive in its turn, it was mixed with graphite, which had a lower cross-section to the radiation.

Less than two months after Hallam had noticed the change in the bottle's contents, Kantrowitsch, in a communication to the editor of *Nuclear Reviews,* with Hallam's name appended as co-author, announced the existence of plutonium-186. Tracy's original determination was thus vindicated but his name was not mentioned, either then or later. With that Hallam's tungsten began to take on an epic scale and Denison began to note the changes that ended by making him a non-person.

The existence of plutonium-186 was bad enough. To have been stable at the start and to display a curiously increasing radioactivity was much worse.

A seminar to handle the problem was organized. Kantrowitsch was in the chair, which was an interesting historical note, for it was the last time in the history of the Electron Pump that a major meeting was held in connection with it that was chaired by anyone but Hallam. As a matter of fact, Kantrowitsch died five months later and the only personality with sufficient prestige to keep Hallam in the shade was removed.

The meeting was extraordinarily fruitless until Hallam announced his Great Insight, but in the version as reconstructed by Lamont, the real turning point came during the luncheon break. At that time, McFarland, who is not credited with any remarks in the official records, although he was listed as an attendee, said "You know, what we need is a little bit of fantasy here. Suppose—"

He was speaking to Diderick van Klemens, and Van Klemens reported it sketchily in a kind of personal shorthand in his own notes. Long before Lamont had succeeded in tracking that down, Van Klemens was dead, and though his notes convinced Lamont himself, he had to admit they would not make a convincing story without further corroboration. What's more, there was no way of proving that Hallam had overheard the remark. Lamont would have been willing to bet a fortune that Hallam was within earshot, but that willingness was not satisfactory proof either.

And then, suppose Lamont could prove it. It might hurt Hallam's egregious pride, but it couldn't really shake his position. It would be argued that to McFarland, the remark was only fantasy. It was Hallam who accepted it as something more. It was Hallam who was willing to stand up in front of the group and say it officially and risk the derision that might be his. McFarland would surely never have dreamed of placing himself on official record with his "little bit of fantasy."

Lamont might have counter-argued that McFarland was a well-known nuclear physicist with a reputation to lose, while Hallam was a young radiochemist who could say anything he pleased in nuclear physics and, as an outsider, get away with it.

In any case, this is what Hallam said, according to the official transcript:

"Gentlemen, we are getting nowhere. I am therefore

going to make a suggestion, not because it necessarily makes sense, but because it represents less nonsense than anything else I've heard. . . . We are faced with a substance, plutonium-186, that cannot exist at all, let alone as an even momentarily stable substance, if the natural laws of the Universe have any validity at all. It follows, then, that since it does indubitably exist and did exist as a stable substance to begin with, it must have existed, at least to begin with, in a place or at a time or under circumstances where the natural laws of the Universe were other than they are. To put it bluntly, the substance we are studying did not originate in our Universe at all, but in another—an alternate Universe—a parallel Universe. Call it what you want.

"Once here—and I don't pretend to know how it got across—it was stable still and I suggest that this was because it carried the laws of its own Universe with it. The fact that it slowly became radioactive and then ever more radioactive may mean that the laws of our own Universe slowly soaked into its substance, if you know what I mean.

"I point out that at the same time that the plutonium-186 appeared, a sample of tungsten, made up of several stable isotopes, including tungsten-186, disappeared. It may have slipped over into the parallel Universe. After all, it is logical to suppose that it is simpler for an exchange of mass to take place than for a one-way transfer to do so. In the parallel Universe, tungsten-186 may be as anomalous as plutonium-186 is here. It may begin as a stable substance and slowly become increasingly radioactive. It may serve as an energy source there just as plutonium-186 would here."

The audience must have been listening with considerable astonishment for there is no record of interruption, at least until the sentence last recorded above, at which time Hallam seemed to have paused to catch his breath and perhaps to wonder at his own temerity.

Someone from the audience (presumably Antoine-Jerome Lapin, though the record is not clear) asked if Professor Hallam were suggesting that an intelligent agent in the para-Universe had deliberately made the exchange in order to obtain an energy source. The expression "para-Universe," inspired apparently as an abbreviation of "parallel-Universe," thus entered the language. This question contained the first recorded use of the expression.

There was a pause and then Hallam, more daring than ever, said—and this was the nub of the Great Insight—"Yes, I think so, and I think that the energy source cannot be made practical unless Universe and para-Universe work together, each at one half of a pump, pushing energy from them to us and from us to them, taking advantage of the difference in the natural laws of the two Universes."

Hallam had adopted the word "para-Universe" and made it his own at this point. Furthermore, he became the first to use the word "pump" (since invariably capitalized) in connection with the matter.

There is a tendency in the official account to give the impression that Hallam's suggestion caught fire at once, but it did not. Those who were willing to discuss it at all would commit themselves no farther than to say it was an amusing speculation. Kantrowitsch, in particular, did not say a word. This was crucial to Hallam's career.

Hallam could scarcely carry through the theoretical and practical implications of his own suggestion all by himself. A team was required and it was built up. But none of the team, until it was too late, would associate himself openly with the suggestion. By the time success was unmistakable, the public had grown to think of it as Hallam's and Hallam's alone. It was Hallam, to all the world, and Hallam alone, who had first discovered the substance, who had conceived and transmitted the Great Insight; and it was therefore Hallam who was the Father of the Electron Pump.

Thus, in various laboratories, pellets of tungsten metal were laid out temptingly. In one out of ten the transfer was made and new supplies of plutonium-186 were produced. Other elements were offered as bait and refused. . . . But wherever the plutonium-186 appeared and whoever it was that brought the supply to the central research organization working on the problem, to the public it was an additional quantity of "Hallam's-tungsten."

It was Hallam again who presented some aspects of the theory to the public most successfully. To his own surprise (as he later said) he found himself to be a facile writer, and he enjoyed popularizing. Besides success has its own inertia, and the public would accept information on the project from no one but Hallam.

In a since famous article in the *North American Sunday Tele-Times Weekly,* he wrote, "We cannot say in how many different ways the laws of the para-Universe differ from our own, but we can guess with some assurance that the strong nuclear interaction, which is the strongest known force in our Universe, is even stronger in the para-Universe; perhaps a hundred times stronger. This means that protons are more easily held together against their own electrostatic attraction and that a nucleus requires fewer neutrons to produce stability.

"Plutonium-186, stable in their Universe, contains far too many protons, or too few neutrons, to be stable in ours with its less effective nuclear interaction. The plutonium-186, once in our Universe, begins to radiate positrons, releasing energy as it does so, and with each positron emitted, a proton within a nucleus is converted to a neutron. Eventually, twenty protons per nucleus have been converted to neutrons and plutonium-186 has become tungsten-186, which is stable by the laws of our own Universe. In the process, twenty positrons per nucleus have been eliminated. These meet, combine with, and annihilate twenty electrons, releasing further energy, so that for every plutonium-186 nucleus sent to us, our Universe ends up with twenty fewer electrons.

"Meanwhile, the tungsten-186 that enters the para-Universe is unstable there for the opposite reason. By the laws of the para-Universe it has too many neutrons, or too few protons. The tungsten-186 nuclei begin to emit electrons, releasing energy steadily while doing so, and with each emitted electron a neutron changes to a proton until, in the end, it is plutonium-186 again. With each tungsten-186 nucleus sent into the para-Universe, twenty more electrons are added to it.

"The plutonium/tungsten can make its cycle endlessly

back and forth between Universe and para-Universe, yielding energy first in one and then in another, with the net effect being a transfer of twenty electrons from our Universe to their per each nucleus cycled. Both sides can gain energy from what is, in effect, an Inter-Universe Electron Pump."

The conversion of this notion into reality and the actual establishment of the Electron Pump as an effective energy source proceeded with amazing speed, and every stage of its success enhanced Hallam's prestige.

3

Lamont had no reason to doubt the basis of that prestige and it was with a certain hero-worshipfulness (the memory of which embarrassed him later and which he strove—with some success—to eliminate from his mind) that he first applied for a chance to interview Hallam at some length in connection with the history he was planning.

Hallam seemed amenable. In thirty years, his position in public esteem had become so lofty one might wonder why his nose did not bleed. Physically, he had aged impressively, if not gracefully. There was a ponderousness to his body that gave him the appearance of circumstantial weightiness and if his face were gross in its features he seemed able to give them the air of a kind of intellectual repose. He still reddened quickly and the easily bruised nature of his self-esteem was a byword.

Hallam had undergone some quick briefing before Lamont's entrance. He said, "You are Dr. Peter Lamont and you've done good work, I'm told, on para-theory. I recall your paper. On para-fusion, wasn't it?"

"Yes, sir."

"Well, refresh my memory. Tell me about it. Informally,

of course, as though you were talking to a layman. After all," and he chuckled here, "in a way, I am a layman. I'm just a radiochemist, you know; and no great theoretician, unless you want to count a few concepts now and then."

Lamont accepted this, at the time, as a straightforward statement, and, indeed, the speech may not have been as obscenely condescending as he later insisted on remembering it to have been. It was typical, though, as Lamont later found out, or at least maintained, of Hallam's method of grasping the essentials of the work done by others. He could talk briskly about the subject thereafter without being overparticular, or particular at all, in assigning credit.

But the younger Lamont of the time was rather flattered, and he began at once with that voluble eagerness one experiences in explaining one's own discoveries. "I can't say I did much, Dr. Hallam. Deducing the laws of nature of the para-Universe—the para-laws—is a tricky business. We have so little to go on. I started from what little we know and assumed no new departures that we had no evidence for. With a stronger nuclear interaction, it seems obvious that the fusion of small nuclei would take place more readily."

"Para-fusion," said Hallam.

"Yes, sir. The trick was simply to work out what the details might be. The mathematics involved was somewhat subtle but once a few transformations were made, the difficulties tended to melt away. It turns out, for instance, that lithium hydride can be made to undergo catastrophic fusion at temperatures four orders of magnitude lower there than here. It takes fission-bomb temperatures to explode lithium hydride here, but a mere dyamite charge, so to speak, would turn the trick in the para-Universe. Just possibly lithium hydride in the para-Universe could be ignited with a match, but that's not very likely. We've offered them lithium hydride, you know, since fusion power might be natural for them, but they won't touch it."

"Yes, I know that."

"It would clearly be too risky for them; like using nitroglycerine in ton-lots in rocket engines—only worse."

"Very good. And you are also writing a history of the Pump."

"An informal one, sir. When the manuscript is ready I will ask you to read it, if I may, so that I might have the benefit of your intimate knowledge of events. In fact, I would like to take advantage of some of that knowledge right now if you have a little time."

"I can make some. What is it you want to know?" Hallam was smiling. It was the last time he ever smiled in Lamont's presence.

"The development of an effective and practical Pump, Professor Hallam, took place with extraordinary speed," began Lamont. "Once the Pump Project—"

"The Inter-Universe Electron Pump Project," corrected Hallam, still smiling.

"Yes, of course," said Lamont, clearing his throat. "I was merely using the popular name. Once the project started, the engineering details were developed with great rapidity and with little waste motion."

"That is true," said Hallam, with a touch of complacence. "People have tried to tell me that the credit was mine for vigorous and imaginative direction, but I wouldn't care to have you overstress that in your book. The fact is that we had an enormous fund of talent in the project, and I wouldn't want the brilliance of individual members to be dimmed by any exaggeration of my role."

Lamont shook his head with a little annoyance. He found the remark irrelevant. He said, "I don't mean that at all. I mean the intelligence at the other end—the para-men, to use the popular phrase. They started it. We discovered them after the first transfer of plutonium for tungsten; but they discovered us first in order to make the transfer, working on pure theory without the benefit of the hint they gave us. And there's the iron-foil they sent across—"

Hallam's smile had now disappeared, and permanently. He was frowning and he said loudly, "The symbols were never understood. Nothing about them—"

"The geometric figures were understood, sir. I've looked into it and it's quite clear that they were directing the geometry of the Pump. It seems to me that—"

Hallam's chair shoved back with an angry scrape. He said, "Let's not have any of that, young man. We did the work, not they."

"Yes—but isn't it true that they—"

"That they *what?*"

Lamont became aware now of the storm of emotion he had raised, but he couldn't understand its cause. Uncertainly, he said, "That they are more intelligent than we— that they did the real work. Is there any doubt of that, sir?"

Hallam, red-faced, had heaved himself to his feet. "There is every doubt," he shouted. "I will not have mysticism here. There is too much of that. See here, young man," he advanced on the still seated and thoroughly astonished Lamont and shook a thick finger at him, "if your history is going to take the attitude that we were puppets in the hands of the para-men, it will not be published from this institution; or at all, if I have my way. I will not have mankind and its intelligence downgraded and I won't have para-men cast in the role of gods."

Lamont could only leave, a puzzled man, utterly upset at having created harsh feeling where he had wanted only to have good will.

And then he found that his historical sources were suddenly drying up. Those who had been loquacious enough a week earlier now remembered nothing and had no time for further interviews.

Lamont was irritated at first and then a slow anger began to build within him. He looked at what he had from a new viewpoint, and now he began to squeeze and insist where earlier he had merely asked. When he met Hallam at department functions, Hallam frowned and looked through him and Lamont began to look scornful in his turn.

The net result was that Lamont found his prime career as para-theoretician beginning to abort and turned more firmly than ever toward his secondary career as science-historian.

6 (continued)

"That damned fool," muttered Lamont, reminiscently. "You had to be there, Mike, to see him go into panic at any suggestion that it was the other side that was the moving force. I look back on it and I wonder—how was it possible to meet him, however casually, and not know he would react that way. Just be grateful you never had to work with him."

"I am," said Bronowski, indifferently, "though there are times you're no angel."

"Don't complain. With your sort of work you have no problems."

"Also no interest. Who cares about my sort of work except myself and five others in the world. Maybe six others —if you remember."

Lamont remembered. "Oh, well," he said.

4

Bronowski's placid exterior never fooled anyone who grew to know him even moderately well. He was sharp and he worried a problem till he had the solution or till he had it in such tatters that he *knew* no solution was possible.

Consider the Etruscan inscriptions on which he had built his reputation. The language had been a living one till the first century A.D., but the cultural imperialism of the Romans had left nothing behind and it had vanished almost completely. What inscriptions survived the carnage of Roman hostility and—worse—indifference were written in Greek letters so that they could be pronounced, but nothing more. Etruscan seemed to have no relationship to any of the surrounding languages; it seemed very archaic; it seemed not even to be Indo-European.

Bronowski therefore passed on to another language that seemed to have no relationship to any of the surrounding languages; that seemed very archaic; that seemed not even to be Indo-European—but which was very much alive and which was spoken in a region not so very far from where once the Etruscans had lived.

What of the Basque language? Bronowski wondered. And he used Basque as his guide. Others had tried this before him and given up. Bronowski did not.

It was hard work, for Basque, an extraordinarily difficult language in itself, was only the loosest of helps. Bronowski found more and more reason, as he went on, to suspect some cultural connection between the inhabitants of early northern Italy and early northern Spain. He could even make out a strong case for a broad swatch of pre-Celts filling western Europe with a language of which Etruscan and Basque were dimly-related survivors. In two thousand years, however, Basque had evolved and had become more than a little contaminated with Spanish. To try, first, to reason out its structure in Roman times and then relate it to Etruscan was an intellectual feat of surpassing difficulty and Bronowski utterly astonished the world's philologists when he triumphed.

The Etruscan translations themselves were marvels of dullness and had no significance whatever; routine funerary inscriptions for the most part. The fact of the translation, however, was stunning and, as it turned out, it proved of the greatest importance to Lamont.

—Not at first. To be perfectly truthful about it, the translations had been a fact for nearly five years before Lamont had as much as heard that there were such people, once, as the Etruscans. But then Bronowski came to the university to give one of the annual Fellowship Lectures and Lamont, who usually shirked the duty of attending which fell on the faculty members, did not shirk this one.

It was not because he recognized its importance or felt any interest in it whatever. It was because he was dating a graduate student in the Department of Romance Languages and it was either that or a music festival he particularly wanted to avoid hearing. The social connection was a feeble one, scarcely satisfactory from Lamont's point of view and only temporary, but it did get him to the talk.

He rather enjoyed it, as it happened. The dim Etruscan civilization entered his consciousness for the first time as a matter of distant interest, and the problem of solving an undeciphered language struck him as fascinating. When young, he had enjoyed solving cryptograms, but had put them away with other childish things in favor of the much grander cryptograms posed by nature, so that he ended in para-theory.

Yet Bronowski's talk took him back to the youthful joys of making slow sense of what seemed a random collection of symbols, and combined it with sufficient difficulty to add great honor to the task. Bronowski was a cryptogrammist on the grandest scale, and it was the description of the steady encroachment of reason upon the unknown that Lamont enjoyed.

All would yet have gone for nothing—the triple coincidence of Bronowski's appearance at campus, Lamont's youthful cryptogrammic enthusiasm, the social pressure of an attractive young lady—were it not for the fact that it was the next day that Lamont saw Hallam and placed himself firmly and, as he eventually found, permanently, in the doghouse.

Within an hour of the conclusion of that interview, Lamont determined to see Bronowski. The issue at hand was the very one that had seemed so obvious to himself and that had so offended Hallam. Because it brought down censure on him, Lamont felt bound to strike back—and in connection with the point of censure specifically. The para-men *were* more intelligent than man. Lamont had believed it before in a casual sort of way as something more obvious than vital. Now it had become vital. It must be proved and the fact of it forced down the throat of Hallam; sideways, if possible, and with all the sharp corners exposed.

Already Lamont found himself so far removed from his so-recent hero worship that he relished the prospect.

Bronowski was still on campus and Lamont tracked him down and insisted on seeing him.

Bronowski was blandly courteous when finally cornered.

Lamont acknowledged the courtesies brusquely, introduced himself with clear impatience, and said, "Dr. Bronowski, I'm delighted to have caught you before you left. I hope that I will persuade you to stay here even longer."

Bronowski said, "That may not be hard. I have been offered a position on the university faculty."

"And you will accept the position?"

"I am considering it. I think I may."

"You must. You will, when you hear what I have to say. Dr. Bronowski, what is there for you to do now that you've solved the Etruscan inscriptions?"

"That is not my only task, young man." (He was five years older than Lamont.) "I'm an archaeologist, and there is more to Etruscan culture than its inscriptions and more to pre-classical Italic culture than the Etruscans."

"But surely nothing as exciting for you, and as challenging, as the Etruscan inscriptions?"

"I grant you that."

"So you would welcome something even more exciting, even more challenging, and something a trillion times as significant as those inscriptions."

"What have you in mind, Dr.—Lamont?"

"We have inscriptions that are not part of a dead culture, or part of anything on Earth, or part of anything in the Universe. We have something called para-symbols."

"I've heard of them. For that matter, I've seen them."

"Surely, then, you have the urge to tackle the problem, Dr. Bronowski? You have had the desire to work out what they say?"

"No desire at all, Dr. Lamont, because there's no problem."

Lamont stared at him suspiciously, "You mean you can read them?"

Bronowski shook his head. "You mistake me. I mean I can't possibly read them, nor can anyone else. There's no base. In the case of Earthly languages, however dead, there is always the chance of finding a living language, or a dead language already deciphered, that bears some relationship to it, however faint. Failing that, there is at least the fact that any Earthly language was written by human beings with human ways of thought. That makes a starting point, however feeble. None of this is the case with the para-symbols, so that they constitute a problem that clearly has no solution. An insolubility is not a problem."

Lamont had kept himself from interrupting only with difficulty, and now he burst out, "You are wrong, Dr. Bronowski. I don't want to seem to be teaching you your profession but you don't know some of the facts that my own profession has uncovered. We are dealing with paramen, concerning whom we know almost nothing. We don't know what they are like, how they think, what kind of world they live on; almost nothing, however basic and fundamental. So far, you are right."

"But it's only *almost* nothing that you know, is that it?" Bronowski did not seem impressed. He took out a package of dried figs from his pocket opened them and began to eat. He offered it to Lamont, who shook his head.

Lamont said, "Right. We do know one thing of crucial importance. They are more intelligent than we are. Item one: They can make the exchange across the inter-Universe gap, while we can play only a passive role."

He interrupted himself here to ask, "Do you know anything about the Inter-Universe Electron Pump?"

"A little," said Bronowski. "Enough to follow you, Doctor, if you don't get technical."

Lamont hastened on. "Item two: They sent us instructions as to how to set up our part of the Pump. We couldn't understand it but we could make out the diagrams just sufficiently well to give us the necessary hints.

Item Three: They can somehow sense us. At least they can become aware of our leaving tungsten for them to pick up, for instance. They know where it is and can act upon it. We can do nothing comparable. There are other points but this is enough to show the para-men to be clearly more intelligent than we are."

Bronowski said, "I imagine, though, that you are in the minority here. Surely your colleagues don't accept this."

"They don't. But what makes you come to that conclusion?"

"Because you're clearly wrong, it seems to me."

"My facts are correct. And since they are, how can I be wrong?"

"You are merely proving the technology of the para-men is more advanced than ours. What has that to do with intelligence? See here"—Bronowski rose to take off his jacket and then sat down in a half-reclining position, the soft rotundity of his body seeming to relax and crease in great comfort as though physical ease helped him think—"about two and a half centuries ago, the American naval commander Matthew Perry led a flotilla into Tokyo harbor. The Japanese, till then isolated, found themselves faced with a technology considerably beyond their own and decided it was unwise to risk resistance. An entire warlike nation of millions was helpless in the face of a few ships from across the sea. Did that prove that Americans were more intelligent than the Japanese were, or merely that Western culture had taken a different turning? Clearly the latter, for within half a century, the Japanese had successfully imitated Western technology and within another half a century were a major industrial power despite the fact that they were disastrously beaten in one of the wars of the time."

Lamont listened gravely, and said, "I've thought that, too, Dr. Bronowski, though I didn't know about the Japanese—I wish I had the time to read history. Yet the analogy is wrong. It's more than technical superiority; it's a matter of difference in degree of intelligence."

"How can you tell, aside from guessing?"

"Because of the mere fact that they sent us directions.

They were eager for us to set up our part of the Pump; they *had* to have us do it. They could not physically cross over; even their thin foils of iron on which their messages were incised (the substance most nearly stable in either world) slowly grew too radioactive to keep in one piece, though, of course, not before we had made permanent copies on our own materials." He paused for breath, feeling himself to be too excited, too eager. He mustn't oversell his case.

Bronowski regarded him curiously. "All right, they sent us messages. What are you trying to deduce from that?"

"That they expected us to understand. Could they be such fools as to send us rather intricate messages, in some cases quite lengthy, if they knew we would not understand? . . . If it hadn't been for their diagrams, we would have ended nowhere. Now if they *had* expected us to understand, it could only be because they felt that any creatures like ourselves with a technology roughly as advanced as their own (and they must have been able to estimate that somehow—another point in favor of my belief) must also be roughly as intelligent as themselves and would experience little difficulty in working out something from the symbols."

"That might also be just their naïveté," said Bronowski, unimpressed.

"You mean they think there is only one language, spoken and written, and that another intelligence in another Universe speaks and writes as they do? Come on!"

Bronowski said, "Even if I were to grant your point, what do you want me to do? I've looked at the para-symbols; I suppose every archaeologist and philologist on Earth has. I don't see what I can do; neither, I'm sure, does anyone else. In over twenty years, no progress has been made."

Lamont said, intensely, "What's true is that in twenty years, there has been no desire for progress. The Pump Authority does not want to solve the symbols."

"Why shouldn't they want to?"

"Because of the annoying possibility that communication with the para-men *will* show them to be distinctly more intelligent. Because that would show human beings to be the puppet-partners in connection with the Pump to the hurt of their ego. And, specifically," (and Lamont strove to keep venom out of his voice) "because Hallam would lose the credit for being the Father of the Electron Pump."

"Suppose they *did* want to make progress. What could be done? The will is not the deed, you know."

"They could get the para-men to cooperate. They could send messages to the para-Universe. This has never been done, but it could be. A message on metal foil might be placed under a pellet of tungsten."

"Oh? Are they still looking for new samples of tungsten, even with Pumps in operation?"

"No, but they'll notice the tungsten and they'll assume we're trying to use it to attract their attention. We might even place the message on tungsten foil itself. If they take the message and make any sense of it at all, even the slightest, they'll send back one of their own, incorporating their findings. They might set up an equivalence table of their words and ours, or they might use a mixture of their words and ours. It will be a kind of alternate push, first on their side, then on ours, then on theirs, and so on."

"With their side," said Bronowski, "doing most of the work."

"Yes."

Bronowski shook his head. "No fun in that, is there? It doesn't appeal to me."

Lamont looked at him with flaring anger. "Why not? Don't you think there'll be enough credit in it for you? Not enough fame? What are you, a connoisseur of fame? What kind of fame did you get out of the Etruscan inscriptions, damn it. You beat out five others in the world. Maybe six. With them you're a household word and a success and they hate you. What else? You go about lecturing on the subject before audiences amounting to a few dozen and they forget your name the day after. Is that what you're really after?"

"Don't be dramatic."

"All right. I won't be. I'll get someone else. It may take

longer but, as you say, the para-men will do most of the work anyway. If necessary, I'll do it myself."

"Have you been assigned this project?"

"No, I haven't. What of it? Or is that another reason you don't want to get involved. Disciplinary problems? There is no law against attempting translation and I can always place tungsten on my desk. I will not choose to report any messages I get in place of the tungsten and to that extent I will be breaking the research-code. Once the translation is made, who will complain? Would you work with me if I guaranteed your safety and kept your part in it secret? You would lose your fame but you may value your security more. Oh, well," Lamont shrugged. "If I do it myself, there's the advantage of not having to worry about someone else's security."

He rose to go. Both men were angry and bore themselves with that stiff-legged courtesy one assumes when addressing someone who is hostile, but still mannerly. "I presume," said Lamont, "you will at least treat this conversation as confidential."

Bronowski was on his feet, too. "Of that you may be assured," he said coldly, and the two shook hands briefly.

Lamont did not expect to hear from Bronowski again. He then began the process of talking himself into believing it would be better to handle the translation effort on his own.

Two days later, however, Bronowski was at Lamont's laboratory. He said, rather brusquely, "I'm leaving the city now, but I'll be back in September. I'm taking the position here and, if you're still interested, I'll see what I can do about the translation problem you mentioned."

Lamont had barely time for a surprised expression of thanks when Bronowski stalked off, apparently angrier at having given in, than at having resisted.

They became friends in time; and, in time, Lamont learned what had brought Bronowski around. The day after their discussion, Bronowski had had lunch at the Faculty Club with a group of the higher officials of the university, including, of course, the president. Bronowski had announced that he would accept the position and send in a formal letter to that effect in due time and all had expressed gratification.

The president had said, "It will be quite a feather in our cap to have the renowned translator of the Itascan Inscriptions at the university. We are honored."

The malapropism had gone uncorrected, of course, and Bronowski's smile, though strained, did not actually waver. Afterward, the head of the Department of Ancient History explained the president to be more of a Minnesotan than a classical scholar and since Lake Itasca was the point of origin of the mighty Mississippi, the slip of the tongue was a natural one.

But, in combination with Lamont's sneer at the extent of his fame, Bronowski found the expression rankling.

When Lamont finally heard the story, he was amused. "Don't go on," he said. "I've been down that road, too. You said to yourself, 'By God, I'll do something even *that* knot-head will have to get straight.'"

"A little like that," said Bronowski.

5

A year's work, however, had netted them very little. Messages had finally come across; messages had come back. Nothing.

"Just guess!" Lamont had said feverishly to Bronowski. "Any wild guess at all. Try it out on them."

"It's exactly what I'm doing, Pete. What are you so jumpy about? I spent twelve years on the Etruscan Inscriptions. Do you expect this job to take less time?"

"Good God, Mike. We can't take twelve years."

"Why not? Look, Pete, it hasn't escaped me that there's been a change in your attitude. You've been impossible this last month or so. I thought we had it clear at the start that this work can't go quickly, and that we've got to be patient. I thought you understood that I had my regular duties at the university, too. Look, I've been asking you this several times, now. Let me ask again. Why are you in such a hurry now?"

"Because I'm in a hurry," said Lamont abruptly. "Because I want to get on with it."

"Congratulations," said Bronowski, dryly, "so do I. Listen, you're not expecting an early death, are you? Your doctor hasn't told you you're hiding a fatal cancer?"

"No, no," groaned Lamont.

"Well, then?"

"Never mind," said Lamont, and he walked away hurriedly.

When he had first tried to get Bronowski to join forces with him, Lamont's grievance had concerned only Hallam's mean-minded obstinacy concerning the suggestion that the para-men were the more intelligent. It was in that respect and that respect only that Lamont was striving for a breakthrough. He intended nothing beyond that—at first.

But in the course of the following months, he had been subjected to endless exasperation. His requests for equipment, for technical assistance, for computer time were delayed; his request for travel funds snubbed; his views at interdepartmental meetings invariably overlooked.

The breaking point came when Henry Garrison, junior to himself in point of service and definitely so in point of ability, received an advisory appointment, rich in prestige, that, by all rights, should have gone to Lamont. It was then that Lamont's resentment built up to the point where merely proving himself right was no longer sufficient. He yearned to smash Hallam, destroy him utterly.

The feeling was reinforced every day, almost every hour, by the unmistakable attitude of everyone else at the Pump Station. Lamont's abrasive personality didn't collect sympathy, but some existed nevertheless.

Garrison himself was embarrassed. He was a quiet-spoken, amiable young man who clearly wanted no trouble and who now stood in the doorway of Lamont's lab with an expression that had more than a small component of apprehension in it.

He said, "Hey, Pete, can I have a few words with you?"

"As many as you like," said Lamont, frowning and avoiding a direct eye-to-eye glance.

Garrison came in and sat down. "Pete," he said, "I can't turn down the appointment but I want you to know I didn't push for it. It came as a surprise."

"Who's asking you to turn it down? I don't give a damn."

"Pete. It's Hallam. If I turned it down, it would go to someone else, not you. What have you done to the old man?"

Lamont rounded on the other. "What do *you* think of Hallam? What kind of man is he, in your opinion?"

Garrison was caught by surprise. He pursed his lips and rubbed his nose. "Well—" he said, and let the sound fade off.

"Great man? Brilliant scientist? Inspiring leader?"

"Well—"

"Let me tell you. The man's a phony! He's a fraud! He's got this reputation and this position of his and he's sitting on it in a panic. He knows that I see through him and that's what he has against me."

Garrison gave out a small, uneasy laugh, "You haven't gone up to him and said—"

"No, I haven't said anything directly to him," said Lamont, morosely. "Some day I will. But he can tell. He knows I'm one person he isn't fooling even if I don't say anything."

"But, Pete, where's the point in letting him know it? I don't say *I* think he's the world's greatest, either, but where's the sense in broadcasting it? Butter him up a little. He's got your career in his hands."

"Has he? I've got his reputation in mine. I'm going to show him up. I'm going to strip him."

"How?"

"My business!" muttered Lamont, who at the moment had not the slightest idea as to how.

"But that's ridiculous," said Garrison. "You can't win. He'll just destroy you. Even if he isn't an Einstein or an Oppenheimer really, he's more than either to the world in general. He *is* the Father of the Electron Pump to Earth's two-billion population and nothing you can possibly do will affect them as long as the Electron Pump is the key to human paradise. While that's true, Hallam can't be touched and you're crazy if you think he can. What the hell, Pete, tell him he's great and eat crow. Don't be another Denison!"

"I tell you what, Henry," said Lamont, in sudden fury. "Why not mind your own business?"

Garrison rose suddenly and left without a word. Lamont had made another enemy; or, at least, lost another friend. The price, however, was right, he finally decided, for one remark of Garrison had set the ball rolling in another direction.

Garrison had said, in essence, ". . . as long as the Electron Pump is the key to human paradise . . . Hallam can't be touched."

With that clanging in his mind, Lamont for the first time turned his attention away from Hallam and placed it on the Electron Pump.

Was the Electron Pump the key to human paradise? Or was there, by Heaven, a catch?

Everything in history had had a catch. What was the catch to the Electron Pump?

Lamont knew enough of the history of para-theory to know that the matter of "a catch" had not gone unexplored. When it was first announced that the basic over-all change in the Electron Pump was the Pumping of electrons from the Universe to the para-Universe, there had not been wanting those who said immediately, "But what will happen when all the electrons have been Pumped?"

This was easily answered. At the largest reasonable rate of Pumping, the electron supply would last for at least a trillion trillion years—and the entire Universe, together, presumably, with the para-Universe, wouldn't last a tiny fraction of that time.

The next objection was more sophisticated. There was

no possibility of Pumping *all* the electrons across. As the electrons were Pumped, the para-Universe would gain a net negative charge, and the Universe a net positive charge. With each year, as this difference in charge grew, it would become more difficult to Pump further electrons against the force of the opposed charge-difference. It was, of course neutral atoms that were actually Pumped but the distortion of the orbital electrons in the process created an effective charge which increased immensely with the radioactive changes that followed.

If the charge-concentration remained at the points of Pumping, the effect on the orbit-distorted atoms being Pumped would stop the entire process almost at once, but of course, there was diffusion to take into account. The charge-concentration diffused outward over the Earth, and the effect on the Pumping process had been calculated with that in mind.

The increased positive charge of the Earth generally forced the positively charged Solar wind to avoid the planet at a greater distance, and the magnetosphere was enlarged. Thanks to the work of McFarland (the real originator of the Great Insight according to Lamont) it could be shown that a definite equilibrium point was reached as the Solar wind swept away more and more of the accumulating positive particles that were repelled from Earth's surface and driven higher into the exosphere. With each increase in Pumping intensity; with each additional Pumping Station constructed, the net positive charge on Earth increased slightly, and the magnetosphere expanded by a few miles. The change, however, was minor, and the positive charge was, in the end, swept away by the Solar wind and spread through the outer reaches of the Solar system.

Even so—even allowing for the most rapid possible diffusion of the charge—the time would come when the local charge-difference between Universe and para-Universe at the points of Pumping would grow large enough to end the process, and that would be a small fraction of the time it would take really to use up all the electrons; roughly, a trillion-trillionth of the time.

But that still meant that Pumping would remain possible for a trillion years. Only a *single* trillion years, but that was enough; it would suffice. A trillion years was far longer than man would last, or the Solar system either. And if man somehow did last that long (or some creature that was man's successor and supplanter) then no doubt something would be devised to correct the situation. A great deal could be done in a trillion years.

Lamont had to agree to that.

But then he thought of something else, another line of thought that he well remembered Hallam himself had dealt with in one of the articles he had written for popular consumption. With some distaste, he dug out the article. It was important to see what Hallam had said before he carried the matter further.

The article said, in part, "Because of the ever-present gravitational force, we have come to associate the phrase 'downhill' with the kind of inevitable change we can use to produce energy of the sort we can change into useful work. It is the water running downhill that, in past centuries, turned wheels which in turn powered machinery such as pumps and generators. But what happens when all the water has run downhill?

"There can then be no further work possible till the water has been returned uphill—and that takes work. In fact, it takes more work to force the water uphill than we can collect by then allowing it to flow downhill. We work at an energy-loss. Fortunately, the Sun does the work for us. It evaporates the oceans so that water vapor climbs high in the atmosphere, forms clouds, and eventually falls again as rain or snow. This soaks the ground at all levels, fills the springs and streams, and keeps the water forever running downhill.

"But not quite forever. The Sun can raise the water vapor, but only because, in a nuclear sense, it is running downhill, too. It is running downhill at a rate immensely greater than any Earthly river can manage, and when all of it has run downhill there will be nothing we know of to pull it uphill again.

"All sources of energy in our Universe run down. We

can't help that. Everything is downhill in just one direction, and we can force a temporary uphill, backward, only by taking advantage of some greater downhill in the vicinity. If we want useful energy forever, we need a road that is downhill both ways. That is a paradox in our Universe; it stands to reason that whatever is downhill one way is uphill going back.

"But need we confine ourselves to our Universe alone? Think of the para-Universe. It has roads, too, that are downhill in one direction and uphill in the other. Those roads, however, don't fit in with our roads. It is possible to take a road from the para-Universe to our Universe that is downhill, but which, when we follow it back from the Universe to the para-Universe, is downhill again—because the Universes have different laws of behavior.

"The Electron Pump takes advantage of a road that is downhill both ways. The Electron Pump—"

Lamont looked back at the title of the piece again. It was "The Road that is Downhill Both Ways."

He began thinking. The concept was, of course, a familiar one to him, as was its thermodynamic consequences. But why not examine the assumptions? That had to be the weak point in any theory. What if the assumptions, assumed to be right by definition, were wrong? What would be the consequences if one started with other assumptions? Contradictory ones?

He started blindly but within a month he had that feeling that every scientist recognizes—the endless click-click as unexpected pieces fall into place, as annoying anomalies become anomalous no more— It was the feel of Truth.

It was from that moment on that he began to put additional pressure on Bronowski.

And one day he said, "I'm going to see Hallam again."

Bronowski's eyebrows lifted. "What for?"

"To have him turn me down."

"Yes, that's about your speed, Pete. You're unhappy if your troubles die down a bit."

"You don't understand. It's important to have him refuse to listen to me. I can't have it said afterward that I by-passed him; that he was ignorant of it."

"Of what? Of the translation of the para-symbols? There isn't any yet. Don't jump the gun, Pete."

"No, no, not that," and he would say no more.

Hallam did not make it easy for Lamont; it was some weeks before he could find time to see the younger man. Nor did Lamont intend to make it easy for Hallam. He stalked in with every invisible bristle on edge and sharply pointed. Hallam waited for him frozen-faced, with sullen eyes.

Hallam said abruptly, "What's this crisis you're talking about?"

"Something's turned up, sir," said Lamont, tonelessly, "inspired by one of your articles."

"Oh?" Then, quickly, "Which one?"

"'The Road that is Downhill Both Ways.' The one you programmed for *Teen-age Life,* sir."

"And what about it?"

"I believe the Electron Pump is not downhill both ways, if I may use your metaphor, which is not, as it happens, a completely accurate way of describing the Second Law of Thermodynamics."

Hallam frowned. "What have you got in mind?"

"I can explain it best, sir, by setting up the Field Equations for the two Universes, sir, and demonstrating an interaction that till now has not been considered—unfortunately so, in my opinion."

With that, Lamont moved directly to the thixo-board and quickly fingered the equations, talking rapidly as he did so.

Lamont knew that Hallam would be humiliated and irritated by such a procedure since he would not follow the mathematics. Lamont counted on that.

Hallam growled, "See here, young man, I have no time now to engage in a full discussion of any aspect of para-theory. You send me a complete report and, for now, if you have some brief statement as to what you're getting at, you may make it."

Lamont walked away from the thixo-board, with an unmistakable expression of contempt on his face. He said, "All right. The Second Law of Thermodynamics describes a process that inevitably chops off extremes. Water doesn't run downhill; what really happens is that extremes of gravitational potential are equalized. Water will just as easily bubble uphill if trapped underground. You can get work out of the juxtaposition of two different temperature levels, but the end result is that the temperature is equalized at an intermediate level; the hot body cools down and the cold body warms up. Both cooling and warming are equal aspects of the Second Law and, under, the proper circumstances, equally spontaneous."

"Don't teach me elementary thermodynamics, young man. What is it you want? I have very little time."

Lamont said, with no change of expression, no sense of being hurried. "Work is obtained out of the Electron Pump by an equalization of extremes. In this case, the extremes are the physical laws of the two Universes. The conditions that make those laws possible, whatever those conditions may be, are being bled from one Universe into the other and the end result of the entire process will be two Universes in which the laws of nature will be identical —and intermediate as compared with the situation now. Since this will produce uncertain but undoubtedly large changes in this Universe, it would seem that serious consideration must be given to stopping the Pumps and shutting down the whole operation permanently."

It was at this point that Lamont expected Hallam to explode, cutting off any chance of further explanation. Hallam did not fail that expectation. He sprang out of his chair, which fell over. He kicked the chair away and took the two steps that separated him from Lamont.

Warily, Lamont pushed his own chair hastily backward and stood up.

"You idiot," shouted Hallam, almost stammering in his anger. "Don't you suppose everyone at the station understands about the equalization of natural law. Are you wasting my time telling me something I knew when you were learning to read? Get out of here, and any time you want to offer me your resignation, consider it accepted."

Lamont left, having obtained exactly what he wanted, and yet he felt himself to be furious over Hallam's treatment of him.

6 (concluded)

"Anyway," said Lamont, "it clears the ground. I've tried to tell him. He wouldn't listen. So I take the next step."

"And what is that?" said Bronowski.

"I'm going to see Senator Burt."

"You mean the head of the Committee on Technology and the Environment?"

"The same. You've heard of him, then."

"Who hasn't. But where's the point, Pete. What have you got that would interest him? It's not the translation. Pete, I'm asking you once again. What have you got on your mind?"

"I can't explain. You don't know para-theory."

"Does Senator Burt?"

"More than you, I think."

Bronowski pointed his finger. "Pete, let's not kid around. Maybe I know things you don't. We can't work together if we work against each other. Either I'm a member of this little two-man corporation or I'm not. You tell me what's on your mind, and I'll tell you something in exchange. Otherwise, let's stop this altogether."

Lamont shrugged. "All right. If you want it, I'll give it to you. Now that I've got it past Hallam, maybe it's just as well. The point is that the Electron Pump is transferring natural law. In the para-Universe, the strong interaction is a hundred times stronger than it is here, which means that nuclear fission is much more likely here than there, and nuclear fusion is much more likely there than here. If the Electron Pump keeps on long enough, there will be a final equilibrium in which the strong nuclear interaction will be equally strong in both Universes, and be at a figure about ten times what it is here now and one-tenth what it is there now."

"Didn't anyone know this?"

"Oh, sure, everyone knew it. It was obvious almost from the start. Even Hallam can see it. That's what got the bastard so excited. I started telling him this in detail as though I didn't think he had ever heard it before and he blew up."

"But what's the point then? Is there danger in the interaction becoming intermediate?"

"Of course. What do you think?"

"I don't think anything. When will it become intermediate?"

"At the present rate, 10^{30} years or so."

"How long is that?"

"Long enough for a trillion trillion Universes like this one to be born, live, grow old, and die, one after the other."

"Oh blazes, Pete. What odds does it make then?"

"Because to reach that figure," said Lamont, slowly and carefully, "which is the official one, certain assumptions were made which I think were wrong. And if certain other assumptions are made, which I think are *right*, we're in trouble *now*."

"What kind of trouble?"

"Suppose the Earth turned into a whiff of gas in a period of about five minutes. Would you consider that trouble?"

"Because of the Pumping?"

"Because of the Pumping!"

"And how about the world of the para-men? Would they be in danger, too?"

"I'm sure of it. A different danger, but danger."

Bronowski stood up and began pacing. He wore his brown hair thick and long in what had once been called a Buster Brown. Now he was clutching at it. He said, "If the para-men are more intelligent than we are, would they be running the Pump? Surely they would know it was dangerous, before we did."

"I've thought of that," said Lamont. "What I guess is that they've started Pumping for the first time and they, like us, got the process started for the apparent good it would bring and worried about consequences later."

"But you say you know the consequences now. Would they be slower than you were?"

"It depends on if and when they look for those consequences. The Pump is too attractive to try to spoil. I wouldn't have looked myself if I hadn't— But what's on *your* mind, Mike?"

Bronowski stopped his pacing, looked full at Lamont, and said, "I think we've got something."

Lamont looked at him wildly, then leaped forward to seize the other's sleeve. "With the para-symbols? Tell me, Mike!"

"It was while you were with Hallam. While you were actually with Hallam. I haven't known exactly what to do about it, because I wasn't sure what was going on. And now—"

"And now?"

"I'm still not sure. One of their foils came through, with four symbols . . ."

"Oh?"

". . . in the Latin alphabet. And it can be pronounced."

"What?"

"Here it is."

Bronowski produced the foil with the air of a conjurer. Incised on it, quite different from the delicate and intricate spirals and differential glistenings of the para-symbols, were four broad, childlike letters: F-E-E-R.

"What do you suppose that means?" asked Lamont, blankly.

"So far all I've been able to think of is that it's F-E-A-R misspelled."

"Is that why you were cross-examining me? You thought someone on the other side was experiencing fear?"

"And I thought it might have some connection with your own obviously increasing excitement over the last month. Frankly, Pete, I didn't like being kept in the dark."

"Okay. Now let's not jump to conclusions. You're the one with experience with fragmentary messages. Wouldn't you say that the para-men were beginning to experience fear concerning the Electron Pump?"

"Not necessarily at all," said Bronowski. "I don't know how much they can sense of this Universe. If they can sense the tungsten we lay out for them; if they can sense our presence; perhaps they are sensing our state of mind. Perhaps they are trying to reassure us; telling us there is no reason to fear."

"Then why don't they say N-O F-E-E-R."

"Because they don't know our language that well yet."

"Hmm. Then I can't take it to Burt."

"I wouldn't. It's ambiguous. In fact, I wouldn't go to Burt till we get something more from the other side. Who knows what they're trying to say."

"No, I can't wait, Mike. I *know* I'm right, and we have no time."

"All right, but if you see Burt you'll be burning your bridges. Your colleagues will never forgive you. Have you thought of talking to the physicists here? You can't put pressure on Hallam on your own, but a whole group of you—"

Lamont shook his head vigorously, "Not at all. The men at this station survive by virtue of their jellyfish quality. There isn't one who would stand against him. Trying to rally the others to put pressure on Hallam would be like asking strands of cooked spaghetti to come to attention."

Bronowski's soft face looked unwontedly grim. "You may be right."

"I know I'm right," said Lamont, just as grimly.

7

It had taken time to pin the senator down; time that Lamont had resented losing; the more so since nothing further in Latin letters had come from the para-men. No message of any kind, though Bronowski had sent across half a dozen, each with a carefully selected combinations of para-symbols and each incorporating both F-E-E-R and F-E-A-R.

Lamont wasn't sure of the significance of the half-dozen variations but Bronowski had seemed hopeful.

Yet nothing had happened and now Lamont was at last in to see Burt.

The senator was thin-faced, sharp-eyed, and elderly. He had been the head of the Committee on Technology and the Environment for a generation. He took his job seriously and had proved that a dozen times.

He fiddled, now, with the old-fashioned necktie that he affected (and that had become his trademark) and said, "I can only give you half an hour, son." He looked at his wristwatch.

Lamont was not worried. He expected to interest Senator Burt enough to make him forget about time limits. Nor did he attempt to begin at the beginning; his intentions here were quite different from those in connection with Hallam.

He said, "I won't bother with the mathematics, Senator, but I will assume you realize that through Pumping, the natural laws of the two Universes are being mixed."

"Stirred together," said the senator, calmly, "with equilibrium coming in about 10^{30} years. Is that the figure?" His eyebrows in repose arched up and then down, giving his lined face a permanent air of surprise.

"It is," said Lamont, "but it is arrived at by assuming

hat the alien laws seeping into our Universe and theirs
pread outward from the point of entry at the speed of
ight. That is just an assumption and I believe it to be
vrong."

"Why?"

"The only measured rate of mixing is within the pluto-
ium-186 sent into this Universe. That rate of mixing is ex-
remely slow at first, presumably because matter is dense,
nd increases with time. If the plutonium is mixed with
ess dense matter, the rate of mixing increases more rapid-
y. From a few measurements of this sort it has been cal-
ulated that the permeation rate would increase to the
peed of light in a vacuum. It would take some time for
he alien laws to work their way into the atmosphere, far
ess time to work their way to the top of the atmosphere
nd then off through space in every direction at 300,000
ilometers per second, thinning into harmlessness in no
ime."

Lamont paused a moment to consider how best to go
n, and the senator picked it up at once. "However——" he
rged, with the manner of a man not willing to waste time.

"It's a convenient assumption that seems to make sense
nd seems to make no trouble, but what if it is not matter
hat offers resistance to the permeation of the alien laws,
ut the basic fabric of the Universe itself."

"What is the basic fabric?"

"I can't put it in words. There is a mathematical expres-
ion which I think represents it, but I can't put it into
vords. The basic fabric of the Universe is that which dic-
ates the laws of nature. It is the basic fabric of our Uni-
erse that makes it necessary for energy to be conserved.
t is the basic fabric of the para-Universe, with a weave, so
o speak, somewhat different from ours, that makes their
uclear interaction a hundred times stronger than ours."

"And so?"

"If it is the basic fabric that is being penetrated, sir,
hen the presence of matter, dense or not, can have only a
econdary influence. The rate of penetration is greater in a
acuum than in dense mass, but not very much greater.
he rate of penetration in outer space may be great in

Earthly terms but it is only a small fraction of the speed of light."

"Which means?"

"That the alien fabric is not dissipating as quickly as we think, but is piling up, so to speak, within the Solar system to a much greater concentration than we have been assuming."

"I see," said the senator, nodding his head. "And how long then will it be before the space within the Solar system is brought to equilibrium? Less than 10^{30} years, I imagine."

"Far less, sir. Less than 10^{10} years, I think. Perhaps fifty billion years, give or take a couple of billion."

"Not much in comparison, but enough, eh? No immediate cause for alarm, eh?"

"But I'm afraid that *is* immediate cause for alarm, sir. Damage will be done long before equilibrium is reached. Because of the Pumping, the strong nuclear interaction is growing steadily stronger in our Universe at every moment."

"Enough stronger to measure?"

"Perhaps not, sir."

"Not even after twenty years of Pumping?"

"Perhaps not, sir."

"Then why worry?"

"Because, sir, upon the strength of the strong nuclear interaction rests the rate at which hydrogen fuses to helium in the core of the Sun. If the interaction strengthens even unnoticeably, the rate of hydrogen fusion in the Sun will increase markedly. The Sun maintains the balance between radiation and gravitation with great delicacy and to upset that balance in favor of radiation, as we are now doing—"

"Yes?"

"—will cause an enormous explosion. Under our laws of nature, it is impossible for a star as small as the Sun to become a supernova. Under the altered laws, it may not be. I doubt that we would have warning. The Sun would build up to a vast explosion and in eight minutes after that

ou and I will be dead and the Earth will quickly vaporize
into an expanding puff of vapor."

"And nothing can be done?"

"If it is too late to avoid upsetting the equilibrium,
nothing. If it is not yet too late, then we must stop Pumping."

The senator cleared his throat. "Before I agreed to see
ou, young man, I inquired as to your background since
ou were not personally known to me. Among those I
queried was Dr. Hallam. You know him, I suppose?"

"Yes, sir." A corner of Lamont's mouth twitched but
his voice held even. "I know him well."

"He tells me," said the senator, glancing at a paper on
his desk, "that you are a troublemaking idiot of doubtful
sanity and he demands that I refuse to see you."

Lamont said in a voice he strove to keep calm. "Are
those his words, sir?"

"His exact words."

"Then why have you agreed to see me, sir?"

"Ordinarily, if I received something like this from Hallam, I wouldn't have seen you. My time is valuable and
Heaven knows I see more troublemaking idiots of doubtful
sanity than bears thinking of, even among those who come
to me with the highest recommendations. In this one case,
though, I didn't like Hallam's 'demand.' You don't make
demands of a senator and Hallam had better learn that."

"Then you will help me, sir?"

"Help you do what?"

"Why—arrange to have the Pumping halted."

"That? Not at all. Quite impossible."

"Why not?" demanded Lamont. "You are the head of
the Committee on Technology and the Environment and it
is precisely your task to stop the Pumping, or any technological procedure that threatens irreversible harm to the
environment. There can be no greater, no more irreversible harm than threatened by Pumping."

"Certainly. Certainly. *If* you are right. But it seems that
what your story amounts to is that your assumptions are
different from the accepted ones. Who's to say which set
of assumptions is right?"

"Sir, the structure I have built explains several things that are left doubtful in the accepted view."

"Well, then, your colleagues ought to accept your modification and in that case you would scarcely have to come to me, I imagine."

"Sir, my colleagues will not believe. Their self-interest stands in the way."

"As your self-interest stands in the way of your believing you might be wrong. . . . Young man, my powers, on paper, are enormous, but I can only succeed when the public is willing to let me. Let me give you a lesson in practical politics."

He looked at his wristwatch, leaned back and smiled. His offer was not characteristic of him, but an editorial in the *Terrestrial Post* that morning had referred to him as "a consummate politician, the most skilled in the International Congress" and the glow that that had roused within him still lingered.

"It is a mistake," he said, "to suppose that the public wants the environment protected or their lives saved and that they will be grateful to any idealist who will fight for such ends. What the public wants is their own individual comfort. We know that well enough from our experience in the environmental crisis of the twentieth century. Once it was well known that cigarettes increased the incidence of lung cancer, the obvious remedy was to stop smoking, but the desired remedy was a cigarette that did not encourage cancer. When it became clear that the internal-combustion engine was polluting the atmosphere dangerously, the obvious remedy was to abandon such engines, and the desired remedy was to develop non-polluting engines.

"Now then, young man, don't ask me to stop the Pumping. The economy and comfort of the entire planet depend on it. Tell me, instead, how to keep the Pumping from exploding the Sun."

Lamont said, "There is no way, Senator. We are dealing with something here that is so basic, we can't play with it. We must stop it."

"Ah, and you can suggest only that we go back to matters as they were before Pumping."

"We must."

"In that case, you will need hard and fast proof that you are right."

"The best proof," said Lamont, stiffly, "is to have the Sun explode. I suppose you don't want me to go that far."

"Not necessary, perhaps. Why can't you get Hallam to back you up?"

"Because he is a small man who finds himself the Father of the Electron Pump. How can he admit his child will destroy the Earth?"

"I see what you mean, but he is still the Father of the Electron Pump to the whole world, and only his word would carry sufficient weight in this respect."

Lamont shook his head. "He would never give in. He would rather see the Sun explode."

The senator said, "Then force his hand. You have a theory but a theory by itself is meaningless. Surely there must be some way of checking it. The rate of radioactive breakdown of, say, uranium depends on the interactions within the nucleus. Has that rate been changing in a fashion predicted by your theory but not the standard one?"

Again, Lamont shook his head. "Ordinary radioactivity depends on the weak nuclear interaction, and unfortunately, experiments of that sort will yield only borderline evidence. By the time it showed sufficiently to be unmistakable, it would be too late."

"What else, then?"

"There are pion interactions of a specific sort that might yield unmistakable data now. Better still there are quark-quark combinations that have produced puzzling results recently that I am sure I can explain—"

"Well, there you are."

"Yes, but in order to obtain that data. I must make use of a large proton synchrotron on the Moon, sir, and no time on that will be available for years—I've checked—unless someone pulls the strings."

"Meaning me?"

"Meaning you, Senator."

"Not as long as Dr. Hallam says this about you, son."
And Senator Burt's gnarled finger tapped the piece of
paper in front of him. "I can't get out on that limb."

"But the existence of the world—"

"*Prove* it."

"Override Hallam and I'll prove it."

"Prove it and I'll override Hallam."

Lamont drew a deep breath, "Senator! Suppose there's
just a trifling chance I'm right. Isn't even that trifling
chance worth fighting for? It means everything; all mankind, the entire planet—"

"You want me to fight the good fight? I'd like to.
There's a certain drama in going down in a good cause.
Any decent politician is masochistic enough to dream now
and then of going down in flames while the angels sing.
But, Dr. Lamont, to do that one has to have a fighting
chance. One has to have something to fight for that may—
just *may*—win out. If I back you, I'll accomplish nothing
with your word alone against the infinite desirability of
Pumping. Shall I demand every man give up the personal
comfort and affluence he has learned to get used to,
thanks to the Pump, just because one man cries 'Doom'
while all the other scientists stand against him, and the revered Hallam calls him an idiot? No, sir, I will not go
down in flames for *nothing*."

Lamont said, "Then just help me find my proof. You
needn't appear in the open if you fear—"

"I'm not afraid," said Burt, abruptly. "I'm being practical. Dr. Lamont, your half-hour is rather more than
gone."

Lamont stared for a moment in frustration but Burt's
expression was a clearly intransigent one now. Lamont left.

Senator Burt did not see his next visitor immediately.
Minutes passed while he stared uneasily at the closed door
and fiddled with his tie. Could the man have been right?
Could he have had the smallest chance of being right?

He had to admit it would be a pleasure to trip Hallam
and push his face into the mud and sit on him till he

choked—but it would not happen. Hallam was untouchable. He had had only one set-to with Hallam nearly ten years ago. He had been right, dead right, and Hallam had been egregiously wrong, and events had since proved it to be so. And yet, at the time, Burt had been humiliated and he had almost lost reelection as a result.

Burt shook his head in admonition to himself. He might risk reelection in a good cause, but he could not risk humiliation again. He signaled for the next visitor and his face was calm and bland as he rose to greet him.

8

If by this time, Lamont had still felt he had something to lose, professionally, he might have hesitated. Joshua Chen was universally unpopular and anyone who dealt with him was in bad odor at once with almost every corner of the Establishment. Chen was a one-man revolutionary whose single voice could somehow always be heard because he brought to his causes an intensity that was utterly overpowering, and because he had built an organization that was more tightly knit than any ordinary political team in the world (as more than one politician was ready to swear).

He had been one of the important factors accounting for the speed with which the Pump had taken over the planet's energy needs. The Pump's virtues were clear and obvious, as clear as non-pollution and as obvious as forfree, yet there might have been a longer rear-guard fight by those who wanted nuclear energy, not because it was better but because it had been the friend of their childhood.

Yet when Chen beat his drums, the world listened just a little harder.

Now he sat there, his broad cheekbones and round face bearing evidence of the approximately three-quarter admixture of Chinese ancestry.

He said, "Let me get this straight. You're speaking only for yourself?"

"Yes," said Lamont tightly. "Hallam doesn't back me. In fact, Hallam says I'm mad. Do you have to have Hallam's approval before you can move?"

"I need no one's approval," said Chen with predictable arrogance, then he lapsed back into thoughtful consideration. "You say the para-men are farther advanced in technology than we are?"

Lamont had gone that far in the direction of compromise. He had avoided saying they were more intelligent. "Farther advanced in technology" was less offensive, but just as true.

"That is clear," said Lamont, "if only because they can send material across the gap between the Universes and we can't."

"Then why did they start the Pump if it is dangerous? Why are they continuing it?"

Lamont was learning to compromise in more than one direction. He might have said that Chen was not the first to ask this, but it would have sounded condescending, perhaps impatient, and he chose not to do so.

Lamont said, "They were anxious to get started with something that was so apparently desirable as a source of energy, just as we were. I have reason to think they're as disturbed about it now as I am."

"That's still your word. You have no definite evidence about their state of mind."

"None that I can present at this moment."

"Then it's not enough."

"Can we afford to risk—"

"It's not enough, Professor. There's no evidence. I haven't built my reputation by shooting down targets at random. My missiles have sped true to the mark every time because I knew what I was doing."

"But when I get the evidence—"

"Then I'll back you. If the evidence satisfies me, I assure you neither Hallam nor the Congress will be able to resist the tide. So get the evidence and come see me again."

"But by then it will be too late."

Chen shrugged. "Perhaps. Much more likely, you will find that you were wrong and no evidence is to be had."

"I'm *not* wrong." Lamont took a deep breath, and said in a confidential tone, "Mr. Chen. There are very likely trillions upon trillions of inhabited planets in the Universe, and among them there may be billions with intelligent life and highly developed technologies. The same is probably true of the para-Universe. It must be that in the history of the two Universes there have been many pairs of worlds that came into contact and began Pumping. There may be dozens or even hundreds of Pumps scattered across junction points of the two Universes."

"Pure speculation. But if so?"

"Then it may be that in dozens or hundreds of cases, the mixture of natural law advanced locally to an extent sufficient to explode a planet's Sun. The effect might have spread outward. The energy of a supernova added to the changing natural law may have set off explosions among neighboring stars, which in turn set off others. In time perhaps an entire core of a galaxy or of a galactic arm will explode."

"But that is only imagination, of course."

"Is it? There are hundreds of quasars in the Universe; tiny bodies the size of several Solar systems but shining with the light of a hundred full-size ordinary galaxies."

"You're telling me that the quasars are what are left of Pumping planets."

"I'm suggesting that. In the century and a half since they were discovered, astronomers have *still* failed to account for their sources of energy. Nothing in this Universe will account for it; nothing. Doesn't it follow then—"

"What about the para-Universe? Is it full of quasars, too?"

"I wouldn't think so. Conditions are different there. Para-theory makes it seem quite definite that fusion takes place much more easily over there, so the stars must be considerably smaller than ours on the average. It would take a much smaller supply of easily-fusing hydrogen to produce the energy our Sun does. A supply as large as that of our Sun would explode spontaneously. If our laws permeate the para-Universe, hydrogen becomes a little more difficult to fuse; the para-stars begin to cool down."

"Well, that's not so bad," said Chen. "They can use Pumping to supply themselves with the necessary energy. By your speculations, they're in fine shape."

"Not really," said Lamont. Until now, he hadn't thought the para-situation through. "Once our end explodes, the Pumping stops. They can't keep it up without us, and that means they'll face a cooling star without Pump-energy. They might be worse off than we; we'd go out in a painless flash while their agony would be long-drawn-out."

"You have a good imagination, Professor," said Chen, "but I'm not buying it. I don't see any chance of giving up Pumping on nothing more than your imagination. Do you know what the Pump means to mankind? It's not just the free, clean, and copious energy. Look beyond that. What it means is that mankind no longer has to work for a living. It means that for the first time in history, mankind can turn its collective brains to the more important problem of developing its true potential.

"For instance, not all the medical advances of two and a half centuries have succeeded in advancing man's full life-span much past a hundred years. We've been told by gerontologists over and over that there is nothing, in theory, to stand in the way of human immortality, but so far not enough attention has been concentrated on this."

Lamont said angrily, "Immortality! You're talking pipe dreams."

"Perhaps you're a judge of pipe dreams, Professor," said Chen, "but I intend to see that research into immortality begins. It won't begin if Pumping ends. Then we are back to expensive energy, scarce energy, dirty energy. Earth's two billions will have to go back to work for a living and the pipe dream of immortality will remain a pipe dream."

"It will anyway. No one is going to be immortal. No one is even going to live out a normal lifetime."

"Ah, but that is your theory, only."

Lamont weighed the possibilities and decided to gamble. "Mr. Chen, a while ago I said I was not willing to explain my knowledge of the state of mind of the para-men. Well, let me try. We have been receiving messages."

"Yes, but can you interpret them?"

"We received an English word."

Chen frowned slightly. He suddenly put his hands in his pockets, stretched his short legs before him, and leaned back in his chair. "And what was the English word?"

"Fear!" Lamont did not feel it necessary to mention the misspelling.

"Fear," repeated Chen; "and what do you think it means?"

"Isn't it clear that they're afraid of the Pumping phenomenon?"

"Not at all. If they were afraid, they would stop it. I think they're afraid, all right, but they're afraid that our side will stop it. You've gotten across your intention to them and if we stop it, as you want us to do, they've got to stop also. You said yourself they can't continue without us; it's a two-ended proposition. I don't blame them for being afraid."

Lamont sat silent.

"I see," said Chen, "that you haven't thought of that. Well, then, we'll push for immortality. I think that will be the more popular cause."

"Oh, popular causes," said Lamont slowly. "I didn't understand what you found important. How old are you, Mr. Chen?"

For a moment, Chen blinked rapidly, then he turned away. He left the room, walking rapidly, with his hands clenched.

Lamont looked up his biography later. Chen was sixty and his father had died at sixty-two. But it didn't matter.

9

"You don't look as though you had any luck at all," said Bronowski.

Lamont was sitting in his laboratory, staring at the toes of his shoes and noting idly that they seemed unusually scuffed. He shook his head. "No."

"Even the great Chen failed you?"

"He would do nothing. He wants evidence, too. They all want evidence, but anything you offer them is rejected. What they really want is their damned Pump, or their reputation, or their place in history. Chen wants immortality."

"What do you want, Pete?" asked Bronowski, softly.

"Mankind's safety," said Lamont. He looked at the other's quizzical eyes. "You don't believe me?"

"Oh, I believe you. But what do you *really* want?"

"Well, then, by God," and Lamont brought his hand down flat on the desk before him in a loud slap. "I want to be *right*, and that I have, for I *am* right."

"You are sure?"

"I am sure! And there's nothing I am worried about, because I intend to win. You know when I left Chen, I came near to despising myself."

"You?"

"Yes, I. Why not? I kept thinking: At every turn Hallam stops me. As long as Hallam refutes me everyone has an excuse not to believe me. While Hallam stands like a rock against me, I must fail. Why, then, didn't I work through him; why didn't I butter him up, indeed; why didn't I maneuver him into supporting me instead of needling him into fighting me?"

"Do you think you could have?"

"No, never. But in my despair, I thought—well, all

64

sorts of things. That I might go to the Moon, perhaps. Of course, when I first turned him against me there was as yet no question of Earth's doom, but I took care to make it worse when that question arose. But, as you imply, nothing could have turned him against the Pump."

"But you don't seem to despise yourself now."

"No. Because my conversation with Chen brought a dividend. It showed me I was wasting time."

"So it would seem."

"Yes, but needlessly. It is not here on Earth that the solution lies. I told Chen that our Sun might blow up but that the para-Sun would not, yet that would not save the para-men, for when our Sun blew up and our end of the Pump halted, so would theirs. They cannot continue without us, do you see?"

"Yes, of course I see."

"They why don't we think in the reverse. We can't continue without them. In which case, who cares whether we stop the Pump or not. Let's get the para-men to stop."

"Ah, but will they?"

"They said F-E-E-R. And it means they're afraid. Chen said they feared us; they feared we would stop the Pump; but I don't believe that for a moment. *They're* afraid. I sat silent when Chen made his suggestion. He thought he had me. He was quite wrong. I was only thinking at that moment that we had to get the para-men to stop. And we've got to. Mike, I abandon everything, except you. You're the hope of the world. Get through to them somehow."

Bronowski laughed, and there was almost a childlike glee in it. "Pete," he said, "you're a genius."

"Aha. You've noticed."

"No, I mean it. You guess what I want to say before I can say it. I've been sending message after message, using their symbols in a way that I guessed might signify the Pump and using our word as well. And I did my best to gather what information I've scrabbled together over many months to use their symbols in a way signifying disapproval, and using an English word again. I had no idea whether I was getting through or was a mile off base and from the fact that I never got an answer, I had little hope."

"You didn't tell me that's what you were trying to do."

"Well, this part of the problem is my baby. You take your sweet time explaining para-theory to me."

"So what happened?"

"So yesterday, I sent off exactly two words, our language. I scrawled: P-U-M-P B-A-D."

"And?"

"And this morning I picked up a return message at last and it was simple enough, and straightforward, too. It went Y-E-S P-U-M-P B-A-D B-A-D B-A-D. Here look at it."

Lamont's hand trembled as it held the foil. "There's no mistaking that, is there? That's confirmation, isn't it?"

"It seems so to me. Who will you take this to?"

"To no one," said Lamont decisively. "I argue no more. They will tell me I faked the message and there's no point in sitting still for that. Let the para-men stop the Pump and it will stop on our side too and nothing we can do unilaterally will start it up again. The entire Station will then be on fire to prove that I was right and the Pump is dangerous."

"How do you figure that?"

"Because that would be the only way they could keep themselves from being torn apart by a mob demanding the Pump and infuriated at not getting it. . . . Don't you think so?"

"Well, maybe. But one thing bothers me."

"What's that?"

"If the para-men are so convinced that the Pump is dangerous, why haven't they stopped it already? I took occasion to check awhile ago and the Pump is working swimmingly."

Lamont frowned. "Perhaps they don't want a unilateral stoppage. They consider us their partners and they want a mutual agreement to stop. Don't you suppose that might be so?"

"It might. But it might also be that communication is less than perfect; that they don't quite understand the significance of the words B-A-D. From what I said to them via their symbols, which I might well have twisted utterly, they may think that B-A-D means what we consider G-O-O-D."

"Oh, no."

"Well, that's your hope, but there's no pay-off on hopes."

"Mike, just keep on sending messages. Use as many of the words they use as possible and keep ringing the changes. You're the expert and it's in your hands. Eventually, they'll know enough words to say something clear and unmistakable and then we'll explain that we're willing to have the Pump stopped."

"We lack the authority to make any such statement."

"Yes, but they won't know, and in the end we'll be mankind's heroes."

"Even if they execute us first?"

"Even so. . . . It's in your hands, Mike, and I'm sure it won't take much longer."

10

And yet it did. Two weeks passed without another message and the strain grew worse.

Bronowski showed it. The momentary lightness of heart had dissipated, and he entered Lamont's laboratory in glum silence.

They stared at each other and finally Bronowski said, "It's all over the place that you've received your show-cause."

Lamont had clearly not shaved that morning. His laboratory had a forlorn look about it, a not-quite-definable packing-up look. He shrugged. "So what? It doesn't bother me. What does bother me is that *Physical Reviews* rejected my paper."

"You said you were expecting that."

"Yes, but I thought they might give me reasons. They

might point out what they thought were fallacies, errors, unwarranted assumptions. Something I could argue about."

"And they didn't?"

"Not a word. Their referees did not consider the paper suitable for publication. Quote, unquote. They just won't touch it. . . . It's really disheartening, the universal stupidity. I think that I wouldn't grieve at mankind's suicide through sheer evilness of heart, or through mere recklessness. There's something so damned undignified at going to destruction through sheer thickheaded stupidity. What's the use of being men if that's how you have to die."

"Stupidity," muttered Bronowski.

"What else do you call it? And they want me to show-cause why I ought not to be fired for the great crime of being right."

"Everyone seems to know that you consulted Chen."

"Yes!" Lamont put his fingers to the bridge of his nose and wearily rubbed his eyes. "I apparently got him annoyed enough to go to Hallam with tales, and now the accusation is that I have been trying to sabotage the Pump project by unwarranted and unsupported fright tactics in an unprofessional manner and that this makes me unsuitable for employment on the Station."

"They can prove that easily, Pete."

"I suppose they can. It doesn't matter."

"What are you going to do."

"Nothing," said Lamont indignantly. "Let them do their worst. I'll rely on red tape. Every step of this thing will take weeks, months, and meanwhile you keep working. We'll hear from the para-men yet."

Bronowski looked miserable. "Pete, suppose we don't. Maybe it's time you think about this again."

Lamont looked up sharply. "What are you talking about?"

"Tell them you're wrong. Do penance. Beat your breast. Give up."

"Never! By God, Mike, we're playing a game in which the stakes are all the world and every living creature on it."

"Yes, but what's that to you? You're not married. You

have no children. I know your father is dead. You never mention your mother or any siblings. I doubt if there is any human being on earth to whom you are emotionally attached as an individual. So go your way and the hell with it all."

"And you?"

"I'll do the same. I'm divorced and I have no children. I have a young lady with whom I'm close and that relationship will continue while it can. Live! Enjoy!"

"And tomorrow!"

"Will take care of itself. Death when it comes will be quick."

"I can't live with that philosophy. . . . Mike. *Mike!* What is all this? Are you trying to tell me that we're not going to get through? Are you giving up on the para-men?"

Bronowski looked away. He said, "Pete, I did get an answer. Last night. I thought I'd wait for today and think about it, but why think? . . . Here it is."

Lamont's eyes were staring questions. He took the foil and looked at it. There was no punctuation:

PUMP NOT STOP NOT STOP WE NOT STOP PUMP WE NOT HEAR DANGER NOT HEAR NOT HEAR YOU STOP PLEASE STOP YOU STOP SO WE STOP PLEASE YOU STOP DANGER DANGER DANGER STOP STOP YOU STOP PUMP

"By God," muttered Bronowski, "they sound desperate."

Lamont was still staring. He said nothing.

Bronowski said, "I gather that somewhere on the other side is someone like you—a para-Lamont. And he can't get his para-Hallams to stop, either. And while we're begging them to save us, he's begging us to save them."

Lamont said, "But if we show this—"

"They'll say you're lying; that it's a hoax you've concocted to save your psychotically-conceived nightmare."

"They can say that of me, maybe; but they can't say it of you. You'll back me, Mike. You'll testify that you received this and how."

Bronowski reddened. "What good would that do?

They'll say that somewhere in the para-Universe there is a nut like yourself and that two crackpots got together. They'll say that the message proves that the constituted authorities in the para-Universe are convinced there's no danger."

"Mike, fight this through with me."

"There's no use, Pete. You said yourself, stupidity! Those para-man may be more advanced than ourselves, even more intelligent, as you insist, but it's plain to see that they're just as stupid as we are and that ends it. Schiller pointed that out and I believe him."

"Who?"

"Schiller. A German dramatist of three centuries ago. In a play about Joan of Arc, he said, 'Against stupidity, the gods themselves contend in vain.' I'm no god and I'll contend no longer. Let it go, Pete, and go your way. Maybe the world will last our time and, if not, there's nothing that can be done anyway. I'm sorry, Pete. You fought the good fight, but you lost, and I'm through."

He was gone and Lamont was alone. He sat in his chair, fingers aimlessly drumming, drumming. Somewhere in the Sun, protons were clinging together with just a trifling additional avidity and with each moment that avidity grew and at some moment the delicate balance would break down . . .

"And no one on Earth will live to know I was right," cried out Lamont, and blinked and blinked to keep back the tears.

2

. . . the gods themselves . . .

1a

Dua did not have much trouble leaving the others. She always expected trouble, but somehow it never came. Never real trouble.

But then why should it? Odeen objected in his lofty way. "Stay put," he would say. "You know you annoy Tritt." He never spoke of his own annoyance; Rationals didn't grow annoyed over trifles. Still, he hovered over Tritt almost as persistently as Tritt hovered over the children.

But then Odeen always let her have her way if she were persistent enough, and would even intercede with Tritt. Sometimes he even admitted he was proud of her ability, of her independence. . . . He wasn't a bad left-ling, she thought with absent-minded affection.

Tritt was harder to handle and he had a sour way of looking at her when she was—well, when she was as she wished to be. But then right-lings were like that. He was a right-ling to her, but a Parental to the children and the latter took precedence always. . . . Which was good because she could always count on one child or the other taking him away just as things grew uncomfortable.

Still, Dua didn't mind Tritt very much. Except for melting, she tended to ignore him. Odeen was another thing. He had been exciting at first; just his presence had made her outlines shimmer and fade. And the fact that he was a Rational made him all the more exciting somehow. She didn't understand her reaction to that; it was part of her queerness. She had grown used to her queerness—almost.

Dua sighed.

When she was a child, when she still thought of herself as an individual, a single being, and not as part of a triad, she was much more aware of that queerness. She was much more made aware of it by the others. As little a thing as the surface at evening—

She had loved the surface at evening. The other Emotionals had called it cold and gloomy and had quivered and coalesced when she described it for them. They were ready enough to emerge in the warmth of midday and stretch and feed, but that was exactly what made the midday dull. She didn't like to be around the twittering lot of them.

She had to eat, of course, but she liked it much better in the evening when there was very little food, but everything was dim, deep red, and she was alone. Of course, she described it as colder and more wistful than it was when she talked to the others in order to watch them grow hardedged as they imagined the chill—or as hard-edged as young Emotionals could. After a while, they would whisper and laugh at her—and leave her alone.

The small sun was at the horizon now, with the secret ruddiness that she alone was there to see. She spread herself out laterally and thickened dorso-ventrally, absorbing the traces of thin warmth. She munched at it idly, savoring the slightly sour, substanceless taste of the long wave lengths. (She had never met another Emotional who would admit to liking it. But she could never explain that she associated it with freedom; freedom from the others, when she could be alone.)

Even now the loneliness, the chill, and the deep, deep red, brought back those old days before the triad; and even more, quite sharply, her own Parental, who would come lumbering after her, forever fearful that she would hurt herself.

He had been carefully devoted to her, as Parentals always were; to their little-mids more than to the other two, as always. It had annoyed her and she would dream of the day when he would leave her. Parentals always did eventually; and how she had missed him, when one day, he finally did.

He had come to tell her, just as carefully as he could, despite the difficulty Parentals had in putting their feelings into words. She had run from him that day; not in malice;

not because she suspected what he had to tell her; but only out of joy. She had managed to find a special place at midday and had gorged herself in unexpected isolation and had been filled with a queer, itching sensation that demanded motion and activity. She had slithered over the rocks and had let her edges overlap theirs. It was something she knew to be a grossly improper action for anyone but a baby and yet it was something at once exciting and soothing.

And her Parental caught her at last and had stood before her, silent for a long time, making his eyes small and dense as though to stop every bit of light reflected from her; to see as much as he could of her; and for as long as possible.

At first, she just stared back with the confused thought that he had seen her rub through the rocks and was ashamed of her. But she caught no shame-aura and finally she said, very subdued, "What is it, Daddy?"

"Why, Dua, it's the time. I've been expecting it. Surely you have."

"What time?" Now that it was here, Dua stubbornly would not let herself know. If she refused to know, there would be nothing to know. (She never quite got out of that habit. Odeen said all Emotionals were like that, in the lofty voice he used sometimes when he was particularly overcome with the importance of being a Rational.)

Her Parental had said, "I must pass on. I will not be with you any more." Then he just stood and looked at her, and she couldn't say anything.

He said, "You will tell the others."

"Why?" Dua turned away rebelliously, her outlines vague and growing vaguer, trying to dissipate. She *wanted* to dissipate altogether and of course she couldn't. After a while, it hurt and cramped and she hardened again. Her Parental didn't even bother to scold her and tell her that it would be shameful if anyone saw her stretched out so.

She said, "*They* won't care," and immediately felt sorrowful that her Parental would be hurt at that. *He* still called them "little-left" and "little-right," but little-left was all involved with his studies and little-right kept talking about forming a triad. Dua was the only one of the three who still felt— Well, she was the youngest. Emotionals always were and with them it was different.

Her Parental only said, "You will tell them anyway." And they stood looking at each other.

She didn't want to tell them. They weren't close any more. It had been different when they were all little. They could hardly tell themselves apart in those days; left-brother from right-brother from mid-sister. They were all wispy and would tangle with each other and roll through each other and hide in the walls.

No one ever minded that when they were little; none of the grown-ups. But then the brothers grew thick and sober and drew away. And when she complained to her Parental, he would only say gently, "You are too old to thin, Dua."

She tried not to listen, but left-brother kept drawing away and would say, "Don't snuggle; I have no time for you." And right-brother began to stay quite hard all the time and became glum and silent. She didn't understand it quite then and Daddy had not been able to make it clear. He would say every once in a while as though it were a lesson he had once learned—"Lefts are Rationals, Dua. Rights are Parentals. They grow up their own way."

She didn't like their way. They were no longer children and she still was, so she flocked with the other Emotionals. They all had the same complaints about their brothers. They all talked of coming triads. They all spread in the Sun and fed. They all grew more and more the same and every day the same things were said.

And she grew to detest them and went off by herself whenever she could, so that they left and called her "Left-Em." (It had been a long time now since she had heard that call, but she never thought of that phrase without remembering perfectly the thin ragged voices that kept it up after her with a kind of half-wit persistence because they knew it hurt.)

But her Parental retained his interest in her even when it must have seemed to him that everyone else laughed at her. He tried, in his clumsy way, to shield her from the others. He followed her to the surface sometimes, even though he hated it himself, in order to make sure she was safe.

She came upon him once, talking to a Hard One. It was hard for a Parental to talk to a Hard One; even though she was quite young, she knew that much. Hard Ones talked only to Rationals.

She was quite frightened and she wisped away but not before she had heard her Parental say, "I take good care of her, Hard-sir."

Could the Hard One have inquired about her? About her queerness, perhaps. But her Parental had not been apologetic. Even to the Hard One, he had spoken of his concern for her. Dua felt an obscure pride.

But now he was leaving and suddenly all the independence that Dua had been looking forward to lost its fine shape and hardened into the pointed crag of loneliness. She said, "But *why* must you pass on?"

"I *must*, little mid-dear."

He must. She knew that. Everyone, sooner or later, must. The day would come when she would have to sigh and say, "I must."

"But what makes you know when you have to pass one? If you can choose your time, why don't you choose a different time and stay longer?"

He said, "Your left-father has decided. The triad must do as he says."

"*Why* must you do what he says?" She hardly ever saw her left-father or her mid-mother. They didn't count any more. Only her right-father, her Parental, her daddy, who stood there squat and flat-surfaced. He wasn't all smooth-curved like a Rational or shuddery uneven like an Emotional, and she could always tell what he was going to say. Almost always.

She was sure he would say, "I can't explain to a little Emotional."

He said it.

Dua said in a burst of woe, "I'll miss you. I know you think I pay you no attention, and that I don't like you for always telling me not to do things. But I would rather not like you for telling me not to do things, than not have you around to tell me not to do things."

And Daddy just stood there. There was no way he could handle an outburst like that except to come closer and pinch out a hand. It cost him a visible effort, but he held it out trembling and its outlines were ever so slightly soft.

Dua said, "Oh, Daddy," and let her own hand flow about it so that his looked misty and shimmery through her substance; but she was careful not to touch it for that would have embarrassed him so.

Then he withdrew it and left her hand enclosing nothing and he said, "Remember the Hard Ones, Dua. They will help you. I—I will go now."

He went and she never saw him again.

Now she sat there, remembering in the sunset, and rebelliously aware that pretty soon Tritt would grow petulant over her absence and nag Odeen.

And then Odeen might lecture her on her duties.

She didn't care.

1b

Odeen was moderately aware that Dua was off on the surface. Without really thinking about it, he could judge her direction and even something of her distance. If he had stopped to think of it, he might have felt displeasure, for this inter-awareness sense had been steadily deadening for a long time now and, without really being certain why, he had a sense of gathering fulfillment about it. It was the way things were supposed to be; the sign of the continuing development of the body with age.

Tritt's inter-awareness sense did not decrease, but it shifted more and more toward the children. That was clearly the line of useful development, but then the role of the Parental was a simple one, in a manner of speaking, however important. The Rational was far more complex and Odeen took a bleak satisfaction in that thought.

Of course, it was Dua who was the real puzzle. She was so unlike all the other Emotionals. That puzzled and frustrated Tritt and reduced him to even more pronounced inarticulacy. It puzzled and frustrated Odeen at times, too, but he was also aware of Dua's infinite capacity to induce satisfaction with life and it did not seem likely that one was independent of the other. The occasional exasperation she produced was a small price to pay for the intense happiness.

And maybe Dua's odd way of life was part of what ought to be, too. The Hard Ones seemed interested in her and ordinarily they paid attention only to Rationals. He felt pride in that; so much the better for the triad that even the Emotional was worth attention.

Things were as they were supposed to be. That was bedrock, and it was what he wanted most to feel, right down to the end. Someday he would even know when it was time to pass on and then he would want to. The Hard Ones assured him of that, as they assured all Rationals, but they also told him that it was his own inner consciousness that would mark the time unmistakably, and not any advice from outside.

"When *you* tell yourself," Losten had told him—in the clear, careful way in which a Hard One always talked to a Soft One, as though the Hard One were laboring to make himself understood, "that you know why you must pass on, then you will pass on, and your triad will pass on with you."

And Odeen had said, "I cannot say I wish to pass on now, Hard-sir. There is so much to learn."

"Of course, left-dear. You feel this because you are not yet ready."

Odeen thought: How could I ever feel ready when I would never feel there wasn't much to learn?

But he didn't say so. He was quite certain the time would come and he would then understand.

He looked down at himself, almost forgetting and

thrusting out an eye to do so—there were always some
childish impulses in even the most adult of the most Rational. He didn't have to, of course. He would sense quite
well with his eye solidly in place, and he found himself satisfactorily solid; nice, sharp outline, smooth and curved
into gracefully conjoined ovoids.

His body lacked the strangely attractive shimmer of
Dua, and the comforting stockiness of Tritt. He loved
them both, but he would not change his own body for either. And, of course, his own mind. He would never say
so, of course, for he would not want to hurt their feelings,
but he never ceased being thankful that he did not have
Tritt's limited understanding or (even more) Dua's erratic
one. He supposed they didn't mind for they knew nothing
else.

He grew distantly aware of Dua again, and deliberately
dulled the sense. At the moment, he felt no need for her. It
was not that he wanted her less, but merely that he had increasing drives elsewhere. It was part of the growing maturity of a Rational to find more and more satisfaction in
the exercise of a mind that could only be practiced alone,
and with the Hard Ones.

He grew constantly more accustomed to the Hard Ones;
constantly more attached to them. He felt that was right
and proper, too, for he was a Rational and in a way the
Hard Ones were super-Rationals. (He had once said that to
Losten, the friendliest of the Hard Ones and, it seemed
to Odeen in some vague way the youngest. Losten had radiated amusement but had said nothing. And that meant
he had not denied it, however.)

Odeen's earliest memories were filled with Hard Ones.
His Parental more and more concentrated his attention on
the last child, the baby-Emotional. That was only natural.
Tritt would do it, too, when the last child came, if it ever
did. (Odeen had picked up that last qualification from
Tritt, who used it constantly as a reproach to Dua.)

But so much the better. With his Parental busy so much
of the time, Odeen could begin his education that much the
earlier. He was losing his baby ways and he had learned a
great deal even before he met Tritt.

That meeting, though, was surely something he would never forget. It might as well have been yesterday as more than half a lifetime ago. He had seen Parentals of his own generation, of course; young ones who, long before they incubated the children that made true Parentals of them, showed few signs of the stolidity to come. As a child he had played with his own right-brother and was scarcely aware of any intellectual difference between them (though, looking back on those days, he recognized that it was there, even then).

He knew also, vaguely, the role of a Parental in a triad. Even as a child, he had whispered tales of melting.

When Tritt first appeared, when Odeen saw him first, everything changed. For the first time in his life, Odeen felt an inner warmth and began to think that there was something he wanted that was utterly divorced from thought. Even now, he could remember the sense of embarrassment that had accompanied this.

Tritt was not embarrassed, of course. Parentals were never embarrassed about the activities of the triad, and Emotionals were almost never embarrassed. Only Rationals had that problem.

"Too much thinking," a Hard One had said when Odeen had discussed the problem with him and that left Odeen dissatisfied. In what way could thinking be "too much"?

Tritt was young when they first met, of course. He was still so childish as to be uncertain in his blockishness so that his reaction to the meeting was embarrassingly clear. He grew almost translucent along his edges.

Odeen said, hesitantly, "I haven't seen you before, have I, right-fellow?"

Tritt said, "I have never been here. I have been brought here."

They both knew exactly what had happened to them. The meeting had been arranged because someone (some Parental, Odeen had thought at the time, but later he knew it was some Hard One) thought they would suit each other, and the thought was correct.

There was no intellectual rapport between the two, of

course. How could there be when Odeen wanted to learn with an intensity that superseded anything but the existence of the triad itself, and Tritt lacked the very concept of learning? What Tritt had to know, he knew beyond either learning or unlearning.

Odeen, out of the excitement of finding out about the world and its Sun; about the history and mechanism of life; about all the abouts in the Universe; sometimes (in those early days together) found himself spilling over to Tritt.

Tritt listened placidly, clearly understanding nothing, but content to be listening; while Odeen, transmitting nothing, was as clearly content to be lecturing.

It was Tritt who made the first move, driven by his special needs. Odeen was chattering about what he had learned that day after the brief midday meal. (Their thicker substance absorbed food so rapidly, they were satisfied with a simple walk in the Sun, while Emotionals basked for hours at a time, curling and thinning as though deliberately to lengthen the task.)

Odeen, who always ignored the Emotionals, was quite happy to be talking. Tritt, who stared wordlessly at them, day after day, was now visibly restless.

Abruptly, he came close to Odeen, formed an appendage so hastily as to clash most disagreeably on the other's form-sense. He placed it in upon a portion of Odeen's upper ovoid where a slight shimmer was allowing a welcome draft of warm air as dessert. Tritt's appendage thinned with a visible effort and sank into the superfices of Odeen's skin before the latter darted away, horribly embarrassed.

Odeen had done such things as a baby, of course, but never since his adolescence. "Don't do that, Tritt," he said sharply.

Tritt's appendage remained out, groping a little. "I want to."

Odeen held himself as compactly as he could, striving to harden the surface to bar entry. "I *don't* want to."

"Why not?" said Tritt, urgently. "There's nothing wrong."

Odeen said the first thing that came into his mind. "It hurt." (It didn't really. Not physically. But the Hard Ones always avoided the touch of the Soft Ones. A careless interpenetration hurt *them*, but they were constructed differently from Soft Ones, completely differently.)

Tritt was not fooled by that. His instinct could not possibly mislead him in this respect. He said, "It didn't hurt."

"Well, it isn't right this way. We need an Emotional."

And Tritt could only say, stubbornly, "I want to, anyway."

It was bound to continue happening, and Odeen was bound to give in. He always did; it was something that was sure to happen even to the most self-conscious Rational. As the old saying had it: Everyone either admitted doing it or lied about it.

Tritt was at him at each meeting after that; if not with an appendage, then rim to rim. And finally Odeen, seduced by the pleasure of it, began to help and tried to shine. He was better at that than Tritt was. Poor Tritt, infinitely more eager, huffed and strained, and could achieve only the barest shimmer here and there, patchily and raggedly.

Odeen, however, could turn translucent all over his surface, and fought down his embarrassment in order to let himself flow against Tritt. There was skin-deep penetration and Odeen could feel the pulsing of Tritt's hard surface under the skin. There was enjoyment, riddled with guilt.

Tritt, as often as not, was tired and vaguely angry when it was all over.

Odeen said, "Now, Tritt, I've told you we need an Emotional to do this properly. You can't be angry at something that just *is*."

And Tritt said, "Let's get an Emotional."

Let's get an Emotional! Tritt's simple drives never led him to anything but direct action. Odeen was not sure he could explain the complexities of life to the other. "It's not that easy, right-ling," he began gently.

Tritt said abruptly. "The Hard Ones can do it. You're friendly with them. Ask them."

Odeen was horrified. "I *can't* ask. The time," he continued, unconsciously falling into his lecturing voice, "is not yet come, or I would certainly know it. Until such time—"

Tritt was not listening. He said, "*I'll* ask."

"*No*," said Odeen, horrified. "You stay out of it. I tell you it's not time. I have an education to worry about. It's very easy to be a Parental and not to have to know anything but—"

He was sorry the instant he had said it and it was a lie anyway. He just didn't want to do anything at all that might offend the Hard Ones and impede his useful relationship with them. Tritt, however, showed no signs of minding and it occurred to Odeen that the other saw no point or merit in knowing anything he did not already know and would not consider the statement of the fact an insult.

The problem of the Emotional kept coming up, though. Occasionally, they tried interpenetration. In fact, the impulse grew stronger with time. It was never truly satisfying though it had its pleasure and each time Tritt would demand an Emotional. Each time, Odeen threw himself deeper into his studies, almost as a defense against the problem.

Yet at times, he was almost tempted to speak to Losten about it.

Losten was the Hard One he knew best; the one who took the greatest personal interest in him. There was a deadly sameness about the Hard Ones, because they did not change; they never changed; their form was fixed. Where there eyes were they always were, and always in the same place for all of them. Their skin was not exactly hard, but it was always opaque, never shimmered, never vague, never penetrable by another skin of its own type.

They were not larger in size, particularly, than the Soft Ones, but they were heavier. Their substance was much denser and they had to be careful about the yielding tissues of the Soft Ones.

Once when he had been little, really little and his body had flowed almost as freely as his sister's, he had been approached by a Hard One. He had never known which one it was, but he learned in later life that they were all of them curious about baby-Rationals. Odeen had reached up for the Hard One, out of nothing but curiosity. The Hard One had sprung backward and later Odeen's Parental had scolded him for offering to touch a Hard One.

The scolding had been harsh enough for Odeen never to forget. When he was older he learned that the close-packed atoms of the Hard One's tissues felt pain on the forcible penetration of others. Odeen wondered if the Soft One felt pain, too. Another young Rational once told him that he had stumbled against a Hard One and the Hard One had doubled up but that he himself had felt nothing —but Odeen wasn't sure this was not just a melodramatic boast.

There were other things he could not do. He liked rubbing against the walls of the cavern. There was a pleasant, warm feeling when he allowed himself to penetrate rock. Babies always did it, but it got harder to do as he grew older. Still, he could do it skin-deep and he liked it, but his Parental found him doing it and scolded him. He objected that his sister did it all the time; he had seen her.

"That's different," said the Parental. "She's an Emotional."

At another time, when Odeen was absorbing a recording—he was older then—he had idly formed a couple of projections and made the tips so thin, he could pass one through the other. He began to do it regularly when he listened. There was a pleasant tickling sensation that made it easier to listen and made him nicely sleepy afterward.

And his Parental caught him at that, too, and what he had said still made Odeen uncomfortable in remembering it.

No one really told him about melting in those days. They fed him knowledge and educated him about everything except what the triad was all about. Tritt had never been told, either, but he was a Parental so he knew without being told. Of course, when Dua came at last, all was clear, even though she seemed to know less about it even than Odeen.

But she didn't come to them because of anything Odeen

did. It was Tritt who broached the matter; Tritt, who ordinarily feared the Hard Ones and avoided them mutely; Tritt, who lacked Odeen's self-assurance, in all but this respect; Tritt, who on this one subject was driven; Tritt—Tritt—Tritt—

Odeen signed. Tritt was invading his thoughts, because Tritt was coming. He could feel him, harsh, demanding, always demanding. Odeen had so little time to himself these days, just when he felt that he needed to think more than ever, to straighten out all the thoughts—

"Yes, Tritt," he said.

1c

Tritt was conscious of his blockiness. He didn't think it ugly. He didn't think about it at all. If he did, he would consider it beautiful. His body was designed for a purpose and designed well.

He said, "Odeen, where is Dua?"

"Outside somewhere," mumbled Odeen, almost as though he didn't care. It annoyed Tritt to have the triad made so little of. Dua was so difficult and Odeen didn't care.

"Why do you let her go?"

"How can I stop her, Tritt? And what harm does it do?"

"You know the harm. We have two babies. We need a third. It is so hard to make a little-mid these days. Dua must be well fed for it to be made. Now she is wandering about at Sunset again. How can she feed properly at Sunset?"

"She's just not a great feeder."

"And we just don't have a little-mid. Odeen," Tritt's voice was caressing, "how can I love you properly without Dua?"

"Now, then," mumbled Odeen, and Tritt felt himself once more puzzled by the other's clear embarrassment at the simplest statement of fact.

Tritt said, "Remember, I was the one who first got Dua." Did Odeen remember that? Did Odeen ever think of the triad and what it meant? Sometimes Tritt felt so frustrated he could—he could— Actually, he didn't know what to do, but he knew he felt frustrated. As in those old days when he wanted an Emotional and Odeen would do nothing.

Tritt knew he didn't have the trick of talking in big, elaborate sentences. But if Parentals didn't talk, they thought. They thought about important things. Odeen always talked about atoms and energy. Who cared about atoms and energy? Tritt thought about the triad and the babies.

Odeen had once told him that the numbers of Soft Ones were gradually growing fewer. Didn't he care? Didn't the Hard Ones care? Did anyone care but the Parentals?

Only two forms of life on all the world, the Soft Ones and the Hard Ones. And food shining down on them.

Odeen had once told him the Sun was cooling off. There was less food, he said, so there were less people. Tritt didn't believe it. The Sun felt no cooler than it had when he was a baby. It was just that people weren't worrying about the triads any more. Too many absorbed Rationals; too many silly Emotionals.

What the Soft Ones must do was concentrate on the important things of life. Tritt did. He tended to the business of the triad. The baby-left came, then the baby-right. They were growing and flourishing. They had to have a baby-mid, though. That was the hardest to get started and without a baby-mid there would be no new triad.

What made Dua as she was? She had always been difficult, but she was growing worse.

Tritt felt an obscure anger against Odeen. Odeen always talked with all those hard words. And Dua listened. Odeen would talk to Dua endlessly till they were almost two Rationals. That was bad for the triad.

Odeen should know better.

It was always Tritt who had to care. It was always Tritt

who had to do what had to be done. Odeen was the friend of the Hard Ones and yet he said nothing. They needed an Emotional and yet Odeen would say nothing. Odeen talked to them of energy and not of the needs of the triad.

It had been Tritt who had turned the scale. Tritt remembered that proudly. He had seen Odeen talking to a Hard One and he had approached. Without a shake in his voice, he had interrupted and said, "We need an Emotional."

The Hard One turned to look at him. Tritt had never been so close to a Hard One. He was all of a piece. Every part of him had to turn when one part did. He had some projections that could move by themselves, but they never changed in shape. They never flowed and were irregular and unlovely. They didn't like to be touched.

The Hard One said, "Is this so, Odeen?" He did not talk to Tritt.

Odeen flattened. He flattened close to the ground; more flattened than Tritt had ever seen. He said, "My right-ling is over-zealous. My right-ling is—is—" He stuttered and puffed and could not speak.

Tritt could speak. He said, "We cannot melt without one."

Tritt knew that Odeen was embarrassed into speechlessness but he didn't care. It was time.

"Well, left-dear," said the Hard One to Odeen, "do you feel the same way about it?" Hard Ones spoke as the Soft Ones did, but more harshly and with fewer overtones. They were hard to listen to. Tritt found them hard, anyway, though Odeen seemed used to it.

"Yes," said Odeen, finally.

The Hard One turned at last to Tritt. "Remind me, young-right. How long have you and Odeen been together?"

"Long enough," said Tritt, "to deserve an Emotional." He kept his shape firmly at angles. He did not allow himself to be frightened. This was too important. He said, "And my name is Tritt."

The Hard One seemed amused. "Yes, the choice was

good. You and Odeen go well together, but it makes the choice of an Emotional difficult. We have almost made up our minds. Or at least I have long since made up *my* mind, but the others must be convinced. Be patient, Tritt."

"I am tired of patience."

"I know, but be patient, anyway." He was amused again.

When he was quite gone, Odeen uplifted himself and thinned out angrily. He said, "How could you do that, Tritt? Do you know who he was?"

"He was a Hard One."

"He was Losten. He is my special teacher. I don't want him angry with me."

"Why should he be angry? I was polite."

"Well, never mind." Odeen was settling into normal shape. That meant he wasn't angry any more. (That relieved Tritt though he tried not to show it.) "It's very embarrassing to have my dumb-right come up and speak out to my Hard One."

"Why didn't you do it, then?"

"There's such a thing as the right time."

"But never's the right time to you."

But then they rubbed surfaces and stopped arguing and it wasn't long after that that Dua came.

It was Losten that brought her. Tritt didn't know that; he didn't look at the Hard One. Only at Dua. But Odeen told him afterward that it was Losten that brought her.

"You see?" said Tritt. "It was I who talked to him. That is why he brought her."

"No," said Odeen. "It was time. He would have brought her even if neither of us had talked to him."

Tritt didn't believe him. He was quite sure that it was entirely because of himself that Dua was with them.

Surely, there was never anyone like Dua in the world. Tritt had seen many Emotionals. They were all attractive. He would have accepted any one of them for proper melting. Once he saw Dua, he realized that none of the others would have suited. Only Dua. Only Dua.

And Dua knew exactly what to do. Exactly. No one had

ever shown her how, she told them afterward. No one had
ever talked to her about it. Even other Emotionals hadn't,
for she avoided them.

Yet when all three were together, each knew what to
do.

Dua thinned. She thinned more than Tritt had ever seen
a person thin. She thinned more than Tritt would ever
have thought possible. She became a kind of colored
smoke that filled the room and dazzled him. He moved
without knowing he was moving. He immersed himself in
the air that was Dua.

There was no sensation of penetration, none at all. Tritt
felt no resistance, no friction. There was just a floating inward and a rapid palpitation. He felt himself beginning to
thin in sympathy, and without the tremendous effort that
had always accompanied it. With Dua filling him, he could
thin without effort into a thick smoke of his own. Thinning
became like flowing, one enormous smooth flow.

Dimly, he could see Odeen approaching from the other
side, from Dua's left. And he, too, was thinning.

Then, like all the shocks of contact in all the world, he
reached Odeen. But it wasn't a shock at all. Tritt felt without feeling, knew without knowing. He slid into Odeen
and Odeen slid into him. He couldn't tell whether he was
surrounding Odeen or being surrounded by him or both or
neither.

It was only—pleasure.

The senses dimmed with the intensity of that pleasure
and at the point where he thought he could stand no more,
the senses failed altogether.

Eventually, they separated and stared at each other.
They had melted for days. Of course, melting always took
time. The better it was the longer it took, though when it
was over all that time seemed as though it had been an instant and they did not remember it. In later life, it rarely
took longer than that first time.

Odeen said, "That was wonderful."

Tritt only gazed at Dua, who had made it possible.

She was coalescing, swirling, moving tremulously. She
seemed most affected of the three.

"We'll do it again," she said, hurriedly, "but later, later. Let me go now."

She had run off. They did not stop her. They were too overcome to stop her. But that was always the way afterward. She was always gone after a melting. No matter how successful it was, she would go. There seemed something in her that needed to be alone.

It bothered Tritt. In point after point, she was different from other Emotionals. She shouldn't be.

Odeen felt differently. He would say on many occasions, "Why don't you leave her alone, Tritt? She's not like the others and that means she's better than the others. Melting wouldn't be as good if she were like the others. Do you want the benefits without paying the price?"

Tritt did not understand that clearly. He knew only that she ought to do what ought to be done. He said, "I want her to do what is right."

"I know, Tritt, I know. But leave her alone, anyway."

Odeen often scolded Dua himself for her queer ways but was always unwilling to let Tritt do so. "You lack tact, Tritt," he would say. Tritt didn't know what tact was exactly.

And now— It had been so long since the first melting and still the baby-Emotional was not born. How much longer? It was already much too long. And Dua, if anything, stayed by herself more and more as time went on.

Tritt said. "She doesn't eat enough."

"When it's time—" began Odeen.

"You always talk about it's being time or it's not being time. You never found it time to get Dua in the first place. Now you never find it time to have a baby-Emotional. Dua should—"

But Odeen turned away. He said, "She's out there, Tritt. If you want to go out and get her, as though you were her Parental instead of her right-ling, do so. But I say, leave her alone."

Tritt backed away. He had a great deal to say, but he didn't know how to say it.

2a

Dua was aware of the left-right agitation concerning her in a dim and faraway manner and her rebelliousness grew.

If one or the other, or both, came to get her, it would end in a melting and she raged against the thought. It was all Tritt knew, except for the children; all Tritt wanted, except for the third and last child; and it was all involved with the children and the still missing child. And when Tritt wanted a melting, he got it.

Tritt dominated the triad when he grew stubborn. He would hold on to some simple idea and never let go and in the end Odeen and Dua would have to give in. Yet now she wouldn't give in; she *wouldn't*—

She didn't feel disloyal at the thought, either. She never expected to feel for either Odeen or Tritt the sheer intensity of longing they felt for each other. She could melt alone; they could melt only through her mediation (so why didn't that make her the more regarded). She felt intense pleasure at the three-way melting; of course she did, it would be stupid to deny it; but it was a pleasure akin to that which she felt when she passed through a rock wall, as she sometimes secretly did. To Tritt and Odeen, the pleasure was like nothing else they had ever experienced or could ever experience.

No, wait. Odeen had the pleasure of learning, of what he called intellectual development. Dua felt some of that at times, enough to know what it might mean; and though it was different from melting, it might serve as a substitute, at least to the point where Odeen could do without melting sometimes.

But not so, Tritt. For him there was only melting and the children. Only. And when his small mind bent entirely upon that, Odeen would give in, and then Dua would have to.

Once she had rebelled. "But what happens when we melt? It's hours, days sometimes, before we come out of it. What happens all that time?"

Tritt had looked outraged at that. "It's always that way. It's *got* to be."

"I don't like anything that's *got* to be. I want to know why."

Odeen had looked embarrassed. He spent half his life being embarrassed. He said, "Now, Dua, it does have to be. On account of—children." He seemed to pulse, as he said the word.

"Well, don't pulse," said Dua, sharply. "We're grown now and we've melted I don't know how many times and we all know it's so we can have children. You might as well say so. Why does it take so long, that's all?"

"Because it's a complicated process," said Odeen, still pulsing. "Because it takes energy. Dua, it takes a long time to get a child started and even when we take a long time, it doesn't always get started. And it's getting worse. . . . Not just with us," he added hastily.

"Worse?" said Tritt anxiously, but Odeen would say no more.

They had a child eventually, a baby-Rational, a left-let, that flitted and thinned so that all three were in raptures and even Odeen would hold it and let it change shape in his hands for as long as Tritt would allow him to. For it was Tritt, of course, who had actually incubated it through the long pre-forming; Tritt who had separated from it when it assumed independent existence; and Tritt who cared for it at all times.

After that, Tritt was often not with them and Dua was oddly pleased. Tritt's obsession annoyed her, but Odeen's —oddly—pleased her. She became increasingly aware of his—importance. There was something to being a Rational that made it possible to answer questions, and somehow Dua had questions for him constantly. He was readier to answer when Tritt was not present.

"*Why* does it take so long, Odeen? I don't like to melt and then not know what's happening for days at a time."

"We're perfectly safe, Dua," said Odeen, earnestly. "Come, nothing has ever happened to us, has it? You've never heard of anything ever happening to any other triad, have you? Besides, you shouldn't ask questions."

"Because I'm an Emotional? Because other Emotionals don't ask questions?—I can't stand other Emotionals, if you want to know, and I *do* want to ask questions."

She was perfectly aware that Odeen was looking at her as though he had never seen anyone as attractive and that if Tritt had been present, melting would have taken place at once. She even let herself thin out; not much, but perceptibly, in deliberate coquettishness.

Odeen said, "But you might not understand the implications, Dua. It takes a great deal of energy to initiate a new spark of life."

"You've often mentioned energy. What is it? Exactly."

"Why, what we eat."

"Well, then, why don't you say food."

"Because food and energy aren't quite the same thing. Our food comes from the Sun and that's a kind of energy, but there are other kinds of energy that are not food. When we eat, we've got to spread out and absorb the light. It's hardest for Emotionals because they're much more transparent; that is, the light tends to pass through instead of being absorbed—"

It was wonderful to have it explained, Dua thought. What she was told, she really knew; but she didn't know the proper words; the long science-words that Odeen knew. And it made sharper and more meaningful everything that happened.

Occasionally now, in adult life, when she no longer feared that childish teasing; when she shared in the prestige of being part of the Odeen-triad; she tried to swarm with other Emotionals and to withstand the chatter and the crowding. After all, she did occasionally feel like a more substantial meal than she usually got and it did make for better melting. There was a joy—sometimes she almost caught the pleasure the others got out ot it—in slithering and maneuvering for exposure to Sunlight; in the luxurious contraction and condensation to absorb the warmth through greater thickness with greater efficiency.

Yet for Dua a little of that went quite a way and the others never seemed to have enough. There was a kind of gluttonous wiggle about them that Dua could not duplicate and that, at length, she could not endure.

That was why Rationals and Parentals were so rarely on the surface. Their thickness made it possible for them to eat quickly and leave. Emotionals writhed in the Sun for hours, for though they ate more slowly, they actually needed more energy than the others—at least for melting.

The Emotional supplied the energy, Odeen had explained (pulsing so that his signals were barely understood), the Rational the seed, the Parental the incubator.

Once Dua understood that, a certain amusement began to blend with her disapproval when she watched the other Emotionals virtually slurp up the ruddy Sunlight. Since they never asked questions, she was sure they didn't know why they did it and couldn't understand that there was an obscene side to their quivering condensations, or to the way in which they went tittering down below eventually—on their way to a good melt, of course, with lots of energy to spare.

She could also stand Tritt's annoyance when she would come down without that swirling opacity that meant a good gorging. Yet why should they complain? The thinness she retained meant a defter melting. Not as sloppy and glutinous as the other triads managed, perhaps, but it was the ethereality that counted, she felt sure. And the little-left and little-right came eventually, didn't they?

Of course, it was the baby-Emotional, the little-mid, that was the crux. That took more energy than the other two and Dua never had enough.

Even Odeen was beginning to mention it. "You're not getting enough Sunlight, Dua."

"Yes I am," said Dua, hastily.

"Genia's triad," said Odeen, "has just initiated an Emotional."

Dua didn't like Genia. She never had. She was empty-headed even by Emotional standards. Dua said, loftily, "I suppose she's boasting about it. She has no delicacy. I suppose she's saying, 'I shouldn't mention it, my dear, but you'll never guess what my left-ling and right-ling have gone and went and done—' " She imitated Genia's tremulous signaling with deadly accuracy and Odeen was amused.

But then he said, "Genia may be a dunder, but she *has* initiated an Emotional, and Tritt is upset about it. We've been at it for much longer than they have—"

Dua turned away. "I get all the Sun I can stand. I do it till I'm too full to move. I don't know what you want of me."

Odeen said, "Don't be angry. I promised Tritt I would talk to you. He thinks you listen to me—"

"Oh, Tritt just thinks it's odd that you explain science to me. He doesn't understand— Do you want a mid-ling like the others?"

"No," said Odeen, seriously. "You're not like the others, and I'm glad of it. And if you're interested in Rational-talk, then let me explain something. The Sun doesn't supply the food it used to in ancient times. The light-energy is less; and it takes longer exposures. The birth rate has been dropping for ages and the world's population is only a fraction of what it once was."

"I can't help it," said Dua, rebelliously.

"The Hard Ones may be able to. Their numbers have been decreasing, too—"

"Do they pass on?" Dua was suddenly interested. She always thought they were immortal somehow; that they weren't born; that they didn't die. Who had ever seen a baby Hard One, for instance? They didn't have babies. They didn't melt. They didn't eat.

Odeen said, thoughtfully, "I imagine they pass on. They never talk about themselves to me. I'm not even sure how they eat, but of course they must. And be born. There's a new one, for instance; I haven't seen him yet— But never mind that. The point is that they've been developing an artificial food—"

"I know," said Dua. "I've tasted it."

"You have? I didn't know that!"

"A bunch of the Emotionals talked about it. They said a Hard One was asking for volunteers to taste it and the sillies were all afraid. They said it would probably turn them permanently hard and they would never be able to melt again."

"That's foolish," said Odeen, vehemently.

"I know. So I volunteered. That shut them up. They are *so* hard to endure, Odeen."

"How was it?"

"Horrible," said Dua, vehemently. "Harsh and bitter. Of course I didn't tell the other Emotionals that."

Odeen said, "I tasted it. It wasn't *that* bad."

"Rationals and Parentals don't care what food tastes like."

But Odeen said, "It's still only experimental. They're working hard on improvements, the Hard Ones are. Especially Estwald—that's the one I mentioned before, the new one I haven't seen—he's working on it. Losten speaks of him now and then as though he's something special; a very great scientist."

"How is it you've never seen him?"

"I'm just a Soft One. You don't suppose they show me and tell me everything, do you? Someday I'll see him, I suppose. He's developed a new energy-source which may save us all yet—"

"I don't want artificial food," said Dua, and she had left Odeen abruptly.

That had been not so long ago, and Odeen had not mentioned this Estwald again, but she knew he would, and she brooded about it up here in the Sunset.

She had seen that artificial food that once; a glowing sphere of light, like a tiny Sun, in a special cavern set up by the Hard Ones. She could taste its bitterness yet.

Would they improve it? Would they make it taste better? Even delicious? And would she have to eat it then and fill herself with it till the full sensation gave her an almost uncontrollable desire to melt?

She feared that self-generating desire. It was different when the desire came through the hectic combined stimulation of left-ling and right-ling. It was the self-generation that meant she would be ripe to bring about the initiation of a little-mid. And——and she didn't want to!

It was a long time before she would admit the truth to herself. She didn't want to initiate an Emotional! It was after the three children were all born that the time would inevitably come to pass on, and she didn't want to. She remembered the day her Parental had left her forever, and it was never going to be like that for her. Of that she was fiercely determined.

The other Emotionals didn't care because they were too empty to think about it, but she was different. She was queer Dua, the Left-Em; that was what they had called her; and she *would* be different. As long as she didn't have that third child, she would not pass on; she would continue to live.

So she wasn't going to have that third child. Never. *Never!*

But how was she going to stave it off? And how would she keep Odeen from finding out? What if Odeen found out?

2b

Odeen waited for Tritt to do something. He was reasonably sure that Tritt would not actually go up to the surface after Dua. It would mean leaving the children and that was always hard for Tritt to do. Tritt waited, without speaking for a while, and when he left, it was in the direction of the children's alcove.

Odeen was almost glad when Tritt left. Not quite, of course, for Tritt had been angry and withdrawn so that interpersonal contact had weakened and the barrier of displeasure had arisen. Odeen could not help but be melancholy at that. It was like the slowing of the life-pulse.

He sometimes wondered if Tritt felt it, too. .... No, that was unfair. Tritt had the special relationship with the children.

And as for Dua, who could tell what Dua felt? Who could tell what any Emotional felt? They were so different they made left and right seem alike in everything but mind. But even allowing for the erratic way of Emotionals, who could tell what Dua—especially Dua—felt?

That was why Odeen managed to be almost glad when Tritt left, for Dua was the question. The delay in initiating the third child was indeed becoming too long and Dua was growing less amenable to persuasion, not more. There was a growing restlessness in Odeen himself, that he could not quite identify, and it was something he would have to discuss with Losten.

He made his way down to the Hard-caverns, hastening his movements into a continuous flow that was not nearly as undignified as the oddly exciting mixture of wavering and rushing that marked the Emotional curve-along, or as amusing as the stolid weight-shift of the Parental—

(He had the keen thought-image of Tritt clumping in pursuit of the baby-Rational, who, of course, was almost as slippery, at his age, as an Emotional, and of Dua having to block the baby and bring him back, and of Tritt cluckingly undecided whether to shake the small life-object or enfold him with his substance. From the start, Tritt could thin himself more effectively for the babies than for Odeen and when Odeen rallied him about that, Tritt answered gravely, for of course he had no humor about such things, "Ah, but the children need it more.")

Odeen was selfishly pleased with his own flow and thought it graceful and impressive. He had mentioned that once to Losten, to whom as his Hard-teacher, he confessed everything, and Losten had said, "But don't you think an Emotional or a Parental feels the same about his own flow-pattern? If each of you think differently and act differently, ought you not to be pleased differently? A triad doesn't preclude individuality, you know."

Odeen wasn't sure he understood about individuality. Did that mean being alone? A Hard One was alone, of course. There were no triads among them. How did they stand it?

Odeen had still been quite young when the matter had come up. His relationship with the Hard Ones had only been beginning, and it suddenly struck him that he wasn't sure that there were no triads among them. That fact was common legend amont the Soft Ones, but how correct was the legend? Odeen thought about that and decided one must ask and not accept matters on faith.

Odeen had said, "Are you a left or a right, sir?" (In later times, Odeen pulsed at the memory of that question. How incredibly naïve to have asked it, and it was very little comfort that every Rational asked the question of a Hard One in some fashion, sooner or later—usually sooner.)

Losten answered quite calmly, "Neither, little-left. There are no lefts or rights among the Hard Ones."

"Or mid-l— Emotionals?"

"Or mid-lings?" And the Hard One changed the shape of his permanent sensory region in a fashion that Odeen eventually associated with amusement or pleasure. "No. No mid-lings either. Just Hard Ones of one kind."

Odeen had to ask. It came out involuntarily, quite against his desire. "But how do you stand it?"

"It is different with us, little-left. We are used to it."

Could Odeen be used to such a thing? There was the Parental triad that had filled his life so far and the sure knowledge that he would at some not-too-distant time form a triad of his own. What was life without that? He thought about it hard now and then. He though about everything hard, as it came up. Sometimes he managed to catch a glimpse of what it might mean. That Hard Ones had only themselves; neither left-brother, nor right-brother, nor mid-sister, nor melting, nor children, nor Parentals. They had only the mind, only the inquiry into the Universe.

Perhaps that was enough for them. As Odeen grew older, he caught bits of understanding as to the joys of inquiry. They were almost enough—almost enough—and then he would think of Tritt and of Dua and decide that even all the Universe beside was not quite enough.

Unless— It was odd, but every once in a while it seemed that there might come a time, a situation, a condition, when— Then he would lose the momentary glimpse, or, rather, glimpse of a glimpse, and miss it all. Yet in time it would return and lately he thought it grew stronger and would remain almost long enough to be caught.

But none of that was what should involve him now. He had to see about Dua. He made his way along the well-known route, along which he had first been taken by his Parental (as Tritt would soon take their own young Rational, their own baby-left.)

And, of course, he was instantly lost in memory again.

It had been frightening, then. There had been other young Rationals, all pulsing and shimmering and changing shape, despite the Parental signals on every side to stay firm and smooth and not disgrace the triad. One small left, a playmate of Odeen, had, in fact, flattened thin, baby-fashion, and would not unflatten, despite all the efforts of his horribly embarrassed Parental. (He had since become a perfectly normal student. . . . Though no Odeen, as Odeen himself could not help realizing with considerable complacency.)

They met a number of Hard Ones on that first day of school. They stopped at each, in order that the young-Rational vibration pattern might be recorded in several specialized ways and for a decision to be reached as to whether to accept them for instruction then, or to wait another interval; and if then, for what kind of instruction.

Odeen, in a desperate effort, had drawn himself smooth as a Hard One approached, and held himself unwavering.

The Hard One said (and the first sound of the odd tones of his voice almost undid Odeen's determination to be grown-up), "This is quite a firm-held Rational. How do you represent yourself, left?"

It was the first time Odeen had ever been called "left" instead of in the form of some diminutive, and he felt firmer than ever as he managed to say, "Odeen, Hard-sir," using the polite address his Parental had carefully taught him.

Dimly, Odeen remembered being taken through the Hard-caverns, with their equipment, their machinery, their libraries, their meaningless, crowding sights and sounds. More than the actual sense perceptions, he remembered his inner feeling of despair. What would they do with him?

His Parental had told him that he would learn, but he didn't know what was really meant by "learn" and when he asked his Parental, it turned out that the older one didn't know either.

It took him a while to find out and the experience was pleasurable, so pleasurable, and yet not without its worrisome aspects.

The Hard One who had first called him "left" was his first teacher. The Hard One taught him to interpret the wave recordings so that after a while what seemed an incomprehensible code became words; words just as clear as those he could form with his own vibrations.

But then that first one didn't appear any more and another Hard One took over. It was a time before Odeen noticed. It was difficult in those early days to tell one Hard One from another, to differentiate among their voices. But then he grew certain. Little by little, he grew certain and he trembled at the change. He didn't understand its significance.

He gathered courage and finally asked, "Where is my teacher, Hard-sir?"

"Gamaldan? . . . He will no longer be with you, left."

Odeen was speechless for a moment. Then he said, "But Hard Ones don't pass on—" He did not quite finish the phrase. It choked off.

The new Hard One was passive, said nothing, volunteered nothing.

It was always to be like that, Odeen found out. They never talked about themselves. On every other subject they discoursed freely. Concerning themselves—nothing.

From dozens of pieces of evidence, Odeen could not help but decide that Hard Ones passed on; that they were not immortal (something so many Soft Ones took for granted). Yet no Hard One ever said as much. Odeen and the other student-Rationals sometimes discussed it, hesitantly, uneasily. Each brought in some small item that pointed inexorably to mortality of the Hard Ones and wondered and did not like to conclude the obvious, so they let it go.

The Hard Ones did not seem to mind that hints of mortality existed. They did nothing to mask it. But they never mentioned it, either. And if the question was asked directly (sometimes it was, inevitably) they never answered; neither denying nor affirming.

And if they passed on, they had to be born also, yet they said nothing of that and Odeen never saw a young Hard One.

Odeen believed the Hard Ones got their energy from rocks instead of from the Sun—at least that they incorporated a powdered black rock into their bodies. Some of the other students thought so, too. Others, rather vehemently, refused to accept that. Nor could they come to a conclusion for no one ever saw them feeding in any way and the Hard Ones never spoke of that either.

In the end, Odeen took their reticence for granted—as part of themselves. Perhaps, he thought, it was their individuality, the fact that they formed no triads. It built a shell about them.

And then, too, Odeen learned things of such grave import that questions concerning the private life of the Hard Ones turned to trivia in any case. He learned, for instance, that the whole world was shriveling—dwindling—

It was Losten, the new teacher, who told him that.

Odeen had asked about the unoccupied caverns that stretched so endlessly into the bowels of the world and Losten had seemed pleased. "Are you afraid to ask about that, Odeen?"

(He was Odeen now; not some general reference to his left-hood. It was always a source of pride to hear a Hard One address him by personal name. Many did so. Odeen was a prodigy of understanding and the use of his name seemed a recognition of the fact. More than once Losten had expressed satisfaction at having him as a pupil.)

Odeen was indeed afraid and, after some hesitation, said so. It was always easier to confess shortcomings to the Hard Ones than to fellow-Rationals; much easier than to confess them to Tritt, unthinkable to confess them to Tritt. . . . Those were the days before Dua.

"Then why do you ask?"

Odeen hesitated again. Then he said slowly. "I'm afraid of the unoccupied caverns because when I was young I was told they had all sorts of monstrous things in them. But I know nothing of that directly; I only know what I have been told by other young ones who couldn't have known directly either. I want to find out the truth about them and the wanting has grown until there is more of curiosity in me than fear."

Losten looked pleased. "Good! The curiosity is useful, the fear useless. Your inner development is excellent, Odeen, and remember it is only your inner development that counts in the important things. Our help to you is marginal. Since you want to know, it is easy to tell you that the unoccupied caverns are truly unoccupied. They are empty. There is nothing in them but the unimportant things left behind in times past."

"Left behind by whom, Hard-sir?" Odeen felt uneasily compelled to use the honorific whenever he was too obviously in the presence of knowledge he lacked that the other had.

"By those who occupied them in times past. There was a time thousands of cycles ago when there were many thousands of Hard Ones and millions of Soft Ones. There are fewer of us now than there were in the past, Odeen. Nowadays there are not quite three hundred Hard Ones and fewer than ten thousand Soft Ones."

"Why?" said Odeen, shocked. (Only three hundred Hard Ones left. This was surely an open admission that Hard Ones passed on, but this was not the time to think of that.)

"Because energy is diminishing. The Sun is cooling. It becomes harder in every cycle to give birth and to live."

(Well, then, did not that mean the Hard Ones gave birth, too? And did it mean that the Hard Ones depended on the Sun for food, too, and not on rocks? Odeen filed the thought away and dismissed it for now.)

"Will this continue?" Odeen asked.

"The Sun must dwindle to an end, Odeen, and someday give no food."

"Does that mean that all of us, the Hard Ones and the Soft Ones, too, will pass on?"

"What else can it mean?"

"We can't all pass on. If we need energy and the Sun is coming to an end, we must find other sources. Other stars."

"But, Odeen, all the stars are coming to an end. The Universe is coming to an end."

"If the stars come to an end, is there no food elsewhere? No other source of energy?"

"No, all the energy-sources in all the Universe are coming to an end."

Odeen considered that rebelliously, then said, "Then other Universes. We can't give up just because the Universe does." He was palpitating as he said it. He had expanded with quite unforgivable discourtesy until he had swelled translucently into a size distinctly larger than the Hard One.

But Losten merely expressed extreme pleasure. He said, "Wonderful, my left-dear. The others must hear of this."

Odeen had collapsed to normal size in mingled embarrassment and pleasure at hearing himself addressed as "left-dear," a phrase he had never heard anyone use to him—except Tritt, of course.

It had not been very long after that that Losten himself had brought them Dua. Odeen had wondered, idly, if there had been any connection, but after a while wonder burned itself out. Tritt had repeated so often that it was his own approach to Losten that had brought them Dua, that Odeen gave up thinking about it. It was too confusing.

But now he was coming to Losten again. A long time had passed since those earlier days when he first learned that the Universe was coming to an end and that (as it turned out) the Hard Ones were resolutely laboring to live on anyway. He himself had become adept in many fields and Losten confessed that in physics there was little he could any longer teach Odeen that a Soft One could profitably learn. And there were other young Rationals to take in hand, so he did not see Losten as frequently as he once did.

Odeen found Losten with two half-grown Rationals in the Radiation Chamber. Losten saw him at once through the glass and came out, closing the door carefully behind him.

"My left-dear," he said, holding out his limbs in a gesture of friendship (so that Odeen, as so often in the past, experienced a perverse desire to touch, but controlled it). "How are you?"

"I did not mean to interrupt, Losten-sir."

"Interrupt? Those two will get along perfectly well by themselves for a time. They are probably glad to see me go, for I am sure I weary them with over-much talk."

"Nonsense," said Odeen. "You always fascinated me and I'm sure you fascinate them."

"Well, well. It is good of you to say so. I see you frequently in the library, and I hear from others that you do well in your advanced courses, and that makes me miss my best student. How is Tritt? Is he as Parentally stubborn in his ways as ever?"

"More stubborn every day. He gives strength to the triad."

"And Dua?"

"Dua? I have come— She is very unusual, you know."

Losten nodded, "Yes, I know that." His expression was one that Odeen had grown to associate with melancholy.

Odeen waited a moment, then decided to tackle the matter directly. He said, "Losten-sir, was she brought to us, to Tritt and myself, just because she was unusual?"

Losten said, "Would you be surprised? You are very unusual yourself, Odeen, and you have told me on a number of occasions that Tritt is."

"Yes," said Odeen, with conviction. "He is."

"Then oughtn't your triad include an unusual Emotional?"

"There are many ways of being unusual," said Odeen, thoughtfully. "In some ways, Dua's odds ways displease Tritt and worry me. May I consult you?"

"Always."

"She is not fond of—of melting."

Losten listened gravely; to all appearances unembarrassed.

Odeen went on. "She is fond of melting when we melt, that is, but it is not always easy to persuade her to do so."

Losten said, "How does Tritt feel about melting? I mean, aside from the immediate pleasure of the act? What does it mean to him besides pleasure?"

"The children, of course," said Odeen. "I like them and Dua likes them, too, but Tritt is the Parental. Do you understand that?" (It suddenly seemed to Odeen that Losten couldn't possibly understand all the subtleties of the triad.)

"I try to understand," said Losten. "It seems to me, then, that Tritt gets more out of melting than melting alone. And how about yourself? What do you get out of it besides the pleasure?"

Odeen considered. "I think you know that. A kind of mental stimulation."

"Yes, I know that, but I want to make sure *you* know. I want to make sure you haven't forgotten. You have told me often that when you come out of a period of melting, with its odd loss of time—during which I admit I sometimes didn't see you for rather long periods—that suddenly you found yourself understanding many things that had seemed obscure before."

"It was as though my mind remained active in the interval," said Odeen. "It was as though there was time which, even though I was unaware of its passing and unconscious of my existence, was necessary to me; during which I could think more deeply and intensely, without the distraction of the less intellectual side of life."

"Yes," agreed Losten, "and you'd come back with a quantum-jump in understanding. It is a common thing among you Rationals, though I must admit no one improved in such great jumps as you did. I honestly think no Rational in history did so."

"Really?" said Odeen, trying not to seem unduly elated.

"On the other hand, I may be wrong"—and Losten seemed slightly amused at the other's sudden loss of shimmer—"but never mind that. The point is that you, like Tritt, get something out of the melt beside the melt itself."

"Yes. Most certainly."

"And what does Dua get out of the melt besides the melt?"

There was a long pause. "I don't know," said Odeen.

"Have you never asked her?"

"Never."

"But then," said Losten, "if all she gets out of a melt is the melt, and if you and Tritt get out of it the melt plus something else, why should she be as eager for it as you two are?"

"Other Emotionals don't seem to require—" began Odeen, defensively.

"Other Emotionals aren't like Dua. You've told me that often enough and, I think, with satisfaction."

Odeen felt ashamed. "I had thought it might be something else."

"What might that be?"

"It's hard to explain. We know each other in the triad; we sense each other; in some ways, all three of us are part of a single individual. A misty individual that comes and goes. Mostly it's unconscious. If we think about it with too great a concentration, we lose it, so we can never get real detail. We—" Odeen stopped rather hopelessly. "It's hard to explain the triad to someone—"

"Nevertheless, I am trying to understand. You think you have caught a portion of Dua's inner mind; something she has tried to keep secret, is that it?"

"I'm not sure. It is the vaguest impression, sensed with a corner of my mind just now and then."

"Well?"

"I sometimes think Dua doesn't want to have a baby-Emotional."

Losten looked at him gravely. "You only have two children so far, I think. A little-left and a little-right."

"Yes, only two. The Emotional is difficult to initiate, you know."

"I know."

"And Dua will not trouble to absorb the necessary energy. Or even try to. She has any number of reasons but I can't believe any of them. It seems to me that for some reason she just doesn't want an Emotional. For myself—if Dua really didn't want one for a while—well, I would let her have her way. But Tritt is a Parental, and he wants one; he must have one; and somehow I can't disappoint Tritt, not even for Dua."

"If Dua had some rational cause for not wanting to initiate an Emotional, would that make a difference with you?"

"With me, certainly, but not with Tritt. He doesn't understand such things."

"But would you labor to keep him patient?"

"Yes, I would, for as long as I could."

Losten said, "Has it occurred to you that hardly any Soft Ones"—here he hesitated as though searching for a word and then he used the customary Soft-One phrase—"ever pass on before the children are born—all three, with the baby-Emotional last."

"Yes, I know." Odeen wondered how Losten could possibly think him ignorant of so elementary a bit of knowledge.

"Then the birth of a baby-Emotional is equivalent to the coming of time to pass on."

"Usually, not till the Emotional is old enough—"

"But the time for passing on will be coming. Might it not be that Dua does not want to pass on?"

"How can that be, Losten? When the time comes to pass on, it is as when the time comes to melt. How can you not want to?" (Hard Ones didn't melt; perhaps they didn't understand.)

"Suppose Dua simply wants never to pass on? What would you then say?"

"Why, that we *must* pass on eventually. If Dua merely

wants to delay the last baby, I might humor her and even persuade Tritt to, perhaps. If she wants never to have it—that simply cannot be allowed."

"Why so?"

Odeen paused to think it out. "I can't say, Losten-sir, but I know we must pass on. I know it more and feel it more with each cycle, and sometimes I almost think I understand why."

"You are a philosopher, I sometimes think, Odeen," said Losten dryly. "Let's consider. By the time the third baby comes and grows, Tritt will have had all his children and can look forward to passing on after a fulfilled life. You yourself will have had the satisfaction of much learning and you, too, can pass on after a fulfilled life. But Dua?"

"I don't *know*," said Odeen, wretchedly. "Other Emotionals cling together all lifelong and seem to get some pleasure out of chattering with each other. Dua, however, will not do that."

"Well, she is unusual. Is there nothing she likes?"

"She likes to listen to me talk about my work," mumbled Odeen.

Losten said, "Well, don't be ashamed of that, Odeen. Every Rational talks about his work to his right and his mid. You all pretend you don't, but you all do."

Odeen said, "But Dua *listens,* Losten-sir."

"I'm quite sure she does. Not like other Emotionals. And does it ever seem to you that she understands rather better after a melt?"

"Yes, I have noticed that at times. I didn't particularly pay any attention, though—"

"Because you are sure Emotionals can't really understand these things. But there seems to be considerable of the Rational in Dua."

(Odeen looked up at Losten with sudden consternation. Once Dua had told him of her childhood unhappiness; only once; of the shrill calls of the other Emotionals; of the filthy name they had called her—Left-Em. Had Losten heard of that, somehow? . . . But he was only looking calmly at Odeen.)

Odeen said, "I have sometimes thought that, too." Then he burst out, "I am *proud* of her for that."

"Nothing wrong with that," said Losten. "Why not tell her so? And if she likes to pamper the Rationalness in herself, why not let her? Teach her what you know more intensively. Answer her questions. Will it disgrace your triad to do that?"

"I don't care if it does. . . . And why should it, anyway? Tritt will think it a waste of time, but I'll handle him."

"Explain to him that if Dua gets more out of life and a truer sense of fulfillment, she might not have the fear of passing on that she now has and might be more ready to have a baby-Emotional."

It was as though an enormous feeling of impending disaster had been lifted from Odeen. He said, hurriedly, "You're right. I feel you're right. Losten-sir, you understand so much. With you leading the Hard Ones, how can we fail to continue succeeding in the other-Universe project?"

"With me?" Losten was amused. "You forget it is Estwald who is guiding us now. He is the real hero of the project. It would be nowhere without him."

"Oh, yes," said Odeen, momentarily discomfited. He had never yet seen Estwald. In fact, he had not yet met a Soft One who had actually met him though some reported having seen him in the distance now and then. Estwald was a new Hard One; new, at least, in the sense that when Odeen had been young, he had never heard him mentioned. Didn't that mean that Estwald was a young Hard One, had been a child Hard One when Odeen had been a child Soft One?

But never mind that. Right now, Odeen wanted to get back home. He couldn't touch Losten in gratitude, but he could thank him again and then hasten away joyfully.

There was a selfish component to his joy. It was not just the distant prospect of the baby-Emotional and the thought of Tritt's pleasure. It was not even the thought of Dua's fulfillment. What counted with him at this very moment was the immediate gleeful prospect ahead. He was going to be able to teach. No other Rational could feel the pleasure of so doing, he was sure, for no other Rational could possibly have an Emotional like Dua as part of the triad.

It would be wonderful, if only Tritt could be made to understand the necessity. He would have to talk to Tritt, somehow persuade him to be patient.

2c

Tritt had never felt less patient. He did not pretend to understand why Dua acted the way she did. He did not want to try. He did not care. He never knew why Emotionals did what they did. And Dua didn't even act like the other Emotionals.

She never thought about the important thing. She would look at the Sun. But then she would thin out so that the light and food would just pass through her. Then she would say it was beautiful. That was not the important thing. The important thing was to eat. What was beautiful about eating? What was beautiful?

She always wanted to melt differently. Once she said, "Let's talk first. We never talk about it. We never think about it."

Odeen would always say, "Let her have her way about it, Tritt. It makes it better."

Odeen was always patient. He always thought things would be better when they waited. Or else he would want to think it out.

Tritt wasn't sure he knew what Odeen meant by "think it out." It seemed to him it just meant that Odeen did nothing.

Like getting Dua in the first place. Odeen would still be thinking it out. Tritt went right up and asked. That was the way to be.

Now Odeen wouldn't do anything about Dua. What

about the baby-Emotional, which was what mattered? Well, Tritt would do something about it, if Odeen didn't.

In fact, he was doing something. He was edging down the long corridor even as all this was going through his mind. He was hardly aware he had come this far. Was this "thinking it out"? Well, he would not let himself be frightened. He would not back away.

Stolidly, he looked about him. This was the way to the Hard-caverns. He knew he would be going that way with his little-left before very long. He had been shown the way by Odeen once.

He did not know what he would do when he got there this time. Still, he felt no fright at all. He wanted a baby-Emotional. It was his right to have a baby-Emotional. *Nothing* was more important than that. The Hard Ones would see he got one. Hadn't they brought them Dua when he had asked?

But who would he ask? Could it be any Hard One? Dimly, he had made up his mind *not* any Hard One. There was the name of one he would ask for. Then he would talk to *him* about it.

He remembered the name. He even remembered when he had first heard the name. It was the time when the little-left had grown old enough to begin changing shape voluntarily. (What a great day! "Come, Odeen, quickly! Annis is all oval and hard. All by himself, too. Dua, look!" And they had rushed in. Annis was the only child then. They had had to wait so long for the second. So they rushed in and he was just plastered in the corner. He was curling at himself and flowing over his resting place like wet clay. Odeen had left because he was busy. But said, "Oh, he'll do it again, Tritt." They had watched for hours and he didn't.)

Tritt was hurt that Odeen hadn't waited. He would have scolded but Odeen looked so weary. There were definite wrinkles in his ovoid. And he made no effort to smooth them out.

Tritt said anxiously, "Is anything wrong, Odeen?"

"A hard day and I'm not sure I'm going to get differential equations before the next melting." (Tritt didn't remember the exact hard words. It was something like that. Odeen always used hard words.)

"Do you want to melt now?"

"Oh, no. I just saw Dua heading topside and you know how she is if we try to interrupt that. There's no rush, really. There's a new Hard One, too."

"A new Hard One?" said Tritt, with distinct lack of interest. Odeen found sharp interest in associating with Hard Ones, but Tritt wished the interest didn't exist. Odeen was more intent on what he called his education than any other Rational in the area. That was unfair. Odeen was too wrapped up in that. Dua was too wrapped up in roaming the surface alone. No one was properly interested in the triad but Tritt.

"He's called Estwald," said Odeen.

"Estwald?" Tritt *did* feel a twinge of interest. Perhaps it was because he was anxiously sensing Odeen's feelings.

"I've never seen him, but they all talk about him." Odeen's eyes had flattened out as they usually did when he turned introspective. "He's responsible for that new thing they've got."

"What new thing?"

"The Positron Pu— You wouldn't understand, Tritt. It's a new thing they have. It's going to revolutionize the whole world."

"What's revolutionize?"

"Make everything different."

Tritt was at once alarmed. "They mustn't make everything different."

"They'll make everything *better*. Different isn't always worse. Anyway, Estwald is responsible. He's very bright. I get the feeling."

"Then why don't you like him?"

"I didn't say I didn't like him."

"You *feel* as though you don't like him."

"Oh, nothing of the sort, Tritt. It's just that somehow— somehow—" Odeen laughed. "I'm jealous. Hard Ones are so intelligent that a Soft One is nothing in comparison, but I got used to that, because Losten was always telling me how bright I was—for a Soft One, I suppose. But now this

Estwald comes along, and even Losten seems lost in admiration, and I'm *really* nothing."

Tritt bellied out his foreplane to have it just make contact with Odeen, who looked up and smiled. "But that's just stupidity on my part. Who cares how smart a Hard One is? Not one of them has a Tritt."

After that they both went looking for Dua after all. For a wonder, she had finished wandering about and was just heading down again. It was a very good melting though the time lapse was only a day or so. Tritt worried about meltings then. With Annis so small, even a short absence was risky, though there were always other Parentals who could take over.

After that, Odeen mentioned Estwald now and then. He always called him "the New One" even after considerable time had passed. He still had never seen him. "I think I avoid him," he said one time, when Dua was with them, "because he knows so much about the new device. I don't want to find out too soon. It's too much fun to learn."

"The Positron Pump?" Dua had asked.

—That was another funny thing about Dua. Tritt thought. It annoyed him. She could say the hard words almost as well as Odeen could. An Emotional shouldn't be like that.

So Tritt made up his mind to ask Estwald because Odeen had said he was smart. Besides, Odeen had never seen him. Estwald couldn't say, "I've talked to Odeen about it, Tritt, and you mustn't worry."

Everyone thought that if you talked to the Rational, you were talking to the triad. Nobody paid attention to the Parentals. But they would have to this time.

He was in the Hard-caverns and everything seemed different. There was nothing there that looked like anything Tritt could understand. It was all wrong and frightening. Still, he was too anxious to see Estwald to let himself really be frightened. He said to himself, "I want my little-mid." That made him feel firm enough to walk forward.

He saw a Hard One finally. There was just this one; doing something; bending over something; doing something. Odeen once told him that Hard Ones were always working at their—whatever it was. Tritt didn't remember and didn't care.

He moved smoothly up and stopped. "Hard-sir," he said.

The Hard One looked up at him and the air vibrated about him, the Odeen said it did when two Hard Ones talked to each other sometimes. Then the Hard One seemed really to see Tritt and said, "Why, it's a right. What is your business here? Do you have your little-left with you? Is today the start of a semester?"

Tritt ignored it all. He said, "Where can I find Estwald, sir?"

"Find whom?"

"Estwald."

The Hard One was silent for a long moment. Then he said, "What is your business with Estwald, right?"

Tritt felt stubborn. "It is important I speak to him. Are *you* Estwald, Hard-sir?"

"No, I am not. . . . What is your name, right?"

"Tritt, Hard-sir."

"I see. You're the right of Odeen's triad, aren't you?"

"Yes."

The Hard One's voice seemed to soften. "I'm afraid you can't see Estwald at the moment. He's not here. If anyone else can help you?"

Tritt didn't know what to say. He simply stood there.

The Hard One said, "You go home now. Talk to Odeen. He'll help you. Yes? Go home, right."

The Hard One turned away. He seemed very concerned in matters other than Tritt, and Tritt still stood there, uncertain. Then he moved into another section quietly, flowing noiselessly. The Hard One did not look up.

Tritt was not certain at first why he had moved in that particular direction. At first, he felt only that it was good to do so. Then it was clear. There was a thin warmth of food about him and he was nibbling at it.

He had not been conscious of hunger, yet now he was eating and enjoying.

The Sun was nowhere. Instinctively, he looked up, but

of course he was in a cavern. Yet the food was better than he had ever found it to be on the surface. He looked about, wondering. He wondered, most of all, that he should be wondering.

He had sometimes been impatient with Odeen because Odeen wondered about so many things that didn't matter. Now he himself—Tritt!—was wondering. But what he was wondering about *did* matter. Suddenly, he saw that it *did* matter. With an almost blinding flash he realized that he wouldn't wonder unless something inside him told it *did* matter.

He acted quickly, marveling at his own bravery. After a while, he retraced his steps. He moved past the Hard One again, the one to whom he had earlier spoken. He said, "I am going home, Hard-sir."

The Hard One merely said something incoherent. He was still doing something, bending over something, doing silly things and not seeing the important thing.

If Hard Ones were so great and powerful and smart, Tritt thought, how could they be so stupid?

3a

Dua found herself drifting toward the Hard-caverns. Partly it was because it was something to do now that the Sun had set, something to keep her from returning home for an additional period of time, something to delay having to listen to the importunities of Tritt and the half-embarrassed, half-resigned suggestions of Odeen. Partly, too, it was the attraction they held for her in themselves.

She had felt that for a long time, ever since she was little in fact, and had given up trying to pretend it wasn't so. Emotionals weren't supposed to feel such attractions. Sometimes little Emotionals did—Dua was old enough and experienced enough to know that—but this quickly faded or they were quickly discouraged if it didn't fade quickly enough.

When she herself had been a child, though, she had continued stubbornly curious about the world, and the Sun, and the caverns, and—anything at all—till her Parental would say, "You're a queer one, Dua, dear. You're a funny little midling. What will become of you?"

She hadn't the vaguest notion at first of what was so queer and so funny about wanting to know. She found, quickly enough, that her Parental could not answer her questions. She once tried her left-father, but he showed none of her Parental's soft puzzlement. He snapped, "Why do you ask, Dua?" and his look seemed harshly inquiring.

She ran away, frightened, and did not ask him again.

But then one day another Emotional of her own age had shrieked "Left-Em" at her after she had said—she no longer remembered—it had been something that had seemed natural to her at the time. Dua had been abashed without knowing why and had asked her considerably older left-brother, what a Left-Em was. He had withdrawn, embarrassed—clearly embarrassed—mumbling, "I don't know," when it was obvious he did.

After some thought, she went to her Parental and said, "Am I a Left-Em, Daddy?"

And he had said, "Who called you that, Dua? You must not repeat such words."

She flowed herself about his near corner, thought about it awhile, and said, "Is it bad?"

He said, "You'll grow out of it," and let himself bulge a bit to make her swing outward and vibrate in the game she had always loved. She somehow didn't love it now, for it was quite clear that he hadn't answered her, really. She moved away thoughtfully. He had said, "You'll grow *out* of it," so she was *in* it now, but in *what*?

Even then, she had had few real friends among the other Emotionals. They liked to whisper and giggle together, but she preferred flowing over the crumbled rocks and enjoying the sensation of their roughness. There were, however, some mids who were more friendly than others and whom she found less provoking. There was Doral, who was as silly as the rest, really, but who would sometimes chatter amusingly. (Doral had grown up to join a triad with Dua's right-brother and a young left from another cavern complex, a left whom Dua did not particularly like. Doral had then gone on to initiate a baby-left, a baby-right, in rapid succession, and a baby-mid not too long after that. She had also grown so dense that the triad looked as though it had two Parentals and Dua wondered if they could still melt. . . . Just the same Tritt was always telling her, pointedly, what a good triad Doral helped make up.)

She and Doral had sat alone one day and Dua had whispered, "Doral, do you know what a Left-Em is?"

And Doral had tittered and compressed herself, as though to avoid being seen, and had said, "It's an Emotional that acts like a Rational; you know, like a left. Get it! Left-Emotional—Left-Em! Get it!"

Of course Dua "got" the phrase. It was obvious once explained. She would have seen it for herself at once if she had been able to bring herself to imagine such a state of affairs.

Dua said, "How do you know?"

"The older girls told me." Doral's substance swirled and Dua found the motion unpleasant. "It's dirty," Doral said.

"Why?" asked Dua.

"Because it's *dirty*. Emotionals shouldn't act like Rationals."

Dua had never thought about the possibility, but now she did. She said, "*Why* shouldn't they?"

"*Because!* You want to know something else that's dirty?"

Dua couldn't help being intrigued. "What?"

Doral didn't say anything, but a portion of herself expanded suddenly and brushed against the unsuspecting Dua before the latter could concavize. Dua didn't like it. She shrank away and said, "Don't do that."

"You know what else is dirty? You can go into a rock."

"No, you can't," said Dua. It had been a silly thing to

say for Dua had often moved through the outer surface of the rock and liked it. But now in the context of Doral's snickering, she felt revolted and denied the whole thing, even to herself.

"Yes, you can. It's called rock-rubbing. Emotionals can do it easy. Lefts and rights can only do it as babies. When they grow up, they do it with each other."

"I don't believe you. You're making it up."

"They do, I tell you. Do you know Dimit?"

"No."

"Sure you do. She's the girl with the thick corner from Cavern c."

"Is she the one who flows funny?"

"Yes. On account of the thick corner. That's the one. She got into a rock all the way once—except for the thick corner. She let her left-brother watch her do it and he told their Parental and what she got for *that*. She never did it again."

Dua left then, quite upset. She didn't talk to Doral again for a long time, and never really grew friendly again, and yet her curiosity had been aroused.

Her curiosity? Why not say her Left-Emmishness?

One day when she was quite sure her Parental wasn't in the vicinity, she let herself melt into a rock, slowly, just a little. It had been the first time she had tried it since she was quite young, and she didn't think she had ever dared go so deep. There was a warmness about the sensation, but when she emerged she felt as though everyone could tell, as though the rock had left a stain on her.

She tried it again now and then, more boldly, and let herself enjoy it more. She never sank in really deeply, of course.

Eventually, she was caught by her Parental, who clucked away in displeasure, and she was more careful after that. She was older now and knew for certain fact that despite Doral's snickering, it wasn't in the least uncommon. Practically every Emotional did it now and then and some quite openly admitted it.

It happened less frequently as they grew older and Dua didn't think that any Emotional she knew ever did it after joining a triad and beginning the proper meltings. It was one of her secrets (she never told anybody) that she had kept it up, and that once or twice she had tried it even after triad-formation. (Those few times she had thought: What if Tritt found out? . . . Somehow that seemed to present formidable consequences and rather spoiled the fun.)

Confusedly, she found excuses for this—to herself—in her ordeal with the others. The cry of "Left-Em" began to follow her everywhere in a kind of public humiliation. There was one period in her life when she had been driven into an almost hermit-like isolation to escape. If she had begun with a liking for aloneness, that had confirmed it. And being alone, she found consolation in the rocks. Rock-rubbing, whether it was dirty or not, was a solitary act, and they were forcing her to be solitary.

At least, so she told herself.

She had tried to strike back once. She had cried out, "You're a bunch of Right-Ems, a bunch of dirty Right-Ems," at the taunting mids.

They had only laughed and Dua had run away in confusion and frustration. They *were*. Almost every Emotional, when she was getting on to the age of triad-formation, became interested in babies, fluttering about them in Parental imitation which Dua had found repulsive. She herself had never felt such interest. Babies were only babies; they were for right-brothers to worry about.

The name-calling died as Dua grew older. It helped that she retained a girlishly rarefied structure and could flow with a smoky curl no other could duplicate. And when, increasingly, lefts and rights showed interest in her, the other Emotionals found it difficult to sneer.

And yet—and yet—now that no one ever dared speak disrespectfully to Dua (for it was well known through all the caverns that Odeen was the most prominent Rational of the generation and Dua was his mid-ling), she herself knew that she was a Left-Em past all redemption.

She didn't think it dirty—not really—but occasionally she caught herself wishing she were a Rational and then she was abashed. She wondered if other Emotionals did— ever—or just once in a while—and if that was why—

partly—she didn't want a baby-Emotional—because she wasn't a real Emotional herself—and didn't fill her triad-role properly—

Odeen hadn't minded her being a Left-Em. He never called her that—but he liked her interest in his life—he liked her questions and he would explain and he liked the way she could understand. He even defended her when Tritt grew jealous—well, not jealous, really—but filled with a feeling that it was all unfit in his stubborn and limited outlook on the world.

Odeen had taken her to the Hard-caverns occasionally, eager to posture before Dua, and openly pleased at the fact that Dua was impressed. And she *was* impressed, not so much with the clear fact of his knowledge and intelligence, but with the fact that he did not resent sharing it. (She remembered her left-father's harsh response that one time she had questioned him.) She never loved Odeen so much as when he let her share his life—and yet even that was part of her Left-Emmishness.

Perhaps (this had occurred to her over and over), by being Left-Emmish, she moved closer to Odeen and farther from Tritt, and this was another reason Tritt's importunities repelled her. Odeen had never hinted at anything like that, but perhaps Tritt felt it vaguely and was unable to grasp it completely but did so well enough to be unhappy over it without being able to explain why.

The first time she was in a Hard-cavern she had heard two Hard Ones talking together. She didn't know they were talking of course. There was air vibration, very rapid, very changing, that made an unpleasant buzz deep inside her. She had to rarefy and let it through.

Odeen had said, "They're talking." Then, hastily, anticipating the objection. "*Their* kind of talk. They understand each other."

Dua had managed to grasp the concept. It was all the more delightful to understand quickly because that pleased Odeen so. (He once said, "None of the other Rationals I've ever met have anything but an empty-head for an Emotional. I'm lucky." She had said, "But the other Rationals seem to like empty-heads. Why are you different from them, Odeen?" Odeen did not deny that the other Rationals liked empty-heads. He just said, "I've never figured it out and I don't think it's important that I do. I'm pleased with you and I'm pleased that I'm pleased.")

She said, "Can *you* understand Hard-One talk?"

"Not really," said Odeen. "I can't sense the changes fast enough. Sometimes I can get a feel for what they're saying, even without understanding, especially after we've melted. Just sometimes, though. Getting feels like that is really an Emotional trick, except even if an Emotional does it, she can never make real sense out of what she's feeling. *You* might, though."

Dua demurred. "I'd be afraid to. They might not like it."

"Oh, go on. I'm curious. See if you can tell what they're talking about."

"Shall I? Really?"

"Go ahead. If they catch you and are annoyed, I'll say I made you do it."

"Promise?"

"I promise."

Feeling rather fluttery, Dua let herself reach out to the Hard Ones, and adopted the total passivity that allowed the influx of feelings.

She said, "Excitement! They're excited. Someone new."

Odeen said, "Maybe that's Estwald."

It was the first time Dua had heard the name. She said, "That's funny."

"What's funny?"

"I have the feeling of a big sun. A really big sun."

Odeen looked thoughtful. "They might be talking about that."

"But how can that be?"

It was just at that time that the Hard Ones spied them. They approached in a friendly manner and greeted them in Soft-One fashion of speech. Dua was horribly embarrassed and wondered if they knew she had been sensing them. If they did, though, they said nothing.

(Odeen told her afterward that it was quite rare to come upon Hard Ones talking among themselves in their own fashion. They always deferred to the Soft Ones and seemed always to suspend their own work when Soft Ones were there. "They like us so much," said Odeen. "They are very kind.")

Once in awhile he would take her down to the Hard-caverns—usually when Tritt was entirely wrapped up in the children. Nor did Odeen go out of his way to tell Tritt that he had taken Dua down. It was sure to evoke some response to the effect that Odeen's coddling simply encouraged Dua's reluctance to sun herself and just made the melting that much more ineffective. . . . It was hard to talk to Tritt for more than five minutes without melting coming into the conversation.

She had even come down alone once or twice. It had always frightened her a little to do so, though the Hard Ones she met were always friendly, always "very kind," as Odeen said. But they did not seem to take her seriously. They were pleased, but somehow amused—she could feel that definitely—when she asked questions. And when they answered it was in a simple way that carried no information. "Just a machine, Dua," they would say. "Odeen might be able to tell you."

She wondered if she had met Estwald. She never quite dared ask the names of the Hard Ones she met (except Losten, to whom Odeen had introduced her, and of whom she heard a great deal). Sometimes it seemed to her that this Hard One or that might be he. Odeen talked about him with great awe and with some resentment.

She gathered that he was too engaged in work of the deepest importance to be in the caverns accessible to the Soft Ones.

She pieced together what Odeen told her and, little by little, discovered that the world needed food badly. Odeen hardly ever called it "food." He said "energy" instead, and said it was the Hard-One word for it.

The Sun was fading and dying but Estwald had discovered how to find energy far away, far beyond the Sun, far beyond the seven stars that shone in the dark, night-sky. (Odeen said the seven stars were seven suns that were very distant, and that there were many other stars that were even more distant and were too dim to be seen. Tritt had heard him say that and had asked of what use it was for stars to exist if they couldn't be seen and he didn't believe a word of it. Odeen had said, "Now, Tritt," in a patient way. Dua had been about to say something very like that which Tritt had said, but changed her mind after that.)

It looked, now, as though there would be plenty of energy forever; plenty of food—at least as soon as Estwald and the other Hard Ones learned to make the new energy taste right.

It had only been a few days ago when she had said to Odeen, "Do you remember, long ago, when you took me to the Hard-caverns and I sensed the Hard Ones and said I caught the feeling of a big sun?"

Odeen looked puzzled for a moment. "I'm not sure. But go ahead, Dua. What about it?"

"I've been thinking. Is the big Sun the source of the new energy?"

Odeen had said, happily, "That's good, Dua. It's not quite right, but that's such good intuition for an Emotional."

And now Dua had been moving slowly, rather moodily, during all this time of reveries. Without particularly noting the passage of either time or space she found herself in the Hard-caverns and was just beginning to wonder if she had really delayed all she safely could and whether she might not turn home now and face the inevitable annoyance of Tritt when—almost as though the thought of Tritt had brought it about—she sensed Tritt.

The sensation was so strong that there was only one confused moment in which she had thought that somehow she was picking up his feelings far away in the home cavern. *No!* He was here, down in the Hard-caverns with her.

But what could he be doing here? Was he pursuing her? Was he going to quarrel with her *here?* Was he foolishly going to appeal to the Hard Ones? Dua didn't think she could endure that—

And then the feeling of cold horror left her and was replaced by astonishment. Tritt was not thinking of her at all. He had to be unaware of her presence. All she could sense about him was an overwhelming feeling of some sort of determination, mixed with fear and apprehension at something he would do.

Dua might have penetrated farther and found out something, at least, about what it was he had done, and why, but nothing was further from her thoughts. Since Tritt didn't know she was in the vicinity, she wanted to make sure of only one thing—that he continued not to know.

She did, then, almost in pure reflex, something that a moment before she would have sworn she would never dream of doing under any circumstances.

Perhaps it was (she later thought) because of her idle reminiscences of that little-girl talk with Doral, or her memories of her own experiments with rock-rubbing. (There was a complicated adult word for it but she found that word infinitely more embarrassing than the one all the children had used.)

In any case, without quite knowing what she was doing or, for a short while afterward, what she had done, she simply flowed hastily into the nearest wall.

Into it! Every bit of her!

The horror of what she had done was mitigated by the perfect manner in which it accomplished its purpose. Tritt passed by within almost touching distance and remained completely unaware that at one point he might have reached out and touched his mid-ling.

By that time, Dua had no room to wonder what Tritt might be doing in the Hard-caverns if he had not come in pursuit of her.

She forgot Tritt completely.

What filled her instead was pure astonishment at her position. Even in childhood she had never melted completely into rock or met anyone who admitted she had (though there were invariably tales of someone else who had). Certainly no adult Emotional ever had or *could*. Dua was unusually rarefied even for an Emotional (Odeen was fond of telling her that) and her avoidance of food accentuated this (as Tritt often said).

What she had just done indicated the extent of her rar-efaction more than any amount of right-ling scolding and for a moment she was ashamed and sorry for Tritt.

And then she was swept by a deeper shame. What if she were caught? She, an adult—

If a Hard One passed and lingered— She could not possibly bring herself to emerge if anyone were watching but how long could she stay within and what if they discovered her *in* the rock?

And even as she thought that, she sensed the Hard Ones and then—somehow—realized they were far away.

She paused, strove to calm herself. The rock, permeating and surrounding her, lent a kind of grayness to her perception but didn't dim it. Instead, she sensed more sharply. She could still sense Tritt in his steady motion downward as sharply as though he were by her side, and she could sense the Hard Ones though they were a cavern complex away. She *saw* the Hard Ones, every single one of them, each in his place, and could sense their vibratory speech to the fullest detail, and even catch bits of what they were saying.

She was sensing as she never had before and never dreamed she could.

So, though she could now leave the rock, secure in the knowledge she was both alone and unobserved, she did not; partly out of amazement, partly out of the curious exultation she felt at understanding and her desire to experience it further.

Her sensitivity was such that she even knew *why* she was sensitive. Odeen had frequently remarked how well he understood something after a period of melting, even though he had not understood it at all before. There was something about the melted state that increased sensitivity incredibly; more was absorbed; more was used. It was because of the greater atomic density during melting, Odeen had said.

Even though Dua was not sure what "greater atomic density" meant, it came with melting and wasn't this present situation rather like melting? Hadn't Dua melted with rock?

When the triad melted, all the sensitivity went to Odeen's benefit. The Rational absorbed it, gained understanding, and retained that understanding after separation. But now Dua was the only consciousness in the melt. It was herself and the rock. There was "greater atomic density" (surely?) with only herself to benefit.

(Was this why rock-rubbing was considered a perversion? Was this why Emotionals were warned off? Or was it just Dua because she was so rarefied? Or because she was a Left-Em?)

And then Dua stopped all speculation and just sensed—in fascination. She was only mechanically aware of Tritt returning, moving past her, passing in the direction back from which he had come. She was only mechanically aware—scarcely feeling the vaguest surprise—that Odeen, too, was coming up from the Hard-caverns. It was the Hard Ones she was sensing, only they, trying to make more out of her perceptions, trying to make the most out of them.

It was a long time before she detached and flowed out of the rock. And when that time came, she was not concerned overmuch as to whether she would be observed. She was confident enough of her sensing ability to know she wouldn't be.

And she returned home deep in thought.

3b

Odeen had returned home to find Tritt waiting for him, but Dua still hadn't returned. Tritt did not seem disturbed at that. Or at least he seemed disturbed, but not at *that*. His emotions were strong enough so that Odeen could sense them clearly, but he let them go without proving. It was Dua's absence that made Odeen restless; to the extent that he found himself annoyed at Tritt's presence simply because Tritt was not Dua.

In this he surprised himself. He could not deny to himself that it was Tritt who, of the two, was the dearer to him. Ideally, all members of the triad were one, and any member should treat the other two exactly on a par—both with each other and with him (her) self. Yet Odeen had never met a triad in which this was so; least of all among those who loudly proclaimed their triad to be ideal in this respect. One of the three was always a little left out, and generally knew it, too.

It was rarely the Emotional, though. They supported each other cross-triad to an extent that Rationals and Parentals never did. The Rational had his teacher, the proverb went, and the Parental his children—but the Emotional had all the other Emotionals.

Emotionals compared notes and if one claimed neglect, or could be made to claim it, she was sent back with a thin patter of instructions to stand firm, to demand! And because melting depended so much on the Emotional and her attitude, she was usually pampered by both left and right.

But Dua was so non-Emotional an Emotional! She didn't seem to care that Odeen and Tritt were so close, and she had no close friendships among the Emotionals to make her care. Of course that was it; she was so non-Emotional an Emotional.

Odeen loved having her so interested in his work; loved having her so concerned and so amazingly ready of comprehension; but that was an intellectual love. The deeper feeling went to steady, stupid Tritt, who knew his place so well and who could offer so little other than exactly what counted—the security of assured routine.

But now Odeen felt petulant. He said, "Have you heard from Dua, Tritt?"

And Tritt did not answer directly. He said, "I am busy. I will see you later. I have been doing things."

"Where are the children? Have you been gone, too? There is a been-gone feel to you."

A note of annoyance made itself plain in Tritt's voice.

"The children are well-trained. They know enough to place themselves in community-care. Really, Odeen, they are not babies." But he did not deny the "been-gone" aura that he faintly exuded.

"I'm sorry. I'm just anxious to see Dua."

"You should feel so more often," Tritt said. "You always tell me to leave her alone. You look for her." And he went on into the deeper recesses of the home cavern.

Odeen looked after his right-ling with some surprise. At almost any other occasion he would have followed in an attempt to probe the unusual uneasiness that was making itself quite evident through the ingrained stolidity of a Parental. What had Tritt done?

—But he was waiting for Dua, and growing more anxious by the moment, and he let Tritt go.

Anxiety keened Odeen's sensitivity. There was almost a perverse pride among Rationals in their relative poverty of perception. Such perception wasn't a thing of the mind; it was most characteristic of Emotionals. Odeen was a Rational of Rationals, proud of reasoning rather than feeling, yet now he flung out the imperfect net of his emotional perception as far as he could; and wished, for just a moment, that he were an Emotional so that he could send it out farther and better.

Yet it eventually served his purpose. He could detect Dua's approach, finally, at an unusual distance—for him —and he hastened out to meet her. And because he made her out at such a distance, he was more aware of her rarefaction than he ordinarily was. She was a delicate mist, no more.

—Tritt was right, Odeen thought with sudden, sharp concern. Dua *must* be made to eat and to melt. Her interest in life *must* be increased.

He was so intent on the necessity of this that when she flung herself flowingly toward him and virtually engulfed him, in utter disregard of the fact that they were not in private and might be observed, and said, "Odeen, I must know—I must know so much—" he accepted it as the completion of his own thought and did not even consider it strange.

Carefully, he slipped away, trying to adopt a more seemly union without making it seem he was repulsing her. "Come," he said, "I've been waiting for you. Tell me what you want to know. I will explain all I can."

They were moving quickly homeward now, with Odeen adapting himself eagerly to the characteristic waver of the Emotional flow.

Dua said, "Tell me about the other Universe. Why are they different? How are they different? Tell me all about it."

It did not occur to Dua she was asking too much. It *did* occur to Odeen. He felt rich with an astonishing quantity of knowledge and was on the point of asking, How do you come to know enough about the other Universe to grow so curious about it?

He repressed the question. Dua was coming from the direction of the Hard-caverns. Perhaps Losten had been talking to her, suspecting that despite everything Odeen would be too proud of his status to help his mid-ling.

Not so, thought Odeen gravely. And he would not ask. He would just explain.

Tritt bustled about them when they returned home. "If you two are going to talk, go into Dua's chamber. I will be busy out here. I must see to it that the children are cleaned and exercised. No time for melting now. No melting."

Neither Odeen nor Dua had any thought of melting, but there was no thought in either mind of disobeying the command. The Parental's home was his castle. The Rational had his Hard-caverns below and the Emotional her meeting places above. The Parental had only his home.

Odeen therefore said, "Yes, Tritt. We'll be out of your way."

And Dua extended a briefly loving part of herself and said, "It's good to see you, right-dear." (Odeen wondered if her gesture was part relief over the fact that there would be no pressure to melt. Tritt did tend to overdo that a bit; even more than Parentals generally.)

In her chamber, Dua stared at her private feeding-place. Ordinarily, she ignored it.

It had been Odeen's idea. He knew that such things did

exist and, as he explained to Tritt, if Dua did not like to
swarm with the other Emotionals, it was perfectly possible
to lead Solar energy down into the cavern so that Dua
might feed there.

Tritt had been horrified. It wasn't done. The others
would laugh. The triad would be disgraced. Why didn't
Dua behave as she should?

"Yes, Tritt," Odeen had said, "but she doesn't behave
as she should, so why not accommodate her? Is it so terrible? She will eat privately, gain substance, make us happier, become happier herself, and maybe learn to swarm in
the end."

Tritt allowed it, and even Dua allowed it—after some
argument—but insisted that it be a simple design. So there
was nothing but the two rods that served as electrodes,
powered by Solar energy, and with room for Dua in between.

Dua rarely used it, but this time she stared at it and
said, "Tritt has decorated it. . . . Unless you did, Odeen."

"I? Of course not."

A pattern of colored-clay designs was at the base of
each electrode. "I suppose it's his way of saying he wishes
I would use it," Dua said, "and I *am* hungry. Besides, if
I'm eating, Tritt wouldn't dream of interrupting us, would
he?"

"No" said Odeen, gravely. "Tritt would stop the world
if he thought its motion might disturb you while you were
eating."

Dua said, "Well—I *am* hungry."

Odeen caught a trace of guilt in her. Guilt over Tritt?
Over being hungry? Why should Dua feel guilty about
being hungry? Or had she done something that had con-
sumed energy and was she feeling—

He wrenched his mind away from that impatiently.
There were times when a Rational could be *too* Rational,
and chase down the tracks of every thought to the detri-
ment of what was important. Right now, it was important
to talk to Dua.

She seated herself between the electrodes and when she
compressed herself to do so, her small size was only too

painfully evident. Odeen was hungry himself; he could te[
because the electrodes seemed brighter than they ordinari[
ly did; and he could taste the food even at that distance
and the savor was delicious. When one was hungry, one
always tasted food more keenly than otherwise and at a
greater distance. . . . But he would eat later.

Dua said, "Don't just sit silently, left-dear. *Tell* me. I
want to know." She had adopted (unconsciously?) the
ovoid character of a Rational, as though to make it clearer
that she wanted to be accepted as one.

Odeen said, "I can't explain it all. All the science I
mean, because you haven't had the background. I will try
to make it simple and you just listen. Later, you tell me
what you didn't understand and I'll try to explain further.
You understand, first, that everything is made up of tiny
particles called atoms and that these are made up of still
tinier subatomic particles."

"Yes, yes," said Dua. "That's why we can melt."

"Exactly. Because actually we are mostly empty space.
All the particles are far apart and your particles and mine
and Tritt's can all melt together because each set fits into
the empty spaces around the other set. The reason matter
doesn't fly apart altogether is that the tiny particles do
manage to cling together across the space that separates
them. There are attractive forces holding them together,
the strongest being one we call the nuclear-force. It holds
the chief subatomic particles *very* tightly together in
bunches that are spread widely apart and that are held together by weaker forces. Do you understand that?"

"Only a little bit," said Dua.

"Well never mind, we can go back later. . . . Matter can
exist in different states. It can be especially spread out, as
in Emotionals; as in you, Dua. It can be a little less spread
out, as in Rationals and in Parentals. Or still less so, as in
rock. It can be very compressed or thick, as in the Hard
Ones. That's why they're hard. They are filled with particles."

"You mean there's no empty space in them."

"No, that's not quite what I mean," said Odeen, puzzled
as to how to make matter clearer. "They still have a great

leal of empty space, but not as much as we do. Particles
need a certain amount of empty space and if all they have
is that much, then other particles can't squeeze in. If particles are forced in, there is pain. That's why the Hard Ones
don't like to be touched by us. We Soft Ones have *more*
space between the particles than are actually needed, so
other particles can fit in."

Dua didn't look at all certain about that.

Odeen hastened onward. "In the other Universe, the
rules are different. The nuclear-force isn't as strong as in
ours. That means the particles need more room."

"Why?"

Odeen shook his head, "Because—because—the particles spread out their wave-forms more. I can't explain better than that. With a weaker nuclear-force, the particles
need more room and two pieces of matter can't melt together as easily as they can in our Universe."

"Can we see the other Universe?"

"Oh, no. That isn't possible. We can deduce its nature
from its basic laws. The Hard Ones can do a great many
things, though. We can send material across, and get material from them. We can study their material, you see.
And we can set up the Positron Pump. You know about
that, don't you?"

"Well, you've told me we get energy out of it. I didn't
know there was a different Universe involved. . . . What is
the other Universe like? Do they have stars and worlds the
way we do?"

"That's an excellent question, Dua." Odeen was enjoying his role as teacher more intensely than usual now that
he had official encouragement to speak. (Earlier he always
had the feeling that there was a kind of sneaking perversion in trying to explain things to an Emotional.)

He said, "We can't see the other Universe, but we can
calculate what it must be like from its laws. You see, what
makes the stars shine is the gradual combination of simple
particle-combinations into more complicated ones. We
call it nuclear fusion."

"Do they have that in the other Universe?"

"Yes, but because the nuclear-force is weaker, fusion is

much slower. This means that the stars must be much, much bigger in the other Universe otherwise not enough fusion would take place to make them shine. Stars of the other Universe that were no bigger than our Sun would be cold and dead. On the other hand, if stars in our Universe were bigger than they are, the amount of fusion would be so great it would blow them up. That means that in our Universe there must be thousands of times as many small stars as there are larger stars in theirs—"

"We only have seven—" began Dua. Then she said, "I forgot."

Odeen smiled indulgently. It was so easy to forget the uncounted stars that could not be seen except by special instruments. "That's all right. You don't mind my boring you with all this."

"You're not boring me," said Dua. "I *love* it. It even makes food taste so good." And she wavered between the electrodes with a kind of luxurious tremor.

Odeen, who had never before heard Dua say anything complimentary about food, was greatly heartened. He said, "Of course, our Universe doesn't last as long as theirs. Fusion goes so fast that all the particles are combined after a million lifetimes."

"But there are so many other stars."

"Ah, but you see they're all going at once. The whole Universe is dying down. In the other Universe, with so many fewer and larger stars, the fusion goes so slowly that the stars last thousands and millions of times as long as ours. It's hard to compare because it may be that time goes at different rates in the two Universes." He added, with some reluctance, "I don't understand that part myself. That's part of the Estwald Theory and I haven't got to that very much so far."

"Did Estwald work out all of this?"

"A great deal of it."

Dua said, "It's wonderful that we're getting the food from the other Universe then. I mean, it doesn't matter if our Sun dies out, then. We can get all the food we want from the other Universe."

"That's right."

"But does nothing bad happen? I have the—the feeling that something bad happens."

"Well," said Odeen. "We transfer matter back and forth to make the Positron Pump and that means the Universes mix together a little. Our nuclear-force gets a tiny bit weaker, so fusion in our Sun slows up a little and the Sun cools down a little faster. . . . But just a little, and we don't need it any more anyway."

"That's not the something-bad feeling I have. If the nuclear-force gets a tiny bit weaker, then the atoms take up more room—is that right?—and then what happens to melting?"

"That gets a tiny bit harder but it would take many millions of lifetimes before it would get noticeably harder to melt. Even if someday melting became impossible and Soft Ones died out, that would happen long, long after we would all have died out for lack of food if we weren't using the other Universe."

"That's still not the something-bad—feeling—" Dua's words were beginning to slur. She wriggled between her electrodes and to Odeen's gratified eyes she seemed noticeably larger and compacter. It was as though his words, as well as the food, were nourishing her.

Losten was right! Education made her more nearly satisfied with life; Odeen could sense a kind of sensual joy in Dua that he had scarcely ever felt before.

She said, "It is so kind of you to explain, Odeen. You are a good left-ling."

"Do you want me to go on?" asked Odeen, flattered and more pleased than he could easily say. "Is there anything else you want to ask?"

"A great deal, Odeen, but—but not now. Not now, Odeen. Oh, Odeen, do you know what I want to do?"

Odeen guessed at once, but was too cautious to say it openly. Dua's moments of erotic advance were too few to treat with anything but care. He hoped desperately that Tritt had not involved himself with the children to the point where they could not take advantage of this.

But Tritt was in the chamber already. Had he been outside the door, waiting? He did not care. There was no time to think.

Dua had flowed out from between the electrodes and Odeen's senses were filled with her beauty. She was between them, now, and through her Tritt shimmered, with his outlines flaming in incredible color.

It had never been like this. Never.

Odeen held himself back desperately, letting his own substance flow through Dua and into Tritt an atom at a time; holding away from the overpowering penetrance of Dua with every bit of strength; not giving himself up to the ecstasy, but letting it be wrenched from him; hanging on to his consciousness to the last possible moment; and then blanking out in one final transport so intense as to feel like an explosion echoing and reverberating endlessly within him.

Never in the lifetime of the triad had the period of melt-unconsciousness lasted so long.

3c

Tritt was pleased. The melting had been so satisfactory. All previous occasions seemed skimpy and hollow in comparison. He was utterly delighted with what had happened. Yet he kept quiet. He felt it better not to speak.

Odeen and Dua were happy, too. Tritt could tell. Even the children seemed to be glowing.

But Tritt was happiest of all—naturally.

He listened to Odeen and Dua talk. He understood none of it, but that didn't matter. He didn't mind that they seemed so pleased with each other. He had his own pleasure and was content to listen.

Dua said, on one occasion. "And do they really try to communicate with us?"

(Tritt never got it quite clear who "they" might be. He gathered that "communicate" was a fancy word for "talk." So why didn't they say "talk"? Sometimes he wondered if he should interrupt. But if he asked questions, Odeen would only say, "Now, Tritt," and Dua would swirl impatiently.)

"Oh, yes," said Odeen. "The Hard Ones are quite sure of that. They have markings on the material that is sent us sometimes and they say that it is perfectly possible to communicate by such markings. Long ago, in fact, they used markings in reverse, when it was necessary to explain to the other-beings how to set up their part of the Positron Pump."

"I wonder what the other-beings look like. What do they look like, do you suppose?"

"From the laws we can work out the nature of the stars because that is simple. But how can we work out the nature of the beings? We can never know."

"Couldn't they communicate what they look like?"

"If we understood what they communicated, perhaps we could make out something. But we don't understand."

Dua seemed aggrieved. "Don't the Hard Ones understand?"

"I don't know. If they do, they haven't told me so. Los ten once told me it didn't matter what they were like, a long as the Positron Pump worked and was enlarged."

"Maybe he just didn't want you bothering him."

Odeen said, huffily. "I don't bother him."

"Oh, you know what I mean. He just didn't want to ge into those details."

By that time Tritt could no longer listen. They went o arguing for quite awhile over whether the Hard One should let Dua look at the markings or not. Dua said tha she could sense what they said, perhaps.

It made Tritt a little angry. After all, Dua was only Soft One and not even a Rational. He began to wonder Odeen was right to tell her all he did. It gave Dua funn ideas—

Dua could see it made Odeen angry, too. First h laughed. Then he said that an Emotional couldn't handl such complicated things. Then he refused to talk at all. Dua had to be very pleasant to him for a while till he came around.

On one occasion it was Dua who was angry—absolutely furious.

It began quietly. In fact, it was on one of the occasions when the two children were with them. Odeen was letting them play with him. He didn't even mind when little-right Torun pulled at him. In fact, he let himself go in most undignified fashion. He didn't seem to mind that he was all out of shape. It was a sure sign he was pleased. Tritt remained in a corner, resting, and was so satisfied with what was happening.

Dua laughed at Odeen's misshapenness. She let her own substance touch Odeen's knobbishness flirtatiously. She knew very well, Tritt knew, that the leftish surface was sensitive when out of ovoid.

Dua said, "I've been thinking, Odeen . . . If the other Universe gets its laws into ours just a bit through the Positron Pump, doesn't our Universe get its laws into theirs the same little bit?"

Odeen howled at Dua's touch and tried to avoid her without upsetting the little ones. He gasped, "I can't answer unless you stop, you mid-ling wretch."

She stopped, and he said, "That's a *very* good thought, Dua. You're an amazing creature. It's true, of course. The mixture goes both ways. . . . Tritt take out the little ones, will you?"

But they scurried off by themselves. They were not such little ones. They were quite grown. Annis would soon be starting his education and Torun was quite Parentally-blockish already.

Tritt stayed and thought Dua looked very beautiful when Odeen talked to her in this way.

Dua said, "If the other laws slow down our Sun and cool them down; don't our laws speed up their suns and heat them up?"

"Exactly right, Dua. A Rational couldn't do better."

"How hot do their suns get?"

"Oh, not much; just slightly hotter, very slightly."

Dua said, "But that's where I keep getting the some-thing-bad feeling."

"Oh, well, the trouble is that their suns are so huge. If our little suns get a little cooler, it doesn't matter. Even if they turned off altogether, it wouldn't matter as long as we have the Positron Pump. With great, huge stars, though, getting even a little hotter is troublesome. There is so much material in one of those stars that turning up the nu-clear fusion even a little way will make it explode."

"*Explode!* But then what happens to the people?"

"What people?"

"The people in the other Universe."

For a moment, Odeen looked blank, then he said, "I don't know."

"Well, what would happen if our own Sun exploded?"

"It couldn't explode."

(Tritt wondered what all the excitement was about. How could a Sun explode? Dua seemed angrier and Odeen looked confused.)

Dua said, "But if it *did?* Would it get very hot?"

"I suppose so."

"Wouldn't it kill us all?"

Odeen hesitated and then said in clear annoyance, "What difference does it make, Dua? Our Sun isn't ex-ploding, and don't ask silly questions."

"You *told* me to ask questions, Odeen, and it *does* make a difference, because the Positron Pump works both ways. We need their end as much as ours."

Odeen stared at her. "I never told you that."

"I feel it."

Odeen said, "You feel a great many things. Dua—"

But Dua was shouting now. She was quite beside her-self. Tritt had never seen her like that. She said, "Don't change the subject, Odeen. And don't withdraw and try to make me out a complete fool—just another Emotional. You said I was almost like a Rational and I'm enough like one to see that the Positron Pump won't work without the other-beings. If the people in the other Universe are de-stroyed, the Positron Pump will stop and our Sun will be colder than ever and we'll all starve. Don't you think that's important?"

Odeen was shouting too, now. "That shows what *you* know. We need their help because the energy supply is in low concentration and we have to switch matter. If the Sun in the other Universe explodes, there'll be an enormous flood of energy; a huge flood that will last for a million lifetimes. There will be so much energy, we could tap it directly without any matter-shift either way; so we *don't* need them, and it *doesn't* matter what happens——"

They were almost touching now. Tritt was horrified. He had better say something, make them get apart, talk to them. He couldn't think of anything to say. Then it turned out he didn't have to.

There was a Hard One just outside the cavern. No, three of them. They had been trying to talk and hadn't made themselves heard.

Tritt shrieked, "Odeen. Dua."

Then he remained quiet, trembling. He had a frightened notion of what the Hard Ones had come to talk about. He decided to leave.

But a Hard One put out one of his permanent, opaque appendages and said, "Don't go."

It sounded harsh, unfriendly. Tritt was more frightened than ever.

4a

Dua was filled with anger; so filled she could scarcely sense the Hard Ones. She seemed stifled under the components of the anger, each one filling her to the brim, separately. There was a sense of wrongness that Odeen should try to lie to her. A sense of wrongness that a whole world of people should die. A sense of wrongness that it was so easy for her to learn and that she had never been allowed to.

Since that first time in the rock, she had gone twice more to the Hard-caverns. Twice more, unnoticed, she had buried herself in rock, and each time she sensed and *knew,* and each time when Odeen would explain matters to her, she knew in advance what it was he would explain.

Why couldn't they teach her, then, as they had taught Odeen? Why only the Rationals? Did she possess the capacity to learn only because she was a Left-Em, a perverted mid-ling? Then let them teach her, perversion and all. It was *wrong* to leave her ignorant.

Finally, the words of the Hard One were breaking through to her. Losten was there, but it was not he speaking. It was a strange Hard One, in front, who spoke. She did not know him, but she knew few of them.

The Hard One said, "Which of you have been in the lower caverns recently: the Hard caverns?"

Dua was defiant. They found out about her rock-rubbing and she didn't care. Let them tell everybody. She would do so herself. She said, *"I* have. Many times.'

"Alone?" said the Hard One calmly.

"Alone. Many times," snapped Dua. It was only three times, but she didn't care.

Odeen muttered, "I have, of course, been to the lower caverns on occasion."

The Hard One seemed to ignore that. He turned to Tritt instead and said sharply. "And you, right?"

Tritt quavered, "Yes, Hard-sir."

"Alone?"

"Yes, Hard-sir."

"How often?"

"Once."

Dua was annoyed. Poor Tritt was in such a panic over nothing. It was she herself who had done it and she wa ready for a confrontation. "Leave him alone," she said "I'm the one you want."

The Hard One turned slowly toward her. "For what? he said.

"For whatever it is." And faced with it directly, sh

couldn't bring herself to describe what she had done after all. Not in front of Odeen.

"Well, we'll get to you. First, the right. . . . Your name is Tritt, isn't it? Why did you go to the lower caverns alone?"

"To speak to Hard-One-Estwald, Hard-sir."

At which again Dua interrupted, eagerly, "Are *you* Estwald?"

The Hard One said briefly, "No."

Odeen looked annoyed, as though it embarrassed him that Dua didn't recognize the Hard One. Dua didn't care.

The Hard One said to Tritt, "What did you take from the lower caverns?"

Tritt was silent.

The Hard One said, without emotion, "We know you took something. We want to know if you know what it was. It could be very dangerous."

Tritt was still silent, and Losten interposed, saying more kindly, "Please tell us, Tritt. We know now it was you and we don't want to have to be harsh."

Tritt mumbled. "I took a food-ball."

"Ah." It was the first Hard One speaking. "What did you do with it?"

And Tritt burst out. "It was for Dua. She wouldn't eat. It was for Dua."

Dua jumped and coalesced in astonishment.

The Hard One turned on her at once. "You did not know about it?"

"No!"

"Nor you?"— to Odeen.

Odeen, so motionless as to seem frozen, said, "No, Hard-sir."

For a moment the air was full of unpleasant vibration as the Hard Ones spoke to each other, ignoring the triad.

Whether her sessions at rock-rubbing had made her more sensitive, or whether it was her recent storm of emotions, Dua couldn't tell, and wouldn't have dreamed of trying to analyze; she simply knew she was catching whiffs —not of words—but of understanding—

They had detected the loss some time ago. They had

been searching quietly. They had turned to the Soft Ones as possible culprits with reluctance. They had investigated and then turned to Odeen's triad with even greater reluctance. (Why? Dua missed that.) They did not see how Odeen could have had the foolishness to take it, or Dua the inclination. They did not think of Tritt at all.

Then the Hard One who had so far not said a word to the Soft Ones recalled seeing Tritt in the Hard-caverns. (Of course, thought Dua. It was the day she had first entered the rock. She had sensed him then. She had forgotten.)

It had seemed unlikely in the extreme, but finally, with all else impossible and with the time lapse having grown intolerably dangerous, they came. They would have liked to consult Estwald, but by the time the possibility of Tritt arose, he was unavailable.

All this Dua sensed in a gasp and now she turned toward Tritt, with a feeling of mingled wonder and outrage.

Losten was anxiously vibrating that no harm had been done, that Dua looked well, that it was a useful experiment actually. The Hard One to whom Tritt had spoken was agreeing; the other still exuded concern.

Dua was not paying attention to them only. She was looking at Tritt.

The first Hard One said, "Where is the food-ball now, Tritt?"

Tritt showed them.

It was hidden effectively and the connections were clumsy but serviceable.

The Hard One said, "Did you do this yourself, Tritt?"

"Yes, Hard-sir."

"How did you know how?"

"I looked at how it was done in the Hard-caverns. I did it exactly the way I saw it done there."

"Didn't you know you might have harmed your midmate?"

"I *didn't*. I *wouldn't*. I—" Tritt seemed unable to speak for a moment. Then he said, "It was not to hurt her. It was to feed her. I let it pour into her feeder and I decorated her feeder. I wanted her to try it and she did. She ate! For the first time in a long while she ate well. We melted." He paused, then said in a huge, tumultuous cry. "She had enough energy at last to initiate a baby-Emotional. She took Odeen's seed and passed it to me. I have it growing inside me. A baby-Emotional is growing inside me."

Dua could not speak. She stumbled back and then rushed for the door in so pell-mell a fashion that the Hard Ones could not get out of the way in time. She struck the appendage of the one in front, passing deep into it, and then pulled free with a harsh sound.

The Hard One's appendage fell limp and his expression seemed contorted with pain. Odeen tried to dodge around him to follow Dua, but the Hard One said, with apparent difficulty. "Let her go for now. There is enough harm done. We will take care."

4b

Odeen found himself living through a nightmare. Dua was gone. The Hard Ones were gone. Only Tritt was still there; silent.

How could it have happened, Odeen thought in tortured fashion. How could Tritt have found his way alone to the Hard-caverns? How could he have taken a storage battery charged at the Positron Pump and designed to yield radiation in much more concentrated form than Sunlight and dared—

Odeen would not have had the courage to chance it. How could Tritt; stumbling, ignorant Tritt? Or was he unusual, too? Odeen, the clever Rational; Dua, the curious Emotional; and Tritt, the daring Parental?

He said, "How could you do it, Tritt?"

Tritt retorted hotly. "What did I do? I fed her. I fed her better than she had ever been fed before. Now we have a baby-Emotional initiated at last. Haven't we waited long enough? We would have waited forever, if we had waited for Dua."

"But don't you understand, Tritt? You might have hurt her. It wasn't ordinary Sunlight. It was an experimental radiational source that could have been too concentrated to be safe."

"I don't understand what you're saying, Odeen. How could it do harm? I tasted the kind of food the Hard Ones made before. It tasted bad. You've tasted it, too. It tasted just awful and it never hurt us. It tasted so bad, Dua wouldn't touch it. Then I came on the food-ball. It tasted *good*. I ate some and it was delicious. How can anything delicious hurt. You see, Dua ate it. She liked it. And it started the baby-Emotional. How can I have done wrong?"

Odeen despaired of explaining. He said, "Dua is going to be very angry."

"She'll get over it."

"I wonder. Tritt, she's not like ordinary Emotionals. That's what makes her so hard to live with, but so wonderful when we *can* live with her. She may never want to melt with us again."

Tritt's outline was sturdily plane-surfaced. Then he said, "Well, what of it?"

"What *of* it? *You* ask. Do you want to give up melting?"

"No, but if she won't she won't. I have my third baby and I don't care any more. I know all about the Soft Ones in the old days. They used to have two triad-births sometimes. But I don't care. One is plenty."

"But, Tritt, babies aren't all there is to melting."

"What else? I heard you say once you learned faster after you melted. Then learn slower. I don't care. I have my third baby."

Odeen turned away, trembling, and flowed jerkily out of the chamber. What was the use of scolding Tritt? Tritt wouldn't understand. He wasn't sure he understood himself.

Once the third baby was born, and grown a little, surely there would come a time to pass on. It would be he,

Odeen, who would have to give the signal, who would have to say when, and it would have to be done without fear. Anything else would be disgrace, or worse, and yet he could not face it without melting, even now that all three children would have been formed.

Melting, somehow, would eliminate the fear. . . . Maybe it was because melting was like passing on. There was a period of time when you were not conscious, yet it did not hurt. It was like not existing and yet it was desirable. With enough melting, he could gain the courage to pass on without fear and without—

Oh, Sun and all the stars, it wasn't "passing on." Why use that phrase so solemnly? He knew the other word that was never used except by children who wanted to shock their elders somehow. It was *dying*. He had to get ready to die without fear, and to have Dua and Tritt die with him.

And he didn't know how. . . . Not without melting . . .

4c

Tritt remained alone in the room, frightened, frightened, but sturdily resolved to remain unmoved. He had his third baby. He could feel it within.

That was what counted.

That was all that counted.

Yet why, then, deep inside, did he have a stubborn faint feeling that it *wasn't* all that counted?

5a

Dua was ashamed almost beyond endurance. It took a long time for her to battle down that shame; battle it down enough to give herself room to think. She had hastened—hastened—moving blindly out and away from the horror of the home-cavern; scarcely caring that she did not know where she was going or even where she was.

It was night, when no decent Soft One would be on the surface, not even the most frivolous Emotional. And it would be a considerable time before the Sun rose. Dua was glad. The Sun was food and at the moment, she *hated* food and what had been done to her.

It was cold, too, but Dua was only distantly aware of it. Why should she care about cold, she thought, when she had been fattened in order that she might do her duty—fattened, mind and body. After that, cold and starvation were almost her friends.

She saw through Tritt. Poor thing; he was so easy to see through; his actions were pure instinct and he was to be praised that he had followed them so bravely. He had come back so daringly from the Hard-caverns with the food-ball (and she—she herself had sensed him and would have known what was happening if Tritt hadn't been so paralyzed at what he was doing that he had dared not think of it, and if *she* had not been so paralyzed at what *she* was doing and at the new depth of sensation it brought her that she would not take care to sense what most she needed to).

Tritt brought it back undetected and had arranged the pitiful booby trap, decorating her feeder to entice her. And she had come back, flushed with awareness of her rock-probing thinness, filled with the shame of it and with

148

pity for Tritt. With all that shame and pity, she ate, and helped initiate birth.

Since then she had eaten but sparingly as was her custom and never at the feeder, but then there had been no impulse to. Tritt had not driven her. He had looked contented (of course) so there was nothing to reactivate the shame. And Tritt left the food-ball in place. He didn't dare risk taking it back; he had what he wanted; it was best and easiest to leave it there and think of it no more.

—Till he was caught.

But clever Odeen must have seen through Tritt's plan, must have spied the new connections to the electrodes, must have understood Tritt's purpose. Undoubtedly, he said nothing to Tritt; that would have embarrassed and frightened the poor right-ling and Odeen always watched over Tritt with loving care.

Of course, Odeen didn't have to say anything. He needed only to fill in the gaps in Tritt's clumsy plan and make it work.

Dua was under no illusions now. She would have detected the taste of the food-ball; noticed its extraordinary tang; caught the way in which it began to fill her while giving her no sensations of fullness—had it not been that Odeen had occupied her with talk.

It had been a conspiracy between the two of them, whether Tritt was consciously part of it or not. How could she have believed that Odeen was suddenly a careful, painstaking teacher? How could she have failed to see the ulterior motive? Their concern for her was their concern for the completion of the new triad, and that in itself was an indication of how little they thought of her.

Well—

She paused long enough to feel her own weariness and she worked herself into a crevice in the rock that would shield her from the thin, cold wind. Two of the seven stars were in her field of vision and she watched them absently, occupying her outer senses in trivia so that she might concentrate the more in internal thought.

She was disillusioned.

"Betrayed," she muttered to herself. "Betrayed!"

Could they see no further than themselves?

That Tritt would be willing to see all destroyed if he were but secure in his babies was to be taken for granted. But he was a creature of instinct. What of Odeen?

Odeen reasoned, and did that mean that for the purpose of exercising his reason, he would sacrifice all else? Was everything produced by reason its own excuse for being—at any cost? Because Estwald had devised the Positron Pump, did it have to be used in order that the whole world, Hard and Soft alike, be placed at its mercy, and at the mercy of the people of the other Universe? What if the other people stopped and if the world was left without a Positron Pump and with a dangerously cooled Sun?

No, they wouldn't stop, those other people; for they had' been persuaded to start and they would be persuaded to keep going until they were destroyed—and then they would be needed no longer by the Rationals, Hard or Soft —just as she, Dua, would have to pass on (be *destroyed*) now that she was needed no longer.

She and the other people, both being betrayed.

Almost without being aware of it, she was cushioning deeper and deeper into the rock. She buried herself, out of sight of the stars, out of touch with the wind, unaware of the world. She was pure thought.

It was Estwald whom she hated. He was the personification of all that was selfish and hard. He had devised the Positron Pump and would destroy a whole world of perhaps tens of thousands without conscience. He was so withdrawn that he never made his appearance and so powerful that even the other Hard Ones seemed afraid of him.

Well, then, she would fight him. She would stop him.

The people of the other Universe had helped set up the Positron Pump through communications of some sort. Odeen had mentioned those. Where would such communications be kept? What would they be like? How could they be used for further communication?

It was remarkable how clearly she could think. Remarkable. There was fierce enjoyment in this, that she would use reason to overcome the cruel reasoners.

They wouldn't be able to stop her, for she could go where no Hard One could go, where no Rational or Parental could—and where no other Emotional would.

She might be caught eventually, but at the moment she didn't care. She was going to fight to have her way—at any price—at any price—though to do it meant she would have to go through rock, live in rock, skirt the Hard-caverns, steal food from their stored energy batteries when she had to, flock with the other Emotionals and feed on Sunlight when she could.

But in the end she would teach them all a lesson and after that they could do as they wished. She would even be ready to pass on then—but only then—

5b

Odeen was present when the new baby-Emotional was born, perfect in every way, but he had not been able to feel enthusiasm over it. Even Tritt, who cared for it perfectly, as a Parental must, seemed subdued in his ecstasies.

A long time had passed and it was as though Dua had vanished. She had not passed on. A Soft One could not pass on except when the whole triad did; but she was not with them, either. It was as though she had passed on, without passing on.

Odeen had seen her once, only once, not very long after her wild fight on the news that she had initiated the new baby.

He had passed a cluster of Emotionals, sunning themselves, when he was moving over the surface on some foolish notion that he might find her. They had tittered at the rare sight of a Rational moving in the vicinity of an Emotional cluster and had thinned in mass-provocation, with no thought among the foolish lot of them but to advertise the fact that they were Emotionals.

Odeen felt only contempt for them and there was no answering stir along his own smooth curves at all. He thought of Dua instead and of how different she was from all of them. Dua never thinned for any reason other than her own inner needs. She had never tried to attract anyone and was the more attractive for that. If she could have brought herself to join the flock of empty-heads she would be easily recognized (he felt sure) by the fact that she alone would *not* thin, but would probably thicken, precisely because the others thinned.

And as he thought that, Odeen scanned the sunning Emotionals and noted that one indeed had not.

He stopped and then hastened toward her, oblivious to the Emotionals in his way, oblivious to their wild screeching as they flicked smokily out of his path and chattered desperately in their attempts to avoid coalescing one with the other—at least not in the open, and with a Rational watching.

It *was* Dua. She did not try to leave. She kept her ground and said nothing.

"Dua," he said, humbly, "aren't you coming home?"

"I have no home, Odeen," she said. Not angrily, not in hate—and all the more dreadfully for that reason.

"How can you blame Tritt for what he did, Dua? You know the poor fellow can't reason."

"But you can, Odeen. And you occupied my mind while he arranged to feed my body, didn't you? Your reason told you that I was much more likely to be trapped by you than by him."

"Dua, *no!*"

"No, what? Didn't you make a big show of teaching me, of educating me?"

"I did, but it wasn't a show, it was real. And it was not because of what Tritt had done. I didn't *know* what Tritt had done."

"I can't believe that." She flowed away without haste. He followed after. They were alone now, the Sun shining redly down upon them.

She turned to him. "Let me ask you one question, Odeen? Why did you want to teach me?"

Odeen said, "Because I *wanted* to. Because I *enjoy* aching and because I would rather teach than do any-ing else—but learn."

"And melt, of course. . . . Never mind," she added to ard him off. "Don't explain that you are talking of rea-n and not of instinct. If you really mean what you say out enjoying teaching; if I can really ever believe what u say; then perhaps you can understand something I'm ing to tell you.

"I've been learning a great deal since I left you, Odeen. ever mind how. I have. There's no Emotional left in me all, except physiologically. Inside, where it counts, I'm Rational, except that I hope I have more feeling for hers than Rationals have. And one thing I've learned is hat we really are, Odeen; you and I and Tritt and all the her triads on this planet; what we really are and always ere."

"What is that?" asked Odeen. He was prepared to listen r as long as might be necessary, and as quietly, if only e would come back with him when she had said her say. e would perform any penance, do anything that might be quired. Only she must come back—and something dim d dark inside him knew that she had to come back vol-ntarily.

"What we are? Why, nothing, really, Odeen," she said ghtly, almost laughing. "Isn't that strange? The Hard nes are the only living species on the face of the world. aven't they taught you that? There is only one species cause you and I, the Soft Ones, are not really alive. e're machines, Odeen. We must be because only the ard Ones are alive. Haven't they taught you that, deen?"

"But, Dua, that's nonsense," said Odeen, nonplused.

Dua's voice grew harsher. "Machines, Odeen! Made by e Hard Ones! Destroyed by the Hard Ones! *They* are ive, the Hard Ones. Only they. They don't talk about it uch. They don't have to. They all know it. But I've arned to think, Odeen, and I've worked it out from the all clues I've had. They live tremendously long lives, t die eventually. They no longer give birth; the Sun

yields too little energy for that. And since they die ver
infrequently, but don't give birth at all, their numbers ar
very slowly declining. And there are no young ones to pro
vide new blood and new thoughts, so the old, long-live
Hard Ones get terribly bored. So what do you suppos
they do, Odeen?"

"What?" There was a kind of fascination about this.
repulsive fascination.

"They manufacture mechanical children, whom the
can teach. You said it yourself, Odeen. You would rathe
teach than do anything else but learn—and melt, c
course. The Rationals are made in the mental image of th
Hard Ones, and the Hard Ones don't melt, and learning i
terribly complex for them since they already know s
much. What is left for them but the fun of teaching. Ration
als were created for no purpose but to be taught. Emo
tionals and Parentals were created because they were nec
essary for the self-perpetuating machinery that made ne
Rationals. And new Rationals were needed constantly be
cause the old ones were used up, were taught all the
could be taught. And when old Rationals had absorbe
what they could, they were destroyed and were taught, i
advance, to call the destruction process "passing on" t
spare their feelings. And of course, Emotionals and Paren
tals passed on with them. As long as they had helped for
a new triad there was no further use for them."

"But that's all wrong, Dua," Odeen managed to sa
He had no arguments to pose against her nightmar
scheme, but he knew with a certainty past argument th
she was wrong. (Or did a little pang of doubt deep insid
suggest that the certainty might have been implanted i
him, to begin with?—No, surely no, for then would n
Dua be certain with an implanted certainty, too, that th
was wrong?—Or was she an imperfect Emotional witho
the proper implantations and without— Oh, what was I
thinking. He was as crazy as she was.)

Dua said, "You look upset, Odeen. Are you sure I'm
wrong? Of course, now they have the Positron Pump ar

hey now have all the energy they need, or will have. Soon
hey will be giving birth again. Maybe they are doing so al-
eady. And they won't need any Soft-One machines at all,
nd we will all be destroyed; I beg pardon, we will all pass
n."

"No, Dua," said Odeen, strenuously, as much to himself
s to her. "I don't know how you got those notions, but
he Hard Ones aren't like that. We are not destroyed."

"Don't lie to yourself, Odeen. They *are* like that. They
re prepared to destroy a whole world of other-beings for
heir benefit; a whole Universe if they have to. Would they
top at destroying a few Soft Ones for their comfort?—
ut they made one mistake. Somehow the machinery went
rong and a Rational mind got into an Emotional body.
m a Left-Em, do you know that? They called me that
hen I was a child, and they were right. I can reason like
Rational and I can feel like an Emotional. And I will
ght the Hard Ones with that combination."

Odeen felt wild. Dua must surely be mad, yet he dared
ot say so. He had to cajole her somehow and bring her
ack. He said with strenuous sincerity, "Dua, we're not
estroyed when we pass on."

"No? What does happen then?"

"I—I don't know. I think we enter another world, a
etter and happier world, and become like—like—well,
uch better than we are."

Dua laughed. "Where did you hear that? Did the Hard
nes tell you that?"

"No, Dua. I'm *sure* that this must be so out of my own
oughts. I've been thinking a great deal about it since you
ft."

Dua said, "Then think less and you'll be less foolish.
oor Odeen! Good-by." She flowed away once more, thin-
There was an air of weariness about her.

Odeen called out, "But wait, Dua. Surely you want to
e your new baby-mid."

She did not answer.

He cried out. "When will you come home?"

She did not answer.

And he followed no more, but looked after her in deepest misery as she dwindled.

He did not tell Tritt he had seen Dua. What was the use? Nor did he see her again. He began haunting the favored sunning-sites of the Emotionals in the region; doing so even though occasional Parentals emerged to watch him in stupid suspicion (Tritt was a mental giant compared to most Parentals).

The lack of her hurt more with each passing day. And with each passing day, he realized that there was a gathering fright inside himself over her absence. He didn't know why.

He came back to home-cavern one day to find Losten waiting for him. Losten was standing there, grave and polite while Tritt was showing him the new baby and striving to keep the handful of mist from touching the Hard One.

Losten said, "It is indeed a beauty, Tritt. Derala is it name?"

"Derola," corrected Tritt. "I don't know when Odeen will be back. He wanders about a lot—"

"Here I am, Losten," said Odeen, hastily. "Tritt, take the baby away; there's a good fellow."

Tritt did so, and Losten turned to Odeen with quite obvious relief, saying, "You must be very happy to have completed the triad."

Odeen tried to answer with some polite inconsequence but could maintain only a miserable silence. He had recently been developing a kind of comradeship, a vague sense of equality with the Hard Ones, that enabled them to talk together on a level. Somehow Dua's madness had spoiled it. Odeen knew she was wrong and yet he approached Losten once more as stiffly as in the long-gone days when he thought of himself as a far inferior creature to them, as a—machine?

Losten said, "Have you seen Dua?" This was a real question, and not politeness. Odeen could tell easily.

"Only once, H—" (He almost said "Hard-sir" as though he were a child again, or a Parental.) "Only once, Losten. She won't come home."

"She *must* come home," said Losten, softly.

"I don't know how to arrange that."

Losten regarded him somberly. "Do you know what he is doing?"

Odeen dared not look at the other. Had he discovered Dua's wild theories? What would be done about that?

He made a negative sign without speaking.

Losten said, "She is a most unusual Emotional, Odeen. You know that, don't you?"

"Yes," sighed Odeen.

"So are you in your way, and Tritt in his. I doubt that any Parental in the world would have had either the courage or the initiative to steal an energy-battery or the perverse ingenuity to put it to use as he did. The three of you make up the most unusual triad of which we have any record."

"Thank you."

"But there are uncomfortable aspects to the triad, too; things we didn't count on. We wanted you to teach Dua as the mildest and best possible way in which to cajole her into performing her function voluntarily. We did not count on Tritt's quixotic action at just that moment. Nor, to tell you the truth, did we count on her wild reaction to the fact that the world in the other Universe must be destroyed."

"I ought to have been careful how I answered her questions," said Odeen miserably.

"It wouldn't have helped. She was finding out for herself. We didn't count on that either. Odeen, I am sorry, but I must tell you this—Dua has become a deadly danger; she is trying to stop the Positron Pump."

"But how can she? She can't reach it, and even if she could, she lacks the knowledge to do anything about it."

"Oh, but she *can* reach it." Losten hesitated, then said, "She remains infused in the rock of the world where she is safe from us."

It took awhile for Odeen to grasp the clear meaning of the words. He said, "No grown Emotional would— Dua would never—"

"She would. She does. Don't waste time arguing the point. . . . She can penetrate anywhere in the caverns.

Nothing is hidden from her. She has studied those communications we have received from the other Universe. We don't know that of certain knowledge, but there is no other way of explaining what is happening."

"Oh, oh, oh." Odeen rocked back and forth, his surface opaque with shame and grief. "Does Estwald know of all this?"

Losten said, grimly, "Not yet; though he must know someday."

"But what will she do with those communications?"

"She is using them to work out a method for sending some of her own in the other direction."

"But she cannot know how to translate or transmit."

"She is learning both. She knows more about those communications than Estwald himself. She is a frightening phenomenon, an Emotional who can reason and who is out of control."

Odeen shivered. Out of control? How machine-like a reference!

He said, "It can't be that bad."

"It can. She has communicated already and I fear she is advising the other creatures to stop their half of the Positron Pump. If they do that before their Sun explodes, we will be helpless at this end."

"But then—"

"She must be stopped, Odeen."

"B—But, how? Are you going to blast—" His voice failed. Dimly, he knew that the Hard One had devices for digging caverns out of the world's rock; devices scarcely used since the world's population had begun declining ages ago. Would they locate Dua in the rock and blast it and her?

"No," said Losten, forcefully. "We cannot harm Dua."

"Estwald might—"

"Estwald cannot harm her, either."

"Then what's to be done?"

"It's you, Odeen. Only you. We're helpless, so we must depend on you."

"On *me?* But what can I do?"

"Think about it," said Losten, urgently. "*Think* about it."

"Think about *what?*"

"I can't say more than that," said Losten, in apparent agony. "Think! There is so little time."

He turned and left, moving rapidly for a Hard One, moving as though he did not trust himself to stay and perhaps say too much.

And Odeen could only look after him, dismayed, confused—lost.

5c

There was a great deal for Tritt to do. Babies required much care, but even two young-lefts and two young-rights together did not make up the sum of a single baby-mid—particularly not a mid as perfect as Derola. She had to be exercised and soothed, protected from percolating into whatever she touched, cajoled into condensing and resting.

It was a long time before he saw Odeen again and, actually, he didn't care. Derola took up all his time. But then he came across Odeen in the corner of his own alcove, iridescent with thought.

Tritt remembered, suddenly. He said, "Was Losten angry about Dua?"

Odeen came to himself with a start. "Losten?—Yes, he was angry. Dua is doing great harm."

"She should come home, shouldn't she?"

Odeen was staring at Tritt. "Tritt," he said, "we're going to have to persuade Dua to come home. We must find her first. You can do it. With a new baby, your Parenal sensitivity is very high. You can use it to find Dua."

"No," said Tritt, shocked. "It's used for Derola. It would be wrong to use it for Dua. Besides, if she wants to

stay away so long when a baby-mid is longing for her—
and she was once a baby-mid herself—maybe we might
just learn to do without her."

"But, Tritt, don't you ever want to melt again?"

"Well, the triad is now complete."

"That's not all there is to melting."

Tritt said, "But where do we have to go to find her? Little Derola needs me. She's a tiny baby. I don't want to
leave her."

"The Hard Ones will arrange to have Derola taken care
of. You and I will go to the Hard-caverns and find Dua."

Tritt thought about that. He didn't care about Dua. He
didn't even care about Odeen, somehow. There was only
Derola. He said, "Someday. Someday, when Derola is
older. Not till then."

"Tritt," said Odeen, urgently, "we must find Dua. Otherwise—otherwise the babies will be taken away from us."

"By whom?" said Tritt.

"By the Hard Ones."

Tritt was silent. There was nothing he could say. He
had never heard of such a thing. He could not conceive of
such a thing.

Odeen said, "Tritt, we must pass on. I know why, now
I've been thinking about it ever since Losten— But never
mind that. Dua and you must pass on, too. Now that
know why, you will feel you must and I hope—I think—
Dua will feel she must, too. And we must pass on *soon*
for Dua is destroying the world."

Tritt was backing away. "Don't look at me like that
Odeen. . . . You're making me. . . . You're making me."

"I'm not making you, Tritt," said Odeen, sadly. "It'
just that I know now and so you must. . . . But we mus
find Dua."

"No, no." Tritt was in agony, trying to resist. There wa
something terribly new about Odeen, and existence wa
approaching an end inexorably. There would be no Trit
and no baby-mid. Where every other Parental had hi
baby-mid for a long time, Tritt would have lost his almos
at once.

It wasn't fair. Oh, it wasn't fair.

Tritt panted. "It's Dua's fault. Let *her* pass on first."

Odeen said, with deadening calm, "There's no other way but for all of us—"

And Tritt knew that was so—that was so—that was so—

6a

Dua felt thin and cold, wispy. Her attempts to rest in the open and absorb Sunlight had ended after Odeen had found her that time. Her feeding at the Hard Ones' batteries was erratic. She dared not remain too long outside the safety of rock, so she ate in quick gulps, and she never got enough.

She was conscious of hunger, continuously, all the more so since it seemed to tire her to remain in the rock. It was as though she were being punished for all that long time in which she haunted the Sunset and ate so skimpily.

If it were not for the work she was doing, she could not bear the weariness and hunger. Sometimes she hoped that the Hard Ones would destroy her—but only after she was finished.

The Hard Ones were helpless as long as she was in the rock. Sometimes she sensed them outside the rock in the open. They were afraid. Sometimes she thought the fear was *for* her, but that couldn't be. How could they be afraid for her; afraid that she would pass on out of sheer lack of food, out of sheer exhaustion. It must be that they were afraid *of* her; afraid of a machine that did not work as they had designed it to work; appalled at so great a prodigy; struck helpless with the terror of it.

Carefully, she avoided them. She always knew where they were, so they could not catch her nor stop her.

They could not watch all places always. She thought she could even blank what little perception they had.

She swirled out of the rock and studied the recorded duplicates of the communications they had received from the other Universe. They did not know that was what she was after. If they hid them, she would find them in whatever new place. If they destroyed them, it didn't matter. Dua could remember them.

She did not understand them, at first, but with her stay in the rocks, her senses grew steadily sharper, and she seemed to understand without understanding. Without knowing what the symbols meant, they inspired feelings within her.

She picked out markings and placed them where they would be sent to the other Universe. The markings were F-E-E-R. What that could possibly mean she had no idea, but its shape inspired her with a feeling of fear and she did her best to impress that feeling of fear upon the markings. Perhaps the other-creatures, studying the markings, would also feel fear.

When the answers came, Dua could sense excitement in them. She did not always get the answers that were sent. Sometimes the Hard Ones found them first. Surely, they must know what she was doing. Still, they couldn't read the messages, couldn't even sense the emotions that went along with them.

So she didn't care. She would not be stopped, till she was done—whatever the Hard Ones found out.

She waited for a message that would carry the feeling she wanted. It came: P-U-M-P B-A-D.

It carried the fear and hatred she wanted. She sent it back in extended form—more fear—more hatred— Now the other people would understand. Now they would stop the Pump. The Hard Ones would have to find some other way, some other source of energy; they must not obtain it through the death of all those thousands of other Universe creatures.

She was resting too much, declining into a kind of stupor, within the rock. Desperately she craved food and waited so that she could crawl out. Even more desperately than she wanted the food in the storage battery, she wanted the storage battery to be dead. She wanted to suck the last bit of food out of it and know that no more would come and that her task was done.

She emerged at last and remained recklessly long, sucking in the contents of one of the batteries. She wanted to withdraw its last, empty it, see that no more was entering —but it was an endless source—endless—endless.

She stirred and drew away from the battery in disgust. The Positron Pumps were still going then. Had her messages not persuaded the other Universe creatures to stop the Pumps? Had they not received them? Had they not sensed their meaning?

She had to try again. She had to make it plain beyond plain. She would include every combination of signals that to her seemed to carry the feeling of danger; every combination that would get across the plea to stop.

Desperately she began to fuse the symbols into metal; drawing without reserve on the energy she had just sucked out of the battery; drawing on it till it was all gone and she was more weary than ever: PUMP NOT STOP NOT STOP WE NOT STOP PUMP WE NOT HEAR DANGER NOT HEAR NOT HEAR YOU STOP PLEASE STOP YOU STOP SO WE STOP PLEASE YOU STOP DANGER DANGER DANGER DANGER STOP STOP YOU STOP PUMP.

It was all she could. There was nothing left in her but a racking pain. She placed the message where it could be transferred and she did not wait for the Hard Ones to send the message unwittingly. Through an agonizing haze, she manipulated the controls as she had seen them do, finding the energy for it somehow.

The message disappeared and so did the cavern in a purple shimmer of vertigo. She was—passing on—out of sheer—exhaustion.

Odeen—Tri—

Odeen came. He had been flowing faster than ever he had flowed before. He had been following Tritt's sharp new-baby sense perception, but now he was close enough for his own blunter senses to detect her nearness. He could on his own account feel the flickering and fading consciousness of Dua, and he raced forward while Tritt did his best to clump along, gasping and calling, "Faster—faster—"

Odeen found her in a state of collapse, scarcely alive, smaller than he had ever seen an adult Emotional.

"Tritt," he said, "bring the battery here. No—no—don't try to carry her. She's too thin to carry. Hurry. If she sinks into the floor—"

The Hard Ones began to gather. They were late, of course, with their inability to sense other life-forms at a distance. If it had depended only on them, it would have been too late to save her. She would not have passed on; she would truly have been destroyed—and—and more than she knew would have been destroyed with her.

Now, as she was slowly gathering life out of the energy supply, the Hard Ones stood silently near them.

Odeen rose; a new Odeen who knew what was happening exactly. Imperiously, he ordered them away with an angry gesture—and they left. Silently. Without objection.

Dua stirred.

Tritt said, "Is she all right, Odeen?"

"Quiet, Tritt," said Odeen. "Dua?"

"Odeen?" She stirred, spoke in a whisper. "I thought I had passed on."

"Not yet, Dua. Not yet. But first you must eat and rest."

"Is Tritt here, too?"

"Here I am, Dua," said Tritt.

"Don't try to bring me back," said Dua. "It's over. I've

164

done what I wanted to do. The Positron Pump will—will stop soon, I'm sure. The Hard Ones will continue to need Soft Ones and they will take care of you two, or at least the children."

Odeen didn't say anything. He kept Tritt from saying anything, either. He let the radiation pour slowly into Dua, very slowly. He stopped at times to let her rest a bit, then he started again.

She began to mutter, "Enough. Enough." Her substance was writhing more strongly.

Still he fed her.

Finally, he spoke. He said, "Dua, you were wrong. We are not machines. I know exactly what we are. I would have come to you sooner, if I had found out earlier, but I didn't know till Losten begged me to think. And I did; very hard; and even so it is almost premature."

Dua moaned and Odeen stopped for a while.

He said, "Listen, Dua. There *is* a single species of life. The Hard Ones *are* the only living things in the world. You gathered that, and so far you were right. But that doesn't mean the Soft Ones aren't alive; it merely means we are part of the same single species. *The Soft Ones are the immature forms of the Hard Ones.* We are first children as Soft Ones, then adults as Soft Ones, then Hard Ones. Do you understand?"

Tritt said, in soft confusion, "What? What?"

Odeen said, "Not now, Tritt. Not now. You'll understand, too, but this is for Dua." He kept watching Dua, who was gaining opalescence.

He said, "Listen, Dua, whenever we melt, whenever the triad melts, we become a Hard One. The Hard One is three-in-one, which is why he is hard. During the time of unconsciousness in melting we are a Hard One. But it is only temporary, and we can never remember the period afterward. We can never stay a Hard One long; we must come back. But all through our life we keep developing, with certain key stages marking it off. Each baby born marks a key stage. With the birth of the third, the Emotional, there comes the possibility of the final stage, where the Rational's mind by itself, without the other two, can remember those flashes of Hard One existence. Then, and only then, he can guide a perfect melt that will form the Hard One forever, so that the triad can live a new and unified life of learning and intellect. I told you that passing on was like being born again. I was groping then for something I did not quite understand, but now I know."

Dua was looking at him, trying to smile. She said, "How can you pretend to believe that, Odeen? If that were so, wouldn't the Hard Ones have told you long ago; told all of us?"

"They couldn't, Dua. There was a time, long ages ago, when melting was just a putting together of the atoms of bodies. But evolution slowly developed minds. Listen to me, Dua; melting is a putting together of the minds, too, and that's much harder, much more delicate. To put it together properly and permanently, just so, the Rational must reach a certain pitch in development. That pitch is reached when he finds out, *for himself,* what it's all about: when his mind is finally keen enough to remember what has happened in all those temporary unions during melting. If the Rational were told, that development would be aborted and the time of the perfect melt could not be determined. The Hard One would form imperfectly. When Losten pleaded with me to think, he was taking a great chance. Even that may have been— I hope not—

"For it's especially true in our case, Dua. For many generations, the Hard Ones have been combining triads with great care to form particularly advanced Hard Ones and our triad was the best they'd ever obtained. Especially you, Dua. Especially you. Losten was once the triad whose baby-mid you were. Part of him was your Parental. He knew you. He brought you to Tritt and me."

Dua sat up. Her voice was almost normal. "Odeen! Are you making all this up to soothe me?"

Tritt broke in. "No, Dua. I feel it, too. I feel it, too. I don't know what exactly, but I feel it."

"He does, Dua," said Odeen. "You will, too. Aren't you beginning to recall being a Hard One during our melt? Don't you want to melt now? One last time? One last time?"

He lifted her. There was a feverishness about her, and though she struggled a bit, she was thinning.

"If what you say is true, Odeen," she gasped. "If we are to be a Hard One; then it seems to me you are saying we'll be an *important* one. Is that so?"

"The most important. The best who was ever formed. I mean that. . . . Tritt, over there. It's not good-by, Tritt. We'll be together, as we always wanted to be. Dua, too. You, too, Dua."

Dua said, "Then we can make Estwald understand the Pump can't continue. We'll force—"

The melting was beginning. One by one, the Hard Ones were entering again at the crucial moment. Odeen saw them imperfectly, for he was beginning to melt into Dua.

It was not like the other times; no sharp ecstasy; just a smooth, cool, utterly peaceful movement. He could feel himself become partly Dua, and all the world seemed pouring into his/her sharpening senses. The Positron Pumps were still going—he/she could tell—why were they still going?

He was Tritt, too, and a keen sharp sense of bitter loss filled his/her/his mind. Oh, my babies—

And he cried out, one last cry under the consciousness of Odeen, except that somehow it was the cry of Dua. "No, we can't stop Estwald. *We* are Estwald. *We*—"

The cry that was Dua's and yet not Dua's stopped and there was no longer any Dua; nor would there ever be Dua again. Nor Odeen. Nor Tritt.

7abc

Estwald stepped forth and said sadly to the waiting Hard Ones, by way of vibrating air waves, "I am permanently with you now, and there is much to do—"

3

. . . contend in vain?

1

Selene Lindstrom smiled brightly and walked with the light springy touch that was startling when first seen by the tourists, but was soon recognized as having a grace of its own.

"It's time for lunch," she said, cheerfully. "All home-grown, ladies and gentlemen. You may not be used to the taste, but it's all nourishing. . . . Right here, sir. You won't mind sitting with the ladies, I know. . . . One moment. There will be seats for all. . . . Sorry, there will be a choice on the beverage, but not on the main course. That will be veal. . . . No, no. Artificial flavor and texture, but it's really quite good."

Then she sat down herself, with a slight sigh and an even slighter wavering of her pleasant expression.

One of the group sat down across from her.

"Do you mind?" he asked.

She looked at him, quickly, penetrating. She had the faculty of making quick judgments, of course, and he did not seem troublesome. She said, "Not at all. But aren't you with someone in this group?"

He shook his head. "No. I'm alone. Even if that were not the case, Earthies are no great thrill to me."

She looked at him again. He was fiftyish and there was a weary look about him which only his bright, inquisitive eyes seemed to belie. He had the unmistakable look of the Earthman, laden down with gravity. She said, " 'Earthie' is a Moon-expression, and not a very nice one."

"I'm from Earth," he said, "so I can use it without offense, I hope. Unless you object."

Selene shrugged as though to say: Please yourself.

She had the faintly oriental look about the eyes so many of the Moon-girls had, but her hair was the color of honey

171

and her nose was prominent. She was undeniably attractive without being in any way classically beautiful.

The Earthman was staring at the nameplate she wore on the blouse covering the upper slope of her high, not-too-large left breast. She decided it was really the nameplate he was looking at, not the breast, though the blouse was semi-transparent when it caught the light at a particular angle and there was no garment beneath it.

He said, "Are there many Selenes here?"

"Oh, yes. Hundreds, I think. Also Cynthias, Dianas, and Artemises. Selene is a little tiresome. Half the Selenes I know are called 'Silly' and the other half 'Lena.' "

"Which are you?"

"Neither. I am Selene, all three syllables. SELL-uh-nee," she said, coming down heavily on the first syllable, "to those who use my first name at all."

There was a small smile on the Earthman's face that sat there as though he weren't quite used to it. He said, "And what if anyone asks you if you sell any, Selene?"

"They never ask me that again!" she said, firmly.

"But do they ask you?"

"There are fools always."

A waitress had reached their table and had placed the dishes before them with quick, smooth motions.

The Earthman was visibly impressed. He said to the waitress, "You make them seem to float down."

The waitress smiled and moved on.

Selene said, "Don't you try to do the same. She's used to the gravity and can handle it."

"And if I try, I'll drop everything? Is that it?"

"You'll make a gorgeous mess," she said.

"Well, I won't try."

"There's a good chance someone will before long, and the plate will flow down to the floor and they'll grab for it and miss, and ten to one knock themselves out of their chair. I'd warn them, but it never helps and they're just all the more embarrassed. Everyone else will laugh—the tourists, that is, because the rest of us have seen it too often to find it funny and because it's just a cleanup job."

The Earthman was lifting his fork carefully. "I see what you mean. Even the simplest motions seem queer."

"Actually, you get used to it quickly enough. At least to little things like eating. Walking is harder. I never saw an Earthman run efficiently out here. Not really efficiently."

For a while they ate in silence. Then he said, "What does the L. stand for?" He was looking at her nameplate again. It said, "Selene Lindstrom L."

"It just means Luna," she said, rather indifferently, "to distinguish me from the immigrants. I was born here."

"Really?"

"That's nothing to be surprised about. We've had a working society here for over half a century. Don't you think babies are born here? We have people here who were born here and are grandparents."

"How old are you?"

"Thirty-two," she said.

He looked startled, then mumbled, "Of course."

Selene raised her eyebrows. "You mean you understand? Most Earthmen have to have it explained."

The Earthman said, "I know enough to know that most of the visible signs of aging are the result of the inexorable victory of gravity over tissue—the sagging of cheek and the drooping of breast. With the Moon's gravity one-sixth that of Earth, it isn't really hard to understand that people will stay young-looking."

Selene said, "Only young-*looking*. It doesn't mean we have immortality here. The life-span is about that of Earth, but most of us are more comfortable in old age."

"That's not to be dismissed. . . . Of course, there are penalties, I suppose." He had just taken his first sip of his coffee. "You have to drink this—" He paused for a word and must have discarded it, for he used none.

"We could import food and beverages from Earth," she said, amused, "but only enough to feed a fraction of us a fraction of the time. There'd be no point to that when we can use the space for more vital items. Besides, we're used to this crud. . . . Or were you going to use a still stronger word?"

"Not for the coffee," he said. "I was going to save that for the food. But crud will do. . . . Tell me, Miss Lindstrom. I didn't see any mention on the tour itinerary of the proton synchrotron."

"The proton synchrotron?" She was finishing her coffee and her eyes were beginning to slide round the room, as though estimating the moment for getting them all to their feet again. "That's Terrestrial property and it's not open to tourists."

"You mean that it's off-limits to Lunarites."

"Oh, no. Nothing of the sort. Most of its staff are Lunarites. It's just that it's the Terrestrial government that sets the rules. No tourists."

"I'd love to see it," he said.

She said, "I'm sure you would. . . . You've brought me luck; not one item of food, not one blessed man or woman has hit the floor."

She got to her feet and said, "Ladies and gentlemen, we'll be leaving in about ten minutes. Please leave the plates where they are. There are rest rooms for those who wish to use them and then we will visit the food-processing plants where meals such as you have just eaten are made possible."

2

Selene's quarters were small, of course, and compact; but they were intricate. The windows were panoramic; star scenes that changed slowly and very randomly, never having any relationship to any real constellation. Each of the three windows could be made to undergo telescopic magnification, when Selene so desired.

Barron Neville hated that part of it. He would tend to turn it off rather savagely and say, "How can you stand it? You're the only one I know who has the bad taste to do such a thing. It's not as though these nebulae and star clusters exist, even."

And Selene would shrug, coolly, and say, "What's existence? How do you know the ones out there exist? Besides it gives me a sensation of freedom and motion. May I have that in my own quarters if I choose?"

Then Neville would mumble something and make a halfhearted attempt to restore the controls to where he had found them and Selene would say, "Let it go!"

The furniture was in smooth curves, and the walls were abstractly decorated in low-key, unobtrusive colors. Nowhere was there any representation of anything that might be considered a living thing.

"Living things are Earth," Selene would say, "not the Moon."

Now, when she entered, she found, as so often, Neville there; Barron Neville, resting on the flimsy couch with one sandal on. The other lay beside him where it had dropped, and there was a line of red marks on his abdomen, just over his umbilicus, where he had been meditatively scratching.

She said, "Get us some coffee, won't you, Barron?" and slipped out of her own clothes in a long, graceful wiggle accompanied by a sigh of relief, letting them drop to the ground and then kicking them into the corner with one toe.

"What a relief to get out of them," she said. "It's the worst part of the job, having to dress like an Earthie."

Neville was in the kitchen corner. He paid no attention; he had heard it before. He said, "What's wrong with your water supply? It's way down."

"Is it?" she asked. "Well, I've been overusing, I suppose. Just be patient."

"Any trouble, today?"

Selene shrugged. "No. Very run of the mill. Just the usual bit about watching them teetering along and pretending they don't hate the food, and knowing they're wondering if they'll be asked to take off their clothes, I shouldn't be surprised. . . . Disgusting possibility."

"Are you taking up prudery?" He brought the two small cups of coffee to the table.

"In this case prudery is required. They're wrinkled, sagging, paunchy, and full of germs. I don't care what the quarantine regulations are like; they're full of germs. . . . What's new on your side?"

Barron shook his head. He was heavily-built for a Lunarite, and there was an almost-sullen narrowing of his eyes that had become a built-in feature. Except for that his features were even, and remarkably handsome, Selene thought.

He said, "Nothing startling. We're still waiting out the change in Commissioner. We'll have to see what this Gottstein is like."

"Can he make difficulties?"

"None more than are being made. After all, what can they do? They can't infiltrate. You can't disguise an Earthie as a Lunarite." But he looked uneasy just the same.

Selene sipped at her coffee and looked at him shrewdly. "Some Lunarites might be Earthies inside."

"Yes, and I'd like to know which. Sometimes I don't think I can trust— Oh, well. I'm wasting incredible amounts of time with my synchrotron project and getting nowhere. I'm having no luck with priorities."

"They probably don't trust you, and I don't blame them. If only you didn't slink around so conspiratorially."

"I do no such thing. It would give me great pleasure to walk out of the synchrotron room and never return, but then they *would* become suspicious. . . . If you've been raising hell with your water supply, Selene, I suppose we can't have a second cup."

"No, we can't. But if it comes to that, you've been helping me waste water. You've had two showers here in the last week."

"I'll give you a water credit. I didn't know you were counting."

"I'm not counting—my water level is."

She finished her own cup of coffee and stared at its emptiness thoughtfully. She said, "They always make faces over it. The tourists do. And I can never figure out why, either. It tastes fine to me. Did you ever taste Earth-coffee, Barron?"

"No," he said, briefly.

"I did. Once. Some tourist had smuggled in packets of what he called instant coffee. He offered me some in exchange for you-know-what. Seemed to think it was an even trade."

"And you had some?"

"I was curious. It was bitter and metallic. I hated it. Then I told him that miscegenation was against Lunarite custom and he turned rather bitter and metallic himself."

"You never told me this. He didn't try anything, did he?"

"It's not particularly your business, is it? And, no, he didn't try anything. If he had tried, at the wrong gravity for him, I'd have bounced him from here to corridor 1."

Then she went on. "Oh, yes. I picked up another Earthie today. Insisted on sitting with me."

"And what did he offer you in exchange for the screwing you so delicately call you-know-what?"

"Just sat there."

"And stared at your breasts?"

"They're there to be stared at, but actually he didn't. He stared at my nameplate. . . . Besides, what's it to you what he fantasied? Fantasies are free and I don't have to fulfill them. What do you think *I'm* fantasying? Bed with an Earthman? With all the action you would expect of someone trying to handle a gravitational field he isn't used to? I wouldn't say it hasn't been done, but not by me, and not that I've ever heard any good of it. Is that settled? Can I get back to the Earthie? Who's nearly fifty? And who obviously wasn't terrifically handsome even when he was twenty? . . . Interesting appearance, though; I'll grant him that."

"All right. I can do without a thumbnail sketch. What about him?"

"He asked about the proton synchrotron!"

Neville rose to his feet, swaying a little as was almost inevitable after quick movement at low gravity. "*What* did he ask about the synchrotron?"

"Nothing. Why are you so excited? You asked me to tell you anything that was out of the way with any tourist at any time and this seemed out of the way. No one ever asked me about the synchrotron before."

"All *right*." He paused a little, then in a normal voice, said, "Why was he interested in the synchrotron?"

Selene said, "I haven't the faintest idea. He just asked if he could see it. It could be that he's a tourist with an interest in science. For all I know, it was just a ploy to get me interested in him."

"And I suppose you are. What's his name?"

"I don't know. I didn't ask him."

"Why not?"

"Because I'm *not* interested in him. Which way do you want it to be? Besides, his asking shows he's a tourist. If he were a physicist, he wouldn't have to ask. He's be there."

"My dear Selene," said Neville. "Let me spell it out. Under the present circumstances, anyone who asks to see the proton synchrotron is a peculiar fellow we want to know about. And why should he ask *you?*" He walked hastily to the other end of the room and back as though wearing off a little energy. Then he said, "You're the expert at that nonsense. Do *you* find him of interest?"

"Sexually?"

"You know what I mean. *Don't play games, Selene.*"

Selene said with clear reluctance. "He's interesting, even disturbing. But I don't know why. He said nothing. He did nothing."

"Interesting and disturbing, is he? Then you will see him again."

"And do what?"

"How do I know? That's your bit. Find out his name. Find out anything else you can. You've got some brains, so use them on a little practical nosiness for a change."

"Oh, well," she said, "orders from on high. All right."

3

There was no way of telling the Commissioner's quarters, by size alone, from those of any Lunarite. There was no space on the Moon, not even for Terrestrial officials; no luxurious waste, even as a symbol of the home planet. Nor, for that matter, was there any way of changing the overwhelming fact about the Moon—that it was underground at low gravity—even for the greatest Earthman who ever lived.

"Man is still the creature of his environment," sighed Luiz Montez. "I've been two years on the Moon and there have been times when I have been tempted to stay on but— I'm getting on in years. I've just passed my fortieth and if I intend ever to go back to Earth, it had better be now. Any older and I won't be able to readjust to full-gravity."

Konrad Gottstein was only thirty-four and looked, if anything, younger. He had a wide, round, large-featured face, the kind of face one didn't see among the Lunarites, the kind of face that was something they would draw as part of an Earthie caricature. He was not heavily-built—it did not pay to send heavily-built Earthmen to the Moon—and his head seemed too large for his body.

He said (and he spoke Planetary Standard with a perceptibly different accent from that of Montez), "You sound apologetic."

"I am. I am," said Montez. Where Gottstein's face was intrinsically good-natured in appearance, the long thin lines of Montez' face were almost comically tragic. "I am apologetic in both senses. I am embarrassed to be leaving the Moon, since it is an attractive world filled with excitement. And I am embarrassed about the embarrassment;

ashamed that I should be reluctant to take up Earth's
burden—gravity and all."

"Yes, I imagine taking back the other five-sixths will be
hard," said Gottstein. "I've been on the Moon only a few
days and already I feel that one-sixth g is perfectly fine."

"You won't feel that when the constipation starts and
you start living on mineral oil," said Montez with a sigh,
"but that will pass. . . . And don't think you can imitate
the light gazelle just because you feel light. There's an art
to it."

"So I understand."

"So you *think* you understand, Gottstein. You haven't
seen the kangaroo walk, have you?"

"On television."

"That doesn't really give you the feel of it. You have to
try it. It's the proper mode for crossing level lunar surface
at high speed. The feet move together backward and
launch you on what would be a simple broad jump on
Earth. While you're in mid-air, they come forward; begin
moving back just *before* they hit the ground again; keep
you launched; and so on. The motion seems slow by Earth
standards with only a low gravity whipping you on, but
each leap is in excess of twenty feet and the amount of
muscular effort required to keep you in the air—if there
were air—is minimal. The sensation is like flying—"

"Have you tried it? Can you do it?"

"I've tried it, but no Earthman can really do it. I've
kept it up for as many as five leaps in a row, enough to get
the sensation; just enough to want to do more, but then
there is the inevitable miscalculation, a loss of synchronization, and you tumble and slide for a quarter of a mile.
The Lunarites are polite and never laugh at you. Of
course, it's easy for them. They start as children and pick
it up at once without trouble."

"It's their world," said Gottstein, chuckling. "Think
how they'd be on Earth."

"They wouldn't be on Earth. They can't. I suppose
that's an advantage on our side. We can be either on
Moon or on Earth. They can live only on the Moon. We

tend to forget that because we confuse the Lunarites with Immies."

"With what?"

"That's what they call the Earth-immigrants; those who live on the Moon more or less permanently but were born and raised on the Earth. The immigrants can, of course, return to the Earth, but the real Lunarites have neither the bones nor the muscles to withstand the Earth's gravity. There were some tragedies in that respect in the Moon's early history."

"Oh?"

"Oh, yes. People who returned with their Moon-born children. We tend to forget. We've had our own Crisis and a few dying children don't seem important in the light of the huge casualties of the late Twentieth and all that followed. Here on the Moon, though, every dead Lunarite who succumbed to the gravity of Earth is remembered. . . . It helps them feel a world apart, I think."

Gottstein said, "I thought I had been thoroughly briefed on Earth, but it seems I will still have a lot to learn."

"Impossible to learn everything about the Moon from a post on Earth, so I have left you a full report as my predecessor did for me. You'll find the Moon fascinating and, in some ways, excruciating. I doubt that you've eaten Lunar rations on Earth and if you're going by description only, you will not be prepared for the reality. . . . But you'll have to learn to like it. It's bad policy to ship Earth-items here. We've got to eat and drink the local products."

"You've been doing it for two years. I guess I'll survive."

"I've not been doing it steadily. There are periodic furloughs to Earth. Those are obligatory, whether you want them or not. They've told you that, I'm sure."

"Yes," said Gottstein.

"Despite any exercises you do here, you will have to subject yourself to full gravity now and then just to remind your bones and muscles what it's like. And when you're on Earth, you'll *eat*. And occasionally, some food is smuggled in."

Gottstein said, "My luggage was carefully inspected, of course, but it turned out there was a can of corned beef in my coat pocket. I had overlooked it. So did they."

Montez smiled slowly and said, hesitantly, "I suspect you are now going to offer to share it."

"No," said Gottstein, judiciously, wrinkling his large button nose. "I was going to say with all the tragic nobility I could muster, 'Here, Montez, have it all! Thy need is greater than mine.'" He stumbled a bit in trying to say this, since he rarely used second person singular in Planetary Standard.

Montez smiled more broadly, and then let it vanish. He shook his head. "No. In a week, I'll have all the Earth-food I can eat. You won't. Your mouthfuls will be few in the next few years and you will spend too much time regretting your present generosity. You keep it all. . . . I insist. I would but be earning your hatred ex post facto."

He seemed serious, his hand on the other's shoulder, his eyes looking straight into Gottstein's. "Besides," he said, "there is something I want to talk to you about that I've been putting off because I don't know how to approach it and this food would be an excuse for further sidetracking."

Gottstein put away the Earth-can at once. There was no way in which his face could match the other's seriousness, but his voice was grave and steady. "Is there something you could not put into your dispatches, Montez?"

"There was something I *tried* to put in, Gottstein, but between my not knowing how to phrase it and Earth's reluctance to grasp my meaning, we ended up not communicating. You may do better. I hope you do. One of the reasons I have not asked to have my tour of duty extended is that I can no longer take the responsibility of my failure to communicate."

"You make it sound serious."

"I wish I could make it sound serious. Frankly, it sounds silly. There are only some ten thousand people in the Lunar colony. Rather less than half are native Lunarites. They're hampered by an insufficiency of resources, an insufficiency of space, a harsh world, and yet—and yet—"

"And yet?" said Gottstein, encouragingly.

"There is something going on here—I don't know exactly what—which may be dangerous."

"How can it be dangerous? What can they do? Make war against the Earth?" Gottstein's face trembled on the brink of a smile-crease.

"No, no. It's more subtle than that." Montez passed his hand over his face, rubbing his eyes petulantly. "Let me be frank with you. Earth has lost its nerve."

"What does that mean?"

"Well, what would you call it? Just about the time the Lunar colony was being established, Earth went through the Great Crisis. I don't have to tell you about that."

"No, you don't," said Gottstein, with distaste.

"The population is two billion now from its six billion peak."

"Earth is much better for that, isn't it?"

"Oh, undoubtedly, though I wish there had been a better way of achieving the drop. . . . But it's left behind a permanent distrust of technology; a vast inertia; a lack of desire to risk change because of the possible side-effects. Great and possibly dangerous efforts have been abandoned because the danger was feared more than greatness was desired."

"I take it you refer to the program on genetic engineering."

"That's the most spectacular case of course, but not the only one," said Montez, bitterly.

"Frankly, I can't get excited over the abandonment of genetic engineering. It was a tissue of failures."

"We lost our chance at intuitionism."

"There has never been any evidence that intuitionism is desirable, and considerable indications of its undesirability. . . . Besides what about the Lunar colony itself? This certainly is no indication of stagnation on Earth."

"It is," said Montez, vigorously. "The Lunar colony is a hangover, a last remnant of the period before the Crisis;

something that was carried through as a last sad forward thrust of mankind before the great retreat."

"That's too dramatic, Montez."

"I don't think so. The Earth has retreated. Mankind has retreated, everywhere but on the Moon. The Lunar colony is man's frontier not just physically, but psychologically, too. Here is a world that doesn't have a web of life to disrupt; that doesn't have a complex environment in delicate balance to upset. Everything on the Moon that is of any use to man is man-made. The Moon is a world constructed by man from the start and out of basics. There is no past."

"Well?"

"On Earth, we are unmanned by our longing for a pastoral past that never really existed; and that, if it had existed, could never exist again. In some respects, much of the ecology was disrupted in the Crisis and we are making do with the remnants so that we are frightened, always frightened. . . . On the Moon, there is no past to long for or dream about. There is no direction but forward."

Montez seemed to be catching fire with his own words. He said, "Gottstein, I have watched it for two years; you will watch it for at least that much longer. There is a fire here on the Moon; a restless burning. They expand in every direction. They expand physically. Every month, new corridors are bored, new living quarters established, a new population potential made room for. They expand as far as resources are concerned. They find new construction materials, new water sources, new lodes of specialized minerals. They expand their sun-power battery-banks, enlarge their electronics factories. . . . I suppose you know that these ten thousand people here on the Moon are now the major source for Earth's supply of mini-electronic devices and fine biochemicals."

"I know they're an important source."

"Earth lies to itself for comfort's sake. The Moon is the major source. At the present rate, it may become the sole source in the near future. . . . It's growing intellectually, too. Gottstein, I imagine there isn't a bright science-oriented youngster on Earth who doesn't vaguely—or perhaps

not so vaguely—dream of going to the Moon one day.
With Earth in retreat from technology, the Moon is where
the action is."

"You're referring to the proton synchrotron, I suppose?"

"That's one example. When was the last new synchrotron built on Earth? But it's just the biggest and most dramatic item; not the only or even the most important. If
you want to know the most important scientific device on
the Moon—"

"Something so secret I haven't been told?"

"No, something so obvious that no one seems to notice.
It's the ten thousand brains here. The ten thousand best
human brains there are. The only close-knit group of ten
thousand human brains that are, in principle and by emotion, science-oriented."

Gottstein moved restlessly and tried to shift his chair's
position. It was bolted to the floor and wouldn't move, but
in the attempt to do so, Gottstein found himself skittering
out of the chair. Montez reached out an arm to steady
him.

Gottstein flushed. "Sorry."

"You'll get used to the gravity."

Gottstein said, "But aren't you making it out a lot
worse than it is? Earth isn't a know-nothing planet altogether. We did develop the Electron Pump. That's a purely Terrestrial accomplishment. No Lunarite had anything
to do with it."

Montez shook his head and muttered a few words in his
native Spanish. They didn't sound like placid words. He
said, "Have you ever met Frederick Hallam?"

Gottstein smiled. "Yes, as a matter of fact I have. The
Father of the Electron Pump. I believe he has the phrase
tattooed on his chest."

"The mere fact that you smile and make that remark
proves my point, really. Ask yourself: Could a man like
Hallam really have fathered the Electron Pump? For the
unthinking multitude, the story will do, but the fact
is—and you must know it if you stop to think about it—
there is no father to the Electron Pump. The para-people,

the people in the para-Universe, whoever they are and whatever that is, invented it. Hallam was their accidental instrument. All of Earth is their accidental instrument."

"We were clever enough to take advantage of their initiative."

"Yes, as cows are clever enough to eat the hay we provide for them. The Pump is no sign that man is forward-looking. Quite the reverse."

"If the Pump is a backward step, then I say good for backwardness. I wouldn't want to do without it."

"Who would? But the point is it fits Earth's present mood perfectly. Infinite energy at virtually zero cost, except for maintenance, and with zero pollution besides. But there are no Electron Pumps on the Moon."

Gottstein said, "I imagine there's no need for them. The Solar batteries supply what the Lunarites require. Infinite energy at virtually zero cost, except for maintenance, and with zero pollution besides. . . . Isn't that the litany?"

"Yes, indeed, but the Solar batteries are entirely man-made. That's the point I'm making. An Electron Pump was projected for the Moon; installation was attempted."

"And?"

"And it didn't work. The para-people didn't accept the tungsten. Nothing happened."

"I didn't know that. Why not?"

Montez lifted his shoulders and eyebrows expressively. "How is one to know? We might assume, for instance, that the para-people live on a world without a satellite; that they have no conception of separate worlds in close proximity, each populated; that, having found one, they did not seek another. Who knows?—The point is, that the para-people didn't bite and we ourselves, without them, could do nothing."

"We ourselves," repeated Gottstein, thoughtfully. "By that, you mean the Earthmen?"

"Yes."

"And the Lunarites?"

"They were not involved."

"Were they interested?"

"I don't know. That's where my uncertainty—and fear

—chiefly rests. The Lunarites—the native Lunarites, particularly—do not feel like Earthmen. I don't know what their plans are or what they intend. I can't find out."

Gottstein looked thoughtful. "But what *can* they do? Do you have any reason to suppose they intend to do us harm; or that they can do Earth harm even if they intend it?"

"I can't answer that question. They are an attractive and intelligent people. It seems to me they lack real hatred or real rage or even real fear. But perhaps that is what only seems to me. What bothers me most is that I don't know."

"The scientific equipment on the Moon is run by Earth, I believe."

"That is correct. The proton synchrotron is. The radio telescope on the trans-terrestrial side is. The three-hundred-inch optical telescope is. . . . The large equipment, that is, all of which has been in existence for fifty years."

"And what's been done since?"

"Very little by Earthmen."

"What about the Lunarites?"

"I'm not sure. Their scientists work in the large installations, but I once tried to check time cards. There are gaps."

"Gaps?"

"They spend considerable time *away* from the large installations. It is as though they had laboratories of their own."

"Well, if they produce mini-electronic devices and fine bio-chemicals, isn't that to be expected?"

"Yes, but— Gottstein, I don't know. I fear my ignorance."

There was a moderately long pause. Gottstein said, "Montez, I take it you are telling me all this so that I will be careful; so that I will try to find out what the Lunarites are doing?"

"I suppose that's about it," said Montez, unhappily.

"But you don't even know that they're doing anything at all."

"I feel that they are."

Gottstein said, "It's odd, then. I should be trying to talk you out of all this fearful mysticism of yours—but it's odd—"

"What is?"

"The same vessel that brought me to the Moon brought someone else to the Moon. I mean, a large party came, but one face in particular triggered something. I didn't talk to him—had no occasion to—and I dismissed the matter. But now our talk is pushing a button, and he suddenly comes back to mind—"

"Yes?"

"I was on a committee once that dealt with Electron Pump matters. A question of safety." He smiled briefly. "Earth's lost nerve, you might say. We worry about safety everywhere—and a good thing, damn it, lost nerve or not. The details escape me but in connection with that hearing, I saw that face that now I saw on the vessel. I'm convinced of it."

"Does that have significance, do you think?"

"I'm not sure. I associate that face with something disturbing. If I keep on thinking, it may come back to me. In any case, I had better get a list of the passengers and see if any name means something to me. Too bad, Montez, but I think you're getting me started."

"Not bad at all," said Montez. "I'm glad of it. As for this man; it may be he is only a tourist of no consequence and will be gone in two weeks, but I am glad to have you thinking about the matter—"

Gottstein did not seem to be listening. "He is a physicist, or a scientist of some sort," he muttered. "I'm certain of it and I associate him with danger—"

4

"Hello," said Selene, cheerfully.

The Earthman turned around. Recognition took almost no time at all. "Selene! Am I right? Selene!"

"Right! Correctly pronounced. Are you enjoying yourself?"

The Earthman said gravely, "Very much. It makes me realize how unique our century is. It was not so long ago I was on Earth, feeling tired of my world, tired of myself. Then I thought: Well, if I were living a hundred years ago, the only way I could leave the world would be to die, but now—I can go to the Moon." He smiled without real gaiety.

Selene said, "Are you happier now that you are on the Moon?"

"A little." He looked about. "Don't you have a crowd of tourists to take care of?"

"Not today," she said, cheerfully. "It's my day off. Who knows, I may take two or three. It's a dull job."

"What a shame, then, that you bump into a tourist on your day off."

"I didn't bump into you. I came looking for you. And a hard job that was, too. You shouldn't wander off by yourself."

The Earthman looked at her with interest. "Why should you look for me? Are you fond of Earthmen?"

"No," she said, with easy frankness. "I'm sick of them. I dislike them on principle and being constantly associated with them in my job makes it worse."

"Yet you come looking for me and there isn't a way on Earth—on the Moon, I mean—that I can convince myself I am young and handsome."

"Even if you were, it wouldn't help. Earthmen don't interest me, as everyone but Barron knows."

"Then why do you come looking for me?"

"Because there are other ways of being interested and because Barron is interested."

"And who is Barron? Your boyfriend?"

Selene laughed. "Barron Neville. He's a lot more than a boy and a lot more than a friend. We have sex when we feel like it."

"Well, that's what I meant. Do you have children?"

"One boy. He's ten. He spends most of his time in the boys'-compound. To spare you the next question, he's not Barron's. I may have a child by Barron if we're still together when I'm assigned another child—*if* I'm assigned another child. . . . I am pretty sure I will be."

"You're quite frank."

"About things I don't consider secret? Of course. . . . Now what would you like to do?"

They had been walking along a corridor of milk-white rock, into the glazed surface of which were inset dusky bits of "Moon-gems" that lay about for the taking in most sections of the Lunar surface. She wore sandals which scarcely seemed to touch the ground; he wore thick-soled boots which leadenly helped weigh him down to keep his steps from becoming torture.

The corridor was one-way. Occasionally, a small electric cart would overtake them and move nearly silently past.

The Earthman said, "Now what would I like to do? That is a broad-beamed invitation. Would you like to set boundary conditions so that my answers will not innocently offend you?"

"Are you a physicist?"

The Earthman hesitated. "Why do you ask?"

"Just to hear what you would say. I know you're a physicist."

"How?"

"No one says 'set boundary conditions' unless they are.

Especially if the first thing they want to see on the Moon is the proton synchrotron."

"Is that why you've come looking for me? Because I seem to be a physicist?"

"That's why Barron sent me looking for you. Because *he's* a physicist. I came because I thought you were rather unusual for an Earthman."

"In what way?"

"Nothing terribly complimentary—if it's compliments you're fishing for. It's just that you seem not to like Earth-men."

"How can you tell that?"

"I watched you look at the others in the party. Besides, I can always tell somehow. It's the Earthies who don't like Earthies who tend to stay on the Moon. Which brings me back to the question. . . . What would you like to do? And I'll set the boundary conditions. I mean, as far as sight-seeing is concerned."

The Earthman looked at her sharply. "That's peculiar, Selene. You have a day off. Your job is sufficiently unin-teresting or distasteful so that you are glad to have the day off and would be willing to make it two or three. Yet your way of spending it is to volunteer to resume your job for me particularly. . . . Just because of a little interest."

"Barron's interest. He's busy now and there's no harm in entertaining you until he's ready. . . . Besides, it's dif-ferent. Can't you see it's different? On my job I'm riding herd on a couple of dozen Earthies— Don't you mind my using the term?"

"I use it myself."

"Because you're an Earthman. Some Earth-people con-sider it a term of derision and resent it when a Lunarite uses it."

"You mean when a Lunie uses it?"

Selene flushed. She said, "Yes. That's about it."

"Well, then, let's neither of us cry out at words. Go ahead, you were telling me about your job."

"On my job, there are these Earthies whom I have to

keep from killing themselves and whom I have to take here and there and give little speeches to and make sure they eat and drink and walk by the book. They see their little pet sights and do their little pet things, and I have to be terribly polite and motherly."

"Awful," said the Earthman.

"But you and I can do as we please, I hope, and you are willing to take your chances and I don't have to watch what I say."

"I told you that you're perfectly welcome to call me Earthie."

"All right, then. I'll have a busman's holiday. What would you like to do?"

"That's an easy one to answer. I want to see the proton synchrotron."

"Not that. Maybe Barron can arrange it after you see him."

"Well, if I can't see the synchrotron, I don't know what else there is to see. I know the radio telescope is on the other side and I don't suppose there's any novelty in it, anyway. . . . You tell me. What doesn't the average tourist get to see?"

"A number of things. There are the algae rooms—not the antiseptic processing plants, which you've seen—but the farms themselves. However, the smell is pretty strong there and I don't suppose an Earthie—Earthman—would find it particularly appetizing. Earth—men have trouble with the food as it is."

"Does that surprise you? Have you ever tasted Earth-food?"

"Not really. I probably wouldn't like it, though. It all depends on what you're used to."

"I suppose so," said the Earthman, sighing. "If you ate a real steak, you'd probably gag at the fat and fiber."

"We could go to the outskirts where the new corridors are being driven into bedrock, but you'll have to wear special protective garments. There are the factories—"

"You make the choice, Selene."

"I will, if you will tell me something honestly."

"I can't promise without hearing the question."

"I said that Earthies that didn't like Earthies tended to stay on the Moon. You didn't correct me. Do you intend to stay on the Moon?"

The Earthman stared at the toes of his clumsy boots. He said, "Selene, I had trouble getting a visa to the Moon. They said I might be too old for the trip and that if I stayed any length of time I might find it impossible to return to Earth. So I told them I planned to stay on the Moon permanently."

"You weren't lying?

"I wasn't sure at the time. But I think I'll stay here now."

"I should have thought that they would have been less willing than ever to let you go under those conditions."

"Why?"

"Generally, the Earth authorities don't like to send physicists to the Moon on a permanent basis."

The Earthman's lips twitched. "In that respect, I had no trouble."

"Well, then, if you're going to be one of us, I think you ought to visit the gymnasium. Earthies often want to but we don't encourage them as a general rule—though it's not forbidden outright. Immigrants are a different thing."

"Why?"

"Well, for one thing, we exercise in the nude or near-nude. Why not?" She sounded aggrieved, as though weary of repeating a defensive position. "The temperature is controlled; the environment is clean. It's just that where people from Earth are expected to be, nudity becomes unsettling. Some Earthies are shocked; some are titillated; and some are both. Well, we're not going to dress in the gymnasium for their sake, and we're not going to cope with them, either; so we keep them out."

"But immigrants?"

"They have to get used to it. In the end, they'll be discarding clothes, too. And they'll need the gymnasium even more than the native Lunarites do."

"I'll be honest with you, Selene. If I encounter female nudity, I'll find it titillating, too. I'm not quite so old that I won't."

"Well, titillate, then," she said, indifferently, "but to yourself. Agreed?"

"Do we have to get undressed too?" He looked at her with amused interest.

"As spectators? No. We could, but we don't have to. You would feel uncomfortable if you did this early in the game and you wouldn't be a particularly inspiring sight to the rest of us—"

"You *are* frank!"

"Do you think it would be? Be honest. And as for myself, I have no wish to put you under a special strain in your private titillation. So we might both just as well stay clothed."

"Will there be any objection? I mean to my being there as an Earthie of uninspirational appearance?"

"Not if I'm with you."

"Very well, then, Selene. Is it far away?"

"We are there. Just through here."

"Ah, then, you were planning to come here all the time."

"I thought it might be interesting."

"Why?"

Selene smiled suddenly. "I just thought."

The Earthman shook his head. "I'm beginning to think you never just think. Let me guess. If I'm to stay on the Moon, I will need to exercise now and then in order to keep muscles, bones, and all my organs, perhaps, in condition."

"Quite true. So do all of us, immigrants from Earth in particular. The day will come when the gymnasium will be a daily grind for you."

They stepped through a door and the Earthman stared in astonishment. "This is the first place I've seen that looks like Earth."

"In what way?"

"Why it's big. I didn't imagine you would have such big rooms on the Moon. Desks, office machinery, women at the desks—"

"Bare-breasted women," said Selene, gravely.

"That part isn't Earthlike, I admit."

"We've got a hold-chute, too, and an elevator for Earthies. There are many levels. . . . But wait."

She approached a woman at one of the nearer desks, talking in a rapid, low voice while the Earthman stared at everything with amiable curiosity.

Selene returned. "No trouble. And it turns out we're going to have a melee. A rather good one; I know the teams."

"This place is very impressive. Really."

"If you still mean its size, it's not nearly big enough. We have three gymnasiums. This is the largest."

"I'm somehow pleased that in the Spartan surroundings of the Moon, you can afford to waste so much room on frivolity."

"Frivolity!" Selene sounded offended. "Why do you think this is frivolity?"

"Melees? Some sort of game?"

"You might call it a game. On Earth you can do such things for sports; ten men doing, ten thousand watching. It's not so on the Moon; what's frivolous for you is necessary for us. . . . This way; we'll take the elevator, which means a little waiting perhaps."

"Didn't mean to get you angry."

"I'm not really angry but you must be reasonable. You Earthmen have been adapted to Earth-gravity for all the three hundred million years since life crawled onto dry land. Even if you don't exercise, you get by. We've had no time at all to adapt to Moon-gravity."

"You look different enough."

"If you're born and reared under Moon-gravity, your bones and muscles are, naturally, slimmer and less massive than an Earthie's would be, but that's superficial. There isn't a bodily function we possess, however subtle— digestion, rates of hormonal secretions—that isn't maladjusted to gravity and that doesn't require a deliberate regimen of exercise. If we can arrange exercise in the form of fun and games that does not make it frivolity. . . . Here's the elevator."

The Earthman hung back in momentary alarm, but Selene, said, with residual impatience, as though still seething over the necessity of defense. "I suppose you're going to tell me it looks like a wickerwork basket. Every Earthman who uses it says so. With Moon-gravity, it doesn't have to be any more substantial."

The elevator moved downward slowly. They were the only ones on board.

The Earthman said, "I suspect this isn't much used."

Selene smiled again. "You're right. The hold-chute is much more popular, and much more fun."

"What is it?"

"Exactly what the name implies. . . . Here we are. We only had to drop two levels. . . . It's just a vertical tube you can drop through, with handholds. We don't encourage Earthies to use it."

"Too risky?"

"Not in itself. You can climb down as though it were a ladder. However, there are always youngsters swinging down at considerable speed and Earthies don't know how to keep out of the way. Collisions are always discomforting. But you'll get to use it in time. . . . In fact, what you'll see now is a kind of large hold-chute designed for reckless-ness."

She led him to a circular railing around which a number of individuals were leaning and talking. All were more or less in the nude. Sandals were common and usually a hip-purse was slung over one shoulder. Some wore briefs. One was scooping a greenish-mash out of a container and was eating it.

The Earthman wrinkled his nose slightly as he passed that one. He said, "The dental problem must be severe on the Moon."

"It isn't good," Selene agreed. "If we ever get the chance, we'll select for an edentate jaw."

"Toothlessness?"

"Maybe not entirely. We might keep the incisors and canines for cosmetic reasons and for occasionally useful tasks. They're easily cleaned, too. But why should we want useless molars? It's just a hangover from an Earthie past."

"Are you making any progress in that direction?"

"No," she said, stiffly. "Genetic engineering is illegal. Earth insists."

She was leaning over the railing. "They call this the Moon's playground," she said.

The Earthman looked down. It was a large cylindrical opening with pink smooth walls to which metal bars were attached in what seemed a random configuration. Here and there, a bar stretched across a portion of the cylinder, sometimes across its entire width. It was perhaps four or five hundred feet deep and about fifty feet across.

No one seemed to be paying particular attention either to the playground or to the Earthman. Some had looked at him indifferently as he passed, seeming to weigh his clothed state, his facial appearance, and then had turned away. Some made a casual hand gesture to Selene's direction before turning away, but all turned away. The no-interest signal, however subdued, could not have been more blatant.

The Earthman turned to the cylindrical opening. There were slim figures at the bottom, foreshortened because they were seen from above. Some wore wisps of clothing in red, some in blue. Two teams, he decided. Clearly the wisps served protective functions, since all wore gloves and sandals, protective bands about knees and elbows. Some wore brief bands about the hips, some about the chests.

"Oh," he muttered. "Men and women."

Selene said, "Right! The sexes compete equally but the idea is to prevent the uncontrolled swinging of parts that might hamper the guided fall. There's a sexual difference there which also involves vulnerability to pain. It's not modesty."

The Earthman said, "I think I've read of this."

"You may have," said Selene, indifferently. "Not much seems to get out. Not that *we* have any objection, but the Terrestrial government prefers to keep news of the Moon to a minimum."

"Why, Selene?"

"You're an Earthman. You tell me. . . . Our theory here

on the Moon is that we embarrass the Earth. Or at least the Earth government."

On either side of the cylinder now, two individuals were rising rapidly and the patter of light drumbeats was heard in the background. At first, the climbers seemed to be going up a ladder, rung by rung, but their speed increased and by the time they were halfway up, they were striking each hold as they passed, making an ostentatious slapping noise.

"Couldn't do that on Earth as gracefully," said the Earthman, admiringly. "Or at all," he amended.

"It's not just low-gravity," said Selene. "Try it, if you think so. This takes endless hours of practice."

The climbers reached the railing and swung up to a headstand. They performed a simultaneous somersault and began to fall.

"They can move quickly when they want to," said the Earthman.

"Umm," said Selene, through the patter of applause. "I suspect that when Earthmen—I mean the real Earthmen, the ones who have never even visited the Moon—think of moving around the Moon, they think of the surface and of spacesuits. That's often slow, of course. The mass, with the spacesuit added, is huge, which means high inertia and a small gravity to overcome it."

"Quite right," said the Earthman. "I've seen the classic motion pictures of the early astronauts that all school children see and the movements are like those underwater. The picture gets imprinted, even when we know better."

"You'd be surprised how fast we can move on the surface these days, spacesuit and all," said Selene. "And here, underground, without spacesuits, we can move as quickly as on Earth. The slower whip of gravity is made up for by the proper use of muscles."

"But you can move slowly, too." The Earthman was watching the acrobats. They had gone up with speed and were going down with deliberate slowness. They were floating, slapping the handholds to delay the drop rather than, as before, to accelerate the rise. They reached the ground and two others replaced them. And then two more.

And then two more. From each team alternately, pairs competed in virtuosity.

Each pair went up in unison; each pair rose and fell in a more complicated pattern. One pair kicked off simultaneously to cross the tube in a low parabola, convex upward, each reaching the handhold the other had abandoned, and somehow skimming past each other in mid-air without touching. That evoked louder applause.

The Earthman said, "I suspect I lack the experience to appreciate the finer points of skill. Are these all native Lunarites?"

"They have to be," said Selene. "The gymnasium is open to all Lunar citizens and some immigrants are fairly good, considering. For this kind of virtuosity, however, you must depend on babies that are conceived and born here. They have the proper physical adaptation, at least more than native Earthmen have, and they get the proper childhood training. Most of these performers are under eighteen."

"I imagine it's dangerous, even at Moon-gravity levels."

"Broken bones aren't very uncommon. I don't think there's been an actual death, but there's been at least one case of broken spine and paralysis. That was a terrible accident; I was actually watching— Oh, wait now; we're going to have the ad libs now."

"The what?"

"Till now, we've had set pieces. The climbs were according to a fixed pattern."

The percussion beat seemed softer as one climber rose and suddenly launched into mid-air. He caught a transverse bar one-handed, circling it once vertically, and let go.

The Earthman watched closely. He said, "Amazing. He gets around those bars exactly like a gibbon."

"A what?" asked Selene.

"A gibbon. A kind of ape; in fact, the only ape still existing in the wild. They—" He looked at Selene's expression and said, "I don't mean it as an insult, Selene; they are graceful creatures."

Selene said, frowning, "I've seen pictures of apes."

"You probably haven't seen gibbons in motion. . . . I dare say that Earthies might call Lunarites 'gibbons' and mean it insultingly, about on the level of what you mean by 'Earthie.' But I don't mean it so."

He leaned both elbows on the railing and watched the movements. It was like dancing in the air. He said, "How do you treat Earth-immigrants here on the Moon, Selene? I mean immigrants who mean to stay here life-long. Since they lack true Lunarite abilities—"

"That makes no difference. Immies are citizens. There's no discrimination; no legal discrimination."

"What does that mean? No *legal* discrimination?"

"Well, you said it yourself. There are some things they can't do. There *are* differences. Their medical problems are different and they've usually had a worse medical history. If they come in middle age, they look—old."

The Earthman looked away, embarrassed. "Can they intermarry? I mean, immigrants and Lunarites."

"Certainly. That is, they can interbreed."

"Yes, that's what I meant."

"Of course. No reason why an immigrant can't have some worthwhile genes. Heavens, my father was an immie, though I'm second-generation Lunarite on my mother's side."

"I suppose your father must have come when he was quite—Oh, *good Lord*—" He froze at the railing, then drew a shuddering sigh. "I thought he was going to miss that bar."

"Not a chance," said Selene. "That's Marco Fore. He likes to do that, reach out at the last moment. Actually, it's bad form to do that and a real champion doesn't. Still— My father was twenty-two when he arrived."

"I suppose that's the way. Still young enough to be adaptable; no emotional complications back on Earth. From the standpoint of the Earthie male, I imagine it must be rather nice to have a sexual attachment with a—"

"Sexual attachment!" Selene's amusement seemed to cover a very real sense of shock. "You don't suppose my father had sex with my mother. If my mother heard you say that, she'd set *you* right in a hurry."

"But—"

"Artificial insemination was what it was for goodness sake. Sex with an *Earthman?*"

The Earthman looked solemn. "I thought you said there was no discrimination."

"That's not discrimination. That's a matter of physical fact. An Earthman can't handle the gravity field properly. However practiced he might be, under the stress of passion, he might revert. I wouldn't risk it. The clumsy fool might snap his arm or leg—or worse, mine. Gene mixtures are one thing; sex is quite another."

"I'm sorry. . . . Isn't artificial insemination against the law?"

She was watching the gymnastics with absorption. "That's Marco Fore again. When he isn't trying to be uselessly spectacular, he really is good; and his sister is almost as good. When they work together it's really a poem of motion. Look at them now. They'll come together and circle the same bar as though they have a single body stretched across. He's a little too flamboyant at times, but you can't fault his muscular control. . . . Yes, artificial insemination is against Earth's law, but it's allowed where medical reasons are involved, and, of course, that's often the case, or said to be."

All the acrobats had now climbed to the top and were in a great circle just below the railing; all the reds on one side, the blues on the other. All arms on the side of the interior were raised and the applause was loud. Quite a crowd had now gathered at the rail.

"You ought to have some seating arrangement," said the Earthman.

"Not at all. This isn't a show. This is exercise. We don't encourage any more spectators than can stand comfortably about the railing. We're supposed to be down there, not up here."

"You mean you can do that sort of thing, Selene?"

"After a fashion, of course. Any Lunarite can. I'm not as good as they are. I haven't joined any teams— There's going to be the melee now, the free-for-all. This is the really dangerous part. All ten are going to be in the air and each side is going to try to send members of the other side into a fall."

"A real fall."

"As real as possible."

"Are there injuries occasionally?"

"Occasionally. In theory, this sort of thing is frowned upon. That *is* considered frivolous, and we don't have so large a population that we can afford to incapacitate anyone without real cause. Still, the melee is popular and we can't raise the votes to outlaw it."

"Which side do you vote on, Selene?"

Selene blushed. "Oh, never mind. You watch this!"

The percussion rhythm had suddenly grown thunderous and each of the individuals in the huge well darted outward like an arrow. There was wild confusion in mid-air but when they parted again, each ended firmly on a bar-grip. There was the tension of waiting. One launched; another followed; and the air was filled with flashing bodies again. Over and over it happened.

Selene said, "The scoring is intricate. There is a point for every launch; a point for every touch; two points for every miss inflicted; ten points for a grounding; various penalties for various kinds of fouling."

"Who keeps the score?"

"There are umpires watching who make the preliminary decisions and there are television tapes in case of appeals. Very often even the tapes can't decide."

There was a sudden excited cry when a girl in blue moved past a boy in red and slapped his flank resoundingly. The boy who received the blow had writhed away, but not successfully, and grabbing at a wall bar with improper balance struck that wall ungracefully with his knee.

"Where were his eyes?" demanded Selene indignantly. "He didn't see her coming."

The action grew hotter and the Earthman tired of trying to make sense of the knotted flights. Occasionally, a leaper touched a bar and did not retain his hold. Those were the times when every spectator leaned over the railing as though ready to launch himself into space in sympathy. A one time, Marco Fore was struck in the wrist and someone cried "Foul!"

Fore missed his handhold and fell. To the Earthman's eyes, the fall, under Moon-gravity, was slow, and Fore's lithe body twisted and turned, reaching for bar after bar, without quite making it. The others waited, as though all maneuvering was suspended during a fall.

Fore was moving quite rapidly now, though twice he had slowed himself without quite being able to maintain a handhold.

He was nearly to the ground when a sudden spidery lunge caught a transverse bar with the right leg and he hung suspended and swinging, head downward, about ten feet above the ground. Arms outspread, he paused while the applause rang out and then he had twisted upright and jumped into a rapid climb.

The Earthman said, "Was he fouled?"

"If Jean Wong actually grabbed Marco's wrist instead of pushing it, it was a foul. The umpire has ruled a fair block, however, and I don't think Marco will appeal. He fell a lot farther than he had to. He likes these last-minute saves and someday he'll miscalculate and hurt himself. . . . Oh, oh."

The Earthman looked up in sudden inquiry, but Selene's eyes weren't upon him. She said, "That's someone from the Commissioner's office and he must be looking for you."

"Why—"

"I don't see why he should come here to find anyone else. You're the unusual one."

"But there's no reason—" began the Earthman.

Yet the messenger, who had the build of an Earthman himself or an Earth-immigrant, and who seemed uneasy to be the center of the stares of a couple of dozen slight, nude figures who seemed to tinge their scorn with indifference, came directly toward him.

"Sir," he began. "Commissioner Gottstein requests that you accompany me—"

5

Barron Neville's quarters were somehow harsher than Selene's. His books were on bold display, his computer-outlet was unmasked in one corner, and his large desk was in disarray. His windows were blank.

Selene entered, folded her arms, and said, "If you live like a slob, Barron, how do you expect to have your thoughts neat?"

"I'll manage," said Barron, grumpily. "How is it you haven't brought the Earthman with you?"

"The Commissioner got to him first. The new Commissioner."

"Gottstein?"

"That's right. Why weren't you ready sooner?"

"Because it took time to find out. I won't work blind."

Selene said, "Well, then, we'll just have to wait."

Neville bit at a thumbnail and then inspected the result severely. "I don't know whether I ought to like the situation or not. . . . What did you think of him?"

"I *liked* him," said Selene, definitely. "He was rather pleasant, considering he was an Earthie. He let me guide him. He was interested. He made no judgments. He didn't patronize. . . . And I didn't go out of my way to avoid insulting him, either."

"Did he ask any further about the synchrotron?"

"No, but then he didn't have to."

"Why not?"

"I told him *you* wanted to see him, and I said you were a physicist. So I imagine he'll ask you whatever he wants to ask you when he sees you."

"Didn't he think it strange that he should be talking to a female tourist guide who just happens to know a physicist?"

"Why strange? I said you were my sex-partner. There's no accounting for sex attraction and a physicist may well condescend to a lowly tourist guide."

"Shut up, Selene."

"Oh— Look, Barron, it seems to me that if he were spinning some sort of fancy web, if he approached me *because* he planned to get to you through me, he would have shown some trace of anxiety. The more complicated and silly any plot, the more rickety it is and the more anxious the plotter. I deliberately acted casual. I talked about everything but the synchrotron. I took him to a gymnastics show."

"And?"

"And he was interested. Relaxed and interested. Whatever he has on his mind, it isn't involuted."

"You're sure of that? Yet the Commissioner got to him before I did. You consider that good?"

"Why should I consider it bad? An open invitation to a meeting of some sort delivered in front of a couple of dozen Lunarites isn't particularly involuted, either."

Neville leaned back with his hands clasped at the nape of his neck. "Selene, please don't insist on making judgments, when I don't ask you to. It's irritating. The man is not a physicist in the first place. Did he tell you he was?"

Selene paused to think. "I called him a physicist. He didn't deny it but I don't recall that he actually said he was. And yet—and yet, I'm *sure* he is."

"It's a lie of omission, Selene. He may be a physicist in his own mind, but the fact is that he isn't trained as a physicist and he doesn't work as one. He has had scientific training; I'll grant him that; but he has no scientific job of any kind. He couldn't get one. There isn't a lab on Earth that would give him working room. He happens to be on Fred Hallam's crud-list and he's been top man there for a long time."

"Are you sure?"

"Believe me, I checked. Didn't you just criticize me for taking so long. . . . And it sounds so good that it's too good."

"Why too good? I don't see what you're getting at."

"Doesn't it seem to you we ought to trust him? After all, he's got a grievance against Earth."

"You can certainly argue that way, if your facts are right."

"Oh, my facts are right, at least in the sense that they're what turns up, if you dig for them. But maybe we're *supposed* to argue that way."

"Barron, that's disgusting. How can you weave these conspiracy theories into everything? Ben didn't sound——"

"Ben?" said Neville, sardonically.

"Ben!" repeated Selene, firmly. "Ben didn't sound like a man with a grievance or like a man trying to make me think he sounded like a man with a grievance."

"No, but he managed to make you think he was someone to be liked. You did say you *liked* him, didn't you? With emphasis? Maybe that's exactly what he was trying to do."

"I'm not that easy to fool and you know it."

"Well, I'll just have to wait till *I* see him."

"The hell with you, Barron. I've associated with thousands of Earthies of all kinds. It's my job. And you have no reason whatsoever to speak sarcastically about my judgment. You know you have every reason to trust it."

"All right. We'll see. Don't get angry. It's just that we'll have to wait now. . . . And as long as we do," he rose lithely to his feet, "guess what I'm thinking?"

"I don't have to." Selene rose as smoothly, and with an almost invisible motion of her feet slid sideways, well away from him. "But think it by yourself. I'm not in the mood."

"Are you annoyed because I've impugned your judgment?"

"I'm annoyed because— Oh, hell, why don't you keep your room in better condition?" And she left.

6

"I would like," said Gottstein, "to offer you some Earth-side luxury, Doctor, but, as a matter of principle, I have been allowed to bring none. The good people of the Moon resent the artificial barriers imposed by special treatment for men from Earth. It seems better to soothe their sensibilities by assuming the Lunarite pose as far as possible though I'm afraid my gait will give me away. Their confounded gravity is impossible."

The Earthman said "I find this so also. I congratulate you on your new post—"

"Not yet quite mine, sir."

"Still, my congratulations. Yet I can't help wondering why you have asked to see me."

"We were shipmates. We arrived not so long ago on the same vessel."

The Earthman waited politely.

Gottstein said, "And my acquaintance with you is a longer one than that. We met—briefly—some years ago."

The Earthman said quietly, "I'm afraid I don't recall—"

"I'm not surprised at that. There is no reason for you to remember. I was, for a time, on the staff of Senator Burt, who headed—still heads, in fact—the Committee on Technology and the Environment. It was at a time when he was rather anxious to get the goods on Hallam—Frederick Hallam."

The Earthman seemed, quite suddenly, to sit a little straighter. "Did you know Hallam?"

"You're the second person to ask me that since my coming to the Moon. Yes, I did. Not intimately. I've known others who've met him. Oddly enough, their opinion usually coincided with mine. For a person who is apparently idolized by the planet, Hallam inspired little personal liking on the part of those who knew him."

"Little? None at all, I think," said the Earthman.

Gottstein ignored the interruption. "It was my job, at the time—or at least, my assignment from the senator—to investigate the Electron Pump and see if its establishment and growth were accompanied by undue waste and personal profit-taking. It was a legitimate concern for what was essentially a watch-dog committee, but the senator was, between us, hoping to find something of damage to Hallam. He was anxious to decrease the strangle-hold that man was gaining on the scientific establishment. There, he failed."

"That much would be obvious. Hallam is stronger than ever right now."

"There was no graft to speak of; certainly none that could be traced to Hallam. The man is rigidly honest."

"In that sense, I am sure. Power has its own market value not necessarily measured in credit-bills."

"But what interested me at the time, though it was something I could not then follow up, was that I did come across someone whose complaint was not against Hallam's power, but against the Electron Pump itself. I was present at the interview, but I did not conduct it. You were the complainant, were you not?"

The Earthman said, cautiously, "I remember the incident to which you refer, but I still don't remember you."

"I wondered then how anyone could possibly object to the Electron Pump on scientific grounds. You impressed me sufficiently so that when I saw you on the ship, something stirred; and then, eventually, it came back. I have not referred to the passenger list but let me check my memory. Aren't you Dr. Benjamin Andrew Denison?"

The Earthman sighed. "Benjamin *Allan* Denison. Yes. But why does this come up now? The truth is, Commissioner, I don't want to drag up matters of the past. I'm here on the Moon and rather anxious to start again; from the start, if necessary. Damn it, I considered changing my name."

"That wouldn't have helped. It was your face I recognized. I have no objection to your new life, Dr. Denison. I would not in any way interfere. But I would like to pry a little for reasons that do not directly involve you. I don't remember, quite, your objection to the Electron Pump. Could you tell me?"

Denison's head bent. The silence lengthened itself and the Commissioner-Appointee did not interrupt. He even stifled a small clearing of the throat.

Denison said, "Truly, it was nothing. It was a guess I made; a fear about the alteration in the intensity of the strong nuclear field. Nothing!"

"Nothing?" Gottstein did clear his throat now. "Please don't mind if I strive to understand this. I told you that you interested me at the time. I was unable to follow it up then and I doubt that I could dig the information out of the records now. The whole thing is classified—the senator did very poorly at the time and he isn't interested in publicity over it. Still, some details come back. You were once a colleague of Hallam's; you were not a physicist."

"That's right. I was a radiochemist. So was he."

"Stop me if I remember incorrectly, but your early record was a very good one, right?"

"There were objective criteria in my favor. I had no illusions about myself. I was a brilliant worker."

"Amazing how it comes back. Hallam, on the other hand, was not."

"Not particularly."

"And yet afterward things did not go well with you. In fact, when we interviewed you—I think you volunteered to see us—you were working for a toy manufacturer—"

"Cosmetics," said Denison, in a strangled voice. "Male cosmetics. That didn't help gain me a respectful hearing."

"No, it wouldn't. I'm sorry. You were a salesman."

"Sales manager. I was still brilliant. I rose to vice-president before breaking off and coming to the Moon."

"Did Hallam have something to do with that? I mean with you leaving science?"

"Commissioner," said Denison. "Please! It really doesn't matter any longer. I was there when Hallam first discovered the tungsten conversion and when the chain of

events began that led to the Electron Pump. Exactly what
would have happened if I had not been there, I can't say.
Hallam and I might both have been dead of radiation poi-
soning a month later or of a nuclear explosion six weeks
later. I don't know. But I *was* there and, partly because of
me, Hallam is what he is now; and because of my part in
it, I am what I am now. The hell with the details. Does
that satisfy you? Because it will have to."

"I think it satisfies me. You had a personal grudge
against Hallam, then?"

"I certainly had no affection for him, in those days. I
have no affection for him now, for that matter."

"Would you say, then, that your objection to the Electron Pump was inspired by your anxiety to destroy
Hallam."

Denison said, "I object to this cross-examination."

"Please? Nothing of what I ask is intended to be used
against you. This is for my own benefit because I am concerned about the Pump and about a number of things."

"Well, then, I suppose you might work out some emotional involvement. Because I disliked Hallam I was ready
to believe that his popularity and greatness had a false
foundation. I thought about the Electron Pump, hoping to
find a flaw."

"And you therefore found one?"

"No," said Denison forcefully, bringing his fist down on
the arm of the chair and moving perceptibly upward from
his seat in reaction. "Not 'therefore.' I found a flaw but it
was an honest one. Or so it seemed to me. I certainly
didn't invent a flaw merely to puncture Hallam."

"No question of *inventing*, Doctor," said Gottstein
soothingly. "I don't dream of making such an implication.
Yet we all know that in trying to determine something on
the boundary line of the known, it is necessary to make assumptions. The assumptions can be made over a gray area
of uncertainty and one can shade them in one direction or
another with perfect honesty, but in accord with—uh—
tthe emotions of the moment. You made your assumptions,
perhaps, on the anti-Hallam edge of the possible."

"This is a profitless discussion, sir. At the time, I

thought I had a valid point. However, I am not a physicist. I am—was—a radiochemist."

"Hallam was a radiochemist, too, but he is now the most famous physicist in the world."

"He's still a radiochemist. A quarter-century out of date."

"Not so, you. You worked hard to become a physicist."

Denison smoldered. "You really investigated me."

"I told you; you impressed me. Amazing how it comes back. But now I'll pass on to something a little different. Do you know a physicist named Peter Lamont?"

Reluctantly—"I've met him."

"Would you say he was brilliant, too?"

"I don't know him well enough to say and I hate to overuse the word."

"Would you say he knew what he was talking about?"

"Barring information to the contrary, I would say, yes."

Carefully, the Commissioner leaned back in his seat. It had a spindly look about it and by Earth standards it would not have supported his weight. He said, "Would you care to say how you came to know Lamont? Was it by reputation only? Did you meet?"

Denison said, "We had some direct conversations. He was planning to write a history of the Electron Pump; how it started; a full account of all the legendary crap that's grown up around it. I was flattered that Lamont came to me; that he seemed to have found out something about me. Damn it, Commissioner, I was flattered that he knew I was alive. But I couldn't really say much. What would have been the use? I would have gained nothing but some sneers and I am tired of it; tired of brooding; tired of self-pity."

"Do you know anything about what Lamont has been doing in the last few years?"

"What is it you're thinking of, Commissioner?" asked Denison, cautiously.

"About a year ago, maybe a little more, Lamont spoke to Burt. I am not on the senator's staff any longer, but we see each other occasionally. He talked to me about it. He was concerned. He thought Lamont might have made a valid point against the Electron Pump and yet could see no practical way of taking up the matter. I, too, was concerned—"

"Concern everywhere," said Denison, sardonically.

"But now, I wonder. If Lamont talked to you and—"

"Stop! Stop right there, Commissioner. I think I see you sidling toward a point and I don't want you to move any further. If you expect me to tell you that Lamont stole my idea, that once again I am being treated badly, you are wrong. Let me tell you as forcefully as I can; I had no valid theory. It was purely a guess. It worried me; I presented it; I was not believed; I was discouraged. Since I had no way of demonstrating its value, I gave up. I did not mention it in my discussion with Lamont; we never went past the early days of the Pump. What he came up with later, however much it may have resembled my guess, was arrived at independently. It seems to be much more solid and to be based on rigid mathematical analysis. I lay claim to no priority; to *none*."

"You seem to know about Lamont's theory."

"It made the rounds in recent months. The fellow can't publish and no one takes him seriously, but it was passed along the grapevine. It even reached *me*."

"I see, Doctor. But *I* take it seriously. To me the warning was second time round, you understand. The report of the first warning—from you—had never reached the senator. It had nothing to do with financial irregularities, which were what was then on his mind. The actual head of the investigating panel—not myself—considered it—you will forgive me—crackpot. I did not. When the matter came up again, I grew disturbed. It was my intention to meet with Lamont, but a number of physicists whom I consulted—"

"Including Hallam?"

"No, I did not see Hallam. A number of those I consulted advised me that Lamont's work was utterly without foundation. Even so, I was considering seeing him when I was asked to take up this position, and here I am, and here *you* are. So you see why I had to see you. In your opinion is there merit in the theories advanced by yourself and by Dr. Lamont?"

"You mean is continued use of the Electron Pump going to blow up the Sun, or maybe the entire arm of the Galaxy?"

"Yes, that's exactly what I mean."

"How can I tell you? All I have is my own guess, which is just a guess. As for Lamont's theory, I have not studied it in detail; it has not been published. If I saw it, the mathematics might be beyond me. . . . Besides, what's the difference? Lamont won't convince anyone. Hallam has ruined him as earlier he ruined me, and the public generally would find it against their short-term interest to believe him even if he went over Hallam's head, so to speak. They don't want to give up the Pump, and it's a lot easier to refuse to accept Lamont's theory than to try to do something about it."

"But you're still concerned about it, aren't you?"

"In the sense that I think we might indeed destroy ourselves and that I wouldn't like to see that happen, of course."

"So you've come to the Moon, now, to do something that Hallam, your old enemy, would prevent your doing on Earth."

Denison said, slowly, "You, too, like to make guesses."

"Do I?" said Gottstein, indifferently. "Perhaps I am brilliant, too. Is my guess correct?"

"It may be. I haven't given up hope of returning to science. If anything I do were to lift the specter of doom from mankind, either by showing that it does not exist or that it does exist and must be removed, I would be pleased."

"I see. Dr. Denison, to discuss another point at the moment, my predecessor, the retiring Commissioner, Mr. Montez, tells me that the growing edge of science is here on the Moon. He seems to think a disproportionate quantity of the brains and initiative of mankind is here."

"He may be right," said Denison. "I don't know."

"He may be right," agreed Gottstein, thoughtfully. "If

so, doesn't it strike you that this may be inconvenient for your purpose. Whatever you do, men may say and think it was accomplished through the Lunar scientific structure. You personally might gain little in the way of recognition, however valuable the results you present. . . . Which, of course, would be unjust."

"I am tired of the rat-race of credit, Commissioner Gottstein. I want some interest in life, more interest than I can find as vice-president in charge of Ultra-sonic Depilatories. I'll find it in a return to science. If I accomplish something in my own eyes, I will be satisfied."

"Let us say that that would be insufficient for me. What credit you earn, you should receive; and it should be quite possible for me, as Commissioner, to present the facts to the Terrestrial community in such a way as to preserve for you what is yours. Surely you are human enough to want what is your own."

"You are kind. And in return?"

"You are cynical. But justly so. In return I want your help. The retiring Commissioner, Mr. Montez, is not certain as to the lines of scientific research being undertaken on the Moon. Communications between the peoples of Earth and Moon are not perfect, and coordination of the efforts on both worlds is clearly for the benefit of all. It is understandable that there's distrust, I suppose, but if you can do anything to break down that distrust, it will be as valuable to us as your scientific findings might be."

"Surely, Commissioner, you can't feel that I'm the ideal man to bear witness to the Lunarites as to how fair-meaning and well-disposed the Earth's scientific establishment is."

"You mustn't confuse one vengeful scientist with the men of the Earth as a whole, Dr. Denison. Let's put it this way. I would appreciate being kept aware of your scientific findings so that I could help you retain your fair share of credit; and in order to understand your findings properly—I am not a professional scientist myself, remember—it would be helpful if you were to explain them in the light of the present state of science on the Moon. Is it agreed?"

Denison said, "You ask a hard thing. Preliminary results, prematurely disclosed, whether through carelessness
or over-enthusiasm, can do tremendous harm to a reputation. I would hate to talk about anything to anyone until I
was sure of my ground. My earlier experience with the
committee on which you served would certainly encourage
me to be cautious."

"I quite understand," said Gottstein, heartily. "I would
leave it to you to decide when I might usefully be in-
formed. . . . But I have kept you late and you probably
want to sleep."

Which was a dismissal. Denison left, and Gottstein
looked after him thoughtfully.

7

Denison opened the door by hand. There was a contact
that would have opened it automatically, but in the blur of
waking, he could not find it.

The dark-haired man, with a face that was somehow
scowling in repose, said, "I'm sorry. . . . Am I early?"

Denison repeated the last word to give him time to absorb matters. "Early? . . . No. I . . . I'm late, I think."

"I called. We made an appointment—"

And now Denison had it. "Yes. You're Dr. Neville."

"That's right. May I come in?"

He stepped in as he asked. Denison's room was small,
and held a rumpled bed that took up most of the available
space. The ventilator was sighing softly.

Neville said with meaningless courtesy, "Slept well, I
hope?"

Denison looked down at his pajamas and passed his
hand over his rumpled hair. "No," he said abruptly. "I
had an abominable night. May I be excused long enough
to make myself more presentable?"

"Of course. Would you like to have me prepare breakfast meanwhile? You may be unacquainted with the equipment."

"It would be a favor," said Denison.

He emerged some twenty minutes later, washed and shaved, wearing trousers and an undershirt. He said, "I trust I didn't break the shower. It went off and I couldn't turn it on again."

"The water's rationed. You only get so much. This is the Moon, Doctor. I've taken the liberty of preparing scrambled eggs and hot soup for the two of us."

"Scrambled—"

"We call it that. Earthmen wouldn't, I suppose."

Denison said, "Oh!" He sat down with something less than enthusiasm and tasted the pasty yellow mixture that clearly was what the other meant by scrambled eggs. He tried not to make a face at the first taste and then manfully swallowed it and dug in for a second forkful.

"You'll get used to it with time," said Neville, "and it's highly nourishing. I might warn you that the high-protein content and the low gravity will cut your need for food."

"Just as well," said Denison, clearing his throat.

Neville said, "Selene tells me that you intend to stay on the Moon."

Denison said, "That was my intention." He rubbed his eyes. "I've had a terrible night, though. It tests my resolution."

"How many times did you fall out of bed?"

"Twice. . . . I take it that the situation is a common one."

"For men of Earth, an invariable one. Awake, you can make yourself walk with due regard for the Moon's gravity. Asleep, you toss as you would on Earth. But at least falling is not painful at low gravity."

"The second time, I slept on the floor awhile before waking. Didn't remember falling. What the hell do you do about it?"

"You mustn't neglect your periodic checks on heartbeat, blood pressure, and so on, just to make sure the gravity change isn't introducing too much of a strain."

"I've been amply warned of that," said Denison with distaste. "In fact, I have fixed appointments for the next month. And pills."

"Well," said Neville, as if dismissing a triviality, "within a week you'll probably have no trouble at all. . . . And you'll need proper clothing. Those trousers will never do and that flimsy upper garment serves no purpose."

"I presume there's some place I can buy clothes."

"Of course. If you can get her when she's off duty, Selene will be glad to help, I'm sure. She assures me you're a decent sort, Doctor."

"I'm delighted she thinks so." Denison, having swallowed a spoonful of the soup, looked at it as though he were wondering what to do with the rest. Grimly, he continued the task of downing it.

"She judged you to be a physicist, but of course she's wrong."

"I was trained as a radiochemist."

"You haven't worked at that either for a long time, Doctor. We may be out of it up here, but we're not that far out of it. You're one of Hallam's victims."

"Are there so many you speak of them as a group?"

"Why not? The whole Moon is one of Hallam's victims."

"The Moon?"

"In a manner of speaking."

"I don't understand."

"We have no Electron Pump Stations on the Moon. None have been established because there has been no cooperation from the para-Universe. No samples of tungsten have been accepted."

"Surely, Dr. Neville, you don't intend to imply that this is Hallam's doing."

"In a negative way, yes. Why must it be only the para-Universe which can initiate a Pump Station. Why not ourselves?"

"As far as I know, we lack the knowledge to take the initiative."

"And we will continue to lack the knowledge if research into the matter is forbidden."

"Is it forbidden?" Denison asked, with a faint note of surprise.

"In effect. If none of the work necessary to expand knowledge in that direction finds adequate priorities at the proton synchrotron or at any of the other large equipment —all controlled by Earth and all under the influence of Hallam—then the research is effectively forbidden."

Denison rubbed his eyes. "I suspect I will have to sleep again before long. . . . I beg your pardon. I did not mean to imply you were boring me. But tell me, is the Electron Pump so important to the Moon? Surely the Solar batteries are effective and sufficient."

"They tie us to the Sun, Doctor. They tie us to the *surface*."

"Well— But why does Hallam take this adverse interest in the matter, do you suppose, Dr. Neville?"

"You know better than I, if you know him personally, as I do not. He prefers not to make it clear to the public generally that the entire Electron Pump establishment is the product of the para-men, with ourselves merely servants of the masters. And if, on the Moon, we advance to the point where we ourselves know what we are doing, then the birth of the true Electron Pump technology will date from our moment, not from his."

Denison said, "Why do you tell me all this?"

"To avoid wasting my time. Ordinarily, we welcome physicists from Earth. We feel cut off here on the Moon, victims of deliberate Terrestrial policy against us, and a physicist-visitor can be helpful, even if only to give us a feeling of lesser isolation. A physicist-immigrant is even more helpful and we like to explain the situation to him and encourage him to work with us. I am sorry that you are not, after all, a physicist."

Denison said, impatiently, "But I never said I was."

"And yet you asked to see the synchrotron. Why?"

"Is that really what's bothering you? My dear sir, let me try to explain. My scientific career was ruined half a lifetime ago. I have decided to see some sort of rehabilitation, some sort of renewed meaning, to my life as far away from Hallam as I could get—which means here on the Moon. I was trained as a radiochemist, but that has not permanently paralyzed me as far as any other field of endeavor is concerned. Para-physics is the great field of today and I have done my best to self-educate myself there, feeling that this will offer me my best hope for rehabilitation."

Neville nodded. "I see," he said with clear dubiousness.

"By the way, since you mentioned the Electron Pump— Have you heard anything about the theories of Peter Lamont?"

Neville eyed the other narrowly. "No. I don't think I know the man."

"Yes, he is not yet famous. And probably never will be; chiefly for the same reason I'll never be. He crossed Hallam. . . . His name came up recently and I've been giving him some thought. It was one way of occupying the sleepless portion of last night." And he yawned.

Neville said, impatiently, "Yes, Doctor? What of this man? What is his name?"

"Peter Lamont. He has some interesting thoughts on para-theory. He believes that with continued use of the Pump, the strong nuclear interaction will grow basically more intense in the space of the Solar system and that the Sun will slowly heat up and, at some crucial point, undergo a phase-change that will produce an explosion."

"Nonsense! Do you know the amount of change produced, on a cosmic scale, of any use of the Pump on a human scale? Even granted that you are only self-educated in physics, you ought have no difficulty in seeing that the Pump can't possibly make any appreciable change in general Universal conditions during the lifetime of the Solar system."

"Do you think so?"

"Of course. Don't you?" said Neville.

"I'm not sure. Lamont's grinding a personal axe. I've met him briefly and he impressed me as an intense and very emotional fellow. Considering what Hallam has done to him, he is probably driven by overwhelming anger."

Neville frowned. He said, "Are you sure he is on the outs with Hallam?"

"I'm an expert on the subject."

"It doesn't occur to you that the initiation of that kind of doubt—that the Pump is dangerous—might be used as but another device to keep the Moon from developing Stations of its own?"

"At the cost of creating universal alarm and despondency? Of course not. That would be cracking walnuts with nuclear explosions. No, I'm sure Lamont is sincere. In fact, in my own bumbling way, I had similar notions once."

"Because you, too, are driven by hate for Hallam."

"I'm not Lamont. I imagine I don't react the same way he does. In fact, I had some dim hope I would be able to investigate the matter on the Moon, without Hallam's interference and without Lamont's emotionalism."

"Here on the Moon?"

"Here on the Moon. I thought perhaps I might get the use of the synchrotron."

"And that was your interest in it?"

Denison nodded.

Neville said, "You really think you will get the use of the synchrotron? Do you know how far back the requisitions have piled up?"

"I thought perhaps I might get the cooperation of some of the Lunar scientists."

Neville laughed and shook his head. "We have almost as little chance as you. . . . However, I'll tell you what we can do. We have established laboratories of our own. We can give you space; we might even have some minor instrumentation for you. How useful our facilities would be to you, I can't say, but you might be able to do something."

"Do you suppose I would have any means there of making observations useful to para-theory?"

"It would depend partly on your ingenuity, I suppose. Do you expect to prove the theories of this man, Lamont?"

"Or disprove them. Perhaps."

"You'll disprove them, if anything at all. I have no fears about that."

Denison said, "It's quite clear, isn't it, that I'm not a

physicist by training? Why do you so readily offer me work-ing-space?"

"Because you're from Earth. I told you that we value that, and perhaps your self-education as a physicist will be of additional value. Selene vouches for you, something I attach more importance to than I should, perhaps. And we are fellow-sufferers at the hands of Hallam. If you wish to rehabilitate yourself, we will help you."

"But pardon me if I am cynical. What do you expect to get out of it?"

"Your help. There is a certain amount of misunder-standing between the scientists of the Earth and the Moon. You are a man of Earth who has come voluntarily to the Moon and you could act as a bridge between us to the benefit of both. You have already had contact with the new Commissioner and it may be possible that, as you re-habilitate yourself, you will rehabilitate us as well."

"You mean that if what I do weakens Hallam's influ-ence, that will benefit Lunar science as well."

"Whatever you do is sure to be useful. . . . But perhaps I ought to leave you to catch up with your sleep. Call on me during the next couple of days and I will see about placing you in a laboratory. And"—he looked about—"getting you somewhat more comfortable quarters as well."

They shook hands and Neville left.

8

Gottstein said, "I suppose that, however annoying this po-sition of yours may have been, you are getting ready to leave it today with a small pang."

Montez shrugged eloquently. "A very large pang, when I think of the return to full gravity. The difficulty of breathing—the aching feet—the perspiration. I'll be a bath of perspiration constantly."

"It will be my turn someday."

"Take my advice. Never stay here longer than two months at a time. I don't care what the doctors tell you or what kind of isometric exercises they put you through—get back to Earth every sixty days and stay at least a week. You've got to keep the feel of it."

"I'll bear that in mind. . . . Oh, I've been in touch with my friend."

"Which friend is that?"

"The man who was on the vessel with me when I came in. I thought I remembered him and I did. A man named Denison; a radiochemist. What I remembered of him was accurate enough."

"Ah?"

"I remembered a certain interesting irrationality of his, and tried to probe it. He resisted in quite a shrewd fashion. He sounded rational; so rational, in fact, that I grew suspicious. There's a kind of attractive rationality developed by certain types of crackpots; a kind of defense mechanism."

"Oh, Lord," said Montez, clearly harassed. "I'm not sure I follow you. If you don't mind, I'm going to sit down for a moment. Between trying to determine whether everything is properly packed and thinking about Earth's gravity, I'm out of breath. . . . What kind of irrationality?"

"He tried to tell us once that there was danger in the use of the Electron Pumps. He thought it would blow up the Universe."

"Indeed? And will it?"

"I hope not. At the time it was dismissed rather brusquely. When scientists work on a subject at the limit of understanding, they grow edgy, you know. I knew a psychiatrist once who called it the 'Who knows?' phenomenon. If nothing you do will give you the knowledge you need, you end by saying, 'Who knows what will happen?' and imagination tells you."

"Yes, but if physicists go around saying such things, even a few of them—"

"But they don't. Not officially. There's such a thing as

scientific responsibility and the journals are careful not to print nonsense. . . . Or what they consider nonsense. Actually, you know, the subject's come up again. A physicist named Lamont spoke to Senator Burt, to that self-appointed environmental messiah, Chen, and to a few others. He also insists on the possibility of cosmic explosion. No one believes him but the story spreads in a thin sort of way and gets better with the retelling."

"And this man here on the Moon believes it."

Gottstein smiled broadly. "I suspect he does. Hell, in the middle of the night, when I have trouble sleeping—I keep falling out of bed, by the way—I believe it myself. He probably hopes to test the theory experimentally, here."

"Well?"

"Well, let him. I hinted we would help him."

Montez shook his head. "That's risky. I don't like the official encouragement of crackpot notions."

"You know, it's just barely possible they may not be entirely crackpot, but that's not the point. The point is that if we can get him established here on the Moon, we may find out, through him, what's going on here. He's anxious for rehabilitation and I hinted that rehabilitation would come through us if he cooperated. . . . I'll see to it that you are discreetly kept posted. As between friends, you know."

"Thank you," said Montez. "And good-by."

9

Neville chafed. "No. I don't like him."

"Why not? Because he's an Earthie?" Selene brushed a bit of fluff from her right breast, then caught it and looked at it critically. "That's not from my blouse. I tell you the air-recirculation is abominable."

"This Denison is worthless. He is not a para-physicist. He's a self-educated man in the field, he says, and proves it by coming here with ready-made damn-fool notions."

"Like what?"

"He thinks that the Electron Pump is going to explode the Universe."

"Did he say that?"

"I know he thinks that. . . . Oh, I know the arguments. I've heard them often enough. But it's not so, that's all."

"Maybe," said Selene, raising her eyebrows, "you just don't want it to be so."

"Don't *you* start," said Neville.

There was a short pause. Selene said, "Well, what will you do with him?"

"I'll give him a place to work. He may be worthless as a scientist, but he'll have his uses just the same. He'll be conspicuous enough; the Commissioner has been talking to him already."

"I know."

"Well, he has a romantic history as someone with a wrecked career trying to rehabilitate himself."

"Really?"

"Really. I'm sure you'll love it. If you ask him about it, he'll tell you. And that's good. If we have a romantic Earthman working on the Moon on a crackpot project, he'll make a perfect object to preoccupy the Commissioner. He'll be misdirection; window-dressing. And it may even be that through him, who knows, we might just possibly get a better idea of what goes on there on Earth. . . . You'd better continue to be friendly with him, Selene."

10

Selene laughed, and the sound was metallic in Denison's earpiece. Her figure was lost in the spacesuit she wore.

She said, "Now come, Ben, there's no reason to be afraid. You're an old hand by now—you've been here a month."

"Twenty-eight days," mumbled Denison. He felt smothered in his own suit.

"A month," insisted Selene. "It was well past half-Earth when you came; it is well past half-Earth now." She pointed to the brilliant curve of the Earth in the southern sky.

"Well, but wait. I'm not as brave out here as I am underground. What if I fall?"

"What if you do? The gravity is weak by your standards, the slope is gentle, your suit is strong. If you fall, just let yourself slide and roll. It's almost as much fun that way, anyhow."

Denison looked about doubtfully. The Moon lay beautiful in the cold light of the Earth. It was black and white; a mild and delicate white as compared with the Sunlit views he had seen when he had taken a trip a week before to inspect the Solar batteries that stretched from horizon to horizon along the floor of Mare Imbrium. And the black was somehow softer, too, through lack of the blazing contrast of true day. The stars were supernally bright and the Earth—the Earth—was infinitely inviting with its swirls of white on blue, and its peeping glimpse of tan.

"Well," he said, "do you mind if I hang on to you?"

"Of course not. And we won't go all the way up. It will be the beginner's slope for you. Just try to keep in time with me. I'll move slowly."

Her steps were long, slow, and swinging, and he tried to keep in synchronization. The up-sloping ground beneath them was dusty and with each step he kicked up a fine powder that settled quickly in the airlessness. He matched her stride for stride, but with an effort.

"Good," said Selene, her arm locked in his, steadying him. "You're very good for an Earthie—no, I ought to say Immie—"

"Thank you."

"That's not much better, I suppose. Immie for Immigrant is as insulting as Earthie for Earthman. Shall I just say you're simply very good for a man your age."

"*No!* That's much worse." Denison was gasping a little and he could feel his forehead moistening.

Selene said, "Each time you reach the point where you're about to put your foot down, give a little push with your other foot. That will lengthen your stride and make it all the easier. No, no—watch me."

Denison paused thankfully and watched Selene, somehow slim and graceful despite the grotesquerie of the suit once she moved, take off into low, loping leaps. She returned and knelt at his feet.

"Now you take a slow step, Ben, and I'll hit your foot when I want it to shove."

They tried several times, and Denison said, "That's worse than running on Earth. I better rest."

"All right. It's just that your muscles aren't used to the proper coordination. It's yourself you're fighting, you know, not gravity. . . . Well, sit down and catch your breath. I won't take you up much farther."

Denison said, "Will I do any damage to the pack if I lie down on my back?"

"No, of course not, but it's not a good idea. Not on the bare ground. It's only at 120 degrees absolute; 150 degrees below zero, if you prefer, and the smaller the area of contact the better. I'd sit down."

"All right." Gingerly, Denison sat down with a grunt. Deliberately, he faced northward, away from the Earth. "Look at those stars!"

Selene sat facing him, at right angles. He could see her face now and then, dimly through the faceplate, when the Earthlight caught it at the proper angle.

She said, "Don't you see the stars on Earth?"

"Not like this. Even when there are no clouds, the air on Earth absorbs some of the light. Temperature differences in the atmosphere make them twinkle, and city lights, even distant city lights, wash them out."

"Sounds disgusting."

"Do you like it out here, Selene? On the surface?"

"I'm not crazy about it really, but I don't mind it too much, now and then. It's part of my job to bring tourists out here, of course."

"And now you have to do it for me."

"Can't I convince you it's not the same thing at all, Ben? We've got a set route for the tourists. It's very tame, very uninteresting. You don't think we'd take them out here to the slide, do you? This is for Lunarites—and Immies. Mostly Immies, actually."

"It can't be very popular. There's no one here but ourselves."

"Oh, well. There are particular days for this sort of thing. You should see this place on race days. You wouldn't like it then, though."

"I'm not sure I like it *now*. Is gliding a sport for Immies, particularly?"

"Rather. Lunarites don't like the surface generally."

"How about Dr. Neville?"

"You mean, how he feels about the surface?"

"Yes."

"Frankly, I don't think he's ever been up here. He's a real city boy. Why do you ask?"

"Well, when I asked permission to go along on the routine servicing of the Solar batteries, he was perfectly willing to have me go, but he wouldn't go himself. I rather asked him to, I think, so I could have someone answer my questions, if there were any, and his refusal was rather strong."

"I hope there was someone else to answer your questions."

"Oh, yes. He was an Immie, too, come to think of it. Maybe that explains Dr. Neville's attitude toward the Electron Pump."

"What do you mean?"

"Well—" Denison leaned back and kicked his legs up alternately, watching them rise and fall slowly with a certain lazy pleasure. "Hey, that's not bad. Look, Selene—What I mean is that Neville is so intent on developing a Pump Station on the Moon when the Solar batteries are so adequate for the job. We couldn't use Solar batteries on the Earth, where the Sun is never as unfailing, as prolonged, as bright, as radiant in all wave lengths. There's not a single planetary body in the Solar system, no body of any size, that is more suitable for the use of the batteries than the Moon is. Even Mercury is too hot.—But the use does tie you to the surface, and if you don't like the surface—"

Selene rose to her feet suddenly, and said, "All right, Ben, you've rested enough. Up! Up!"

He struggled to his feet and said, "A Pump Station, however, would mean that no Lunarite would ever have to come out on the surface, if he didn't want to."

"Uphill we go, Ben. We'll go to that ridge up ahead. See it, where the Earthlight cuts off in a horizontal line?"

They made their way up the final stretch silently. Denison was aware of the smoother area to their side; a wide swathe of slope from which most of the dust had been brushed.

"That's too smooth for a beginner to work up," Selene said, answering his thoughts. "Don't get too ambitious or you'll want me to teach you the kangaroo-hop next."

She made a kangaroo-hop as she spoke, turned about face almost before landing, and said, "Right here. Sit down and I'll adjust—"

Denison did, facing downhill. He looked down the slope uncertainly. "Can you really glide on it?"

"Of course. The gravity is weaker on the Moon than on the Earth, so you press against the ground much less strongly, and that means there is much less friction. Everything is more slippery on the Moon than on the Earth. That's why the floors in our corridors and apartments seemed unfinished to you. Would you like to hear me give my little lecture on the subject? The one I give the tourists?"

"No, Selene."

"Besides, we're going to use gliders, of course." She had a small cartridge in her hand. Clamps and a pair of thin tubes were attached to it.

"What is that?" asked Ben.

"Just a small liquid-gas reservoir. It will emit a jet of vapor just under your boots. The thin gas layer between boots and ground will reduce friction to virtually zero. You'll move as though you were in clear space."

Denison said uneasily. "I disapprove. Surely, it's wasteful to use gas in this fashion on the Moon."

"Oh, now. What gas do you think we use in these gliders? Carbon dioxde? Oxygen? This is waste gas to begin with. It's argon. It comes out of the Moon's soil in ton-lots, formed by the billions of years of breakdown of potassium-40. . . . That's part of my lecture, too, Ben. . . . The argon has only a few specialized uses on the Moon. We could use it for gliding for a million years without exhausting the supply. . . . All right. Your gliders are on. Now wait till I put mine on."

"How do they work?"

"It's quite automatic. You just start sliding and that will trip the contact and start the vapor. You've only got a few minutes supply; but that's all you'll need."

She stood up and helped him to his feet. "Face downhill. . . . Come on, Ben, this is a gentle slope. Look at it. It looks perfectly level."

"No, it doesn't," said Denison, sulkily. "It looks like a cliff to me."

"Nonsense. Now listen to me and remember what I told you. Keep your feet about six inches apart and one just a few inches ahead of the other. It doesn't matter which one is ahead. Keep your knees bent. Don't lean into the wind because there isn't any. Don't try to look up or back, but you can look from side to side if you have to. Most of all, when you finally hit level, don't try to stop too soon; you'll be going faster than you think. Just let the glider expire and then friction will bring you to a slow halt."

"I'll never remember all that."

"Yes, you will. And I'll be right at your side to help. And if you do fall and I don't catch you, don't try to do anything. Just relax and let yourself tumble or slide. There are no boulders anywhere that you can collide with."

Denison swallowed and looked ahead. The southward slide was gleaming in Earthlight. Minute unevennesses caught more than their share of light, leaving tiny uphill patches in darkness so that there was a vague mottling of the surface. The bulging half-circle of Earth rode the black sky almost directly ahead.

"Ready?" said Selene. Her gauntleted hand was between his shoulders.

"Ready," said Denison faintly.

"Then off you go," she said. She pushed and Denison felt himself begin to move. He moved quite slowly at first. He turned toward her, wobbling, and she said, "Don't worry. I'm right at your side."

He could feel the ground beneath his feet—and then he couldn't. The glider had been activated.

For a moment he felt as though he were standing still. There was no push of air against his body, no feel of anything sliding past his feet. But when he turned toward Selene again, he noticed that the lights and shadows to one side were moving backward at a slowly increasing speed.

"Keep your eyes on the Earth," Selene's voice said in his ear, "till you build up speed. The faster you go, the more stable you'll be. Keep your knees bent. . . . You're doing very well, Ben."

"For an Immie," gasped Denison.

"How does it feel?"

"Like flying," he said. The pattern of light and dark on either side was moving backward in a blur. He looked briefly to one side, then the other, trying to convert the sensation of a backward flight of the surroundings into one of a forward flight of his own. Then, as soon as he succeeded, he found he had to look forward hastily at the Earth to regain his sense of balance. "I suppose that's not a good comparison to use to you. You have no experience of flying on the Moon."

"Now I know, though. Flying must be like gliding—I know what *that* is."

She was keeping up with him easily.

Denison was going fast enough now so that he got the sensation of motion even when he looked ahead. The Moonscape ahead was opening before him and flowing past on either side. He said, "How fast do you get to go in a glide?"

"A good Moon-race," said Selene, "has been clocked at speeds in excess of a hundred miles an hour—on steeper slopes than this one, of course. You'll probably reach a top of thirty-five."

"It feels a lot faster than that somehow."

"Well, it isn't. We're leveling off now, Ben, and you haven't fallen. Now just hang on; the glider will die off and you'll feel friction. Don't do anything to help it. Just keep going."

Selene had barely completed her remarks when Denison felt the beginning of pressure under his boots. There was at once an overwhelming sensation of speed and he clenched his fists hard to keep from throwing his arms up in an almost reflex gesture against the collision that wasn't going to happen. He knew that if he threw up his arms, he would go over backward.

He narrowed his eyes, held his breath till he thought his lungs would explode, and then Selene said, "Perfect, Ben, perfect. I've never known an Immie to go through his first slide without a fall, so if you do fall, there'll be nothing wrong. No disgrace."

"I don't intend to fall," whispered Denison. He caught a large, ragged breath, and opened his eyes wide. The Earth was as serene as ever, as uncaring. He was moving more slowly now—more slowly—more slowly—

"Am I standing still now, Selene?" he asked. "I'm not sure."

"You're standing still. Now don't move. You've got to rest before we make the trip back to town. . . . Damn it, I left it somewhere around here when we came up."

Denison watched her with disbelief. She had climbed up with him, had glided down with him. Yet he was half-dead with weariness and tension, and she was in the air with long kangaroo-leaps. She seemed a hundred yards away when she said, "Here it is!" and her voice was as loud in his ears as when she was next to him.

She was back in a moment, with a folded, paunchy sheet of plastic under her arm.

"Remember," she said, cheerily, "when you asked what it was on our way up and I said we'd be using it before we came down?" She unfolded it and spread it on the dusty surface of the Moon.

"A Lunar Lounge is its full name," she said, "but we just call it a lounge. We take the adjective for granted here on this world." She inserted a cartridge and tripped a lever.

It began to fill. Somehow Denison had expected a hissing noise, but of course there was no air to carry sound.

"Before you question our conservation policies again," said Selene, "this is argon also."

It blossomed into a mattress on six, stubby legs. "It will hold you," she said. "It makes very little actual contact with the ground and the vacuum all around will conserve its heat."

"Don't tell me it's hot," said Denison, amazed.

"The argon is heated as it pours in, but only relatively. It ends up at 270 degrees absolute, almost warm enough to melt ice, and quite warm enough to keep your insulated suit from losing heat faster than you can manufacture it. Go ahead. Lie down."

Denison did so, with a sensation of enormous luxury.

"Great!" he said with a long sigh.

"Mamma Selene thinks of everything," she said.

She came from behind him now, gliding around him, her feet placed heel to heel as though she were on skates, and then let them fly out from under her, as she came down gracefully on hip and elbow on the ground just beside him.

Denison whistled. "How did you do that?"

"Lots of practice! And don't you try it. You'll break your elbow. I warn you though. If I get too cold, I'm going to have to crowd you on the lounge."

"Safe enough," he said, "with both of us in suits."

"Ah, there speaks my brave lecher. . . . How do you feel?"

"All right, I guess. What an experience!"

"What an experience? You set a record for non-falls. Do you mind if I tell the folks back in town about this?"

"No. Always like to be appreciated. . . . You're not going to expect me to do this again, are you?"

"Right now? Of course not. I wouldn't myself. We'll just rest awhile, make sure your heart action is back to normal, and then we'll go back. If you'll reach your legs in my direction, I'll take your gliders off. Next time, I'll show you how to handle the gliders yourself."

"I'm not sure that there will be a next time."

"Of course there'll be. Didn't you enjoy it?"

"A little. In between terror."

"You'll have less terror next time, and still less the time after, and eventually you'll just experience the enjoyment and I'll make a racer out of you."

"No, you won't. I'm too old."

"Not on the Moon. You just *look* old."

Denison could feel the ultimate quiet of the Moon soaking into him as he lay there. He was facing the Earth this time. Its steady presence in the sky had, more than anything else, given him the sensation of stability during his recent glide and he felt grateful to it.

He said, "Do you often come out here, Selene? I mean, by yourself, or just one or two others? You know, when it isn't fiesta time?"

"Practically never. Unless there are people around, this is too much for me. That I'm doing it now, actually, surprises me."

"Uh-huh," said Denison, noncommittally.

"You're not surprised?"

"Should I be? My feeling is that each person does what he does either because he wants to or he must and in either case that's his business, not mine."

"Thanks, Ben. I mean it; it's good to hear. One of the nice things about you, Ben, is that for an Immie, you're willing to let us be ourselves. We're underground people, we Lunarites, cave people, corridor people. And what's wrong with that?"

"Nothing."

"Not to hear the Earthies talk. And I'm a tourist guide and have to listen to them. There isn't anything they say that I haven't heard a million times, but what I hear most of all"—and she dropped into the clipped accents of the typical Earthie speaking Planetary Standard "—'But, dear, however can all you people live in *caves* all the time? Doesn't it give you a terrible *closed-in* feeling? Don't you ever want to see blue sky and trees and ocean and feel wind and smell flowers—'

"Oh, I could go on and on, Ben. Then they say, 'But I suppose you don't know what blue sky and sea and trees are like so you don't miss them.' . . . As if we don't receive Earth-television and as if we don't have full access to Earth-literature, both optical and auditory—and olfactory sometimes, too."

Denison was amused. He said, "What's the official answer to remarks like that?"

"Nothing much. We just say, 'We're quite used to it, madam.' Or 'sir' if it's a man. Usually it's a woman. The men are too interested in studying our blouses and wondering when we take them off, I suppose. You know what I'd like to tell the idiots?"

"Please tell me. As long as you have to keep the blouse on, it being inside the suit, at least get that off your chest."

"Funny, funny word play! . . . I'd like to tell them, 'Look, madam, why the hell should we be interested in your damned world? We don't want to be hanging on the outside of any planet and waiting to fall off or get blown off. We don't want raw air puffing at us and dirty water falling on us. We don't want your damned germs and your smelly grass and your dull blue sky and your dull white clouds. We can see Earth in our own sky when we want to, and we don't often want to. The Moon is our home and it's what we make it; exactly what we make it. We own it and we build our own ecology, and we don't need you here being sorry for us going our own way. Go back to your own world and let your gravity pull your breasts down to your knees.' That's what I'd say."

Denison said, "All right. Whenever you get too close to saying that to some Earthie, you come say it to me and you'll feel better."

"You know what? Every once in a while, some Immie suggests that we build an Earth-park on the Moon; some little spot with Earth-plants brought in as seeds or seedlings; maybe some animals. A touch of home—that's the usual expression."

"I take it you're against that."

"Of course, I'm against it. A touch of whose home? The *Moon* is our home. An Immie who wants a touch of home had better get back to *his* home. Immies can be worse than Earthies sometimes."

"I'll keep that in mind," said Denison.

"Not you—so far," said Selene.

There was silence for a moment and Denison wondered if Selene were going to suggest a return to the caverns. On the one hand, it wouldn't be long before he would feel a fairly strenuous craving to visit a rest-room. On the other, he had never felt so relaxed. He wondered how long the oxygen in his pack would hold out.

Then Selene said, "Ben, do you mind if I ask you a question?"

"Not at all. If it's my private life that interests you, I am without secrets. I'm five-foot-nine, weigh twenty-eight pounds on the Moon, had one wife long ago, now divorced, one child, a daughter, grown-up and married, attended University of—"

"No, Ben. I'm serious. Can I ask about your work?"

"Of course you can, Selene. I don't know how much I can explain to you, though."

"Well— You know that Barron and I—"

"Yes, I know," said Denison, brusquely.

"We talk together. He tells me things sometimes. He said you think the Electron Pump might make the Universe explode."

"Our section of the Universe. It might convert a part of our Galactic arm into a quasar."

"Really? Do you really think so?"

Denison said, "When I came to the Moon, I wasn't sure. Now I am. I am personally convinced that this will happen."

"When do you think it will happen?"

"That I can't say exactly. Maybe a few years from now. Maybe a few decades."

There was a short silence between them. Then Selene said, in a subdued voice, "Barron doesn't think so."

"I know he doesn't. I'm not trying to convert him. You don't beat refusal to believe in a frontal attack. That's Lamont's mistake."

"Who's Lamont?"

"I'm sorry, Selene. I'm talking to myself."

"No, Ben. Please tell me. I'm interested. Please."

Denison turned to one side, facing her. "All right," he said. "I have no objection to telling you. Lamont, a physicist back on Earth, tried in his way to alert the world to the dangers of the Pump. He failed. Earthmen want the Pump; they want the free energy; they want it enough to refuse to believe they can't have it."

"But why should they want it, if it means death?"

"All they have to do is refuse to believe it means death. The easiest way to solve a problem is to deny it exists. Your friend, Dr. Neville, does the same thing. He dislikes the surface, so he forces himself to believe that Solar batteries are no good—even though to any impartial observer they would seem the perfect energy source for the Moon. He wants the Pump so he can stay underground, so he refuses to believe that there can be any danger from it."

Selene said, "I don't think Barron would refuse to believe something for which valid evidence existed. Do you really have the evidence?"

"I think I do. It's most amazing really, Selene. The whole thing depends on certain subtle factors of quark-quark interactions. Do you know what that means?"

"You don't have to explain. I've talked so much to Barron about all sorts of things that I might be able to follow."

"Well, I thought I would need the Lunar proton

synchrotron for the purpose. It's twenty-five miles across, has superconducting magnets, and can dispose of energies of 20,000 Bev and more. It turns out, though, that you people have something you call a Pionizer, which fits into a moderately sized room and does all the work of the synchrotron. The Moon is to be congratulated on a most amazing advance."

"Thank you," said Selene, complacently. "I mean on behalf of the Moon."

"Well, then, my Pionizer results can show the rate of increase of intensity of strong nuclear interaction; and the increase is what Lamont says it is and not what the orthodox theory would have it be."

"And have you shown it to Barron?"

"No, I haven't. And if I do, I expect Neville to reject it. He'll say the results are marginal. He'll say I've made an error. He'll say that I haven't taken all factors into account. He'll say I've used inadequate controls. . . . What he'll really be saying is that he wants the Electron Pump and won't give it up."

"You mean there's no way out."

"Of course there is, but not the direct way. Not Lamont's way."

"What's that?"

"Lamont's solution is to force abandonment of the Pump, but you can't just move backward. You can't push the chicken back into the egg, wine back into the grape, the boy back into the womb. If you want the baby to let go of your watch, you don't just try to explain that he ought to do it—you offer him something he would rather have."

"And what's that?"

"Ah, that's where I'm not so sure. I do have an idea, a simple idea—perhaps too simple to work—based on the quite obvious fact that the number two is ridiculous and can't exist."

There was a silence that lasted for a minute or so and then Selene, her voice as absorbed as his, said, "Let me guess your meaning."

"I don't know that I have any," said Denison.

"Let me guess, anyway. It could make sense to suppose

that our own Universe is the only one that can exist or does exist, because it is the only one we live in and directly experience. Once, however, evidence arises that there is a second Universe as well, the one we call the para-Universe, then it becomes absolutely ridiculous to suppose that there are two and only two Universes. If a second Universe can exist, then an infinite number can. Between one and the infinite in cases such as these, there are no sensible numbers. Not only two, but any finite number, is ridiculous and can't exist."

Denison said, "That's exactly my reas—" And silence fell again.

Denison heaved himself into a sitting position and looked down on the suit-encased girl. He said, "I think we had better go back to town."

She said, "I was just guessing."

He said, "No, you weren't. Whatever it was, it wasn't *just* guessing."

11

Barron Neville stared at her, quite speechless for a while. She looked calmly back at him. Her window panorama had been changed again. One of them now showed the Earth, a little more than half full.

Finally, he said, "Why?"

She said, "It was an accident, really, I saw the point and I was too enthusiastic not to speak. I should have told you days ago but I was afraid your reaction would be exactly what it is."

"So he knows. You *fool!*"

She frowned. "What does he know? Only what he would have guessed sooner or later—that I'm not really a tourist guide—that I'm your Intuitionist. An Intuitionist who knows no mathematics, for heaven's sake. So what if he knows that? What does it matter if I have intuition? How many times have you told me that my intuition has no value till it is backed by mathematical rigor and experimental observation? How many times have you told me that the most compelling intuition could be wrong? Well, then, what value will he place on mere Intuitionism?"

Neville grew white, but Selene couldn't tell whether that was out of anger or apprehension. He said, "You're different. Hasn't your intuition always proved right? When you were sure of it?"

"Ah, but he doesn't know that, does he?"

"He'll guess it. He'll see Gottstein."

"What will he tell Gottstein? He still has no idea of what we're really after."

"Doesn't he?"

"No." She had stood up, walked away. Now she turned to him and shouted, "*No!* It's cheap of you to imply that I would betray you and the rest. If you don't accept my integrity then accept my common sense. There's no point in telling them. What's the use of it to them, or to us, if we're all going to be destroyed?"

"Oh, please, Selene!" Neville waved his hand in disgust. "Not that."

"No. You listen. He talked to me and described his work. You hide me like a secret weapon. You tell me that I'm more valuable than any instrument or any ordinary scientist. You play your games of conspiracy, insisting that everyone must continue to think me a tourist guide and nothing more so that my great talents will always be available to the Lunarites. To *you*. And what do you accomplish?"

"We have you, haven't we? How long do you suppose you would have remained free, if they—"

"You keep saying things like that. But who's been imprisoned? Who's been stopped? Where is the evidence of the great conspiracy you see all around you? The Earthmen keep you and your team from their large instruments much more because you goad them into it than out of any malice on their part. And that's done us good, rather than harm, since it's forced us to invent other instruments that are more subtle."

"Based on *your* theoretical insight, Selene."

Selene smiled. "I know. Ben was very complimentary about them."

"You and your Ben. What the *hell* do you want with that miserable Earthie?"

"He's an Immigrant. And what I want is information. Do you give me any? You're so damned afraid I'll be caught, you don't dare let me be seen talking to any physicist; only you, and you're my— For that reason only, probably."

"Now, Selene." He tried to manage a soothing tone, but there was far too much impatience to it.

"No, I don't care about that really. You've told me I have this one task and I've tried to concentrate on it and sometimes I think I have it, mathematics or not. I can visualize it; the kind of thing that must be done—and then it slips away. But what's the use of it, when the Pump will destroy us all anyway. . . . Haven't I told you I distrusted the exchange of field intensities?"

Neville said, "I'll ask you again. Are you ready to tell me that the Pump *will* destroy us? Never mind might, never mind 'could'; never mind anything but 'will.' "

Selene shook her head angrily. "I can't. It's so marginal. I can't say it will. But isn't a simple 'might' sufficient in such a case?"

"Oh, Lord."

"Don't turn up your eyes. Don't *sneer!* You've never tested the matter. I told you how it might be tested."

"You were never this worried about it till you started listening to this Earthie of yours."

"He's an Immigrant. Aren't you going to test it?"

"No! I told you your suggestions were impractical. You're not an experimentalist, and what looks good in your mind doesn't necessarily work in the real world of instruments, of randomness, and of uncertainty."

"The so-called real world of your *laboratory*." Her face

was flushed and angry and she held her clenched fists at chin-level. "You waste so much time trying to get a vacuum good enough—There's a vacuum up there, up *there* on the surface where I'm pointing, with temperatures that, at times, are halfway down toward absolute zero. Why don't you try experiments on the surface?"

"It would have been useless."

"How do you *know?* You just won't try. Ben Denison tried. He took the trouble to devise a system he could use on the surface and he set it up when he went to inspect the Solar batteries. He wanted you to come and you wouldn't. Do you remember? It was a very simple thing, something even I could describe to you now that it's been described to me. He ran it at day-temperatures and again at night-temperatures and that was enough to guide him to a new line of research with the Pionizer."

"How simple you make it sound."

"How simple it *is*. Once he found out I was an Intuitionist, he talked to me as you never did. He explained his reasons for thinking that the strengthening of the strong nuclear interaction is indeed accumulating catastrophically in the neighborhood of Earth. It will only be a few years before the Sun explodes and sends the strengthening, in ripples—"

"No, no, no, *no*," shouted Neville. "I've seen his results and I'm not impressed."

"You've *seen* them?"

"Yes, of course. Do you suppose I let him work in our laboratories without making sure I know what he's doing? I've seen his results and they're worth *nothing*. He deals with tiny deviations that are well within the experimental error. If he wants to believe that those deviations have significance and if you want to believe them, go ahead. But no amount of belief will make them have that significance if, in fact, they don't."

"What do *you* want to believe, Barron?"

"I want the truth."

"But haven't you decided in advance what the truth must be by your own gospel? You want the Pump Station of the Moon, don't you, so that you need have nothing to do with the surface; and anything that might prevent that is not the truth—by definition."

"I won't argue with you. I want the Pump Station, and even more—I want the other. One's no good without the other. Are you sure you haven't—"

"I *haven't*."

"Will you?"

Selene whirled on him again, her feet tapping rapidly on the ground in such a way as to keep her bobbing in the air to the tune of an angry clatter.

"I won't tell him anything," she said, "but I must have more information. You have no information for me, but he may have; or he may get it with the experiments you won't do. I've got to talk to him and find out what he is going to find out. If you get between him and me, you'll never have what you want. And you needn't fear his getting it before I do. He's too used to Earth thinking; he won't make that last step. I will."

"All right. And don't forget the difference between Earth and Moon, either. This is your world; you have no other. This man, Denison, this Ben, this *Immigrant,* having come from Earth to the Moon, can, if he chooses, return from Moon to Earth. You can never go to the Earth; never. You are a Lunarite forever."

"A Moon-maiden," said Selene, derisively.

"No maiden," said Neville. "Though you may have to wait a long while before I confirm the matter once again."

She seemed unmoved at that.

He said, "And about this big danger of explosion. If the risk involved in changing the basic constants of a Universe is so great, why haven't the para-men, who are so far advanced beyond us in technology, stopped Pumping?"

And he left.

She faced the closed door with bunched jaw muscles. Then she said, "Because conditions are different for them and for us, you incredible jerk." But she was speaking to herself; he was gone.

She kicked the lever that let down her bed, threw herself into it and seethed. How much closer was she now to the real object for which Barron and those others had now been aiming for years?

No closer.

Energy! Everyone searched for energy! The magic word! The cornucopia! The one key to universal plenty! . . . And yet energy wasn't all.

If one found energy, one could find the other, too. If one found the key to energy, the key to the other would be obvious. She *knew* the key to the other would be obvious if she could but grasp some subtle point that would appear obvious the moment it was grasped. (Good heavens, she had been so infected by Barron's chronic suspicion that even in her thoughts she was calling it "the other.")

No Earthman would get that subtle point because no Earthman had reason to look for it.

Ben Denison would find it for her, then, without finding it for himself.

Except that— If the Universe was to be destroyed, what did anything matter?

12

Denison tried to beat down his self-consciousness. Time and again, he made a groping motion as though to hitch upward the pants he wasn't wearing. He wore only sandals and the barest of briefs, which were uncomfortably tight. And, of course, he carried the blanket.

Selene, who was similarly accoutered, laughed. "Now, Ben, there's nothing wrong with your bare body, barring a certain flabbiness. It's perfectly in fashion here. In fact, take off your briefs if they're binding you."

"No!" muttered Denison. He shifted the blanket so that it draped over his abdomen and she snatched it from him.

She said, "Now give me that thing. What kind of a Lunarite will you make if you bring your Earth puritanism here? You *know* that prudery is only the other side of prurience. The words are even on the same page in the dictionary."

"I have to get used to it, Selene."

"You might start by looking at me once in awhile, without having your glance slide off me as though I were coated with oil. You look at other women quite efficiently, I notice."

"If I look at you—"

"Then you'll seem too interested and you'll be embarrassed. But if you look hard, you'll get used to it, and you'll stop noticing. Look, I'll stand still and you stare. I'll take off my briefs."

Denison groaned, "Selene, there are people all around and you're making intolerable fun of me. Please keep walking and let me get used to the situation."

"All right, but I hope you notice the people who pass us don't look at us."

"They don't look at *you*. They look at me all right. They've probably never seen so old-looking and ill-shaped a person."

"They probably haven't," agreed Selene, cheerfully, "but they'll just have to get used to it."

Denison walked on in misery, conscious of every gray hair on his chest and of every quiver of his paunch. It was only when the passageway thinned out and the people passing them were fewer in number that he began to feel a certain relief.

He looked about him curiously now, not as aware of Selene's conical breasts as he had been, nor of her smooth thighs. The corridor seemed endless.

"How far have we come?" he asked.

"Are you tired?" Selene was contrite. "We could have taken a scooter. I forget you're from Earth."

"I should hope you do. Isn't that the ideal for an immigrant? I'm not the least bit tired. Hardly the least bit tired at any rate. What I am is a little cold."

"Purely your imagination, Ben," said Selene, firmly. "You just think you ought to feel cold because so much of you is bare. Put it out of your head."

"Easy to say," he sighed. "I'm walking well, I hope."

"Very well. I'll have you kangarooing yet."

"And participating in glider races down the surface slopes. Remember, I'm moderately advanced in years. But really, how far have we come?"

"Two miles, I should judge."

"Good Lord! How many miles of corridors are there altogether?"

"I'm afraid I don't know. The residential corridors make up comparatively little of the total. There are the mining corridors, the geological ones, the industrial, the mycological. . . . I'm sure there must be several hundred miles altogether."

"Do you have maps?"

"Of course there are maps. We can't work blind."

"I mean you, personally."

"Well, no, not with me, but I don't need maps for this area; it's quite familiar to me. I used to wander about here as a child. These are old corridors. Most of the new corridors—and we average two or three miles of new corridors a year, I think—are in the north. I couldn't work my way through them, without a map, for untold sums. Maybe not even with a map."

"Where are we heading?"

"I promised you an unusual sight—no, not me, so don't say it—and you'll have it. It's the Moon's most unusual mine and it's completely off the ordinary tourist trails."

"Don't tell me you've got diamonds on the Moon?"

"Better than that."

The corridor walls were unfinished here—gray rock, dimly but adequately lit by patches of electroluminescence. The temperature was comfortable and at a steady mildness, with ventilation so gently effective there was no sensation of wind. It was hard to tell here that a couple of hundred feet above was a surface subjected to alternate frying and freezing as the Sun came and went on its grand biweekly swing from horizon to horizon and then underneath and back.

"Is all this airtight?" asked Denison, suddenly uncomfortably aware that he was not far below the bottom of an ocean of vacuum that extended upward through all infinity.

"Oh, yes. Those walls are impervious. They're all booby-trapped, too. If the air pressure drops as much as ten per cent in any section of the corridors there is such a hooting and howling from sirens as you have never heard and such a flashing of arrows and blazing of signs directing you to safety as you have never seen."

"How often does this happen?"

"Not often. I don't think anyone has been killed through air-lack for at least five years." Then, with sudden defensiveness, "You have natural catastrophes on Earth. A big quake or a tidal wave can kill thousands."

"No argument, Selene." He threw up his hands. "I surrender."

"All right," she said. "I didn't mean to get excited. . . . Do you hear that?"

She stopped, in an attitude of listening.

Denison listened, too, and shook his head. Suddenly, he looked around. "It's so quiet. Where is everybody? Are you sure we're not lost?"

"This isn't a natural cavern with unknown passageways. You have those on Earth, haven't you? I've seen photographs."

"Yes, most of them are limestone caves, formed by water. That certainly can't be the case of the Moon, can it?"

"So we can't be lost," said Selene, smiling. "If we're alone, put it down to superstition."

"To what?" Denison looked startled and his face creased in an expression of disbelief.

"Don't do that," she said. "You get all lined. That's right. Smooth out. You look much better than you did when you first arrived, you know. That's low gravity and exercise."

"And trying to keep up with nude young ladies who have an uncommon amount of off-time and an uncommon lack of better things to do than to go on busmen's holidays."

"Now you're treating me like a tourist guide again, and I'm not nude."

"At that, even nudity is less frightening than Intuitionism. . . . But what's this about superstition?"

"Not really superstition, I suppose, but most of the people of the city tend to stay away from this part of the corridor-complex."

"But why?"

"Because of what I'm going to show you." They were walking again. "Hear it now?"

She stopped and Denison listened anxiously. He said, "You mean that small tapping sound? Tap—tap— Is that what you mean?"

She ran ahead in slow, loping strides with the slow-motion movement of the Lunarite in unhurried flight. He followed her, attempting to ape the gait.

"Here—here—"

Denison's eye followed Selene's eagerly pointing finger. "Good Lord," he said. "Where's it coming from?"

There was a drip of what was clearly water. A slow dripping, with each drip striking a small ceramic trough that led into the rock wall.

"From the rocks. We do have water on the Moon, you know. Most of it we can bake out of gypsum; enough for our purposes, since we conserve it pretty well."

"I know. I know. I've never yet been able to manage one complete shower. How you people manage to stay clean I don't know."

"I *told* you. First, wet yourself. Then turn off the water and smear just a little detergent on you. You rub it— Oh, Ben, I'm not going through it yet again. And there's nothing on the Moon to get you all that dirty anyway. . . . But that's not what we're talking about. In one or two places there are actually water deposits, usually as ice near the surface in a mountain shadow. If we locate it, it drips out. This one has been dripping since the corridor was first driven through, and that was eight years ago."

"But why the superstition?"

"Well, obviously, water is the great material resource

on which the Moon depends. We drink it, wash with it, grow our food with it, make our oxygen with it, keep everything going with it. Free water can't help but get a lot of respect. Once this drip was discovered, plans to extend the tunnels in this direction were abandoned till it stopped. The corridor walls were even left unfinished."

"That sounds like superstition right there."

"Well—a kind of awe, maybe. It wasn't expected to last for more than a few months; such drips never do. Well, after this one had passed its first anniversary, it began to seem eternal. In fact, that's what it's called: 'The Eternal.' You'll even find it marked that way on the maps. Naturally people have come to attach importance to it; a feeling that if it stops it will mean some sort of bad fortune."

Denison laughed.

Selene said, warmly, "No one *really* believes it, but everyone part-believes it. You see, it's not really eternal and it must stop some time. As a matter of fact, the rate of drip is only about a third of what it was when it was first discovered, so that it is slowly drying. I imagine people feel that if it happened to stop when they were actually here, they would share in the bad fortune. At least, that's the rational way of explaining their reluctance to come here."

"I take it that you don't believe this."

"Whether I believe it or not isn't the point. You see I'm quite certain that it won't stop sharply enough for anyone to be able to take the blame. It will just drip slower and slower and slower and no one will ever be able to pinpoint the exact time when it stopped. So why worry?"

"I agree with you."

"I do, however," she said, making the transition smoothly, "have other worries, and I'd like to discuss them with you while we're alone." She spread out the blanket and sat on it, cross-legged.

"Which is why you really brought me here?" He dropped to hip and elbow, facing her.

She said, "See, you can look at me easily now. You're getting used to me. . . . And, really, there were surely times on Earth when near nudity wasn't something to be exclaimed over."

"Times and places," agreed Denison, "but not since the passing of the Crisis. In my lifetime——"

"Well, on the Moon, do as the Lunarites do is a good enough guide for behavior."

"Are you going to tell me why you really brought me here? Or shall I suspect you of planning seduction?"

"I could carry through seduction quite comfortably at home, thank you. This is different. The surface would have been best, but getting ready to go out on the surface would have attracted a great deal of attention. Coming here didn't, and this place is the only spot in town where we can be reasonably safe from interruption." She hesitated.

"Well?" said Denison.

"Barron is angry. Very angry, in fact."

"I'm not surprised. I warned you he would be if you told him that I knew you were an Intuitionist. Why did you feel it so necessary to tell him?"

"Because it is difficult to keep things for long from my —companion. Probably, though, he doesn't consider me that any longer."

"I'm sorry."

"Oh, it was turning sour anyway. It's lasted long enough. What bothers me more—much more—is that he violently refuses to accept your interpretation of the Pionizer experiments you ran after the surface observations."

"I told you the way it would be."

"He said he had seen your results."

"He glanced at them and grunted."

"It's rather disillusioning. Does everyone just believe what he wants to?"

"As long as possible. Sometimes longer."

"What about you?"

"You mean, am I human? Certainly. I don't believe I'm really old. I believe I'm quite attractive. I believe you seek out my company because you think I'm charming—even when you insist on turning the conversation to physics."

"No! I mean it!"

"Well, I suspect Neville told you that the data I had gathered were not significant beyond the margin of error, which makes them doubtful, and that's true enough. . . . And yet I prefer to believe they have the meaning I expected them to have to begin with."

"Just because you want to believe that?"

"Not *just* because. Look at it this way. Suppose there is no harm in the Pump, but that I insist on thinking there *is* harm. In that case, I will turn out to be a fool and my scientific reputation will be badly damaged. But I *am* a fool in the eyes of the people who count, and I have no scientific reputation."

"Why is that, Ben? You've hinted around the tale several times. Can't you tell me the whole story?"

"You'd be surprised how little there is to tell. At the age of twenty-five I was still such a child that I had to amuse myself by insulting a fool for no reason other than that he was a fool. Since his folly was not his fault, I was the greater fool to do it. My insult drove him to heights he couldn't possibly have scaled otherwise—"

"You're talking of Hallam?"

"Yes, of course. And as he rose, I fell. And eventually, it dropped me to—the Moon."

"Is that so bad?"

"No, I rather think it's good. So let's say he did me a favor, long-way round. . . . And let's get back to what I'm talking about. I've just explained that if I believe the Pump to be harmful and am wrong, I lose nothing. On the other hand, if I believe the Pump to be harmless and am wrong, I will be helping to destroy the world. To be sure, I've lived most of my life already and I suppose I can argue myself into believing that I have no great cause to love humanity. However, only a few people have hurt me, and if I hurt everyone in return that is unconscionable usury.

"Then, too, if you'd rather have a less noble reason, Selene, consider my daughter. Just before I left for the Moon, she had applied for permission to have a child. She'll probably get it and before long I'll be—if you don't mind my saying so—a grandfather. Somehow I'd like to see my grandchild have a normal life expectancy. So I prefer to believe the Pump is dangerous and to act on that belief."

Selene said, intensely, "But here's my point. Is the Pump dangerous or is it not? I mean, the truth, and not what anyone wants to believe."

"I should ask *you* that. You're the Intuitionist. What does your intuition say?"

"But that's what bothers me, Ben. I can't make it really certain either way. I tend to feel the Pump is harmful, but maybe that's because I want to believe that."

"All right. Maybe you do. Why?"

Selene smiled ruefully and shrugged her shoulders. "It would be fun for Barron to be wrong. When he thinks he's certain, he's so *vituperatively* certain."

"I know. You want to see his face when he's forced to back down. I'm well aware of how intense such a desire can be. For instance, if the Pump *were* dangerous and I could prove it, I might conceivably be hailed as the savior of humanity, and yet I swear that I'd be more interested in the look on Hallam's face. I'm not proud of that feeling so I suspect that what I'll do is insist on an equal share of the credit with Lamont, who deserves it after all, and confine my pleasure to watching Lamont's face when *he* watches Hallam's face. The pettishness will then be one place removed. . . . But I'm beginning to speak nonsense. . . . Selene?"

"Yes, Ben?"

"When did you find out you were an Intuitionist?"

"I don't quite know."

"You took physics in college, I imagine."

"Oh, yes. Some math, too, but I was never good at that. Come to think of it, I wasn't particularly good in physics, either. I used to guess the answers when I was desperate; you know, guess what I was supposed to do to get the right answers. Very often, it worked and then I would be asked to explain why I had done what I did and I couldn't do that very well. They suspected me of cheating but could never prove it."

"They didn't suspect Intuitionism?"

"I don't think so. But then, I didn't either. Until—well, one of my first sex-mates was a physicist. In fact, he was the father of my child, assuming he really supplied the sperm-sample. He had a physics problem and he told me about it when we were lying in bed afterward, just to have something to talk about, I suppose. And I said, 'You know what it sounds like to me?' and told him. He tried it just for the fun of it, he said, and it worked. In fact, that was the first step to the Pionizer, which you said was much better than the proton synchrotron."

"You mean that was *your* idea?" Denison put his finger under the dripping water and paused as he was about to put it in his mouth. "Is this water safe?"

"It's perfectly sterile," said Selene, "and it goes into the general reservoir for treatment. It's saturated with sulfates, carbonates, and a few other items, however. You won't like the taste."

Denison rubbed his finger on his briefs. "*You* invented the Pionizer?"

"Not invented. I had the original concept. It took lots of development, mostly by Barron."

Denison shook his head. "You know, Selene, you're an amazing phenomenon. You should be under observation by the molecular biologists."

"Should I? That's not my idea of a thrill."

"About half a century ago, there came the climax to the big trend toward genetic engineering—"

"I know. It flopped and was thrown out of court. It's illegal now—that whole type of study—insofar as research can be made illegal. I know people who've done work on it just the same."

"I dare say. On Intuitionism?"

"No. I don't think so."

"Ah. But that's my point. At the height of the push for genetic engineering, there was this attempt to stimulate Intuitionism. Almost all the great scientists had intuitive ability, of course, and there was the feeling that this was the single great key to creativity. One could argue that superior capacity for intuition was the product of a particular gene combination and there were all sorts of speculations as to which gene combination that was."

"I suspect that there are many possible types that would satisfy."

"And I suspect that if you are consulting your intuition here, you are correct. But there were also those who insisted that one gene, or one small related group of genes, was of particular importance to the combination so that you might speak of an Intuition Gene. . . . Then the whole thing collapsed."

"As I said."

"But before it collapsed," Denison went on, "there had been attempts to alter genes to increase the intensity of Intuitionism and there were those who insisted that some success had been achieved. The altered genes entered the gene pool, I'm positive, and if you happened to inherit— Were any of your grandparents involved in the program?"

"Not as far as I know," said Selene, "but I can't rule it out. One of them might have been, for all I can say. . . . If you don't mind, I'm not going to investigate the matter. I don't want to know."

"Perhaps not. The whole field grew fearfully unpopular with the general public and anyone who can be considered the product of genetic engineering would not exactly be greeted gladly. . . . Intuitionism, they said, for instance, was inseparable from certain undesirable characteristics."

"Well, thank you."

"*They* said. To possess intuition is to inspire a certain envy and enmity in others. Even as gentle and saint-like an Intuitionist as Michael Faraday aroused the envy and hatred of Humphry Davy. Who's to say that it doesn't take a certain flaw in character to be capable of arousing envy. And in your case—"

Selene said, "Surely, I don't rouse your envy and hatred?"

"I don't think so. What about Neville, though?"

Selene was silent.

Denison said, "By the time you got to Neville, you were well-known as an Intuitionist, I suppose."

"Not *well* known, I would say. Some physicists suspected it, I'm sure. However, they don't like to give up credit here any more than on Earth, and I suppose they convinced themselves, more or less, that whatever I had said to them was just a meaningless guess. But Barron knew, of course."

"I see." Denison paused.

Selene's lips twitched. "Somehow I get the feeling that you want to say: 'Oh, *that's* why he bothers with you.'"

"No, of course not, Selene. You're quite attractive enough to be desired for your own sake."

"I think so, too, but every little bit helps and Barron was bound to be interested in my Intuitionism. Why shouldn't he be? Only he insisted I keep my job as tourist guide. He said I was an important natural resource of the Moon and he didn't want Earth monopolizing me the way they monopolized the synchrotron."

"An odd thought. But perhaps it was that the fewer who knew of your Intuitionism, the fewer would suspect your contribution to what would otherwise be put to his sole credit."

"Now you sound like Barron himself!"

"Do I? And is it possible he gets rather annoyed with you when your Intuitionism is working particularly well."

Selene shrugged. "Barron is a suspicious man. We all have our faults."

"Is it wise to be alone with me, then?"

Selene said, sharply, "Now don't get hurt because I defend him. He doesn't really suspect the possibility of sexual misbehavior between us. You're from Earth. In fact, I might as well tell you he encourages our companionship. He thinks I can learn from you."

"And have you?" asked Denison, coldly.

"I have. . . . Yet though that may be *his* chief reason for encouraging our friendship, it isn't mine."

"What's yours?"

"As you well know," said Selene, "and as you want to hear me say, I enjoy your company. Otherwise, I could get what I want in considerably less time."

"All right, Selene. Friends?"

"Friends! Absolutely."

"What have you learned from me, then? May I know?"

"That would take awhile to explain. You know that the reason we can't set up a Pump Station anywhere we want to is that we can't locate the para-Universe, even though they can locate us. That might be because they are much more intelligent or much more technologically advanced than we are——"

"Not necessarily the same thing," muttered Denison.

"I know. That's why I put in the 'or.' But it might also be that we are neither particularly stupid nor particularly backward. It might be something as simple as the fact that they offer the harder target. If the strong nuclear interaction is stronger in the para-Universe, they'd be bound to have much smaller Suns and, very likely, much smaller planets. Their individual world would be harder to locate than ours would be.

"Or then again," she went on, "suppose it's the electromagnetic field they detect. The electromagnetic field of a planet is much larger than the planet itself and is much easier to locate. And that would mean that while they can detect the Earth, they can't detect the Moon, which has no electromagnetic field to speak of. That's why, perhaps, we've failed to set up a Pump Station on the Moon. And, if their small planets lack a significant electromagnetic field, we can't locate them."

Denison said, "It's an attractive thought."

"Next, consider the inter-Universal exchange in properties that serves to weaken their strong nuclear interaction, cooling their Suns, while strengthening ours, heating and exploding our Suns. What might that imply? Suppose they can collect energy one-way without our help but only at ruinously low efficiencies. Under ordinary circumstances that would therefore be utterly impractical. They would need us to help direct concentrated energy in their direction by supplying tungsten-186 to them and accepting plutonium-186 in return. But suppose our Galactic arm implodes into a quasar. That would produce an energy concentration in the neighborhood of the Solar system enormously greater than now exists and one that might persist for over a million years.

"Once that quasar forms, even a ruinously low efficiency becomes sufficient. It wouldn't matter to them, therefore, whether we are destroyed or not. In fact, we might argue that it would be safer for them if we did explode. Until we do, we might end the Pump for any of a variety of reasons and they would be helpless to start it again. After the explosion, they are home free; no one could interfere. . . . And that's why people who say, 'If the Pump is dangerous, why don't those terribly clever para-men stop it?' don't know what they're talking about."

"Did Neville give you that argument?"

"Yes, he did."

"But the para-Sun would keep cooling down, wouldn't it?"

"What does that matter?" said Selene, impatiently. "With the Pump, they wouldn't be dependent on their Sun for anything."

Denison took a deep breath. "You can't possibly know this, Selene, but there was a rumor on Earth that Lamont received a message from the para-men to the effect that the Pump was dangerous, but that they couldn't stop it. No one took it seriously, of course, but suppose it's true. Suppose Lamont did receive such a message. Might it be that some of the para-men were humanitarian enough to wish not to destroy a world with cooperating intelligences upon it, and were prevented by the opposition of an oh-so-practical majority?"

Selene nodded. "I suppose that's possible. . . . All this I knew, or rather, intuited, before you came on the scene. But then you said that nothing between one and the infinite made any sense. Remember?"

"Of course."

"All right. The differences between our Universe and the para-Universe lie so obviously in the strong nuclear interaction that so far it's all that's been studied. But there is more than one interaction; there are four. In addition to the strong nuclear, there is the electromagnetic, the weak nuclear, and the gravitational, with intensity ratios of $130:1:10^{-10}:10^{-42}$. But if four, why not an infinite number, with all the others too weak to be detectable or to influence our Universe in any way."

Denison said, "If an interaction is too weak to be detectable or to exert influence in any way, then by any operational definition, it doesn't exist."

"In *this* Universe," said Selene, with a snap. "Who knows what does or does not exist in the para-Universe? With an infinite number of possible interactions, each of which can vary infinitely in intensity compared to any one of them taken as standard, the number of different possible Universes that can exist is infinite."

"Possibly the infinity of the continuum; aleph-one, rather than aleph-null."

Selene frowned. "What does that mean?"

"It's not important. Go on."

Selene said, "Instead, then, of trying to work with the one para-Universe that has impinged itself on us and which may not suit our needs at all, why don't we instead try to work out which Universe, out of all the infinite possibilities, best suits us, and is most easily located. Let us *design* a Universe, for after all whatever we design must exist, and search for it."

Denison smiled. "Selene, I've thought of exactly the same thing. And while there's no law that states I can't be completely wrong, it's very unlikely that anyone as brilliant as myself can be completely wrong when anyone as brilliant as yourself comes to exactly the same conclusion independently. . . . Do you know what?"

"What?" asked Selene.

"I'm beginning to like your damned Moon food. Or getting used to it, anyway. Let's go back home and eat, and then we can start working out our plans. . . . And you know what else?"

"What?"

"As long as we'll be working together, how about one kiss—as experimentalist to intuitionist."

Selene considered. She said, "We've both of us kissed and been kissed a good many times, I suppose. How about doing it as man to woman?"

"I think I can manage that. But what do I do so as not to be clumsy about it? What are the Moon-rules for kissing?"

"Follow instinct," said Selene, casually.

Carefully, Denison placed his arms behind his back and leaned toward Selene. Then, after a while, he placed his arms behind her back.

13

"And then I actually kissed him back," said Selene, thoughtfully.

"Oh, did you?" said Barron Neville, harshly. "Well, that's valor beyond the call of duty."

"I don't know. It wasn't that bad. In fact," (and she smiled) "he was rather touching about it. He was afraid he would be clumsy and began by putting his arms behind his back so that he wouldn't crush me, I suppose."

"Spare me the details."

"Why, what the hell do you care?" she fired up, suddenly. "You're Mister Platonic, aren't you?"

"Do you want it differently? Now?"

"You needn't perform to order."

"But *you* had better. When do you expect to give us what we need?"

"As soon as I can," she said, tonelessly.

"Without his knowing?"

"He's interested only in energy."

"And in saving the world," mocked Neville. "And in being a hero. And in showing everybody. And in kissing you."

"He admits to all that. What do you admit to?"

"Impatience," said Neville, angrily. "Lots of impatience."

14

"I am glad," said Denison, deliberately, "that the daytime is over." He held out his right arm and stared at it, encased in its protective layers. "The Lunar Sun is one thing I can't get used to and don't want to get used to. Even this suit seems a natural thing to me in comparison."

"What's wrong with the Sun?" asked Selene.

"Don't tell me you like it, Selene!"

"No, of course not. I hate it. But then I never see it. You're an— You're used to the Sun."

"Not the way it is here on the Moon. It shines out of a black sky here. It dazzles the stars away, instead of muffling them. It is hot, hard, and dangerous. It is an enemy, and while it's in the sky, I can't help but feel that none of our attempts at reducing field intensity will succeed."

"That's superstition, Ben," said Selene, with a distant edge of exasperation. "The Sun has nothing to do with it. We were in the crater shadow anyway and it was just like night. Stars and all."

"Not quite," said Denison. "Anytime we looked northward, Selene, we could see that stretch of Sunlight glittering. I hated to look northward, yet the direction dragged at my eyes. Every time I looked at it I could feel the hard ultraviolet springing at my viewplate."

"That's imagination. In the first place there's no ultraviolet to speak of in reflected light; in the second, your suit protects you against radiation."

"Not against heat. Not very much."

"But it's night now."

"Yes," said Denison with satisfaction, "and this I like." He looked about with a continuing wonder. Earth was in the sky, of course, in its accustomed place; a fat crescent, now, bellying to the southwestward. The constellation

259

Orion was above it, a hunter rising up out of the brilliant curved chair of Earth. The horizon glittered in the dim crescent-Earth light.

"It's beautiful," he said. Then: "Selene, is the Pionizer showing anything?"

Selene, who was looking at the skies with no comment, stepped toward the maze of equipment that, over the past three alternations of day and night, had been assembled there in the shadow of the crater.

"Not yet," she said, "but that's good news really. The field intensity is holding at just over fifty."

"Not low enough," said Denison.

Selene said, "It can be lowered further. I'm sure that all the parameters are suitable."

"The magnetic field, too?"

"I'm not sure about the magnetic field."

"If we strengthen that, the whole thing becomes unstable."

"It shouldn't. I know it shouldn't."

"Selene, I trust your intuition against everything but the facts. It *does* get unstable. We've tried it."

"I know, Ben. But not quite with this geometry. It's been holding to fifty-two a phenomenally long time. Surely, if we begin to hold it there for hours instead of minutes, we ought to be able to strengthen the magnetic field tenfold for a period of minutes instead of seconds. . . . Let's try."

"Not yet," said Denison.

Selene hesitated, then stepped back, turning away. She said, "You still don't miss Earth, do you, Ben?"

"No. It's rather odd, but I don't. I would have thought it inevitable that I miss blue sky, green earth, flowing water—all the cliché adjective-noun combinations peculiar to Earth. I miss none of them. I don't even dream about them."

Selene said, "This sort of thing does happen sometime. At least, there are Immies who say they experience no homesickness. They're in the minority, of course, and no one has ever been able to decide what this minority has in common. Guesses run all the way from serious emotional deficiency, no capacity to feel anything; to serious emotional excess, a fear to admit homesickness lest it lead to breakdown."

"In my case, I think it's plain enough. Life on Earth was not very enjoyable for two decades and more, while here I work at last in a field I have made my own. And I have your help. . . . More than that, Selene, I have your company."

"You are kind," said Selene, gravely, "to place company and help in the relationship you do. You don't seem to need much help. Do you pretend to seek it for the sake of my company?"

Denison laughed softly. "I'm not sure which answer would flatter you more."

"Try the truth."

"The truth is not so easy to determine when I value each so much." He turned back to the Pionizer. "The field intensity still holds, Selene."

Selene's faceplate glinted in the Earthlight. She said, "Barron says that non-homesickness is natural and the sign of a healthy mind. He says that though the human body was adapted to Earth's surface and requires adjustment to the Moon, the human brain was not and does not. The human brain is so different, qualitatively, from all other brains that it can be considered a new phenomenon. It has had no time to be really fixed to Earth's surface and can, without adjustment, fit other environments. He says that enclosure in the caverns of the Moon may actually suit it best of all, for that is but a larger version of its enclosure in the cavern of the skull."

"Do you believe that?" asked Denison, amused.

"When Barron talks, he can make things sound very plausible."

"I think it can be made equally plausible to claim that the comfort to be found in the caverns of the Moon is the result of the fulfillment of the return-to-the-womb fantasy. In fact," he added, thoughtfully, "considering the controlled temperature and pressure, the nature and digestibility of the food, I could make a good case for considering the Lunar colony—I beg your pardon, Selene—the Lunar city a deliberate reconstruction of the fetal environment."

Selene said, "I don't think Barron would agree with you for a minute."

"I'm sure he wouldn't," said Denison. He looked at the Earth-crescent, watching the distant cloud banks on edge. He fell into silence, absorbed in the view, and even though Selene moved back to the Pionizer, he remained in place.

He watched Earth in its nest of stars and looked toward the serrated horizon where, every once in a while, it seemed to him he saw a puff of smoke where a small meteorite might be landing.

He had pointed out a similar phenomenon, with some concern, to Selene during the previous Lunar night. She had been unconcerned.

She said, "The Earth does shift slightly in the sky because of the Moon's libration and every once in a while a shaft of Earth-light tops a small rise and falls on a bit of soil beyond. It comes into view like a tiny puff of rising dust. It's common. We pay no attention."

Denison had said, "But it could be a meteorite sometimes. Don't meteorites ever strike?"

"Of course they do. You're probably hit by several every time you're out. Your suit protects you."

"I don't mean micro-dust particles. I mean sizable meteorites that would really kick up the dust. Meteorites that could kill you."

"Well, they fall, too, but they are few and the Moon is large. No one has been hit yet."

And as Denison watched the sky and thought of that, he saw what, in the midst of his momentary preoccupation, he took to be a meteorite. Light streaking through the sky could, however, be a meteorite only on Earth with its atmosphere and not on the airless Moon.

The light in the sky was man-made and Denison had not yet sorted out his impressions when it became, quite clearly, a small rocket-vessel sinking rapidly to a landing beside him.

A single suited figure emerged, while a pilot remained within, barely seen as a dark splotch against the highlights.

Denison waited. The etiquette of the spacesuit required the newcomer joining any group to announce himself first.

"Commissioner Gottstein here," the new voice said, "as you can probably tell from my wobble."

"Ben Denison here," said Denison.

"Yes. I thought as much."

"Have you come here looking for me?"

"Certainly."

"In a space-skipper? You might—"

"I might," said Gottstein, "have used Outlet P-4, which is less than a thousand yards from here. Yes, indeed. But I wasn't looking only for you."

"Well, I won't ask for the meaning of what you say."

"There's no reason for me to be coy. Surely you have not expected me to be uninterested in the fact that you have been carrying on experiments on the Lunar surface."

"It's been no secret and anyone might be interested."

"Yet no one seems to know the details of the experiments. Except, of course, that in some way you are working on matters concerning the Electron Pump."

"It's a reasonable assumption."

"Is it? It seemed to me that experiments of such a nature, to have any value at all, would require a rather enormous setup. This is not of my own knowledge, you understand. I consulted those who would know. And, it is quite obvious, you are not working on such a setup. It occurred to me, therefore, that you might not be the proper focus of my interest. While my attention was drawn to you, others might be undertaking more important tasks."

"Why should I be used as distraction?"

"I don't know. If I knew, I would be less concerned."

"So I have been under observation."

Gottstein chuckled. "That, yes. Since you have arrived. But while you have been working here on the surface, we have observed this entire region for miles in every direction. Oddly enough, it would seem that you, Dr. Denison, and your companion, are the only ones on the Lunar surface for any but the most routine of purposes."

"Why is that odd?"

"Because it means that you really think you're doing

something with your gimcrack contraption, whatever it is. I can't believe that you are incompetent, so I think it would be worth listening to you if you tell me what you are doing."

"I am experimenting in para-physics, Commissioner, precisely as rumor has it. To which I can add that so far my experiments have been only partly successful."

"Your companion is, I imagine, Selene Lindstrom L., a tourist guide."

"Yes."

"An unusual choice as an assistant."

"She is intelligent, eager, interested, and extremely attractive."

"And willing to work with an Earthman?"

"And quite willing to work with an Immigrant who will be a Lunar citizen as soon as he qualifies for that status."

Selene was approaching now. Her voice rang in their ears. "Good day, Commissioner. I would have liked not to overhear, and intrude on a private conversation, but, in a spacesuit, overhearing is inevitable anywhere within the horizon."

Gottstein turned. "Hello, Miss Lindstrom. I did not expect to talk in secrecy. Are you interested in para-physics?"

"Oh, yes."

"You are not disheartened by the failures of the experiment."

"They are not entirely failures," she said. "They are less a failure than Dr. Denison thinks at present."

"What?" Denison turned sharply on his heel, nearly overbalancing himself and sending out a spurt of dust.

All three were facing the Pionizer now, and above it, just about five feet above it, light shone like a fat star.

Selene said, "I raised the intensity of the magnetic field, and the nuclear field remained stable in being—then eased further and further and—"

"Leaked!" Denison said. "Damn it. I didn't see it happen."

Selene said, "I'm sorry, Ben. First you were lost in your own thoughts, then the Commissioner arrived, and I couldn't resist the chance of trying on my own."

Gottstein said, "But just what is it that I see there?"

Denison said, "Energy being spontaneously given off by matter leaking from another Universe into ours."

And even as he said that the light blinked out and many yards away, a farther, dimmer star came into simultaneous being.

Denison lunged toward the Pionizer, but Selene, all Lunar grace, propelled herself across the surface more efficiently and was there first. She killed the field structure and the distant star went out.

She said, "The leak-point isn't stable, you see."

"Not on a small scale," said Denison, "but considering that a shift of a light-year is as theoretically possible as a shift of a hundred yards, one of a hundred yards only is miraculous stability."

"Not miraculous enough," said Selene, flatly.

Gottstein interrupted. "Let me guess what you're talking about. You mean that the matter can leak through here, or there, or anywhere in our Universe—at random."

"Not quite at random, Commissioner," said Denison. "The probability of leakage drops with distance from the Pionizer, and rather sharply I should say. The sharpness depends on a variety of factors and I think we've tightened the situation remarkably. Even so, a flip of a few hundred yards is quite probable and, as a matter of fact, you saw it happen."

"And it might have shifted to somewhere within the city or within our own helmets, perhaps."

Denison said, impatiently, "No, no. The leak, at least by the techniques we use, is heavily dependent on the density of matter already present in this Universe. The chances are virtually nil that the leak-position would shift from a place of essential vacuum to one where an atmosphere even a hundredth as dense as that within the city or within our helmets would exist. It would be impractical to expect to arrange the leak anywhere but into a vacuum in the first place, which is why we had to make the attempt up here on the surface."

"Then this is not like the Electron Pump?"

"Not at all," said Denison. "In the Electron Pump there

is a two-way transfer of matter, here a one-way leak. Nor are the Universes involved the same."

Gottstein said, "I wonder if you would have dinner with me this evening, Dr. Denison?"

Denison hesitated. "Myself only?"

Gottstein attempted a bow in the direction of Selene but could accomplish only a grotesque parody of it in his spacesuit. "I would be charmed to have Miss Lindstrom's company on another occasion, but on this one I must speak with you alone, Dr. Denison."

"Oh, go ahead," said Selene, crisply, as Denison still hesitated. "I have a heavy schedule tomorrow anyway and you'll need time to worry about the leak-point instability."

Denison said, uncertainly, "Well, then—Selene, will you let me know when your next free day is?"

"I always do, don't I? And we'll be in touch before then anyway. . . . Why don't you two go on? I'll take care of the equipment."

15

Barron Neville shifted from foot to foot in the fashion made necessary by the restricted quarters and by the Moon's gravity. In a larger room under a world's stronger pull, he would have walked hastily up and back. Here, he tilted from side to side, in a repetitive back-and-forth glide.

"Then you're positive it works. Right, Selene? You're positive?"

"I'm positive," said Selene. "I've told you five times by actual count."

Neville didn't seem to be listening. He said in a low, rapid voice, "It doesn't matter that Gottstein was there then? He didn't try to stop the experiment?"

"No. Of course not."

"There was no indication that he would try to exert authority—"

"Now, Barron, what kind of authority could he exert? Will Earth send a police force? Besides—oh, you know they can't stop us."

Neville stopped moving, stood motionless for a while. "They don't know? They still don't know?"

"Of course they don't. Ben was looking at the stars and then Gottstein came. So I tried for the field-leak, got it, and I had already gotten the other. Ben's setup—"

"Don't call it his setup. It was your idea, wasn't it?"

Selene shook her head. "I made vague suggestions. The details were Ben's."

"But you can reproduce it now. For Luna's sake, we don't have to go to the Earthie for it, do we?"

"I think I can reproduce enough of it now so that our people can fill it in."

"All right, then. Let's get started."

"Not yet. Oh, damn it, Barron, not yet."

"Why not yet?"

"We need the energy, too."

"But we have that."

"Not *quite*. The leak-point is unstable; pretty badly unstable."

"But that can be fixed up. You said so."

"I said I *thought* it could."

"That's good enough for me."

"Just the same, it would be better to have Ben work out the details and stabilize it."

There was a silence between them. Neville's thin face slowly twisted into something approaching hostility. "You don't think I can do it? Is that it?"

Selene said, "Will you come out on the surface with me and work on it?"

There was another silence. Neville said, unsteadily, "I don't appreciate your sarcasm. And I don't want to have to wait long."

"I can't command the laws of nature. But I think it won't be long. . . . Now if you don't mind, I need my sleep. I've got my tourists tomorrow."

For a moment, Neville seemed on the point of gesturing to his own bed-alcove as though offering hospitality, but the gesture, if that was what it was, did not really come to birth and Selene made no sign of understanding or even anticipating. She nodded wearily, and left.

16

"I had hoped, to be frank," said Gottstein, smiling over what passed for dessert—a sticky, sweet concoction—"that we would have seen each other more often."

Denison said, "It is kind of you to take such an interest in my work. If the leak-instability can be corrected, I think my achievement—and that of Miss Lindstrom—will have been a most significant one."

"You speak carefully, like a scientist. . . . I won't insult you by offering the Lunar equivalent of a liqueur; that is the one approximation to Earth's cuisine I have simply made up my mind not to tolerate. Can you tell me, in lay language, what makes the achievement significant?"

"I can try," said Denison, cautiously. "Suppose we start with the para-Universe. It has a more intense strong nuclear interaction than our Universe has so that relatively small masses of protons in the para-Universe can undergo the fusion reaction capable of supporting a star. Masses equivalent to our stars would explode violently in the para-Universe which has many more, but much smaller stars than ours does.

"Suppose, now, that we had a much less intense strong nuclear interaction than that which prevails in our Universe. In that case, huge masses of protons would have so little tendency to fuse that a very large mass of hydrogen would be needed to support a star. Such an anti-para-Universe—one that was the opposite of the para-Universe, in other words—would consist of considerably fewer but far larger stars than our Universe does. In fact, if the strong nuclear interaction were made sufficiently weak, a Universe would exist which consisted of a single star containing all the mass in that Universe. It would be a very dense star, but relatively non-reactive and giving off no more radiation than our single Sun does, perhaps."

Gottstein said, "Am I wrong, or isn't that the situation that prevailed in our own Universe before the time of the big bang—one vast body containing all the universal mass."

"Yes," said Denison, "as a matter of fact, the anti-para-Universe I am picturing consists of what some call a cosmic egg; or 'cosmeg' for short. A cosmeg-Universe is what we need if we are to probe for one-way leakage. The para-Universe we are now using with its tiny stars is virtually empty space. You can probe and probe and touch nothing."

"The para-men reached us, however."

"Yes, possibly by following magnetic fields. There is some reason to think that there are no planetary magnetic fields of significance in the para-Universe, which deprives us of the advantage they have. On the other hand, if we probe the cosmeg-Universe, we cannot fail. The cosmeg is, itself, the entire Universe, and wherever we probe we strike matter."

"But how do you probe for it?"

Denison hesitated. "That is the part I find difficult to explain. Pions are the mediating particles of the strong nuclear interaction. The intensity of the interaction depends on the mass of the pions and that mass can, under certain specialized conditions, be altered. The Lunar physicists have developed an instrument they call the Pionizer, which can be made to do just such a thing. Once the pion's mass is decreased, or increased for that matter, it is, effectively, part of another Universe; it becomes a gateway, a crossing point. If it is decreased sufficiently, it can be made part of a cosmeg-Universe and that's what we want."

Gottstein said, "And you can suck in matter from the—the—cosmeg-Universe?"

"That part is easy. Once the gateway forms, the influx is spontaneous. The matter enters with its own laws and is stable when it arrives. Gradually the laws of our own Universe soak in, the strong interaction grows stronger, and the matter fuses and begins to give off enormous energy."

"But if it is super-dense, why doesn't it just expand in a puff of smoke?"

"That, too, would yield energy, but that depends on the electromagnetic field and in this particular case the strong interaction takes precedence, because we control the electromagnetic field. It would take quite a time to explain that."

"Well, then, the globe of light that I saw on the surface was cosmeg material fusing?"

"Yes, Commissioner."

"And that energy can be harnessed for useful purposes?"

"Certainly. And in any quantity. What you saw was the arrival in our Universe of micromicrogram masses of cosmeg. There's nothing, in theory, to prevent our bringing it over in ton-lots."

"Well, then, this can be used to replace the Electron Pump."

Denison shook his head. "No. The use of cosmeg energy also alters the properties of the Universes in question. The strong interaction gradually grows more intense in the cosmeg-Universe and less intense in ours as the laws of nature cross over. That means that the cosmeg slowly undergoes fusion at a greater rate and gradually warms up. Eventually—"

"Eventually," sad Gottstein, crossing his arms across his chest and narrowing his eyes, thoughtfully, "it explodes in a big bang."

"That's my feeling."

"Do you suppose that's what happened to our own Universe ten billion years ago?"

"Perhaps. Cosmogonists have wondered why the original cosmic egg exploded at some one point in time and not at another. One solution was to imagine an oscillatin

Universe in which the cosmic egg was formed and then *at once* exploded. The oscillating Universe has been eliminated as a possibility and the conclusion is that the cosmic egg had to exist for some long period of time and then went through a crisis of instability which arose for some unknown reason."

"But which may have been the result of the tapping of its energy across the Universes."

"Possibly, but not necessarily by some intelligence. Perhaps there are occasional spontaneous leaks."

"And when the big bang takes place," said Gottstein, "can we still extract energy from the cosmeg-Universe?"

"I'm not sure, but surely that is not an immediate worry. The leakage of our strong-interaction field into the cosmeg-Universe must very likely continue for millions of years before pushing it past the critical point. And there must be other cosmeg-Universes; an infinite number, perhaps."

"What about the change in our own Universe?"

"The strong interaction weakens. Slowly, very slowly, our Sun cools off."

"Can we use cosmeg energy to make up for that?"

"That would not be necessary, Commissioner," said Denison, earnestly. "While the strong interaction here in our Universe weakens as a result of the cosmeg pump, it strengthens through the action of the ordinary Electron Pump. If we adjust the energy productions of the two then, though the laws of nature change in the cosmeg-Universe and in the para-Universe, they do not change in ours. We are a highway but not the terminus in either direction.

"Nor need we be disturbed on behalf of the terminuses. The para-men on their side may have adjusted themselves to the cooling off of their Sun which may be pretty cool to begin with. As for the cosmeg-Universe, there is no reason to suspect life can exist there. Indeed, it is by inducing the conditions required for the big bang that we may be setting up a new kind of Universe that will eventually grow hospitable to life."

For a while, Gottstein said nothing. His plump face, in repose, seemed emotionless. He nodded to himself as though following the line of his own thoughts.

Finally, he said, "You know, Denison, I think this is what will set the world on its ear. Any difficulty in persuading the scientific leadership that the Electron Pump is destroying the world should now disappear."

Denison said, "The emotional reluctance to accept that no longer exists. It will be possible to present the problem and the solution at the same time."

"When would you be willing to prepare a paper to this effect if I guarantee speedy publication?"

"Can you guarantee that?"

"In a government-published pamphlet, if no other way."

"I would prefer to try to neutralize the leak-instability before reporting."

"Of course."

"And I think it would be wise," said Denison, "to arrange to have Dr. Peter Lamont as co-author. He can make the mathematics rigorous; something I cannot do. Besides, it was through his work that I took the course I have followed. One more point, Commissioner—"

"Yes."

"I would suggest that the Lunar physicists be involved. One of their number, Dr. Barron Neville, might well be a third author."

"But why? Aren't you introducing unnecessary complications now?"

"It was their Pionizer that made everything possible."

"There can be appropriate mention of that. . . . But did Dr. Barron actually work on the project with you?"

"Not directly."

"Then why involve him?"

Denison looked down and brushed his hand thoughtfully over the weave of his pants leg. He said, "It would be the diplomatic thing to do. We would need to set up the cosmeg pump on the Moon."

"Why not on Earth?"

"In the first place, we need a vacuum. This is a one-way

transfer and not a two-way as in the case of the Electron Pump, and the conditions necessary to make it practical are different in the two cases. The surface of the Moon has its vacuum ready-made in vast quantities; while to prepare one on Earth would involve an enormous effort."

"Yet it could be done, couldn't it?"

"Secondly," said Denison, "if we have two vast energy sources from opposite directions with our own Universe between, there would be something like a short circuit if the two outlets were too close together. Separation by a quarter-million miles of vacuum, with the Electron Pump operating only on Earth and the cosmeg pump operating only on the Moon, would be ideal—in fact, necessary. And if we are to operate on the Moon, it would be wise, even decent, to take the sensibilities of the Lunar physicists into account. We ought to give them a share."

Gottstein smiled. "Is this the advice of Miss Lindstrom?"

"I'm sure it would be, but the suggestion is reasonable enough to have occurred to me independently."

Gottstein rose, stretched, and then jumped in place two or three times in the eerily slow fashion imposed by Lunar gravity. He flexed his knees each time. He sat down again and said, "Ever try that, Dr. Denison?"

Denison shook his head.

"It's supposed to help the circulation in the lower extremities. I do it whenever I feel my legs may be going to sleep. I'll be heading back for a short visit to Earth before long and I'm trying to keep from getting too used to Lunar gravity. . . . Shall we talk of Miss Lindstrom, Dr. Denison?"

Denison said in a quite changed tone, "What about her?"

"She is a tourist guide."

"Yes. You said so earlier."

"As I also said, she is an odd assistant for a physicist."

"Actually, I'm an amateur physicist only, and I suppose she is an amateur assistant."

Gottstein was no longer smiling. "Don't play games, Doctor. I have taken the trouble to find out what I can about her. Her record is quite revealing, or would have been if it had occurred to anyone to look at it before this. I believe she is an Intuitionist."

Denison said, "Many of us are. I have no doubt you are an Intuitionist yourself, after a fashion. I certainly know that I am, after a fashion."

"There is a difference, Doctor. You are an accomplished scientist and I, I hope, am an accomplished administrator. . . . Yet while Miss Lindstrom is enough of an Intuitionist to be useful to you in advanced theoretical physics, she is, in actual fact, a tourist guide."

Denison hesitated. "She has little formal training, Commissioner. Her Intuitionism is at an unusually high level but it is under little conscious control."

"Is she the result of the one-time genetic engineering program?"

"I don't know. I wouldn't be surprised if that were so, however."

"Do you trust her?"

"In what way? She has helped me."

"Do you know that she is the wife of Dr. Barron Neville?"

"There is an emotional connection; not a legal one, I believe."

"None of the connections are what we would call legal here on the Moon. The same Neville you want to invite as third author of the paper you are to write?"

"Yes."

"Is that merely a coincidence?"

"No. Neville was interested in my arrival and I believe he asked Selene to help me in my work."

"Did she tell you this?"

"She said he was interested in me. That was natural enough, I suppose."

"Does it occur to you, Dr. Denison, that she may be working in her own interests and in those of Dr. Neville?"

"In what way would their interests differ from ours? She has helped me without reservation."

Gottstein shifted position and moved his shoulders as though he were going through muscle-pulling exercises. He said, "Dr. Neville must know that a woman so close to himself is an Intuitionist. Wouldn't he use her? Why would she remain a tourist guide, if not to mask her abilities—for a purpose."

"I understand Dr. Neville frequently reasons in this fashion. I find it difficult to suspect unnecessary conspiracies."

"How do you know they are unnecessary. . . . When my space-skipper was hovering over the Moon's surface just before the ball of radiation formed over your equipment, I was looking down at you. You were not at the Pionizer."

Denison thought back. "No, I wasn't. I was looking at the stars; rather a tendency of mine on the surface."

"What was Miss Lindstrom doing?"

"I didn't see. She said she strengthened the magnetic field and the leak finally broke through."

"Is it customary for her to manipulate the equipment without you?"

"No. But I can understand the impulse."

"And would there have been some sort of an ejection?"

"I don't understand you."

"I'm not sure I understand myself. There was a dim sparkle in the Earthlight, as though something was flying through the air. I don't know what."

"I don't either," said Denison.

"You can't think of anything that might naturally have to do with the experiment that—"

"No."

"Then what was Miss Lindstrom doing?"

"I still don't know."

For a moment, the silence was heavy between them. Then the Commissioner said, "As I see it then, you will try to correct the leak-instability and will be thinking about the preparation of a paper. I will get matters into motion at the other end and on my shortly forthcoming visit to Earth will make arrangements to have the paper published and will alert the government."

It was a clear dismissal. Denison rose and the Commissioner said easily, "And think about Dr. Neville and Miss Lindstrom."

17

It was a heavier star of radiation, a fatter one, a brighter one. Denison could feel its warmth on his faceplate, and backed away. There was a distinct x-ray component in the radiation and though this shielding should take care of that there was no point in placing it under a strain.

"I guess we can't question it," he muttered. "The leak-point is stable."

"I'm sure of it," said Selene, flatly.

"Then let's turn it off and go gack to the city."

They moved slowly and Denison felt oddly dispirited. There was no uncertainty any more; no excitement. From this point on, there was no chance of failure. The government was interested; more and more, it would be out of his own hands.

He said, "I suppose I can begin the paper now."

"I suppose so," said Selene, carefully.

"Have you talked to Barron again?"

"Yes, I have."

"Any difference in his attitude?"

"None at all. He will not participate. Ben—"

"Yes?"

"I really don't think it's any use talking to him. He will not cooperate in any project with the Earth government."

"But you've explained the situation?"

"Completely."

"And he still won't."

"He's asked to see Gottstein, and the Commissioner agreed to an interview after he returns from his Earth visit. We'll have to wait till then. Maybe Gottstein can have some effect on him, but I doubt it."

Denison shrugged, a useless maneuver inside his space-suit. "I don't understand him."

"I do," said Selene, softly.

Denison did not respond directly. He shoved the Pionizer and its attendant apparatus into its rocky shelter and said, "Ready?"

"Ready."

They slipped into the surface entrance at Outlet P-4 in silence and Denison climbed down the entry ladder. Selene dropped past him, braking in quick holds at individual rungs. Denison had learned to do that, but he was dispirited and climbed down in a kind of rebellious refusal to accept acclimation.

They removed their suits in the staging areas, placed them in their lockers. Denison said, "Would you join me for lunch, Selene?"

Selene said uneasily, "You seem upset. Is something wrong?"

"Reaction, I think. Lunch?"

"Yes, of course."

They ate in Selene's quarters. She insisted, saying, "I want to talk to you and I can't do it properly in the cafeteria."

And when Denison was chewing slowly at something that had a faint resemblance to peanut-flavored veal, she said, "Ben, you haven't said a word, and you've been like this for a week."

"No, I haven't," said Denison, frowning.

"Yes, you have." She looked into his eyes with concern. "I'm not sure how good my intuition is outside physics, but I suppose there's something you don't want to tell me."

Denison shrugged. "They're making a fuss about all this back on Earth. Gottstein has been pulling at strings as tough as cables in advance of his trip back. Dr. Lamont is being lionized, and they want me to come back once the paper is written."

"Back to Earth?"

"Yes. It seems I'm a hero, too."

"You should be."

"Complete rehabilitation," said Denison, thoughtfully,

"is what they offer. It's clear I can get a position in any suitable university or government agency on Earth."

"Isn't that what you wanted?"

"It's what I imagine Lamont wants, and would enjoy, and will certainly get. But I don't want it."

Selene said, "What *do* you want then?"

"I want to stay on the Moon."

"Why?"

"Because it's the cutting edge of humanity and I want to be part of that cutting edge. I want to work at the establishment of cosmeg pumps and that will be only here on the Moon. I want to work on para-theory with the kind of instruments you can dream up and handle, Selene. . . . I want to be with you, Selene. But will you stay with me?"

"I am as interested in para-theory as you are."

Denison said, "But won't Neville pull you off the job now?"

"Barron pull me off?" She said, tightly, "Are you trying to insult me, Ben?"

"Not at all."

"Well, then, do I misunderstand you? Are you suggesting that I'm working with you because Barron ordered me to?"

"Didn't he?"

"Yes, he did. But that's not why I'm here. I *choose* to be here. He may think he can order me about but he can only do so when his orders coincide with my will, as in your case they did. I resent his thinking he can order me otherwise, and I resent your thinking it, too."

"You two are sex-partners."

"We have been, yes, but what has that to do with it? By that argument, I can order him about as easily as he me."

"Then you *can* work with me, Selene?"

"Certainly," she said, coldly. "If I choose to."

"But do you choose to?"

"As of now, yes."

And Denison smiled. "The chance that you might not choose to, or even might not be able to, is, I think, what has really been worrying me this past week. I dreaded the end of the project if it meant the end of you. I'm sorry, Selene, I don't mean to plague you with a sentimental attachment of an old Earthie—"

"Well, there's nothing old Earthie about your mind, Ben. There are other attachments than sexual. I like being with you."

There was a pause and Denison's smile faded, then returned, perhaps a thought more mechanically. "I'm glad for my mind."

Denison looked away, shook his head slightly, then turned back. She watched him carefully, almost anxiously.

Denison said, "Selene, there's more than energy involved in the cross-Universe leaks. I suspect you've been thinking about that."

The silence stretched out now, painfully, and finally Selene said, "Oh, that—"

For a while the two stared at each other—Denison embarrassed, Selene almost furtive.

18

Gottstein said, "I haven't got my Moon-legs quite yet, but this isn't anything compared to what it cost me to get my Earth-legs. Denison, you had better not dream of returning. You'll never make it."

"I have no intention of returning, Commissioner," said Denison.

"In a way, it's too bad. You could be emperor by acclamation. As for Hallam—"

Denison said, wistfully, "I would have liked to see his face, but that's a small ambition."

"Lamont, of course, is receiving the lion's share. He's on the spot."

"I don't mind that. He deserves a good deal. . . . Do you think Neville will really join us?"

"No question. He's on his way at this moment. . . . Listen," Gottstein's voice dropped one conspiratorial note in pitch. "Before he comes, would you like a bar of chocolate?"

"What?"

"A bar of chocolate. With almonds. *One.* I have some."

Denison's face, from initial confusion, suddenly lit with comprehension. "*Real* chocolate?"

"Yes."

"Certain—" His face hardened. "No, Commissioner."

"No?"

"No! If I taste real chocolate then, for the few minutes it's in my mouth, I'm going to miss Earth; I'm going to miss everything about it. I can't afford that. I don't want it. . . . Don't even show it to me. Don't let me smell it or see it."

The Commissioner looked discomfited. "You're right." He made an obvious attempt to change the subject. "The excitement on Earth is overwhelming. Of course, we made a considerable effort to save Hallam's face. He'll continue to hold some position of importance, but he'll have little real say."

"He's getting more consideration than he gave others," said Denison, resignedly.

"It's not for his sake. You can't smash a personal image that has been built to a level of such importance; it would reflect on science itself. The good name of science is more important than Hallam either way."

"I disapprove of that in principle," said Denison, warmly. "Science must take what blows it deserves."

"A time and place for— There's Dr. Neville."

Gottstein composed his face. Denison shifted his chair to face the entrance.

Barron Neville entered solemnly. Somehow there was less than ever of the Lunar delicacy about his figure. He greeted the two curtly, sat down, and crossed his legs. He was clearly waiting for Gottstein to speak first.

The Commissioner said, "I am glad to see you, Dr. Neville. Dr. Denison tells me that you refused to append your name to what I am sure will be a classic paper on the cosmeg pump."

"No need to do so," said Neville. "What happens on Earth is of no interest to me."

"You are aware of the cosmeg pump experiments? Of its implications?"

"All of them. I know the situation as well as you two do."

"Then I will proceed without preliminaries. I have returned from Earth, Dr. Neville, and it is quite settled as to what will be the course of future procedure. Large cosmeg pump stations will be set up on three different places on the Lunar surface in such a way that one will always be in the night-shadow. Half the time, two will be. Those in the night-shadow will be constantly generating energy, most of which will simply radiate into space. The purpose will be not so much to use the energy for practical purposes, as to counteract the changes in field intensities introduced by the Electron Pump."

Denison interrupted. "For some years, we will have to overbalance the Electron Pump to restore our section of the Universe to the point at which it was before the pump began operation."

Neville nodded. "Will Luna City have the use of any of it?"

"If necessary. We feel the Solar batteries will probably supply what you need, but there is no objection to supplementation."

"That is kind of you," said Neville, not bothering to mask the sarcasm. "And who will build and run the cosmeg pump stations?"

"Lunar workers, we hope," said Gottstein.

"Lunar workers, you know," said Neville. "Earth workers would be too clumsy to work effectively on the Moon."

"We recognize that," said Gottstein. "We trust the men of the Moon will cooperate."

"And who will decide how much energy to generate, how much to apply for any local purpose, how much to radiate away? Who decides policy?"

Gottstein said, "The government would have to. It's a matter of planetary decision."

Neville said, "You see, then, it will be Moonmen who do the work; Earthmen who run the show."

Gottstein said, calmly, "No. All of us work who work best; all of us administer who can best weigh the total problem."

"I hear the words," said Neville, "but it boils down anyway to us working and you deciding. . . . No, Commissioner. The answer is no."

"You mean you won't build the cosmeg pump stations?"

"We'll build them, Commissioner, but they'll be ours. We'll decide how much energy to put out and what use to make of it."

"That would scarcely be efficient. You would have to deal constantly with the Earth government since the cosmeg pump energy will have to balance the Electron Pump energy."

"I dare say it will, more or less, but we have other things in mind. You might as well know now. Energy is not the only conserved phenomenon that becomes limitless once universes are crossed."

Denison interrupted. "There are a number of conservation laws. We realize that."

"I'm glad you do," said Neville, turning a hostile glare in his direction. "They include those of linear momentum and angular momentum. As long as any object responds to the gravitational field in which it is immersed, and to that only, it is in free fall and can retain its mass. In order to move in any other way than free fall, it must accelerate in a non-gravitational way and for that to happen, part of itself must undergo an opposite change."

"As in a rocketship," said Denison, "which must eject mass in one direction in order that the rest might accelerate in the opposite direction."

"I'm sure you understand, Dr. Denison," said Neville, "but I explain for the Commissioner's sake. The loss of mass can be minimized if its velocity is increased enormously, since momentum is equal to mass multiplied by velocity. Nevertheless, however great the velocity, some mass must be thrown away. If the mass which must be accelerated is enormous in the first place, then the mass which must be discarded is also enormous. If the Moon, for instance—"

"The *Moon!*" said Gottstein, explosively.

"Yes, the Moon," said Neville, calmly. "If the Moon were to be driven out of its orbit and sent out of the Solar system, the conservation of momentum would make it a colossal undertaking, and probably a thoroughly impractical one. If, however, momentum could be transferred to the cosmeg in another Universe, the Moon could accelerate at any convenient rate without loss of mass at all. It would be like poling a barge upstream, to give you a picture I obtained from some Earth-book I once read."

"But why? I mean why should you want to move the Moon?"

"I should think that would be obvious. Why do we need the suffocating presence of the Earth? We have the energy we need; we have a comfortable world through which we have room to expand for the next few centuries, at least. Why not go our own way? In any case, we will. I have come to tell you that you cannot stop us and to urge you to make no attempt to interfere. We shall transfer momentum and we shall pull out. We of the Moon know precisely how to go about building cosmeg pump stations. We will use what energy we need for ourselves and produce excess in order to neutralize the changes your own power stations are producing."

Denison said, sardonically, "It sounds kind of you to produce excess for our sake, but it isn't for our sake, of course. If our Electron Pumps explode the Sun, that will happen long before you can move out of even the inner Solar system and you will vaporize wherever you are."

"Perhaps," said Neville, "but in any case we *will* produce an excess, so that won't happen."

"But you can't do that," said Gottstein, excitedly. "You can't move out. If you get out too far, the cosmeg pump will no longer neutralize the Electron Pump, eh, Denison?"

Denison shrugged. "Once they are as far off as Saturn, more or less, there may be trouble, if I may trust a mental calculation I have just made. It will, however, be many years before they recede to such a distance and by that time, we will surely have constructed space stations in what was once the orbit of the Moon and place cosmeg pumps on them. Actually, we don't need the Moon. It can leave—except that it won't."

Neville smiled briefly. "What makes you think we won't? We can't be stopped. There is no way Earthmen can impose their will on us."

"You won't leave, because there's no sense to doing so. Why drag the entire Moon away? To build up respectable accelerations will take years where the Moon-mass is concerned. You'll creep. Build starships instead; miles-long ships that are cosmeg-powered and have independent ecologies. With a cosmeg momentum-drive, you can then do wonders. If it takes twenty years to build the ships, they will nevertheless accelerate at a rate that will enable them to overtake the Moon's place within a year even if the Moon starts accelerating today. The ships will be able to change course in a tiny fraction of the time the Moon will."

"And the unbalanced cosmeg pumps? What will that do to the Universe?"

"The energy required by a ship, or even by a number, will be far less than that required by a planet and will be distributed throughout large sections of the Universe. It will be millions of years before any significant change takes place. That is well worth the maneuverability you gain. The Moon will move so slowly it might as well be left in space."

Neville said, scornfully, "We're in no hurry to get anywhere—except away from Earth."

Denison said, "There are advantages in having Earth as a neighbor. You have the influx of the Immigrants. You have cultural intercourse. You have a planetary world of two billion people just over the horizon. Do you want to give all that up?"

"Gladly."

"Is that true of the people of the Moon generally? Or just of you? There's something intense about you, Neville. You won't go out on the surface. Other Lunarites do.

They don't like it particularly, but they do. The interior of the Moon isn't their womb, as it is in your case. It isn't their prison, as it is yours. There is a neurotic factor in you that is absent in most Lunarities, or at least considerably weaker. If you take the Moon away from Earth, you make it into a prison for all. It will become a one-world prison from which no man—and not you only—can emerge, not even to the extent of seeing another inhabited world in the sky. Perhaps that is what you want."

"I want independence; a free world; a world untouched by the outside."

"You can build ships, any number. You can move outward at near-light velocities without difficulty, once you transfer momentum to the cosmeg. You can explore the entire Universe in a single lifetime. Wouldn't you like to get on such a ship?"

"No," said Neville, with clear distaste.

"Wouldn't you? Or is it couldn't? Is it that you must take the Moon with you wherever you go Why must all the others accept your need?"

"Because that's the way it's going to be," said Neville.

Denison's voice remained level but his cheeks reddened. "Who gave you the right to say that? There are many citizens of Luna City who may not feel as you do."

"That is none of your concern."

"That is *precisely* my concern. I am an Immigrant who will qualify for citizenship soon. I do not wish to have my choice made for me by someone who cannot emerge on the surface and who wants his personal prison made into a prison for all. I have left Earth forever, but only to come to the Moon, only to remain a quarter-million miles from the home-planet. I have not contracted to be taken forever away for an unlimited distance."

"Then return to Earth," said Neville, indifferently. "There is still time."

"And what of the other citizens of Luna? The other Immigrants?"

"The decision is made."

"It is not made. . . . Selene!"

Selene entered, her face solemn, her eyes a little defiant.

Neville's legs uncrossed. Both shoes came down flat upon the ground.

Neville said, "How long have you been waiting in the next room, Selene?"

"Since before you arrived, Barron," she said.

Neville looked from Selene to Denison and back again. "You two—" he began, finger pointing from one to the other and back.

"I don't know what you mean by 'you two,'" said Selene, "but Ben found out about the momentum quite a while ago."

"It wasn't Selene's fault," said Denison. "The Commissioner spotted something flying at a time when no one could possibly have known he would be observing. It seemed to me that Selene might be testing something I was not thinking of and transfer of momentum eventually occurred to me. After that—"

"Well, then, you knew," said Neville. "It doesn't matter."

"It does, Barron," said Selene. "I talked about it with Ben. I found that I didn't always have to accept what you said. Perhaps I can't ever go to Earth. Perhaps I don't even want to. But I found I liked it in the sky where I could see it if I wanted to. I didn't want an empty sky. Then I talked to others of the Group. Not everybody wants to leave. Most people would rather build the ships and let those go who wish to go while allowing those to remain behind who wish to remain."

Neville's breath was coming hard. "You *talked* about it. Who gave you the right to—"

"I *took* the right, Barron. Besides, it doesn't matter any more. You'll be outvoted."

"Because of—" Neville rose to his feet and took a menacing step toward Denison.

The Commissioner said, "Please don't get emotional, Dr. Neville. You may be of Luna, but I don't think you can man-handle both of us."

"All three," said Selene, "and I'm of Luna, too. I did it, Barron; not they."

Then Denison said, "Look, Neville— For all Earth

cares, the Moon can go. Earth can build its space stations. It's the citizens of Luna City who care. Selene cares and I care and the rest. You are not being debarred from space, from escape, from freedom. In twenty years at the outside, all who want to go will go, including you if you can bring yourself to leave the womb. And those who want to stay will stay."

Slowly, Neville seated himself again. There was the look of defeat on his face.

19

In Selene's apartment, every window now had a view of the Earth. She said, "The vote did go against him, you know, Ben. Quite heavily."

"I doubt that he'll give up, though. If there's friction with Earth during the building of the stations, public opinion on the Moon may swing back."

"There needn't be friction."

"No, there needn't. In any case, there are no happy endings in history, only crisis points that pass. We've passed this one safely, I think, and we'll be sorry about the others as they come and as they can be foreseen. Once the starships are built, the tension will surely subside considerably."

"We'll live to see that, I'm sure."

"*You* will, Selene."

"You, too, Ben. Don't overdramatize your age. You're only forty-eight."

"Would you go on one of the starships, Selene?"

"No. I'd be too old and I still wouldn't want to lose Earth in the sky. My son might go. . . . Ben."

"Yes, Selene."

"I have applied for a second son. The application has been accepted. Would you contribute?"

Denison's eyes lifted and looked straight into hers. She did not look away.

He said, "Artificial insemination?"

She said, "Of course. . . . The gene combination should be interesting."

Denison's eyes dropped. "I would be flattered, Selene."

Selene said, defensively, "That's just good sense, Ben. It's important to have good gene combinations. There's nothing wrong with some *natural* genetic engineering."

"None at all."

"It doesn't mean that I don't want it for other reasons, too. . . . Because I like you."

Denison nodded and remained silent.

Selene said, almost angrily, "Well, there's more to love than sex."

Denison said, "I agree to that. At least, I love you even with sex subtracted."

And Selene said, "And for that matter, there's more to sex than acrobatics."

Denison said, "I agree to that, too."

And Selene said, "And besides— Oh, damn it, you could try to learn."

Denison said softly, "If you would try to teach."

Hesitantly, he moved toward her. She did not move away.

He stopped hesitating.